THE RAVEN

A COFFEY & HILL NOVEL

MIKE NAPPA

Revell

a division of Baker Publishing Group
Grand Rapids, Michigan

Published by Revell
a division of Baker Publishing Group
P.O. Box 6287, Grand Rapids, MI 49516-6287
www.revellbooks.com

Printed in the United States of America

Library of Congress Cataloging-in-Publication Data
Names: Nappa, Mike, 1963– author.
Title: The raven : a Coffey & Hill novel / Mike Nappa.
Description: Grand Rapids, MI : Revell, a division of Baker Publishing Group,
    [2016] | Series: Coffey & Hill ; 2
Identifiers: LCCN 2016010255 | ISBN 9780800726454 (pbk.)
Subjects: LCSH: Private investigators—Alabama—Fiction. | GSAFD: Mystery
    fiction. | Suspense fiction. | Christian fiction.
Classification: LCC PS3564.A624 R39 2016 | DDC 813/.54—dc23
LC record available at https://lccn.loc.gov/2016010255

This book is a work of fiction. Names, characters, places, and incidents are the product of the author's imagination or are used fictitiously.

The Raven is published in association with Nappaland Literary Agency, an independent agency dedicated to publishing works that are: Authentic. Relevant. Eternal. Visit us online at: NappalandLiterary.com.

16 17 18 19 20 21 22   7 6 5 4 3 2 1

"*The Raven* is a delightful romp. Mike Nappa holds to a breathless pace in his new story, one that is sure to thrill his growing and well-deserved readership."

—**Thomas Locke**, bestselling and award-winning novelist,
author of *Emissary* and *Trial Run*

"I love Mike Nappa's style! With intrigue, action, and a main character snarky enough to cheer for, *The Raven* is a thrill ride into the stark territory between grace and the letter of the law."

—**Tosca Lee**, *New York Times* bestselling author

Praise for *Annabel Lee*

"The start to Nappa's Coffey & Hill series begins with an exciting event, and the adventure doesn't let up. With hidden secrets, questionable motives, and interesting characters, this book has a bit of everything that suspense lovers will enjoy. The characters make this book shine; they are distinct, memorable, and fascinating."

—*RT Book Reviews*, 4½ stars, Top Pick

"Mike Nappa's *Annabel Lee* is a fast-paced thriller, filled with unexpected twists and peopled by unique and memorable characters. From the first chapter on, I found it impossible to put down."

—**Lois Duncan**, *New York Times* bestselling author, *I Know What You Did Last Summer* and *Killing Mr. Griffin*

"*Annabel Lee* is compelling, fast-paced, and filled with fascinating characters. One hopes that Mike Nappa's eleven-year-old wunderkind from the title will reappear in future novels of this promising new suspense series!"

—**M. K. Preston**, Mary Higgins Clark Award–winning novelist, *Song of the Bones* and *Perhaps She'll Die*

"A relentless surge of suspense and mounting tension coupled with an engaging mix of characters. With *Annabel Lee*, Mike Nappa skillfully sets the stage for a compelling series of Coffey & Hill Investigation thrillers."

—**Jack Cavanaugh**, award-winning author of 26 novels

THE
RAVEN

Books in the Coffey & Hill Series

For Amy!

It's my favorite time of day,

driving you . . .

Here I opened wide the door;—
Darkness there and nothing more.

—Edgar Allan Poe,
in "The Raven"

NOW

Sixteen minutes to Nevermore . . .

1

RAVEN

Atlanta, GA
Downtown
Friday, April 14, 8:11 p.m.

My daddy used to tell me the best way to stay out of trouble was to think about tomorrow before you act today. Every Friday night in high school, just before I stepped out to go crazy with my friends, he'd look up from whatever he was reading—the Bible, a new Sharon Carter Rogers thriller, a boring book about Roman history, whatever—and he'd give me that same lecture: *"Son, ask yourself if Tomorrow-You is going to thank you for the circumstances you get him into tonight."*

Of course he was right. Pops generally gave good advice—it was kind of his job, after all. And of course I mostly ignored him. I figured that was my job.

Right now, though, I'm kind of wishing Last-Night-Me had been paying attention to Dad's most famous lecture. Even if LNM had just made some kind of contingency plan or something, that would've been helpful. But, as usual, that guy was winging it, hoping things would work out anyway, regardless of what he did.

Eternal optimist, I guess that's me. Hope it doesn't get me killed today.

The timer app on my cell phone beeps to tell me there's only sixteen minutes left.

I take in a deep breath and let it out slowly to calm my nerves. *No time to panic, not yet at least. Gotta keep my wits.*

The Big Dude in the wheelchair twitches and groans. I can see that his subconscious mind is fighting the drug that knocked him out, but there's nothing I can do about it right now. All I can do is punch the elevator button again, swear a little bit, and hope that sixteen minutes is going to be enough time to get done what needs to get done.

And then I see her.

Wow.

Trudi Coffey pops through the door to the stairwell without hesitating, like she knew I'd be here, like she knew I'd be waiting for this stupid elevator on the sixth floor of the Ritz-Carlton Atlanta hotel.

She's cleaned up for the occasion, a rare treat if you ask me. Sleeveless red dress, sexy but not trashy—I think they call it a body-con style. It's sleek, with ribbed material that hugs her hips until the fabric ends just above her knees. Below that is a pair of black ankle books, flirty, with a gold buckle, metal sequins, and chunky heels. Stylish, but also convenient for running. Or kicking.

Her thick brown hair is casually twisted and tacked up on her head in a way that just drives a man crazy. Dangly diamond earrings are her only jewelry, except for that long, black-marble chopstick-thingy holding her hair in place. And stuck to her left hand is a little black purse—Mom would've called it a "clutch." The way she's holding the purse—I mean *clutch*—with the snap undone, tells me what I would've expected from her anyway: She wants to be able to get to her Beretta Tomcat quickly. Just in case.

I know she's just jogged up six flights of stairs, but she's barely breathing hard, like she could run up the next eighteen floors of this hotel without any problem. *She keeps in shape, this one.* Of course, one peek at that red dress told me that. She pauses long enough to glance up and down the hall, checking to see if we have company. Then she turns her full attention to me.

"So, Raven," she says, "this is interesting."

"Don't call me that, Trudi," I say too quickly. "I mean, you don't have to call me that. You can call me—"

"Raven," she interrupts. "I can't help noticing you've got my ex-husband, unconscious for some reason, strapped into Mama's wheelchair."

I cringe at that. This could be hard to explain. I decide to postpone that conversation. "You look great, Trudi," I say.

I'm stalling, obviously, but I mean it too. My mom always taught me it's important to acknowledge a woman's efforts toward looking pretty. Plus, if this ends badly, I'll never forgive myself for missing an opportunity to tell Trudi Coffey that I think she's heartbreakingly beautiful. Seems like she doesn't believe that about herself anymore. And she definitely deserves to believe it.

"I mean, wow, Trudi. Spectacular. You should dress like this all the time. Are those Vince Camuto boots? Very nice."

"We're talking fashion now? That's the best you can do?"

I shrug and try out what I think is my adorably sheepish grin. "I'm just saying, you're dressed nice today. It's a compliment."

Her stupid ex-husband groans again, interrupting the flow of our conversation. She presses a hand to her hip and frowns. "This doesn't look good, Raven."

The timer app on my cell phone beeps again.

"What's that?" she says.

Only fifteen minutes left. I jab at the elevator button a few times. What is taking so long?

"Raven." She says my name again, intensity building in her voice. She steps toward me, and I suddenly get a maddening whiff of Bvlgari perfume.

How's a guy supposed to concentrate when a woman like this is standing just two feet away? I cannot catch a break today.

"They shut down the lifts in the whole hotel," she's saying. "SWAT's going to be here any minute. So . . . you want to explain what's going on, or do I step out of the way and let them take you down? I'm giving you a chance here. Maybe you should take it."

I close my eyes and take in a sweet breath of violet, orange blossom, and jasmine. I try to make a mental list of my options at this point, and it's not very long. In the end, though, all I can think is . . .

This is going to get really messy really soon.

THEN

Four weeks ago . . .

2

RAVEN

Atlanta, GA
The Old Fourth Ward Neighborhood
Friday, March 17, 11:04 a.m.
28 days to Nevermore

Part of me thinks that maybe I deserve this beating.

I did, after all, try to blackmail a captain of Atlanta industry. A man with political clout and many ardent supporters here in Georgia's fine state capital. Then I feel my tooth wiggle, taste the blood from that last leather-fisted blow, and feel the stinging in my split lips.

Nope, I decide. *This one's on them. The punishment does not fit the crime.*

Regardless, it's back to the business at hand.

"Jack of spades," I say to the guy at the table with me. "Is that your card?"

It sounds garbled, like I'm deliberately mumbling just to be annoying. But whatever, right? If they wanted me to speak clearly, they wouldn't be trying to break my jaw.

The dumpy Ukrainian guy standing behind me crows with laughter. "Got you again, Vicky! You don't get to hit this kid all night long. Tell truth, he got you again."

I try moving my chin forward and back, left and right. *Okay, good. Jaw's not broken. At least, I don't think it's broken.*

The quiet one sitting at the table with me exhales slowly. His name is Viktor, and he looks Ukrainian too, or maybe Russian, even though it feels like a movie stereotype to admit that. He's got dark hair, pale skin, and a medium build, taut and wiry, like he's nothing but muscle underneath his navy blue suit. And maybe he's got something else, like a gun, stashed under that coat, as well. Why else would he wear an expensive suit on an errand to beat up a luckless nobody like me?

Viktor blinks. Once at the card. Once at me. Then, with purposeful silence, he blinks twice at Pavlo, the dumpy guy standing behind me. I think maybe there's a family resemblance between Viktor and the chubby Pavlo, but I'm not about to make that suggestion. Don't want to risk being wrong about that.

The sluggish laughter stops.

"I am just saying," Pavlo mutters. "Maybe you got 'tell,' like in poker. This is all."

Now it's time for the third guy to start chuckling from the kitchen. He's a beefy, linebacker type, with cocoa skin and knotted muscles. No one has said his name, so I've taken to thinking of him as "Scholarship." He reminds me of every careless college football stud who thought he'd make it to the NFL, only to have his scholarship revoked "for academic reasons" during sophomore year, thereby making him a college dropout and ending his pro football career before it began. Apparently this guy never quit lifting weights, though.

"Pavlo, don't mess your pants right there in the living room,"

Scholarship says. He's spreading jelly onto stale bread while he talks. "This place is bad enough without you adding to the urban decay in here. I mean, look at me. I'm eating a PB&J sandwich like a five-year-old. Why can't people keep a little lunch meat in the fridge anymore? Even scrambled eggs and bacon would be better."

He takes a bite of the sandwich, licks peanut butter off the corner of his mouth, and grimaces. To me, he says, "You gotta get some eggs, kid."

He says it warmly, like we're old college buddies, reconnecting after a few years apart. I'm not sure what to make of that. Then he turns back to his Ukrainian pal.

"Besides, Pav," he says, "you know Viktor's not gonna embarrass you in front of this guy today. He'll wait until we're in the alley before he punctures your eardrum. Again."

Well, that explains why Pavlo seems hard of hearing sometimes.

The dumpy one crosses his arms and turns away.

Part of me feels good about the linebacker's little revelation. Pavlo's been the hardest to read all night long, and the sloppiest puncher too. I like the idea that maybe he gets bullied a bit by the quiet boss man. Still, another part of me wonders what ol' Vik would do to me if he got the chance. Which parts of my body might he try to alter permanently?

I decide I don't want to find out.

At the table, Viktor looks back in my direction and softens his gaze just a bit. I see a grudging admiration in his gray eyes. "*Vrazhayuchyy*," he says to himself in what I can only guess is Russian or Ukrainian or some other foreign language. Then he translates for me. "Impressive. Nice work." He stands up, stretches, and speaks to the room. "What time is it?"

Viktor speaks flawless English, even though he's obviously from somewhere in Eastern Europe. It makes me wonder why

Pavlo still struggles with the language—and also makes me question my earlier assumption that the two Ukrainians are related. Maybe they came to America at different ages? Maybe Viktor came as a kid, and Pavlo came as a teenager? Or maybe Viktor just cares more about things like communicating clearly? Maybe that's why he's in charge.

"It eleven o'clock, Vicky," Pavlo chirps.

Viktor flicks a look at the football player in the kitchen.

"Eleven-oh-seven," the linebacker says. He waits for Viktor to nod before taking another bite of his sandwich. Apparently the boss man is used to precision.

"Yes," Pavlo says. "This is what I mean. Of course. Eleven-oh-seven. Eleven-oh-eight now."

Everybody ignores him.

I can barely feel my hands anymore. They've been handcuffed behind my chair for so long I worry I won't be able to use them if they ever get loose. Of course, every once in a while I'll shift and feel the pins and needles stab through my palms and into my fingers, so I figure at least some blood is getting down there. But that doesn't make it better. My feet ache too, which I guess is a good sign, since they're tied to the legs of my chair. At least that means circulation is happening, despite the zip ties around my ankles.

Gotta be thankful for the little things. That's what Pops always said.

My jaw feels loose and misshapen but seems to be all in one piece. My lips are caked with a mixture of dried blood and fresh blood. My gums are also bleeding, and my nose feels puffy. Not my best day, I'll say that.

I'm guessing, because Scholarship is a lefty and because he got to hit me three times with that thin leather strap wrapped around his fist, that my right eye is bruised and black. It's swollen enough for that. Barely a slit that I can peek through now.

Pavlo is a body puncher, so I might have a cracked rib or two, as well. I can't really tell since I kind of hurt all over. I guess he could have bruised some internal organs too, but what am I supposed to do about that?

Still, all in all, it could've been worse. They might've cut me with knives or shot me with guns. Or made me eat okra.

My dad used to say that nobody likes a smart guy—usually right after I'd just said something sarcastic about his parenting skills. I know Pops was right, but I can't resist anyway. I mean, what are they gonna do, hit me again?

"So, Scholarship," I say to the linebacker eating the last of my food. "Ready to get your butt kicked again? Looks like I've got an opening at my table."

Even the quiet Viktor sniggers at that.

"Whaddya think, Mr. Kostiuk?" Scholarship says to Viktor, taking another leisurely bite. "Should I put down this delicious sandwich and recommence beating the living daylights outta this magician kid?"

Viktor smirks and shakes his head.

I feel my insides loosen in relief. After all, Scholarship hits like a rodeo bull. Then I clench up again. Don't want to make a mess in my otherwise reasonably clean underwear.

Viktor Kostiuk reaches over and pats my chest. It's almost affectionate, which seems kind of weird to me, considering the situation.

It wasn't quite midnight last night when they knocked on my door.

"Pizza delivery," one of them said. I think it was Pavlo.

Now, I didn't order any pizza. Sure, I know that. But the blue-collar folks here in the Boulevard Home Apartments order pizza anytime, day or night, sometimes into the wee hours of the morning. And sometimes delivery drivers make mistakes. When they make mistakes late at night here in Atlanta's Old Fourth Ward, well, sometimes they just cut their losses. So I was kinda hoping to get a free pizza out of the deal—at least then I'd have something to eat for breakfast.

"Pizza!" the voice on the other side of the door said again. Then I did what every stupid blackmailer does.

I opened the door.

They had me shirtless and my legs bound to one of my three kitchen chairs before I even knew who they were. Only after they'd gagged me and cuffed my hands behind me did I start to piece things together.

They all stood around me for a minute, the heavy Ukrainian breathing hard and giggling in little hiccups. Then Viktor nodded and Pavlo let me have it, right in the solar plexus. It felt like a hammer, and I wasn't really prepared for it. They all laughed while I struggled to breathe. Pavlo pulled back for another shot, but this time Scholarship stepped between us.

"You know why we're here, kid?" he said, leaning down close to my face. He was almost smiling. I think he liked this part.

I shook my head as an answer to his question. I was still gagged, not breathing, and not able to form words anyway.

"Because you have something that doesn't belong to you." He pulled away and leaned against the table, grinning. He started wrapping a leather strap, like a makeshift glove, around the knuckles on his left hand.

Yeah, he was definitely enjoying himself.

This is bad, I thought. I knew what he was talking about. *Bad. Bad. Bad.*

"You have something . . . personal . . . that belongs to Mr. Maksym Romanenko. And for some reason, you thought Mr.

Roman should pay you ten thousand dollars just to get back what was already his in the first place. What have you got to say about that?" He snatched the gag out of my mouth.

"Well, technically," I gasped out, "the two women who were naked with Councilman Roman in those pictures could also claim copyright ownership of that property. Unless they signed model releases or something. But I'm guessing they didn't sign anything. Probably didn't even know they were being photographed. That right, Scholarship?"

Yeah, nobody likes a smart guy. Thanks, Pops.

He hit me so fast I thought my right eye had popped out of its socket. When the black spots in my vision finally faded, all three goons were still standing around me. So no, it wasn't just a bad dream. And nobody was laughing now.

Viktor spoke into the silence. "I hear you're some kind of magician," he said.

"Deception specialist," I said automatically.

It was stupid, I know, but I heard myself say it before I thought it, so I guess my mouth was working without my brain attached again. This seems to happen regularly with me. It's just that, a few years back, I heard the great Apollo Robbins call himself that, and I realized immediately that "deception specialist" sounded a lot better than "magician." I decided to be like my hero and started telling anyone and everyone I was a deception specialist too, not just a lowly magician. Apparently my subconscious thought this was an important point to make at this moment, right when I was about to get my first truly professional beating.

Viktor nodded amiably toward me. "All right," he said, "how did a *deception specialist* come to acquire Max Roman's private . . . art photography?"

No sense in lying at this point. Here goes nothing.

"A week ago last Saturday, I was working down at Piedmont Park, doing street magic for a few extra bucks."

"This is where I see you!" Pavlo said suddenly. "You mister magic guy, The Raven! I do not recognize you without purple cape and little black eye mask." He turned to his fellow goons. "This *khlopchyk* the real deal. He make stuff disappear—poof! Gone! Read your mind too. Crazy." He patted me on the back enthusiastically.

"Well, um, thanks?" I said. "Always nice to meet a fan. Anyway, Councilman Roman and his girlfriends—"

"Personal assistants," Scholarship interrupted.

"Right," I said. And I flinched because I thought he was going to thump me again. But he didn't, at least not that time. "Right, right. Well, Mr. Roman and his personal assistants stopped for the Permission to Pickpocket show."

Viktor tapped a finger on the table, getting impatient.

"That's the one where I steal your stuff while you're watching," I explained quickly. "I lift your watch, your wallet, your scarf, even the hat off your head if you're wearing one. You're watching me the whole time, but the laws of deception dictate that you can't keep track of everything I'm doing. So I end up with your stuff. Then I return it all, we have a good laugh, and you leave me a good tip."

"Except?"

Viktor knew what happened next. He just wanted me to say it out loud.

Fine, I'll admit it.

"Well, Councilman Roman thought the show would be entertaining for his girlfr—assistants. So I did the pickpocket spiel. When I discovered he had two wallets, I thought maybe I'd keep the smaller one, just to see if I could score a few extra dollars before turning it in to the police as a lost-and-found. I thought it was a cash wallet—I didn't know the second one was actually a photo wallet. And I didn't know Mr. Roman kept *those* kinds of pictures in there."

Viktor nodded and wandered into the tiny, shabby living room of my apartment, absently checking out the fold-out couch as if deciding whether or not it carried any infectious diseases before he would take a seat.

"I looked him up online," I continued, "and saw he's a city councilman and a big-time real estate developer here in the Atlanta metro. Also saw he's running for mayor this year. And that he's married. So I figured, why not take a shot? Ten thousand dollars in blackmail money wouldn't mean much to a big shot like that, but it'd sure make a difference for a small-timer like me."

I was hoping the whole small-timer self-deprecating shtick would make me seem more likeable, just a poor, good-natured-but-stupid guy trying to make ends meet. Somebody kind of like them, only making a little mistake here and there. Apparently that was too subtle for these guys.

"Where's the wallet?" Scholarship said, flexing his fingers to stretch out the leather strap.

At first I was tempted to hold back on him, but I was still seeing spots in my right eye, and that made me think twice about things. I decided to be like a pizza delivery guy. Cut my losses and move on. "Taped to the back of the toilet," I said.

Pavlo went and got the dirty pictures. He came back flipping through the images, wearing a look of hungry admiration. Then he saw the way Viktor was frowning, apparently not approving of the fact that he was skimming Maksym Romanenko's private property. Pavlo slapped the wallet closed and tossed it over to his boss.

"It all there, Vicky," he said.

I sighed, relieved. I thought that was going to be the end of things. Shows how much I know.

Now it's eleven hours later, and Viktor Kostiuk is giving me a look of grudging approval. "You've done well," he says. Again I can't help but notice how easily the English language rolls off his tongue, especially when compared to Pavlo. "All night long. What, fifty or sixty tries? And you were only struck five or six times."

Feels like more than that to me, mainly because Scholarship loosened my fillings with his last left hook. But that number seems about right, not counting the preliminary action before the game started.

"That's close to a ninety-percent success rate," he continues. "Impressive for a young man in a stressful situation. *Nervy staly.* Nerves of steel. That's good."

"I got 'im four times myself, Vicky," Pavlo pipes up. "Pretty good, huh?"

Viktor ignores him. But yeah, the dumpy Ukrainian was actually a challenge for me.

The game had been Pavlo's idea, after they got the picture wallet back. I think he just wanted an excuse to hit me again. It was a variation on the This Is You Lying game he'd seen me do at the park. In that trick, I ask the mark to tell me three lies—something like "I am a ninety-six-year-old woman. I'm currently in Zimbabwe. I'm wearing Bart Simpson underwear." While they're fibbing to me, I get a read on their unconscious lying habits, their bluffing "tells," so to speak.

Next I have them pick a card from the deck and then reshuffle it back in. After that, I separate the deck into four stacks, face up, and make them tell me, "No, my card's not in that stack" until

I see them lying. I keep making smaller stacks and narrowing it down until there's only one card left that I know they're lying about. That, of course, is their card. Then I get a nice tip and everybody goes home happy.

According to the rule my new buddies added, though, every time I got the card wrong . ... well, I got beat up a little.

Viktor was pretty easy to read. His left eye twitched whenever he told a lie. It wasn't a big deal, but I saw it right away and, thankfully, he never laid a hand on me all night.

Scholarship wasn't too difficult, although at one point he figured out I was reading the way he clenched his fists when he lied. He suckered me twice before I understood that he'd corrected that tell. After that, I was more attentive.

Pavlo, though, was unpredictable, unreliable, like he never knew himself whether he was lying or telling the truth. I had to try and read him fresh every time, which was fine early on but took its toll once it got past four in the morning. This violent little game has gone on until late this morning. By now, we are all a little exhausted.

"Yeah, he did well," Scholarship mutters to nobody in particular. "I almost feel sorry for what the kid's got coming next."

I see that the clock in my kitchen now reads 11:31 a.m. Time has kept ticking on, in spite of everything. The room falls eerily silent, so much so that I can track Pavlo's labored breathing behind me. Seems like everybody's waiting, but I'm not sure what for.

Almost like it's happening in slow motion, I watch Scholarship take another bite of his sandwich.

And then I hear a knock on my apartment door.

3

BLISS

Atlanta, GA
Little Five Points Neighborhood
Friday, March 17, 11:11 a.m.
28 days to Nevermore

Bliss June Monroe saw the silver Ford GT sports car and knew it was coming for her. She held it in her gaze when it stopped at the red light where Mansfield Avenue North crossed Moreland Avenue—but just for a moment. Just long enough to make sure.

She patted the worn picture in her left breast pocket and suddenly felt like crying all over again. She didn't, of course. She was long past that weepy, weak woman she once was. But still, seeing that GT made her think it was a nice gesture that he'd come today to pay his respects. That he, at least, hadn't forgotten.

She adjusted her wheelchair to face the parking lot a little better, opening her posture to be more welcoming. People, in general, knew not to interrupt Bliss while she was painting a portrait in the backroom office of her retail store. But when she spread her oils and canvas on the sidewalk, out in front here, well, that meant she was in a mood for company.

When she'd opened this place—what, forty-four years ago now?—she'd named it Sister Bliss's Secret Stash. At first it was just a little shop with all the funky, junky, fun stuff Bliss could find at local auctions and estate sales. But people liked it, and they kept coming back, and after a time, it even became sort of a popular tourist destination here in the Little Five Points corner of Atlanta. Today it was a ten-thousand-square-foot superstore of unique and unusual items imported from all over the world. In here, rock stars, actors, and everyday folks found one-of-a-kind swan dresses, priceless stage costumes from the Roaring Twenties, worthless junk jewelry, Batman toasters and Joker wigs, antique books and magazines, vaudeville posters, collector cards, funky hats from model runways, and even bejeweled combat boots for underground dance clubs. If it was retro or out of the ordinary, if it was an outfit no other store could even imagine—if it was a gift you couldn't find anywhere else—it would be at Sister Bliss's Secret Stash.

Of course, no one called her "Sister" anymore. Some things came with being seventy-one years old, and one of them was losing the name Sister. But she was okay with that.

"Mornin', Mama Bliss," a young woman said on her way into the store.

She was a pretty little thing. Honey-colored skin and dark eyes that glittered. Bliss liked her, liked seeing her visit every so often. Didn't like that new thug boyfriend with her today, though—some guy wearing the orange Nike basketball shoes that represented the Kipo gangs from down south. Riverdale maybe, or maybe one of the starter sets in East Point. Wherever he was from, he didn't belong here in Little Five Points; none of the "Knights in pimp orange" did. Mama Bliss knew it, and he did too—she could tell, by the way he ducked his head at the sight of her and barely mumbled his greeting before disappearing into the store. The girl, though, paused long enough to say a kind word. Mama always appreciated a little southern hospitality in the younger generations.

"Mornin', sugar," Mama said. She was sometimes bad at remembering names, but nobody seemed to mind being called *sugar*. "Where's that sweetie pie of yours?"

"Grandma's watching Baby Girl this morning. Got birthday money to spend today, and this way I don't have to share it!" The girl giggled with a genuineness that made Bliss's heart ache. Davis could've done well by this one.

Out of the corner of her eye, Bliss saw the GT ease through the stoplight at Mansfield and swing right into the parking lot. It was crowded today; he was going to have to park down by the dry cleaner and walk his way up to see her, but he didn't know that yet. He drove slowly past where she was sitting, found nothing open, and then circled back to where he'd come from before finding a space near the front of the Redi-Dry, at the end of the lot. She saw him exit his sports car and pause to stretch his cramped muscles beside the door before slamming it shut.

He was still a handsome man, Bliss decided—still in good shape for a guy who had to be, what, thirty-four or thirty-five years old now? Apparently his CIA cover in Army Special Forces had taught him to stay lean and active into his middle age. His skin was lighter than most in this neighborhood but held enough sunlight in it to confirm he spent a lot of time outdoors. His dark hair was sensibly short—a man who liked to look good but didn't like the hassle of gel and blow-dry after a shower. He wore denim jeans and a tan suit coat over a blue, collarless shirt that favored his muscled torso. Comfortable black boots finished his outfit. He looked ready for either business or pleasure, and Bliss wondered which of those was on his mind this morning.

She turned her attention away from the man and back to the girl at her side. "Well, happy birthday, sugar," Bliss said. "You go on inside and tell 'em that Mama Bliss said you get the birthday discount. They'll treat you right."

"Thanks, Mama!" The girl leaned in for a quick kiss on the cheek and got a good look at the painting in front of Bliss's wheelchair. "Oh, that's so pretty," she said, pointing to the canvas. "You're so talented, Mama Bliss."

Bliss tilted her head to the side in mock disapproval. "Oh, go on now, honey. You already got your discount. No need to butter up the old crippled woman anymore."

The girl laughed again, a hopeful, honest sound. "No, Mama, I'd never do that. It really is beautiful. When will it be done?"

Bliss saw the man nearing them now and figured it was okay to make him wait. "I don't know," she said. "Maybe never. Just something to keep myself busy on the long days."

The girl looked up and saw the man waiting, saw her time was done. She was suddenly shy and uncomfortable. "Okay, well, thanks. I'll show you what I come up with when I'm done shopping." She smiled, avoiding eye contact with the man.

"You do that, sugar. Have fun, and happy birthday."

Bliss reached for her paintbrush while the girl went into the store. She began adding color to a particularly troublesome corner of her creation, leaning forward in her wheelchair until her face was only inches away from the canvas. The man waited, not speaking, while she tackled her work.

Always a gentleman, she thought. *I do like that about him*. Still, she made him stand in silence a full minute before she spoke.

"Samuel Eric Douglas Hill," she said to her painting. "What

brings a fine, upstanding detective like you into our humble little circumstances?"

He chuckled. "Yeah, I've missed you too, Mama Bliss. How're you doing this beautiful day?"

She set down the paintbrush and turned her chair to face him. She didn't smile. "I think you know how I'm doing, Samuel," she said, "or you wouldn't be here."

Samuel's face lost its mirth. He nodded and said nothing. His eyes were lost in hers, and she felt the familiar sadness again. She saw that he was holding a small bouquet of tulips and a tall cup of what looked like lemonade.

"Those for me?" she said at last. He nodded. "Well, hand 'em over, honey. And go tell Darrent to get you a folding chair so you can come sit by me for a bit, like when you and old Truck used to come by together."

"Okay, Mama," he said. He set the lemonade near the easel holding the painting and put the flowers in her lap. He tapped a short kiss on her forehead in the process, and she patted the back of his neck at the same time. The tulips really were pretty, she decided, an assortment of reds, yellows, and deep purples.

Across the street, a man eating an early lunch at the table on the patio outside of Planet Bombay aimed his dark sunglasses in her direction.

He was of medium build, dark skinned, maybe late twenties, wearing a black T-shirt covered by a light gray hoodie. She caught his eye and returned his gaze with deliberate care, daring him to do . . . well, whatever it was he was thinking of doing. He saw the challenge, and she could see him considering it behind his sunglasses, but in the end he turned away. He wrapped up the rest of his lunch and walked south toward the Clothing Warehouse, a big, red building with giant praying hands painted on the side, just above a caption that read, *Pray for*

ATL. She lost sight of him when he turned the corner, heading away from the Clothing Warehouse, and disappeared.

A moment later Samuel Hill returned with a folding chair.

Mama Bliss favored him with a grim smile. "It's nice of you to come out today," she said. "Respectful. I appreciate that. Davis would have appreciated it. But I'm guessing that's not the only reason you're here."

Samuel looked at the ground for a moment, then said, "Well, I am sorry about Davis. What is this, eight years since your grandson was . . . well, since he passed?"

"Since he was taken from me," Bliss said. "You can say it, Samuel. You know what happened good as I do."

"I am sorry, Bliss."

"I know, Samuel. We all are. And yes, eight years today." She patted the picture in her breast pocket again.

"Is there anything I can do for you today?"

She leaned back and shot him a contemptuous look. "What you gonna do that Mama can't do for herself?" she said.

Samuel tried to stop his gaze from reaching her wheelchair, but failed.

"This chair of mine is a convenience, not a habit," she snapped. "Diabetes hasn't taken my feet yet, and maybe it never will. You best watch yourself before Mama Bliss hops outta this wheelchair and wraps these flowers around your pretty little neck."

Samuel laughed out loud. "You're right, Mama. Even though I have never—not ever, not in all the years I've known you—seen you get out of that chair, I believe you can just because you say you can. Now don't hurt me. I'm just trying to be helpful, just trying to be your friend today."

Bliss couldn't help but smile back in his direction. "That's better. But I know you, Samuel Hill. Now that you're officially a hotshot detective in the Atlanta PD, you want Mama Bliss to fill you in on some secrets again, like she used to do when you were CIA, isn't that right?"

"Mama, shh," Samuel said, grinning and immediately scanning the area for eavesdroppers.

"Shoot, Samuel, anybody can take one look at you and know you're police. Why you think that girl ran into the store as soon as she saw you walk up? Maybe you knew how to fit in overseas where people slip in and out all the time, but here in Little Five Points we know our own. And we can smell a cop all the way from Inman Park."

"All right, Mama, all right. I'll give you that most people here know I'm a police officer. But nobody's supposed to know I used to work with the CIA. Most of the people down at the Zone 6 precinct headquarters don't even know that. They think I'm just another army veteran working in law enforcement after serving in the military."

"Ah, so now I got another secret about you!" Bliss crowed. "That might come in helpful someday." She slapped his shoulder and leaned back in victory.

They shared a quick moment of silence, then Samuel said, "Okay, yes, I could use a little help from you. You know, just to keep me in the loop. Everybody knows that Mama Bliss knows everything about Little Five Points. I'd be pretty foolish not to check in with you from time to time, right?"

She patted his hand. "That's right, honey. Mama knows everything. You just remember that and we'll be all right, like always."

"Like always." He looked sober again. "Mama, do you know the name Nevermore?"

She turned her head sideways in his direction. "You mean like in that poem? 'Quoth The Raven, "Nevermore"'? Seems like your wife would know more about that than me. Ain't Trudi the one with a college degree in fine literature and such?"

Samuel's lips pressed tightly together for just an instant, then he said, "Well, *ex-wife* you mean. But no, not the poem. I keep hearing whispers that something big is about to break in Atlanta, something people are calling 'Nevermore.' But no one I've talked to seems to know exactly what it refers to, only that it's going to be bad, and that it might be some kind of homegrown terrorist plot like the bombing in Centennial Olympic Park back in 1996."

"And what's that got to do with me?"

"Well, Mama, the only solid info I can get is that Nevermore is coming out of Little Five Points. So, of course, I came to you."

Bliss nodded thoughtfully.

Out on the street, a car screeched—a near miss on a fender bender. She listened to someone shout and also thought she heard music coming from somewhere in the parking lot nearby. She heard signs of life all around her—a bird chirping overhead, a conversation going on between two friends just down the sidewalk, Samuel Hill breathing lightly, waiting for her to say something.

A flicker of movement drew her eyes back to her painting, and she silently cursed herself for not stopping a tear from leaking.

"He was a good boy, my grandson," she said quietly. "A good boy."

"I know, Mama," Samuel said. "Davis had the whole world before him. I only wish I'd been able to help him before the Kipo got their hooks in him. Before it was too late."

"Wasn't nothing you could do, honey." She squeezed his hand. "He was flirting with them gang boys before you ever made Georgia your home. Ol' Truck, your CIA boss, he should of done something. Davis was supposed to grow up to be one of his boys. But Truck was off playing house in 'Bama or some other awful place."

"Truck was kind of busy with his own problems. It was complicated."

Bliss felt the anger rising again, had to remind herself that Samuel meant well, that he didn't know everything. That he'd come out today to sit with her, not to argue with her. She let go of his hand and looked into his face. "How's it going with your Miss Trudi?" she said. "You patch things up with that girl yet?"

Samuel's head dipped for a quick second. "That's really complicated," he said. He looked up at the sky. "No, we haven't really 'patched things up.' But we're talking now at least. Almost friends again, sort of. And sometimes working together on cases, though I can't say she was happy when I took the job with the Atlanta police department last Christmas."

"Well, why should she be? You left her alone back at the detective agency. Again."

"Yeah, but it's more than just that. It's . . . well, it's complicated."

"You keep saying that," Mama said. She turned and picked up her paintbrush. "But all right, honey, I believe you. Tell you what. You go inside and pick out something nice for Miss Trudi. Tell Darrent it's on me today—"

"Oh no, Mama, I can pay for—"

"Hush now, Samuel. You pick out something for Trudi. Tell her it's from me, and that I want to see her come 'round sometime. As for your Nevermore problem, I'll start sending out feelers, see what I can find out. Mama Bliss'll do what she can for you. She always does, right? I'll let you know if I hear anything."

"Thank you."

"Now get out of my way, honey, because I'm feeling the urge to desecrate a canvas again."

"All right, Mama." Samuel stood. "You take care, okay? You need anything, you call me. You got the number for my cell, right?"

She nodded, but he was already a distant memory to her.

She barely heard him mumble his goodbyes and disappear into the store.

Bliss looked back at her painting. It was about two-thirds done, an image of Davis Walker Monroe, her grandson, created from memory, without even having to look at the picture in her shirt pocket. Davis was floating in the sky, arms outstretched, wearing angel wings, with light from above filling the air behind him. She had wanted to paint him smiling, but it hadn't come out that way. Instead, he was just looking at her, a question in his eyes. Asking her what happened. Asking her what came next.

Samuel stopped on his way out to deliver a hug, but Bliss didn't notice, not really. She played along until he and his fancy little sports car were long gone. Then she dipped her paintbrush in the red oils.

She dabbed a bullet hole into Davis's head.

She let the paint drip down from there, just for a moment.

She scratched her red brush, hard, across his angel wings, down into his chest, down to the ground below his feet. Still his eyes asked their questions.

And today, like every March 17 since the shooting, Bliss June Monroe just didn't have a good answer.

4

TRUDI

Atlanta, GA
Old Fourth Ward
Friday, March 17, 11:24 a.m.
28 days to Nevermore

Trudi Sara Coffey walked toward the east entrance of the Boulevard Home Apartments and found herself wishing, just for a moment, that Samuel was with her.

It wasn't that she needed a bodyguard, or even that she was worried about the possible confrontation she was walking into—more than a decade of studying martial arts and self-defense had pretty much eliminated that kind of insecurity. Besides, she'd seen pictures of her target; she didn't see him as the violent type. She expected a conversation that would, hopefully, end in her favor.

It was just that, well, she kind of wished she had a friend going along for the ride on this one. An errand buddy. Someone who knew what she was about to do and understood what it took to do it. Somebody who'd laugh when she quoted an obscure line from a forgotten sitcom, just because he knew the line and knew the way she was misusing it to suit her own situational sense of humor.

Someone who shares my history.

Someone like that, she'd learned, was hard to come by.

After the divorce, after losing what she'd thought was impossible to lose, she'd hated Samuel for a while. Then she'd mourned him until finally coming to the point where she was over him, she thought, but still missed him sometimes. It wasn't great, but it was livable, and she'd gotten on with her life, burying herself in her detective agency, finding purpose in her faith and a few friends at her church, filling her days with work until she felt almost normal again.

Almost.

Then the whole Annabel Lee situation had exploded, bringing Samuel back into her life and forcing them to solve that case together. When it was over, she'd expected him to return to his globe-trotting work as a CIA field operative, but he'd surprised her once more.

"So," Samuel had said, "they're telling me to take a sabbatical."

"What?"

It had been October, about a year and a half ago. Trudi had been standing behind her desk at the Coffey & Hill Investigations office in Atlanta, and she couldn't follow what Samuel was saying. Wasn't this supposed to be another awkward goodbye? One of the many they'd grown accustomed to sharing?

"The CIA. They want me out of the field for a bit. They say that the whole Annabel Lee situation makes me 'hot' overseas right now, and they want me to cool off stateside for a while."

"Wow, I'm sorry, Samuel. I know how that must be hard for you."

Her ex-husband had shrugged. "At first I was a little upset about it. But now I'm thinking maybe it's for the best."

"Good for you."

Samuel had taken a long look across the hall toward the cluttered storage room.

"I notice you still have an empty office here at Coffey & Hill Investigations." He placed an unnecessary emphasis on the *Hill* part of Coffey & Hill. "And, you know, I've got some free time ahead of me."

"What are you suggesting?" Trudi had said. She bit her lip.

"I'm suggesting that maybe I could come back."

"Samuel." Trudi sat down heavily. "You know we can't do that. Not after, well, everything."

"No, no," he said, "I understand that part. I understand we can't get back together that way, not as husband and wife. But, you know, we're a good P.I. team, Tru-Bear. We were a great team working on the Annabel Lee case. We can't be lovers, I get that, but why can't we be partners? It is called Coffey & Hill Investigations, after all. That's both our names on the sign out there."

Trudi hadn't known what to say. She'd let the idea roll around in her head. *It would be nice to have Samuel Hill around again*, she'd told herself. He was a superb asset to any private investigation. Smart. Resourceful. Connected out the wazoo. *And a girl always appreciates looking at pretty things, right?* But still . . .

"I don't know, Samuel," she'd said at last. "It seems like it could be a big mistake."

"I know," he said, "it could be. Or it could be just the thing we've both been looking for since . . . since a few years ago."

"I don't know . . ."

Trudi interrupted her train of thought and frowned at the street-side entrance on this section of the Boulevard Home

Apartments. She'd been careful to park her teal Ford Focus as near to the easternmost entrance as she could, the nose of her car pointing toward a quick exit up Glen Iris Drive. That was just common sense as far as she was concerned. *Always check exit paths before entering unfamiliar territory*, she'd told herself a thousand times. Now her private detective training took over for the moment, and she let her eyes sweep over the grounds outside the doorway.

Here in the Old Fourth Ward, mature trees lined the streets, and graffiti decorated the dumpsters. The 1920s architecture stayed sturdily in place but hinted that this area had seen better times. Across the street from her was an empty lot, grassy and green, with tall trees shading it in beauty. She wasn't surprised to see a mother with two preschool-aged children enjoying an early-spring picnic over there. She kind of wished she could join them.

Instead, Trudi tilted her head back and looked up at the second floor of the red-brick apartment building. Every unit had a small covered patio or balcony. The balcony for the left, upstairs apartment had a lightweight, city-friendly bicycle stored on one side. *Useful*, she decided, *if you don't have to go very far from home to work*.

From what she could tell, the main entrance to each section of the building gave access to four apartments at a time. Enter through the main door and there would be two more doors on the first floor, with stairs up to two doors on the second floor. The traditional way out of Apartment 249, then, would be through the front door, down the indoor stairs, out the main door, and into the street. The nontraditional way out would be through the balcony door, over the side, and a ten-foot drop to the ground. Not pleasant, but certainly doable if it was required and if she was paying attention to her fall.

She glanced west, down the street, and frowned.

Like hers, most of the cars parallel-parked up and down this road fit right in—working-class vehicles, a few small trucks, almost all a few years old. But parked about five spaces behind her Focus was what appeared to be a current-year-model, black Cadillac Escalade ESV. That kind of luxury utility vehicle was a favorite of the suits over at CNN and City Hall—but it stuck out like an ugly Christmas sweater in this part of the Old Fourth Ward.

"Now why are you here?" she murmured to the car. "Seems like you belong in a *Sesame Street* song." The forgotten five-year-old inside her mind involuntarily sang out the tune, *One of these things is not like the others . . .*

She scanned down the street, looking past the Escalade, past the row of apartments on her left, toward the single-family homes that filled the rest of the block up to Boulevard Northeast, but the only people she could see outside at this moment were that single mom and her two happy kids on a picnic. Finally, she shrugged. She had an errand to do, and it was probably best to get it over with quickly. No sense obsessing about misplaced motor vehicles. Maybe a rich uncle was visiting, or somebody here had won the lottery.

At the top of the stairwell inside the building, Trudi checked her watch. It was 11:31 a.m. when she knocked on Apartment 249. She heard mumbling voices on the other side of the door and thought maybe a chair scraped the floor, as well. But no one answered.

Had the guy seen her come in? Maybe gone out over the balcony? She waited until 11:32 had come and lingered a bit before knocking again, a little louder this time.

She heard a grunt on the other side, and then a voice called out, "Who is it?"

Trudi weighed her options. If she said, "Trudi Coffey, private detective," the chances of the door to Apartment 249 opening were slim to none. If she said nothing, and just knocked again, that might be annoying enough to get a physical response. But somebody on the other side was obviously trying to hide something, and that made her more than a little curious.

She took a chance.

Trudi reached down to the doorknob and gave it a twist, surprised and pleased when it turned easily in her grasp. She pushed on the door but stayed in the hallway while it opened before her. She'd learned from experience that it was dangerous to walk into a room without clearing sightlines first. A terrorist with a gun might be hiding just inside the door, just out of view.

Apartment 249 was a basic Atlanta rat-hole, built decades ago, maybe refurbished once or twice over the years but mostly just a place to eat, sleep, and kill your dreams. Someone with a little incentive might've made it a nice, comfy, even stylish rat-hole, but the guy who lived here obviously wasn't that kind of renter.

The front door of the apartment opened into a drab, tiny living area that featured a beat-up green couch and a lawn chair placed together, both facing a wooden coffee table and a small, wall-mounted TV set. Trudi peeked toward her right and saw a narrow hallway that she figured must lead to the kitchen and bedroom. She also saw a heavyset Russian man with a startled look on his face standing by the window on the opposite wall.

"Hey, what you think you doing? You can't be in here."

After hearing the accent, she thought maybe the man wasn't Russian, but from somewhere else in Eastern Europe. Chechnya maybe? Or Ukraine?

Either way, Trudi didn't bother responding to him. Instead, she stepped into the room and headed toward the kitchen. The heavy man was too surprised to stop her. She reached the entrance to the kitchen, then paused.

The first thing she saw was the shirtless young guy, legs strapped to a wooden dining room chair, hands cuffed behind his back, sporting the requisite bruises and bleeding from a systematic beating.

She guessed he was maybe mid-twenties, fit, but not a gym rat. Probably more familiar with running or riding a bicycle than he was with lifting weights or punching a guy in the face. His skin was pale, but not sickly white, more like basic Pilgrim Settler stock mixed in with other European brand names down through the generations until it had arrived at this slightly bland, Caucasian hue. His hair was dirty blond, short and spiky, and his eyes—well, at least the non-swollen one Trudi could see—were startling blue, like water in an ice-covered lake.

Bet he thinks he's kind of cute when he's not bleeding all over himself, she thought briefly.

Trudi didn't let herself stay there too long, though. The surprisingly big athlete by the refrigerator attracted the lion's share of her attention. He'd be tough to handle, she knew, if things got confrontational. And judging by the bulge on the left side of his black blazer, he was also carrying a little firepower in a holster next to his heart. That was something to worry about.

The athlete was eating a sandwich when she came in, and she was glad to see he hadn't put it down when he saw her. That meant he wasn't ready to do anything violent—at least not yet.

Behind her, the chubby guy was trying to get his lightweight Adidas jacket off the ugly green couch, in a hurry to put it on instead of trying to chase Trudi, like he'd left something in a pocket that made him feel safe. Something he might want to use in the near future.

His mistake, she told herself. That goon she could deal with when the time came.

Next, in the space of a thought, Trudi scrutinized the third man in the kitchen. He had a medium build and was clearly related to Piggy in the Adidas jacket. *If not Russian, then Ukrainian*, she decided. That in itself was something. Ninety-percent-plus of the Atlanta population was either African American or melting-pot Caucasian, so finding two menacing, ethnic Ukrainian guys in an obscure OFW apartment was fairly unexpected; as far as she knew, the Ukrainian Mafia types stayed mainly in New York and Los Angeles. Were they branching out, testing the waters here in the Deep South? A question to explore later.

She could see that this third man was solid inside his expensive suit, and he was standing very still. She also saw his eyes evaluating her in the same way she was assessing him.

That one's dangerous, she decided. *The boss.*

She plastered a grin on her face and tried to look flirtatious.

"Well," she said to the room, "looks like The Raven's having a party and he forgot to invite me."

5

RAVEN

Atlanta, GA
Old Fourth Ward
Friday, March 17, 11:36 a.m.
28 days to Nevermore

First things first: I think I'm in love.

It's not often that a beautiful woman just walks into your dumpster-decorated apartment and acts like she belongs there. It's even rarer for that beautiful woman not to run screaming the minute she sees a bunch of mobsters beating you into a bloody pulp in the kitchen.

"Well," My Future Wife says, "looks like The Raven's having a party and he forgot to invite me."

Nice. She knows who I am. I try not to cough blood when I smile at her.

"I'm not going to lie to you, Raven," she continues casually. "You don't look good."

I shrug, but I can't stop smiling. I can't keep my eyes off her, either.

It may just be the exhaustion talking, but I'm fairly certain I've never seen anyone or anything more captivating than this woman is right now. I'm guessing she's about five foot, six inches tall and around one hundred and twenty-five pounds. She's older than me, I think, maybe a year or two. Maybe five. Or maybe a hundred years older, it doesn't matter. Age is just a number when you're in love.

She's wearing boot-cut Levis under a stylish, spring-weight leather jacket. The coat is black, short-waisted with long arms, and unzipped. Sexy as all get-out, if you ask me. Her short, black boots match the jacket, which just looks really cool on her. She's trim, but not delicate like the pampered girls I see pretending to jog around Piedmont Park or Freedom Park. Her calf muscles bulge against the snug fabric of her jeans, and I can see there's a tight, flat stomach barely hidden behind her untucked, pale yellow, button-up shirt. She's a workout warrior, I can tell. I'll have some catching up to do in that area if we're going to make our future marriage work. She'll be worth the effort.

Much as I like her athletic figure, though, it's her face that captures my imagination. She's a natural beauty, wearing only a little eyeliner and nothing else in the way of makeup. Her hair is thick, nut-brown, and tangled slightly, happily, just past her shoulders. Hazel eyes look at me, and her lips make me lick my mouth in anticipation of a kiss. Of course that hurts, since my lips are cut and bleeding, but hey, what's a guy in love gonna do?

"Weren't you that main girl in the *Ant-Man* movie?" I say to her.

I think it's a pretty good line for the spur of the moment—I mean, who wouldn't be flattered by a comparison to the beautiful actress Evangeline Lilly? She just rolls her eyes, though, and I think she might have said a bad word in her head. Even Scholarship, over by the refrigerator, snorts at how lame that came out. She doesn't acknowledge the compliment and instead turns her attention to Viktor, standing behind me.

"You can't be in here, lady." It's Pavlo again, whining from the living room. I'm almost gleeful at the fact that she ignores him completely. Instead, she speaks to Viktor.

"Seems like it's about time for this party to break up, don't you think?"

Is she threatening him? Is she actually daring him to threaten her?

Pavlo makes a move behind her and, faster than I would've imagined possible, she reaches into the back waistband of her jeans and produces some kind of small handgun. Everybody freezes, and I feel like applauding. It's like I'm watching a really cool western unspool in 3D right in my kitchen. I suddenly crave a large bag of buttery, salty popcorn.

Now she's turning to face Pavlo, slow, deliberate, like he barely deserves her attention.

"I think you'd be wise to step away from me," she says to him. Her voice is even and deadly. Then she puts up a lazy smile. "My therapist tells me I'm a little neurotic about my personal space."

"Uh . . ."

Pavlo doesn't know what to do. He looks to Viktor for guidance. I peek back at the boss man and he's mirroring My Future Wife's tight grin, but he doesn't say anything.

Now the girl is giving Pavlo an exaggerated appraisal, looking him up and down like he's a used car and she's trying to decide whether it's worth the hassle to kick the tires. She relaxes visibly.

"You know," she says to him, "I don't think I'm even going to need this, after all."

She turns her back completely to Pavlo and looks Viktor dead in the eye. She carefully lays the pistol on the table in front of me. "Want to tell your baby brother to back away," she says, "before I break parts of him?"

Holy cow, did that just happen? I am so going to marry this girl and have lots of babies who grow up to be just like her.

"Uh, what—" I think Pavlo is about to wet his pants.

There's a stale moment of silence before Viktor finally comes out of his coma. "You heard the lady, Cousin," he says. "Party's over."

Viktor is still smiling, but his eyes have the look of a wolf, or like a fox about to raid a henhouse. Scholarship doesn't hesitate. He shoves the last bite of his sandwich into his mouth and steps toward the door. He taps my shoulder affectionately on his way out, like we're old buddies or I'm his nephew or something. He nods in the direction of My Future Wife as he squeezes past her to leave the kitchen. She never takes her eyes off Viktor.

"Uh . . ." Pavlo still doesn't get what's happening.

"Come on, Pav," Scholarship says as he gently pushes the chubby guy toward the front door. "Time to go."

A few seconds later, there's only me, My Future Wife, and Viktor Kostiuk in the apartment.

Nobody says anything for a minute. It feels kind of awkward, but I know better than to add words to this silence. The girl and Viktor are still just looking at each other, sizing each other up. I'm really wishing I could scratch my left ear, but I wait it out like a pro.

How cool would that be? My mind wanders. *A professional league of ear-scratchers. I would so be a star in that league.*

Yeah, I think I might have an attention-deficit problem.

Finally Viktor breaks the eye-lock and reaches into his pocket. He pulls out a gold money clip that's fat with green bills and peels one off the top. He leans over my shoulder and places a one-hundred-dollar bill next to the girl's gun. With his fingers still pressing Ben Franklin onto the table, he looks up at My Future Wife.

"Thanks for the show, miss," he says. "I was very entertained."

She says nothing as he lifts his hand off the table and walks casually past her into the living room. She follows him, and I hear them both stop at the front door. "Might want to lock this," he says lightly. "In this neighborhood, you never know who might come barging in." Then the door shuts, and it's just me and the girl. I hear her twist the deadbolt, hard and fast.

A breath later, she's drifted back into the living room, where I can see her from my seat in the kitchen.

"Huh," I say. "I mean, thank you. I—"

"Hush," she says.

"I just—"

She glares at me, and I take the hint. To pass the time, I read the lettering on her gun: *3032 TOMCAT—32 AUTO Made in USA*, it says. A Beretta Tomcat, now my favorite type of weapon, even though I know I don't have the right personality to ever own, let alone use, a gun. Still, that doesn't mean I can't have a favorite.

I notice now that she's peering through the curtains on the balcony window, being careful not to disturb them. *Doesn't want Viktor to know she's watching him leave*, I reason. So I just enjoy the view for a minute.

She really is stunning.

I wonder if she'll want to honeymoon overseas or if I can talk her into someplace in the States, like maybe Disney World or a beach resort on Hilton Head Island. Finally she turns away from the balcony and comes back to where I'm still tied up in the kitchen.

She sighs. "Like I said, you don't look good, Raven."

I try smiling again. It hurts, but it feels good at the same time. It's been a long night.

"What, this?" I say. "Just a few scratches. Now, let's talk about you."

She almost smiles, I can tell. At least I hope that's what that is. She picks up her gun from the table and re-holsters it but leaves the hundred-dollar bill. *Maybe I'll get to keep that money? Score!*

"I feel like I should ask what that was all about," she says slowly, "but honestly, I don't want to know."

"Can I ask you a question?" I say. "I mean, two questions?"

She starts to say something, then stops herself. She nods instead.

"First question: Who are you?"

She laughs in spite of herself. "Yeah, I guess that's fair at this point." She pulls out identification. *Man, she even looks good in an ID-card photo.* "My name is Trudi Coffey. I'm the principal private detective at Coffey & Hill Investigations over in West Midtown."

"So my father sent you," I say. I feel my world start to crumble. I'm not smiling anymore. *We would've been so happy together.*

She tilts her head to the right, a question on her lips, but she doesn't let it pass. "No," she says, "I was hired by someone else."

Ah, heavenly rapture. I'm in love again.

She reaches inside her jacket and pulls out a small, white envelope, then she hesitates. "Well, this can wait. I'd better get you to a hospital. Where do you keep scissors? I'll cut off those zip ties on your feet."

"No," I say, and maybe I say it too quickly. "No, I'm fine. I mean, yes, please cut me loose. Scissors are in the top drawer by the refrigerator. But no, I don't need to go to the hospital. I'm fine, really."

It takes her only a minute to cut my feet loose, but she's

stymied by the handcuffs. "I don't have the right tool with me for those," she says. "You have a key somewhere? Otherwise, the way they're threaded through the slats there, you'll have to carry that chair with you for the rest of your life."

"No, but it's okay. I'll figure something out. I've been in worse."

She nods slowly.

"I think, really, I should take you to the hospital."

"No, no. Honestly not necessary. All good here. Just need a little sleep and a hot bowl of oatmeal or something mushy like that."

"I see," she says. "Don't want to answer the questions that come with medical treatment or face the police officers who'll come when the hospital staff reports an assault victim in their emergency room."

I shrug. She's pretty much nailed it. Of course, My Future Wife is a private detective, so why should I be surprised? *She's got brains*, I tell myself. *Our children will be pretty and smart.*

She presses hard under my nose, and it makes me wince. But I love it anyway because she's so near to me now I can make out the faint smell of lavender soap on her skin. Heavenly.

"That was risky," I say to change the subject, "putting your gun on the table."

Now it's her turn to shrug. "I was negotiating," she says. "I was offering the boss guy a way out and asking him to let you go. He clearly had the advantage, especially with that football player in the corner there. But if he'd wanted to kill you, he would have done it hours ago. So I took a chance that he might be close to finished with you."

"He might have called your bluff. I mean, turned down your negotiation offer."

"Then I would've incapacitated the chubby guy with spear-fingers to the throat and tried to get the gun out of his right jacket pocket before that football player could get to me."

She says it so matter-of-factly that I think she probably could've done it.

"How did you know he had a—no, never mind. Don't want to waste my second question on something trivial like that. All right. Show me what's in your envelope," I say. "Whatever you need, you got it. I owe you at least that much."

She pauses to look at me, and I feel lost in her eyes. At first they tip toward green, then brown, then both. Mesmerizing. *So this is why Paul McCartney wrote so many cheesy love songs.*

"All right," she says. She produces the envelope again and pulls out two pictures of a Glashütte Original Lady Pavonina, a luxury watch with diamond studs in all twelve number spots on the face. She lays them on the table in front of me, and I feel a little embarrassed. Still, this girl just saved my life.

What's a stolen six-thousand-dollar watch between us?

"My client gave this watch to his fiancée as a wedding present," she says. "You know that old tradition, 'Something old, something new, something borrowed, something blue'? Well, this was going to be the 'something new' she wore at the ceremony. But she got cold feet, and they had a big, blowout fight the week before the wedding. Canceled the whole thing. A few months later, my client asked for the watch back. She told him she'd lost it. He thought she was lying, so he hired me to find it. I started checking area pawn shops, and that trail led me to you. Apparently you're something of a regular in a few of those places."

Busted.

I nod toward the bathroom down the hall. "It's taped under the bathroom rug."

She looks surprised. "Aren't you worried about damaging it in there? That's an expensive piece of jewelry."

"Nah," I say. "The rug is kind of shoved in a corner, and I know never to step on it. Fortunately, I don't get many visitors, either." I try flashing what I think is a winsome smile, but I'm beginning to worry I may be losing her.

"Hmm."

She turns away and heads to the bathroom. It feels good to move my feet and legs again. The pins and needles of blood flow down there are almost all gone. I'm thinking of standing up, carrying the chair, and following her into the bathroom when she appears suddenly in the kitchen doorway.

Busted again.

She drops four clear poly bags onto the table. One of them holds the watch she was looking for. The other three . . . well, the other three I was hoping she wouldn't find since they were taped to the porcelain underneath the sink. Apparently Trudi Coffey is thorough in her work.

Gonna be tough to make rent this month.

"Looks like you've been busy over there in Freedom Park," she says. She picks up the largest poly bag. "This sapphire bracelet is breathtaking. No wonder the pawn shops like you so much."

"You've got the wrong idea," I say. "I'm not a hardcore thief. I just need a little help to pay rent sometimes."

"So you steal from your fans? That's not really a magic trick, you know."

"No, of course not. I don't steal from fans, not the locals at least." An image of Max Roman flashes in my mind. "Well, not usually. But sometimes when there's a group of rich tourists passing through, when I can see they don't really need all the glitz they're holding on to and I know they'll be gone in a few days anyway, I just sort of redistribute the wealth. No harm, no foul, right?"

She drops the bracelet next to a poly-bagged Apple Watch with a stainless steel case and a thick, braided gold chain. She picks up the Glashütte Original Lady Pavonina and stuffs it into her inside coat pocket along with the envelope that holds the pictures. Then she sits across from me at the table, thinking.

"Thanks for coming," I say into the silence. "Who knows, you might have saved my life." I laugh at the joke, but I can see she doesn't think it's funny.

"Those guys"—she nods toward the door—"might come back. Are you prepared for that?"

"What's to prepare?" I say.

She nods and then reaches into her coat and produces a small pocketbook. She pulls out a card. "Pen?" she says.

"Same drawer as the scissors."

She scribbles something on the back of the card and drops it on the table.

"That's my card," she says. "On the back are the email address and phone number for my ex-husband, Samuel Hill. He's with the Atlanta PD. Tell him I sent you and that you'd like to anonymously turn over some stolen goods. He'll make sure everything gets sorted out."

Ex-husband is all I hear from that speech. *My Future Wife is single!*

". . . stop stealing from random people in parks," she's saying. "And if those thugs come back, remember your best exit is out that balcony door. It's about a ten-foot drop, so hang by your hands first. Don't just jump off the top. Then run away and find Samuel. He'll help you. He's good at helping."

"I'll be fine, really. No worries. But thanks."

"Go see Samuel Hill. I'm giving you a chance here, Raven. Maybe you should take it. Your life can be better than this."

I nod. And smile. I can't stop smiling.

She turns to go, and I realize I still haven't asked my second question. "Wait, uh, wait please," I say. "One more thing."

She stops in the hallway and looks back at me in the kitchen. I figure I should do this right, so I stand up, lifting the chair with my hands that are cuffed behind my back. Then I creak my way down onto one knee and give her what I think is a dreamy-eyed look.

"Trudi Coffey, will you marry me?"

My Future Wife walks out the door without giving me an answer.

"It's okay," I tell myself, sitting back on the chair again. "She just needs a little time to think about it."

6

BLISS

Atlanta, GA
Little Five Points
Friday, March 17, 12:15 p.m.
28 days to Nevermore

Bliss tried not to slam the door to her spacious office at the back of the Secret Stash. It rattled with a small thud anyway.

Oh well, she thought. *Nobody's paying any mind today.*

She rolled her wheelchair toward the desk on the far side of the room but didn't complete that journey. She didn't know what she wanted to do in here right now, she just knew she didn't want to have to talk to people anymore for a while. She scanned the room and nodded to herself.

It was a nice office. Though sparsely decorated, there was plenty of room for her to inhabit. It had once been a conference room, before the last remodel. Now it had been converted for her into a handicapped-accessible haven, a combination business office and studio apartment of sorts. The big desk took up the back corner, to the left, sitting underneath a large bay window in case she wanted a little sun on her back while she was going over inventory or tallying up receipts. There were also two file cabinets, a printer, scanner, copier, and other requisite office equipment. There was even a spot where she could set up her painting supplies and lose herself in oils and canvas if the fever hit her just right.

On the right side of the room, against the wall, was a small bed with a pillow and a plain comforter on top. Nearby was a mini-refrigerator, a microwave, a row of cupboards, and an undersized table for eating, or reading, or just doing a crossword puzzle in the morning time. Bliss had a traditional home not far from here, a nice four-bedroom house filled with all the comforts. But most days it just felt better to sleep here, in the simplicity of her office near the back of the store.

"What I got to go home to anyway?" she muttered to herself. "William long dead and gone. Lenore out to who-knows-where in the world. And Davis . . . Davis no more." She sighed. "At least here I don't have to fill up a whole house all by myself."

The clock on the microwave told her it was time to eat lunch, but she wasn't hungry and didn't feel like fiddling with her insulin pump just yet anyway. She dipped into her shirt pocket and pulled out the picture she carried wherever she went. It hurt to look at it sometimes, but today it made her smile. Davis, age eighteen, standing in front of a new car—well, new for him—with arms raised and keys flashing in the sunlight. He was grinning, and she liked that. She loved that boy's smile. It cheered her on many weary days after his mother left them both. And then the thought of Lenore made her own fledgling smile hide itself back inside her face.

"I got to do this, Mama," Lenore Monroe had told her. "It's a once-in-a-lifetime."

"But what about your boy?" Bliss had said. "You can't just pull

Davis outta his life and take him globe-trotting through South America on some rock-and-roll concert tour. He's only four years old. He's already registered for kindergarten next year."

"You don't understand how hard and how long I've been working for this, Mama—"

"Pshaw. 'Course I do. I was there for all of it, remember?"

"Daddy was there," Lenore said, and there was ice in her tone. "Daddy knew. He understood how music burns inside you, how it gets hold of you like a drug and never lets go."

Bliss had said nothing to that. She was right—William Monroe knew the addiction of sound, knew the comfort of fingers blistered by guitar strings and the lullabies of melodies no one else could hear. Her husband had passed that passion on to his daughter, and they'd been thick as thieves in their time, listening to old vinyl records of Billie Holiday or Sarah Vaughan, crowing over some long-lost power ballad by Aerosmith or Journey. He'd taught her well, insisted she discover all styles of music, not just the ones that catered to the current tastes. They were kindred spirits, and for some reason she never quite understood, Bliss was always on the outside of that circle, invited to listen but never allowed to join their private little club.

"I got to do it, Mama," Lenore said again. "They want me to be the number-one backup singer, and the tour is already booked. I'll be traveling the world, singing in front of thousands of people at every venue. It's *my chance*. I make good on this, and I just might have a career, a life outside of Atlanta for once."

"It's eight months gone! Eight months flitting about like you got no responsibilities, nobody else to think about. What about Davis, honey? Life on the road, new hotel room every night, drugs and alcohol and who knows what else spread all around all the time? That's no life for a baby boy. No life for my baby grandson."

Lenore nodded, and a serious layer added itself to her face. "I know. You're right. You're one hundred percent right. And that's why I'm here."

Mama Bliss had felt suddenly stupid. Of course that was why Lenore was here. She should have seen it coming.

"Eight months," Mama said.

"Eight months," Lenore said. "I'll only be gone eight months. And I'll be getting paid. I can send money back to you every two weeks to help with his care and expenses."

"You already owe me more money than you can ever pay back."

"See, so you should be glad I'll be working! It's only eight months, Mama. You can take him for eight months, cantcha? This is my chance, my big break." She breathed hard before saying, "Daddy would want me to go."

And so Davis had moved in with Gran-Mama.

And eight months had gotten extended to thirteen, with one quick visit from Lenore in between—lunch at a fast-food place—and that was it. Then another tour called, and Davis's time with Gran-Mama became two years. And by the time year three rolled around, Lenore finally gave up all pretense of wanting to be a mother, and they all just accepted the fact that she wasn't coming back for her son. She was caught up in world tours, mesmerized by her place standing ten feet from stardom on every stage, always working toward that next "big break" that never seemed to come.

They heard from her at Christmas, and sometimes on Davis's birthday, but after he turned twelve, Lenore seemed to lose touch with anybody from her old life back in Atlanta—including Mama and Davis. She quit trying, and Mama decided that was fine with her. Her grandson had become more than just a grandson. With her husband long passed away and her daughter as good as dead, Davis Jensen Monroe had become an old woman's sole reason for living, the light that shone in the morning and the comfort that hugged her good night. As far as Davis was concerned, he'd never had a mother—barely remembered her, really. He just had a grandmother who promised him that someday, just you wait, he was going to be greater than anything and anyone his family had ever seen.

"I broke that promise," Bliss muttered to the photo in her hand. "We both broke it, I guess."

Bliss heard a knock and shoved the picture back into her pocket.

"In!" she hollered.

A moment later, Darrent poked his head through the doorway. "Just wanted to check in before I go home for the afternoon," he said. "I'm working a split shift today, since we got that shipment rolling in tonight."

Mama looked at Darrent's graying beard and wondered where the time had gone and why it had been in such a hurry to pass by.

William had hired Darrent Hayes right out of college, fresh from his MBA program at Georgia State University. Back then, he was a bright-eyed, handsome young man in his mid-twenties, driven to be the best, ready to make his mark on the world. He started out helping Mama as assistant manager on the sales floor, but he was too smart for that. It wasn't long before William stole him away to work on the back side of the business, in inventory management with him.

"I hired him." William had laughed when Bliss objected. "I just loaned him to you for a bit." Then he kissed his wife hard on the lips and promised to find her another assistant manager "just as good, or almost at least."

Darrent was a quick learner, and before five years were up,

he'd become the right-hand man to both William and Bliss. They trusted him more than they trusted each other sometimes.

After William passed away, Darrent didn't allow the store to miss a beat. "You do what you need to do, Mama," he'd said as she'd grieved her new widowhood. "The Secret Stash and your husband's hard work will be waiting whenever you're ready to come back." Of course she did come back—how could she stay away from something she and William had built together?—but she left more and more of the day-to-day responsibilities to Darrent until he was doing even more than William used to do.

Now, truth was, he ran Sister Bliss's Secret Stash, and it had prospered under his care. Mama was still the boss, of course—ownership did have its privileges. But she mostly just looked over his shoulder to make sure everything was going smoothly and made sure Darrent had the resources he needed to keep doing his job. It was a system that worked, but sometimes she wished she still had the energy to do all the things Darrent did for her now. Still, other concerns took her attention, and she knew it was best to leave things as they were.

Mama Bliss looked at Darrent, saw hair and beard speckled with gray but eyes that were still as bright as she remembered on that handsome young kid who'd first walked in her door and said, "What can I do to help you today?" She smiled inside. Sometimes she missed that innocent young man, but the grown-up version before her interrupted the reverie.

"You need anything before I go?" he said.

"What time you coming back, honey?" Bliss asked.

"Shipment hits around ten tonight," he said, "so I figure I'll show up around eight, help close down the sales day, and then get everybody ready to take in the new product when it arrives."

Mama nodded. "Okay," she said. "You go on, then. I'll check in on you after ten o'clock."

He started to close the door, but Bliss stopped him. "Darrent," she said suddenly, "how long you been with the Stash?"

He paused and looked toward the window. "Let's see," he said, "I was twenty-five when William hired me, and I'm forty-nine now, so I guess about twenty-four years, Mama. Give or take. You know how time blends together."

"Uh-huh," she said.

"Anything else?"

"Samuel Hill came by to see me this morning."

Darrent stepped inside the room now. "Yeah, Detective Hill stopped to see me too. Said you told him to pick out something for his ex-wife, but he insisted on paying for it anyway."

"Mm."

"Everything okay, Mama?"

"He says there's something going on in Little Five Points."

"Always something going in Little Five Points."

"He heard people talking about something called Nevermore."

Darrent took another step into Mama's office and sat down in one of the guest chairs at her table. He waited.

"Darrent, who you think is talking about that in this neighborhood?" Mama Bliss fixed her manager with a steady gaze. "I promised Samuel I'd see what I could find for him."

"I don't know, Mama." Darrent shifted his weight in the chair and spoke slowly, like he was composing the words that came out next, aware of them and the power they might hold. "You want me to start asking around?"

She nodded. "Thank you, Darrent. That's all. You go get some rest so you're ready for tonight."

"All right, Mama. I'll see you later."

After her number-one manager left, Bliss felt uneasiness slither through her midsection. "I've known Darrent Hayes near a quarter-century," she said to the empty office. "So what got me thinking he just lied in my face?"

She stared at the closed door to her office for a long time, thinking.

7

TRUDI

Atlanta, GA
West Midtown Neighborhood
Friday, March 17, 2:22 p.m.
28 days to Nevermore

Trudi found the place empty when she arrived at Coffey & Hill Investigations on Howell Mill Road. She was glad to see that her assistant, Eulalie, had remembered to lock the plate-glass door out front before she'd left. Eulalie was good about doing the things that Trudi often forgot, simple things like locking a front door or making sure the electric bill got paid each month. Trudi's assistant was smart too. Insightful. She noticed things that other people sometimes missed, a trait that Trudi was learning to rely on these days.

Eulalie Marie Jefferson had come to work as the receptionist at Coffey & Hill Investigations a little more than a year ago, just before Samuel had come back from the Middle East—just before the Annabel Lee affair had blown up in their faces. To her credit, she stuck around—even after Trudi had been forced to fire her during the confusion of the Annabel Lee case. After that was over, Trudi had made Samuel rehire her, and she came back without complaint or questions. Loyal, that one. A trait Trudi liked to reward. Plus, Eulalie had taken to a detective's life like a natural, never complaining about the tedious grunt work, always thorough, always willing to learn and ready to contribute in whatever way was needed. Trudi liked that.

"Teachability," she said to herself, thinking out loud as she unlocked the front door to her office. "Someone who's teachable can succeed at anything."

An image of The Raven flashed in her mind. For some reason, it made her smile, just a little. She wondered if she'd wasted her time trying to help him, trying to get him to connect with Samuel. She wondered if he was the teachable type who could learn from mistakes and ultimately become a better person for it . . . or if he was just another stubborn kid destined to keep repeating himself until he ended up in jail, or worse.

She decided to think about other things.

Trudi checked her watch: 2:25 p.m. That meant Eulalie was at her tae kwon do lesson and Trudi would have the office to herself for the next forty-five minutes or so. Enough time to catch up on the tasks she'd put off this morning. She headed back to her office and was pleased to see that Eula had left the *Atlanta Journal-Constitution*, opened and waiting, on her desk.

It had become Trudi's daily custom to skim this newspaper at least once, no matter how busy she was or how many items were on her to-do list. If she ever had to miss a day, she felt almost neurotic until she could find a copy to look at again. And no matter what, even if she was gone for a week, she always went back and checked the classified ads from any day that she missed. She had to do that, she told herself. But she knew the truth was that she *wanted* to do that, even though she knew others were doing the same thing. She thought of Annabel and knew she always would check the *Constitution*, even when it didn't matter anymore.

Trudi flipped the paper to the classifieds section before sitting down at her desk. She scanned the personals until the familiar advertisement came into view. It was only one line, one word actually, easy to miss, but it was there nonetheless. She let out a sigh when she read its message today.

Safe.

She pulled her gun out of the hybrid hip holster nestled in the back waistband of her jeans and dropped it into a drawer on the right side of her desk. She saw a set of skeleton keys and a shim sliding around inside the drawer and wondered if The Raven had been able to get out of his handcuffs. She almost grabbed the tools and headed back out, thinking she'd go ahead and help him one last time, but then she stopped herself.

"That's his problem," she mumbled to the drawer and to the keys now in her hand.

Eulalie came in around 3:15, just as expected. Trudi heard the front door open and then watched on the security monitor as her assistant came into the little reception area just down the short hall from her office. Eula was dressed in a white dobok— her tae kwon do uniform—decorated by a thick blue belt tied into a knot in the front. She carried a red chest protector and her purse in one hand.

"Sparring today?" Trudi hollered down the hall. A moment later, Eulalie was standing in the doorway to the office.

"Yep." She dimpled, holding up the chest protector and nodding her head in a way that made the tight curls in her hair bounce up and down like miniature Slinky toys on her shoulders.

"You'd have been proud, boss. That mean old sparring partner of mine never landed a solid blow the whole time."

"Good."

Trudi liked that Eulalie was learning self-defense. After she'd decided that this one was going to be more than a receptionist, after she'd started thinking of Eula as an "assistant" instead, Trudi had suggested the tae kwon do class. *Detective work is messy sometimes*, she'd said. *It could be important for you to be able to defend yourself.* Because her assistant was going to school part-time at night, Trudi had arranged for her to take tae kwon do classes during the day, three or four times a week, as part of her hourly work at Coffey & Hill Investigations. Eulalie had jumped in with both feet, soaking it all in, and proving herself a quick learner. She was well on her way to earning a red belt, which was only one level below the black belt in that martial art.

"Don't say it," Eulalie said, heading toward the bathroom to get cleaned up. "No, I still don't want to spar with you. Not yet. I've seen what you can do already."

"Can't run from me forever, Eula," she called down the hall. She smiled.

Eulalie was still in the bathroom when the phone rang. Caller ID said it was an unknown number. Trudi was tempted to let it roll into voicemail and have Eulalie deal with it when she was ready, but the neurotic within her wouldn't let that happen.

"Coffey & Hill Investigations," she said into the receiver. There was silence at first. "May I help you?" She was feeling immediately impatient.

"Yeah," a woman's voice said. "Yeah."

"What can I do for you?" Trudi asked. She couldn't quite place the accent.

"You're a detective place? Yeah?"

"Mm-hmm."

"Okay. So you look for people and stuff. Yeah?"

Trudi didn't like the way this conversation was going. "What is it you want, miss?"

"I couldn't find you on the internets."

"No," Trudi said. "We prefer to work through referrals. Did someone refer you to me?"

"Yeah. Well, yeah."

"What's this about, miss? You'll have to get to the point."

Eulalie came and stood by the office door, now dressed for business but still drying her hair with a towel. She cocked her head in silent question. In response, Trudi waved her in and tapped the speaker button on the telephone.

"So, you on Howell Mill Road?" The woman's voice filled the whole room now. "By that Arby's?"

"Mm-hmm. Yes. Would you like to make an appointment?"

"Um, yeah."

Trudi had an uncomfortable thought. "Miss, are you in danger right now? Is someone listening while you make this call?"

Silence was the only answer.

"Miss?"

She heard a sharp exhale on the other side, then a click, and the phone line went dead. Trudi looked up at Eulalie, and the two women fumbled with their thoughts for a moment.

"What do you think that was about?" Eulalie said at last.

"No way to tell," Trudi said. "No ID on the caller. No real information from the woman on the other end."

"Do you think she was in danger?"

Trudi shrugged as if unconcerned, but the crease in her forehead said otherwise.

"What was that accent?" Eula said. "Didn't sound like it was from around here."

A frown. "No," Trudi said. "No, it didn't, did it?"

"'You on Howell Mill Road?'" Eulalie mimicked. "'By that Arby's?'"

Trudi gave her assistant an admiring gaze. "Hey, that's pretty good. Do it again, but blur the *l*'s a little more."

Eulalie complied, and Trudi nodded. "Now say, 'You're a detective place? Yeah?'"

"You're a detective place? Yeah?"

Trudi shook her head. "No, replay that woman's voice in your head for a minute, and then try it again." Eulalie gave it another try, and then a third. By the fourth time, Trudi thought it sounded right. She scribbled a name on a Post-it Note and handed it to her assistant.

"Call this guy. One of my old professors over at the University of Georgia. He's a linguist. You'll have to look up the number, but call him, tell him it's for me. Then say a few things in that accent and ask if he knows where it might come from."

"On it, yeah," Eulalie said, staying in character and keeping the accent alive.

It took only about twenty minutes before Eulalie was back in Trudi's office. "Okay," she said. "First, Professor Frandsen says hello, and that he wants you to come back and speak to his class sometime about careers for English majors."

"There are no careers for English majors. That's why I'm a detective."

Eulalie snorted. "Well, I told him you'd be glad to set something up. He's checking dates."

"I hate you."

"You'll be great. Think of it as a 'What Would Jesus Do?' moment."

"Fine. I don't hate you. But I'm not buying your coffee tomorrow morning."

"Fair enough. But Professor Frandsen also said he thought

the accent sounded familiar. He checked a few websites while we were on the phone, then said it sounded like something that had elements of Eastern Europe in it, but that had been influenced by the American South, as well."

"Eastern Europe?"

"He said that if he were to guess, he'd pick someplace like Russia or Poland. Or maybe Ukraine."

Trudi stood up at her desk. She felt like saying a bad word.

"What? What is it?"

The pieces fell into place too easily, which set off a chorus of alarm bells ringing inside Trudi's head.

"So," she said to Eulalie, "let's imagine you're a poor young woman living in Ukraine. Somebody promises you a job and a new life-of-plenty in America. You accept the offer, pack up, and sneak into the U.S. with your benefactor. You find yourself in Atlanta in the glorious American South. Heaven. Only you've been settled by handlers from your home country into a seedy side of town. They tell you you're an illegal alien, that if anybody finds out about you that you're going to jail, or worse. And now that you're trapped here in a foreign country, your new host *explains* that your job is to make American businessmen and other customers, um, *happy*."

"So you spend the next several years living in a brothel?" Eulalie said. Her face furrowed too.

"Right. Working for an offshoot of the Ukrainian Mafia. Now, if that's been your life up to this point, is there any chance you'd sound like that woman who just called us here? Like a Ukrainian prostitute stuck in Atlanta, just trying to get from today to tomorrow without adding more troubles than you already have?"

Eulalie looked grim. She nodded. "So, either this woman wants out and called us for help . . ."

"Mm-hmm," Trudi said. "Or she's just a cover voice for the man who's really looking for us. For me."

Once again, Trudi's mind wandered back to The Raven and their encounter earlier at his apartment. This time, though, the memory didn't make her smile.

"Trudi, did you happen to make any Ukrainians mad recently?"

She thought for a moment but didn't say anything.

Eulalie nodded. "Okay, what else is new, right? Well, I didn't come to work for Trudi Coffey because I wanted to live a boring life." She grinned. "At least we got a warning. We can be ready. So what's the next step? Should we call Mr. Hill?"

Trudi shook her head and grimaced.

The last thing she wanted was to call for Samuel to play knight-in-shining-armor to her damsel-in-distress. *I take care of myself, Mr. Samuel Hill*, she spat at him in her head. *Done it my whole life. I don't need you, or any man, to be my own personal protector.* She felt her jaw set and her muscles go hard. She grabbed her keys off the desk. "Come on," she said. "I'm suddenly in the mood for a good sparring session over at the gym."

Eulalie's eyes widened but, to her credit, she followed her boss out the front door.

8

BLISS

Atlanta, GA
Little Five Points
Friday, March 17, 11:11 p.m.
28 days to Nevermore

"We have a problem."

Mama Bliss felt heaviness in her bones.

Only ten minutes ago, she'd left the narrow loading dock in Darrent's capable hands, things running smoothly as normal, crates dropping onto the conveyor belts at one end of the warehouse and being carefully unpacked at the other end. *Clockwork, that's what William always called it*, she reminded herself. No surprises, things just moving forward as planned, the system working like it was supposed to work.

Only ten minutes ago, she'd said, "I'm tired out, Darrent. Been a long, long day for me. I'm going to lie down in my office tonight. Sleep away this weariness and wake up better—"

"And richer," he'd interrupted.

"Yes, and richer, tomorrow." She watched him pen a stroke

on his clipboard, listened to the hum of activity buzzing around them both. They didn't need her here for this, not really. These people were well-trained. They knew what to do, and if they didn't, Darrent would sort them out pretty quickly. She said, "You got things handled here, right?"

"All clockwork, Mama," he'd said, checking his clipboard and watching the busyness that filled the warehouse.

Only six minutes ago, Mama had rolled into her office near the back of the Secret Stash. She'd needed to visit the toilet, but she also needed to lie down and rest. She was tempted to do both at the same time, but the thought of an old woman wetting her own bed—on purpose—was just comical enough to make her laugh and head to the bathroom.

Only two minutes ago, she'd finally rolled her wheelchair next to her functional little bed in the corner of her office. She'd sleep in her clothes tonight, she'd decided, then go home in the morning and change. Maybe even take a nice, warm bath as part of the morning ritual. She liked the sound of that.

She was just beginning to make the arduous transfer of her body from chair to bed when she heard the knock on the door.

"Mama?" a voice said on the other side. Bliss wanted to ignore it. It wasn't unfamiliar to her, but she couldn't place it in her memory right away, either. "You awake?" the voice asked again. "Mr. Hayes told me to come wake you up."

"Didn't even get to turn off the light," she mumbled to herself.

"Mama Bliss?"

"In," she called to the door. But she wasn't happy about it.

The young man who stepped into the office was visibly nervous, like he was entering into territory where he knew he didn't belong.

"What's your name, honey?" Bliss said. She tried not to sound unkind. "I know your face, but my old mind sometimes lets the names slip away."

"Alvin," he said. He ducked his head a little. Bliss could see him trying not to be too obvious about checking out her office for the first time. If he'd had a hat, she was sure he'd have been fumbling with it in his hands. "Been working for the Stash for about a year now, but only with Mr. Hayes on the night shipments for the last month or so."

"You like working here, Alvin?"

"Oh, yes, ma'am," he said. "I plan to stay awhile, if you and Mr. Hayes'll have me."

"Mm-hmm." Bliss knew how careful Darrent was about choosing his night-shift workers. They were paid well—and they tended to stay on for a long time, loyal either to Darrent, or to Mama, or to the money. If he'd sent this one to personally interrupt her sleep, then she figured she would trust him. For now.

"Well, what is it, Alvin? What's the problem, and why didn't Darrent come tell me about it himself?"

"Mr. Hayes was kind of busy about the problem, ma'am."

"So he told you to come get me instead?"

"Well, he didn't actually tell me. He kind of signaled me. I'm new to the night shift, and I think he figured no one would notice me slip out of the warehouse."

Bliss frowned. That didn't sound good. She started rolling her wheelchair toward the door.

"Now you got me curious and agitated, young man. Lay it out plain. What's the problem?"

"Max Roman just showed up. Said he was here to oversee the shipment."

Bliss let fly an expletive that seemed to surprise even a veteran warehouse worker like Alvin. He actually flinched, but his feet stayed rooted in his spot.

"Push this chair, Alvin," she commanded. "I don't have time

for Max Roman's shenanigans tonight, and I suspect Darrent's not too happy about it either."

"Yes, ma'am. And no, ma'am, he didn't seem happy at all."

Alvin was a good motor for Bliss's wheelchair, and they swung into the warehouse in only two minutes or so. She saw Darrent catch her entrance out of the corner of his eye, but he didn't give her away, not yet. He was busy holding out his clipboard for Max Roman to inspect.

Bliss motioned for Alvin to get back to his station and privately ground her teeth at the fact that no one was working anymore. All of her crew was standing around the edges of the scene, waiting for someone to tell them what to do next. She headed toward Darrent and tried to take in the situation.

Standing near Max were two men she recognized. One was a large, athletic type who'd played football a few years at Georgia Southern. The other was Ukrainian, like Roman. A wiry man with tight, dark eyes and hair to match. The football player was imposing, but Bliss knew from experience that the wiry Ukrainian was the more dangerous of the two.

It was the Ukrainian who nudged his boss and pointed in her direction.

Max Roman gave her the "official" smile, the one he used when making a campaign appearance or doing a TV interview. She could see why people liked him in politics. He was handsome in his way, with a reassuring face, like a CNN news anchor or a late-night talk show host, but not so pretty it was distracting. He was clean-shaven but had a weathered face, like he was just old enough to understand your suffering, but still young enough to be good company at a party too. She'd read somewhere that he was in his early fifties, but he looked younger than that, more fit, like he worked out some, but not muscle-bound like the athlete that was his bodyguard. His eyes were basic brown, as was his hair, which he kept short and parted on the side.

Bliss could never remember seeing Max Roman wear anything other than a finely-tailored suit, always a solid color like black or blue or tan. Tonight he wore a blue suit, with a bright red tie for effect.

Max's grandfather, Nestor Romanenko, had come to America in the early 1900s, using money and support from networks in "the old country" to build himself a presence in the textile industry during the Great Depression. By the mid-1950s, he'd traded that success for the banking industry in which he—and his children—became millionaires. By the time Maksym Romanenko came around, Granddaddy's money had bought law degrees, real estate holdings, network TV shares, and even a career in local politics for the one who now went by the name of Max Roman.

In spite of his significant financial assets and seat at the table of power, Max still maintained a common-man persona that made him inherently appealing to people from all walks of life. Not Bliss, of course. She knew him too well for that. Still, when he flashed that campaign smile in her direction, she put on her own plastic face, as well.

"Max," she said, rolling her wheelchair up to the little party. "This is a surprise. We weren't expecting you until the thirtieth of the month, as usual."

"Always a pleasure to see you, Ms. Bliss," he said, flashing a brighter glimpse of his porcelain veneers. His two bodyguards stepped back behind their boss in deference to both Bliss and Max.

Darrent was not similarly cowed, nor was he in the mood for small talk. "Mama," Darrent said, nodding in the direction of their unexpected guests, "Mr. Roman here has *suggested* that we let him take ten percent of tonight's shipment in advance of his normal payment at the end of the month."

The Ukrainian bodyguard standing behind Max Roman snorted lightly at that, but the athlete beside him remained impassive.

Bliss felt her plastic smile melt away. Now it was time for business. "You find something funny, Viktor?" she snapped at the bodyguard. "You think my man here is making a joke?"

"No, of course not, Ms. Bliss."

"Then why the laughter? I distinctly heard laughter from your general direction."

"All due respect, Ms. Bliss," he said, nodding slightly. "Your man here simply misspoke, or he misunderstand the reason for our visit tonight."

Now it was Max Roman's turn. He grinned fiercely and patted Darrent's shoulder in condescension. "Viktor's right, Ms. Bliss," Roman said. "We are not *suggesting* anything."

"My mistake," Darrent said placidly, but his eyes flashed in fury. He folded his arms across his chest, encircling the clipboard within them.

"Mm-hmm," Bliss said. She looked from Max to Viktor and back to Darrent. Then she put her plastic smile back on. "You in a pickle, honey? You need Mama Bliss to bail you outta some problem this week? Can't handle your business?"

Now it was Roman's turn to flush with anger at the insult. The bodyguards didn't respond this time, but Bliss saw them tense and lean forward just a bit. Out of the corner of her eye, she saw the football player do a quick scan of the room and slide his arms behind his back, as if he were a military man resting at ease. She knew he was really just getting his hands closer to a gun that was likely hidden underneath the back of his suit coat.

As quickly as the flame had burned in Max's eyes, it was extinguished, and now he seemed to shrug off the insult in favor of the business at hand. "I find myself in special circumstances at the moment," he said. "Someone down south tipped law enforcement as to where one of my, ah, private groups kept a cache of unlicensed weapons. They confiscated everything about three weeks ago."

"Your PR machine hailed that as a victory in the war on crime that you've been leading from City Hall," Darrent said.

"And your PR says you're just a mild-mannered retail manager, right, Mr. Hayes?" Max lasered a look at Darrent before returning his attention to Bliss. "Regardless, we're not asking anything of you tonight, Ms. Bliss. We're *taking*. Ten percent. I have need right now, and you have surplus. We'll even things out at the end of the month. You have my word on that."

Bliss felt like spitting. She'd heard that promise before. "That was your boy today, wasn't it, Max? Watching me from across the street at Planet Bombay. That how you found out about tonight's shipment? Spying on an old crippled woman?"

Max shrugged.

"How many guns coming in tonight, Darrent?" Bliss asked, not taking her eyes off Max Roman.

"Seven hundred seventy-eight."

"Where they from?"

"Brazil."

"Mm-hmm." She looked up. "These guns don't feel right for you, Max. These are Taurus MT-9 G2 submachine guns. War weapons, headed to Donbass."

Max leaned down close to Bliss. His voice was hard. "My people in the old country thank you for your support, but I also know they are paying you quite well to launder these guns for them, so don't try to play the immigrant sympathy card on me. I was born here in Georgia, same as you, same as my father before me."

Bliss tried a different approach. "Look, we got a shipment of Glock handguns coming in ten days straight from Austria. They're going to Boston on a collateral deal, then on to what's left of the IRA in Europe, so they don't need a full shipment. They'll never miss them. Besides, your 'private groups,' they love the Glock. Why not wait for those? I'll pick out seventy-eight guns special just for you. Shoot, I'll give you a hundred at no extra cost. How's that sound?"

"It sounds like you've forgotten the deal we made, the deal my father and I made with your late husband."

Bliss felt herself losing this fight, and she didn't like losing anything to Maksym Romanenko. He'd already cost her more than she could suffer anyway.

"Mama," Darrent said urgently, "our deal was that none of our guns ever stays in Atlanta. Not Taurus, not Glock, not any of them. Not one, not ever. That's the deal William made, and Mr. Roman here knows that."

"How about this?" Max said suddenly, stretching up to his full height and markedly ignoring Darrent in the process. "You do me this little favor tonight, Ms. Bliss, and I'll do you a big favor in return. In fact, maybe I've already done you a favor today. What do you think of that?"

Bliss didn't like the sound of it, but she could see this wasn't going to end well no matter what she did. She decided it was time to fold her cards.

"Darrent," she said without taking her gaze off Max, "have your crew pack up seventy-eight submachine guns for Mr. Roman. Viktor here can handle loading them into his truck."

Max flashed his bright white veneers again and clapped Darrent heartily on the back. "Yes, Darrent," he crowed, "do as your Mama says." To Viktor and the football player, he simply nodded. A moment later, he and Bliss were standing alone.

"Now, Ms. Mama Bliss," Max said generously, "would you like to see the favor I did for you today?"

9

RAVEN

Atlanta, GA
Old Fourth Ward
Friday, March 17, 11:55 p.m.
28 days to Nevermore

I wonder what it's like to be a Disney cartoon.

I think that's how I'm feeling right now, like one of those animated heroes bouncing through a sugary forest. Light. Bright. Rested. Optimistic. Like I want to grin for no real reason, except that it hurts my lips to do that.

Sure, I'm sore all over, and my face still feels tender and bruised, but I'm not bleeding anymore. And I can see out of my right eye again, so I've got that going for me. My bed feels soft and comfortable, almost like a warm puppy has curled up beside me. I'm pretty sure that, despite my earlier worries, all my ribs have remained intact. Plus, I went to the bathroom a few minutes ago and didn't pass any blood. I think that means there's no significant internal injury to speak of, which is a relief.

All in all, considering how this day started, I'm calling today a win for The Amazing Raven.

The street outside is quiet, with just the dullest of moonlight sneaking through the open curtains of my bedroom. It's a shadowy paradise, and I'm the king of it all. Feels good. Peaceful. A welcome respite after the storm that passed through here earlier.

This is the kind of moment when I'd normally drift off to sleep and dream of flying carpets or hidden rooms filled with rare comic books, but I've already slept the entire day away. Now that it's just about midnight, I'm lying awake, feeling lazy, and wishing I had a pizza in the fridge. Of course, I don't know if I'll ever be able to answer the door for pizza delivery again. But that doesn't stop me wishing.

After Trudi Coffey left my place this morning, the world dwindled down to just me, my apartment—and an angry little pair of handcuffs.

I made my marriage proposal, and even though she kind of rejected it by walking out the door, Trudi Coffey didn't actually say no, so I'm taking that as an opening. As an invitation to ask again someday. But next time, I think it'll probably be better if I pop the question in a more, um, suitable situation. Like when I'm all healed up and not being terrorized by a group of Ukrainian hit men. Like maybe when we're having a nice dinner in a place where she doesn't have to pull her gun just to keep us both from getting killed.

That'd probably be a good idea.

"I don't have the right tool with me for those," she'd said about the handcuffs holding me in my chair. She thought I might be stuck in them, but I knew better. Handcuffs are no match for a guy who knows the great scam artist/magician Brian Brushwood . . . well, for a guy who bought Brian Brushwood's Rogue's Ring

off www.shwood.com and hopes to meet him someday. Even as Trudi was clipping away the zip ties on my ankles, I couldn't help twisting in circles the helpful little piece of jewelry they'd left on the middle finger of my right hand.

Still, when the apartment was finally empty, I didn't have the energy to get right to my escape. I was exhausted from getting beat up all night long and then falling in love the next morning. So I sat back in my rickety kitchen chair and just waited for my heart to settle back into a normal resting rate. Can't say it was terribly comfortable, but I can say it was tempting just to take a little nap in the chair. Of course, the chair didn't feel like cooperating with that idea. Just the act of sitting felt like someone was jabbing a crowbar in my back. And there was the problem of having my handcuffs threaded through the slats in a way that made it impossible for me to wrest my hands out from behind me.

It almost felt good to smash that wooden chair onto the floor to get my hands free. It made a little mess, and I only had two kitchen chairs left after that, but so what? At least then I could get to the ring on my finger.

Here's the beauty of the Rogue's Ring: It's titanium, decorated with rock-and-roll hieroglyphs that make it look like pretty much any guy's lame attempt at cool, urban jewelry. Forgettable, but not out of place if someone notices it, either. What most people don't know is that it's hollow, and coiled inside it is a narrow, serrated shim—just the tool I need to break out of handcuffs or even cut through zip ties.

I'd like to say I've never had to use the Rogue's Ring before but, well, once or twice it's come in handy. *Thanks, Brian.*

After breaking my chair, it was a simple chore to unspool my shim out of the ring and slip it into the locking mechanism on the handcuffs. A few seconds later, the metal bracelets slid right off my wrists and onto the table. That was when I remembered Trudi had left me Viktor's one-hundred-dollar bill, and I felt grateful for that girl all over again.

Now free of the handcuffs and rubbing my wrists to get circulation going full-steam again, I thought about taking a shower. It'd be nice just to wash away the day's troubles with the grime and blood, but in the end, I decided against it. Too exhausting. Next I thought about eating something, but given the shape I was in, that made me feel a little sick to my stomach.

"Sleep," I finally told myself. "Everything's better after a few hours of sleep." I left the money on the table next to the handcuffs, left the shattered chair on my kitchen floor, and headed to my bedroom.

I only stopped long enough to lock the front door.

I slept until my dreams became an endless search for a work-ing toilet, until I realized that I kept finding bathroom stalls that were always empty closets because I needed to wake up and let my bladder lose itself in sweet release.

Now, freshly voided and twenty-four hours after being ac-costed by mobsters, I feel warm and relaxed at last. I watch the glowing light on my digital alarm clock announce "12:02" on my nightstand.

Two minutes after midnight. It's tomorrow. Finally. Yesterday can just be a bad memory. Yay.

The night is still, quiet, and if I don't move too much, my body feels almost normal. With my eyes closed, it feels like I'm a boy again, safe in my little, orange bedroom back in Oklahoma City. I listen to myself breathe, a comfortable, familiar sound.

I'm in that in-between world between waking and dreaming.

I can almost hear my dad speaking gently in my ear, almost feel his hand stroking my head before I drift off to sleep.

"It's in the quiet when you can best hear God's voice, son."
That never happens for me, Daddy.
"Maybe that's because you've never been truly quiet. You have a restless little soul, son, like that raven in the Great Flood."
That was the bird that never landed anywhere. Right, Daddy? Noah sent him out, and he just kept flying around until the water went away.
A smile in the darkness. "So you have been paying attention in Sunday school."
Sometimes.
A hand patting softly on my chest. "Rest well, my little Raven. And listen for God. You'd be surprised at how often he speaks in the quiet."
G'night, Daddy.
"G'night, Da—" I twitch fully awake at the sound of my own voice.

The quiet around me now feels foreign, unwelcome. I stare at the ceiling above me, waiting for something and not knowing what it is. The shadows on the ceiling act like they're going to merge into a recognizable thing, or into the face of someone familiar, but before that can happen, they all melt into one another and fade into indistinguishable gray and black smears.
Sometimes I miss you, Daddy.
I'm surprised that I admit that to myself, even though I know it's true.
But I know . . . I know what I did to you.
I sit up in bed, suddenly angry at myself. At my father. At God.
"So," I say to the emptiness, "here I am in the quiet. How about it, Jesus? You got anything you want to say to me?"

A siren in the distance interrupts the solitude. A fire truck this time, I think. Maybe two. *I should've known Old Fourth Ward couldn't stay peaceful for long.*

"Yeah, I didn't think so," I say to the absent presence in my room. "You and I haven't been on speaking terms since high school graduation, right? Hey, don't take it personally. I haven't spoken to my own flesh-and-blood father for over four years, either. But you already knew that."

My mind drifts to Trudi Coffey and the business card she left on my kitchen table. *I don't actually have to do anything*, I reason. *She left the stolen swag right there on the table with her card. She'll never know that I didn't call her stupid cop ex-husband.*

But . . .

If I don't call her stupid ex-husband, does that mean I can't see her again? Can't move forward with my plan to make her fall crazy in love with me?

I play out our next meeting in my head.

"Trudi, you look beautiful," I say.

"Thanks, Raven. You look handsome too."

"Aw shucks."

No, change that. I'm never going to say *aw shucks* to any woman, let alone Trudi Coffey. Let's see. Okay, just smile and acknowledge. That's what I do. Sometimes words are unnecessary, right?

"Listen, Trudi," I say after an appreciative conversational break, "I was wondering if I might take you out to dinner. I know a sweet little fusion place that has live entertainment on Fridays."

"Oh, is this a place where you perform?"

A sly shrug, like, well, yeah, I am that cool, but I don't want to say it out loud. *Nice.*

And then she'll say, "I'd love to go out with you."

Or maybe she'll say, "Did you call my ex-husband and return those things you stole? Or are you still a dirty, dishonest, thieving thug?"

I don't like this little game anymore.

I get up and move to the kitchen. The gnawing in my stomach makes me wish that Scholarship hadn't eaten all my food, but I try to focus on the table anyway. The three poly bags are still where she left them: a sapphire bracelet, an Apple Watch, and a thick, braided gold chain. Spread those out between pawn shops paying ten to twenty percent of the value and it should be enough to cover a month's rent on this awful apartment and maybe two weeks of tasteless, prepackaged groceries to boot.

Are you still a dirty, dishonest, thieving thug?

For some reason, an old movie pops into my head, one of mom's favorites, *As Good As It Gets*. It was that movie that made me add celebrity impressions to my act, I think because my mom was so delighted to hear Jack Nicholson's voice come out of my mouth. Right now, I see grizzled, cranky old Jack sitting across a table from the lovely Helen Hunt. It's a moment of truth for him, the moment that's going to decide whether she stays or leaves forever. "You make me want to be a better man," he growls finally, and that's exactly what Helen wants to hear. It was a choice he made, one that changed everything for them both.

You make me want to be a better man.

Is that what Trudi Coffey wants from me?

Maybe this is all a test. Maybe she left these valuable trinkets on my table to see if I'm more than the guy she met. Maybe she wants to see if I'm someone she can trust, if I'm more than just a petty thief using a magician's act to scam and shoplift from tourists at Piedmont Park.

But maybe that's all I am, Trudi.

I pick up my hard-earned, expertly stolen, poly-bagged prizes and take them into the bathroom. It'd be easy just to tape them back under the sink. I've done that kind of thing a hundred times. It's super simple.

The guy staring at me in the mirror is not happy about that idea, though. I get the feeling he'd like to punch me in the jaw like old Scholarship did.

It's past midnight now, I try to reason with Mirror-Man. *No time to be making phone calls to law enforcement officials. Especially ones that can put you in jail.* But that's just an excuse. I know I'm in a moment of truth right now, like Jack Nicholson in *As Good As It Gets.*

So what if I call Samuel Hill's cell phone after midnight? I think. He's a police detective; he probably gets calls at all hours of the day and night anyway. And probably my call will just dump into voicemail, which, when I think about it, is better than having to talk to the guy in person anyway. I can leave a message, tell him I'm dropping off the stolen goods at the Zone 6 police station. *Done and done.*

And then I get to call Trudi Coffey tomorrow, clean slate, clear conscience. Maybe even visit her in a few days, after I'm healed up a bit.

The guy in the mirror is staring hard at me. His face is dirty, bruised, and still a little swollen, with his right eye half shut. But he won't look away. He wants an answer. He wants to know what I'm going to do. Who I really am.

He blinks first. Or was it me?

"Trudi," I growl in my best Jack Nicholson impersonation, "you make me want to be a better man."

THREE
WEEKS
AGO . . .

10

TRUDI

Atlanta, GA
West Midtown
Friday, March 24, 9:08 a.m.
21 days to Nevermore

He looked good. The pig.

And he smelled good—not like cologne or strange aftershave, but like a guy who showered regularly and used plenty of green-apple shampoo. She missed that early-morning smell of her ex-husband, even kind of missed hearing him knock around in the bathroom getting ready for work, making her late for work by taking so long in there. It reminded her of home, or at least the home she'd once taken for granted.

The ordinary things—that's what you miss when it's all gone. Not all the big moments or the wild romantic gestures. Just having someone there, someone who makes doing nothing something worth doing.

"So," he was saying, "what do you think?"

Trudi tried not to let her face flush. She hadn't been paying

91

attention. Did he know that? Was he baiting her? She tried a bluff.

"I don't know," she said slowly. "Tell it all to me again, and I'm going to close my eyes and watch it in my head while you tell it."

"Okay," he said.

It was a good bluff, she decided. That was a habit she had when she was trying to puzzle through a problem, and he knew it. Close her eyes, go through it detail by detail, find the answer inside her head. She risked peeking through slitted eyes at her ex-husband and thought he bought the bluff, or if he didn't, at least he was gentlemanly enough to let her get away with it this time.

"Well, they're calling it 'Nevermore,' and—"

"No, no," Trudi said, leaning back in her office chair and putting her feet up on the desk. "Start back at the stakeout. And tell it slow, so I can see it while I hear it."

"All right."

She could hear him settling back in his chair, as well. Before he could start, though, she opened her eyes and put up a hand. It took a little effort since she kept her feet propped on the desktop, but she leaned forward to her phone and tapped the intercom button.

"Eulalie," Trudi said to her receptionist, "when's my next appointment?"

"Nine-thirty," the assistant's voice chirped into the speaker. "New client. His name is Marvin L. Deasy."

Samuel tilted his head, and Trudi shrugged. "What do we know about Mr. Deasy?" Samuel asked. He always was the curious type.

"Initial consultation only," Eulalie responded. "He made the appointment by phone, said it was a private matter."

"Referral?" Trudi asked.

There was a small silence on the other end. "Well," she said at last, "when I asked for a referral name, he mentioned Mr. Hill. I assumed he meant Detective Hill. Should I have asked for more information?"

Now it was Trudi's turn to tilt her jaw at Samuel. "No, it's fine, Eula. We're in the detective business, and walk-ins are welcome. But I'll check with Samuel anyway." She raised an eyebrow. "Might be one of his old war buddies or something."

Samuel put his palms out and up and shrugged at Trudi before she could even finish turning off the intercom. "Don't know him," he said as if that settled it. "Guess you'll have to be surprised."

Trudi shrugged in return. She'd find out who he was and what he wanted in the next twenty minutes or so. For now, she needed to concentrate on Samuel's problem.

"Ask him if he's a comic book fan, though," Samuel said suddenly.

"What?"

He just grinned like he knew a secret but wasn't telling what it was.

"Fine, I'll ask him." She leaned back in her chair and closed her eyes. "Now tell me a story, Mr. Storyman, and maybe I can help you solve a terrible mystery."

From across the desk, she heard Samuel resettling into the ornate metal chair that served as client furniture and listened to the comfortable rhythms of his baritone voice.

"All right, so a few weeks ago I'm working a stakeout down in Inman Park."

"How many weeks ago?"

"I don't know. Three? Four? Four weeks ago, how's that?"

Lie, she thought. *I know where you were four weeks ago, and it wasn't at a stakeout.*

One of the perks of owning your own detective agency was that sometimes, on a Friday night when you were feeling lonely, you could hack your ex-husband's Find My iPhone app to keep tabs on your dashing ex-lover. You know, just to see if he'd met anybody new, or if he might be at home, feeling lonely too. You could also discover that he'd downloaded the pricey Urban Enhancement—Atlanta Edition app extension that pinpointed his iPhone's location on blueprint maps of any building in Atlanta's public records. *Four weeks ago,* she silently accused, *you were on the seventy-first floor of the Westin Peachtree Plaza building. Dining at the Sun Dial Restaurant. Probably with some airheaded, Barbie-shaped weathergirl who works at CNN.*

Out loud she said only, "Continue."

"We got word that a Kipo gang was going to hit a jewelry store on Euclid, so I was waiting to see if the tipster was reliable."

"By yourself?"

"Backup was just a call away. But I didn't need it because the tip turned out to be a diversion. They hit a different place over in Adair Park. Anyway, around two a.m. I'm getting ready to call it a night when one of my locals comes knocking on the door of my car."

"Gang informant, or general informant?"

"Probably shouldn't tell you that. Just understand that he's an informant for the Atlanta PD."

"So it's a man, huh?"

"Unless I deliberately lied about that to misdirect you. Then it would be a woman, wouldn't it?"

Trudi smiled behind her eyes. This felt good, like old times.

"Anyway, my informant says that someone is trying to recruit Kipo—"

"Gang informant. You're too easy."

"Huh. Whatever. Anyway, he tells me someone's trying to

poach a few 'Knights in pimp orange' for a big show. Something on a terrorist level, but homegrown, like the Oklahoma City Bombing back in 1995. Something that's on the calendar, but that he can't get people to talk about, like they're more afraid of the ghost who's recruiting than they are of the police. Or maybe they don't really know who the ghost is. So now my captain has me working on this full-time, says it's up to me to prevent tomorrow's bad news."

"Anything else?"

"Well, I worked my network a bit, but all I can get is that somebody thinks Nevermore is coming out of Little Five Points, and that it has a connection to Edgar Allan Poe."

Trudi's eyes popped open. "How is that possible? Poe's been dead for more than a century."

"No, no, not Mr. Poe himself. Something about his writings. That's why it's called Nevermore, I guess, because it somehow relates to that poem about the creepy bird."

"You mean, 'The Raven.'"

"I just said that."

"No, you said, oh, never mind." She lifted her feet off the desk and slid them to the floor. "Little Five Points," she said. "You talk to Mama Bliss?"

"Yep. She didn't know anything. Said she'd send out a few feelers for me, though, see what she could find out."

Trudi nodded. It was unusual for Mama Bliss to be caught unaware about anything happening in Little Five Points. Did that mean Samuel's source was wrong on that? Or just that Mama was getting older and maybe was no longer as thorough as she'd once been?

"That all?"

"Oh, one more thing." Samuel reached into the inside pocket of his sports jacket. "Mama said to give you this."

Trudi let a tiny smile peek through the edges of her lips. Mama might have sent this gift, but she knew Samuel must have picked it out. He held out a delicate gold chain with a gold ring on it, about the size of a wedding band. The ring was etched with what appeared to be an otherworldly script all the way around it.

"Actual movie prop?" she said. Mama Bliss was good at finding things other people couldn't get ahold of.

"Replica," he said, "but eighteen-carat gold anyway."

She reached out and accepted the gift. "You know, *The Lord of the Rings* has all kinds of Christian allegory in it. You sure you want to support that?"

"Literature and faith all mixed into a little piece of sparkly jewelry. What else was there to get for you?" Samuel shrugged and grinned. "Besides, being agnostic doesn't mean I'm antagonistic. Just means I don't share your certainty of belief."

"And Mama sent this anyway, right?"

He shifted in his seat. "Of course. I said that already."

"Well, next time you see her, you tell Mama Bliss that I loved it. That it's lovely." She opened a drawer on the left side of her desk and nestled the necklace and ring safely inside. "Or maybe I'll drop by and tell her myself sometime soon."

"I'm sure she'd like that." There was an awkward silence for a moment, and then Samuel was ready to get back to business. "So," he said, "what do you think?"

Trudi leaned back and let her legs cause the chair to swivel back and forth just a bit. She tented her fingers in front of her, elbows resting on her lap, and started thinking out loud.

"Okay, first of all," she said in Samuel's direction, "there was no stakeout. That's a load of hooey you made up just because you didn't want to give away the identity of your informant."

"Wait, what?"

"Hush. Don't argue with me when you know I'm right." She

waited for him to keep protesting, but he kept his mouth shut. *Choosing his battles*, she thought. Then she said, "Second, your informant can't be local if he's working on a terrorist plot. That screams federal agency, but the CIA has you in a holding pattern, so it must be someone from one of the other domestic alphabets. NSA maybe? Or Homeland Security?"

"Trudi, is this—"

"Shh. I'm thinking. You know I hate to be interrupted while I'm thinking." She swiveled a full circle in her chair and ended up facing the laptop situated on her desk. She pulled up a web browser on her computer, typed a few keywords, then looked pleased.

"Okay, so about four weeks ago, the Bureau of Alcohol, Tobacco, and Firearms staged a joint raid with Atlanta PD, trying to bust up some kind of gun-smuggling ring. According to the newspapers, your ATF boys collared a half dozen Kipo gang members, some unnamed others, and about one hundred Russian-made AK-47 automatic rifles."

"Okay, but—"

"That means your 'informant' is probably ATF, right? And that he found out about the whole Nevermore thing while he was interrogating some of those Kipo boys back at the station. Or maybe he was working undercover in the gang sets and he's the tipster that led everybody to the big gun bust?" She tapped a finger absently on her desk. "That'd mean the whole Nevermore thing was probably something he stumbled across while gathering intel on the gun smugglers, but didn't have time to pursue. So he bounced it down to your captain who, in turn, dropped it onto your desk because you have federal agency connections from your CIA past. Am I right?"

Samuel sighed.

"Look, Trudi," he said, "that's all just conjecture and, besides, what does it matter if my informant is street level or agency level?"

"It matters to me, cowboy, because it mattered enough for you to try and hide it from me. And because it's the only way I can track what's going on in that pretty little head of yours."

He waved a hand in dismissal. "And yet Nevermore still exists, and I'm still hitting a brick wall trying to figure out what it is, who's behind it, how it connects to Poe's poem, and when this impending disaster is going down. If this is a real threat, it could be awful. You know it must be serious if I'm here begging you for help, right?"

She nodded slowly. It was hard, sometimes, not to make everything a competition when it came to her ex-husband. *Compulsive need to show him I can live just fine without him*, she thought. *Maybe I should try to grow up a little bit in that area.*

"All right," she said, "you're right."

She stood up and faced the bookshelves built into the wall behind her. There were several volumes of world mythology, a few books of fairy tales and folk stories. And the pride of her shelves, the best of her collection, was a fine gathering of detective fiction, all in one place and, when possible, first editions of the books. The complete Edgar Allan Poe. Same with Sir Arthur Conan Doyle. Memoirs of Eugène François Vidocq. A number of Miss Marple tales, Lord Wimsey, Ellery Queen, and the rest. Sometimes people commented on the collection, wondering why there was so much in the way of pleasure reading and so little in the way of practical manuals, but most often her clients barely noticed the books. It was her own little literary sanctuary, and she loved it. It inspired her. On at least one occasion, it had put her life in danger—which, in a strange way, made her love it more.

She stretched her fingers and removed the collector's edition of *The Complete Tales and Poems of Edgar Allan Poe* from the shelf. She flipped it open to "The Raven" on page 943, then set it on the desk where both she and Samuel could look at it.

"Okay, if this maybe-plot is using Nevermore as a code name, then there's probably something in this poem that can give us a clue as to what's going on. Do you want to start there?" She sat down and craned her neck to read the first few lines.

Samuel glanced at the page on the desk and nodded. "I'm going to be honest with you, Tru-Bear," he said, "I've already read this a dozen times. It just seems like nonsense to me, so I'm hoping your English Lit degree might see something I can't."

Inside, Trudi cringed. She hated it when he called her by that little nickname. It had been sweet, even welcome, back when they were married, back when it was okay to be in love with him. But after his betrayal, after the affair, after the divorce, after everything, it just brought back unwelcome memories. She tried to ignore it. "English Literature with a minor in World Mythology and Religions," she said. "I worked hard for that, so get it right, mister."

"I stand corrected."

They looked at the poem in silence for a moment. *Once upon a midnight dreary*, Trudi read to herself, *while I pondered weak and weary . . .*

"What we need to ask," she said aloud, "is whether 'The Raven' is a symbol of the planner's motivation or his intended outcome."

"Explain," Samuel said.

"Well, obviously the poem is some sort of totem for your planner. A symbol of some sort. Is that because he relates to the poem as a reminder of his motivation for planning the attack? Or is it because he sees in the poem the desired outcome of his attack, something that he wants to make 'nevermore'?"

"Mm," Samuel said. "What if it's both? Or what if it's his-torical in nature?"

"What do you mean?"

"What if there's some kind of history about the publishing of this poem that makes it a relatable totem for the justification of terrorism?"

"Well—" Trudi started, but she was interrupted by the sound of her intercom switching on.

"Ms. Coffey," Eulalie's voice said, "your nine-thirty appoint-ment is here."

Already? Time does fly when Samuel Hill's in the room.

"Want me to sit in?" Samuel asked. She could see he wasn't ready to leave her yet. Maybe he was a little bit lonely nowadays too?

"No. Thanks." Trudi added a head shake for emphasis.

She took a second to peek at the live-feed video monitor situated under her desk, tucked away on the left side. Thanks to the security camera hidden in the lighting sconce, she had a full view of the small reception area just down the hall. Eulalie was at her desk, waiting patiently for a reply. Standing in front of Eula's desk was—

She stood up out of reflex. "You've got to be kidding me," Trudi said aloud.

"What?" Samuel said, twisting in his seat to try and peek down the hallway into the reception area. "Is it a celebrity?"

Trudi pursed her lips and shook her head again. "Get out, Samuel," she said, though not unkindly. "I've got to take care of this one on my own." Then she spoke into the intercom. "Thank you, Eulalie. Please send Mr. Deasy in."

11

RAVEN

Atlanta, GA
West Midtown
Friday, March 24, 9:31 a.m.
21 days to Nevermore

I actually feel nervous.

I haven't had stage fright since I was eleven years old, performing my very first magic tricks at a church potluck. As soon as the applause started, I never looked back, never lost my nerve again. And yet here I am today, standing in the reception area of Coffey & Hill Investigations, and I can feel a frog croaking inside my lungs. I think my hands may even be sweating, just a little, which is crazy. My hands are my greatest asset as a deception specialist—they never let me down.

Of course, I've never met a woman like Trudi Coffey before, either. She makes me feel like a junior high kid, like I'm trying to get up the nerve to call her, but I always chicken out and hang up before the phone rings.

Well, if that's the way it is, then I'm going to enjoy it.

The receptionist returns my smile, which makes me feel a little embarrassed because I didn't realize I was grinning. But she's being nice, and I appreciate it. She's younger than Trudi. I'm guessing she's closer to my age, maybe a year or two older.

"Ms. Coffey," she says, "your nine-thirty appointment is here."

"You can call me Marv," I say. There's a brief silence while we both wait for Trudi to answer. I decide to practice the Age, Weight, Relationship Status game with the receptionist.

Sixty seconds or until Trudi responds on the intercom, I tell myself. *Go.*

This trick is all about comparison. I've got to take in all the clues the mark has on display and then compare them to what I know about me. First, weight. This is easiest when working with women, because they're already self-conscious about that kind of thing. A woman who's feeling heavy wears looser, billowy tops to disguise the true circumference of her midsection. This receptionist doesn't have that insecurity. She wears a smart, sleeveless, button-up shirt and business slacks. She's young, trim, and reasonably fit, not afraid to be seen for who she is. Probably still eats cheeseburgers from time to time—but that won't last once she hits twenty-eight or so. She's sitting, but I'm guessing her height at about five foot five, which means . . .

All right. I picture the balancing scales in my head. *I weigh 170. How many of her would it take to match my weight on the scale? Got it.*

Now, quickly, I check the age indicators. Her dark skin is smooth and creamy, like chocolate frosting poured out as body paint and then spread with a spatula to eliminate all creases. The corners of her eyes and lips are unlined, fresh, young. No loose skin or wear and tear on the knuckles or backs of the hands. Root color in the hair is consistent with the tips, which isn't too difficult to tell with this one because the receptionist has a head full of thick, bouncy ringlets, about shoulder-length. Her hair is black-widow-spider black, with deep red highlights tinted throughout. Very pretty. *Okay, move to skin on the neck, and . . . Got it.*

Relationship status. *Hurry, boy, you're going to lose this one!* No wedding ring, but she wears several fashion rings on both hands. And—

"Thank you, Eulalie." Trudi's voice pops through the intercom without warning. "Please send Mr. Deasy in."

"Single," I say, "but dating." *Oops. Didn't mean to say that out loud.* "Sorry. Just a little game I was playing inside my head."

She cocks her head in curiosity. "Was I playing it too?" Thankfully, she's not offended.

"I, ah, well . . . Hmm."

I ask for a pen and Post-it Note from the reception desk, which she hands over without comment. "It's a game where I try to guess your age, weight, and relationship status." I scribble on the Post-it Note. I make a point to underestimate her weight. Don't want to insult Trudi Coffey's receptionist the first time I meet her. "This is what I would've guessed for you."

She looks at the note.

Twenty-four years old. Weight at 117. Relationship status, single but dating a few guys casually.

"Few pounds heavier than that," she says with a smile. "But thanks for the compliment."

"Oh, well. I was close."

"Actually pretty impressive given that you've only been in here about two and a half minutes and you got everything else correct. How did you figure out the relationship status? That one seems kind of arbitrary."

"Sorry, a magician never reveals his secrets."

She stands and nods. "This way," she says. "I'll walk you back." Then, "I bet you're a force to be reckoned with at night-clubs. Pretty good wingman for your friends on a Friday night at the bar?"

"Haven't gone out drinking with my buddies in years," I say, and I feel a stab of pride about that. "Not in years."

She stops and looks at me. "My turn, then," she says. "You're a recovering alcoholic? Probably started drinking in high school, just for the thrill of it, and then one day you realized the thrill was gone but you still needed the drink. Am I right?"

Not bad, I think. *Am I that transparent?* "Well, I—"

"No, you don't have to answer," she says. "I know the answer anyway. And don't ask how I know, because a detective's assistant never reveals her secrets, either." She dimples and leads me down the short hallway from the reception area to Trudi's office.

Trudi is standing near a medium-sized wooden desk. Behind her is an impressive collection of books on shelves built into the wall. In front of her desk are a couple of metal chairs and a fairly large dude in black jeans and a blue sports coat. He stands when I come into the room.

"Ms. Coffey," Eulalie says by way of introduction, "this is Marvin L. Deasy. Excuse me, sorry, he goes by Marv."

The Big Dude covers a laugh and makes eye contact with the receptionist. Her eyes are smiling back in his direction, apparently sharing an inside joke.

Are they sharing my joke?

"Raven," Trudi says, "please have a seat."

"Am I interrupting?" I say, trying hard not to stare at the big guy.

"No, no," he says to me. I notice the edge of a shoulder holster peeking out from inside his sports coat, and I hear the buzz of a cell phone from somewhere on him too. He pulls a fairly new iPhone out of his coat pocket and continues. "I was just leaving. Plus, I apparently missed a call from my boss, so I'd better check that or heads will roll, right? Sorry for the intrusion, Marv." He starts for the door.

"I'll walk out with you, Mr. Hill," the receptionist says. A moment later, it's just me and Trudi. Crazy thing is, she somehow looks even more perfect than I remember her from a week ago. I hope she thinks I look a little better too.

"Please," she repeats, "have a seat."

Right. Forgot I was still standing. Kind of hard to concentrate when I'm staring at a woman like this.

"Marv L. Deasy," she says, taking her seat after I've taken mine. There's a slight wrinkle in her nose, like she's just gotten a whiff of bad fish or something. "I get it now."

"Excuse me?"

"If you didn't want to tell me your real name, why didn't you just use The Raven? Then at least I would've known to expect you."

"No, my name's Marv. I just figured that—"

She puts a hand up, and I close my flapping lips.

"Here's the deal, Raven. I don't care what your real name is, or whether you like comic books, or candy, or both."

Ah, so it was obvious. Have to do better next time.

"All I care about is the truth, so if you're going to come into my office, if you want to talk to me, or hire my agency, or whatever, you're going to have to tell me the truth. Fair enough?"

She leans back in her chair, fingers steepled in front of her chin.

"Sorry," I say. "Old habits die hard, I guess."

I think I see her face softening, so I try to look sheepish.

"Your right eye is looking a lot better," she says at last. "How's the rest of you holding up?"

"Still a little sore around the rib cage," I say, relieved, "but pretty much back to normal." I hope she likes the way my "normal" looks. I'm all cleaned up and wearing my best T-shirt, after all.

"You look good," she says. "I mean, you look like you're in better shape than you were a week ago. Any trouble with those bad guys returning?"

I shake my head.

"They're probably going to come back. Are you ready for that?"

"Ah, I think they're done with me at this point."

"Why do you believe that?"

I can see she thinks I'm naïve, but really, why would they come back? They got what they were after, plus they got to have a little sadistic fun before they left. I haven't seen any trace of them at all for a week now. I'm pretty sure my troubles with Max Roman's thugs are over.

"Well, I gave them what they wanted." I shrug. "I'm not worth anything to them anymore, so why would they bother?"

She nods slowly. "Those kinds of guys don't usually need a reason." She can tell I'm ready to change the subject now. Thankfully, she decides to help me out on this. She says, "I see you got out of the handcuffs. Did you have to break the chair?"

"Yeah. Made a little mess, but such is the price of freedom."

She offers a wan smile in acknowledgment of my lame joke. It seems like we've made all the chitchat we can make at this point. Junior-High Me is starting to panic, looking for a way to hang up the phone. Finally she sighs and drops her hands into her lap.

"So," she says, "what can I do for you today, Raven?"

"I called your ex-husband, Detective Samuel Hill," I say suddenly. I want her to know I took her advice, but I'm confused by the hard look that suddenly crosses her eyes.

"Really," she says. She drags out the syllables like a prosecuting attorney getting ready to pounce. *Reeaallly.*

"Yep. And I turned over those, uh, items we talked about before."

"I see." She leans forward and locks her eyes on to mine. "Just out of curiosity, what does my ex-husband look like?"

I freeze.

Didn't anticipate that.

"Mm-hmm." She leans back in her chair again.

This isn't going quite the way I envisioned it.

"That's what I thought," she says. I can see she thinks the case is closed.

Come on, kid, I tell myself, *pull this one out of the flames.*

And then a thought flashes in my head. I hear that receptionist talking again. *"I'll walk out with you, Mr. Hill,"* she said. *Could that be . . . ?* No, surely she would have called him "Detective Hill," not "Mr. Hill." Unless she was trying to be discreet about his occupation in front of a client? I take a chance.

"He's, uh, about six foot two, I'd guess. Big dude. You can tell he works out. I think women would say he's handsome. Dark hair, short." I hesitate, just checking my progress. I'm winning her back, I can tell. "Carries a gun inside his blazer."

"All right," she says, palms out. "I can see you're trying at least. But maybe you can explain why you and my ex-husband just saw each other here in my office and neither one of you recognized the other?"

"Oh!" I say, and I stand up without thinking. I guess I'm excited, like in grade school when I actually knew the answer to the math problem on the board. "That's because we never met in person. But I did call him. I left a message and made arrangements to drop off the stolen stuff for him at the Zone 6 police station. Which I did, just like you asked me to do. It's all good." I suddenly realize I'm standing, and I sit back down, maybe too quickly. "It's all good. I'm a new man."

She doesn't say anything, but I can see she's tempted to believe me.

"Cross my heart."

I want to give her my stage grin, the one that puts people at ease and makes them believe I'm telling the truth even when they know I'm lying to them. But I'm actually telling the truth to Trudi, and I want her to believe I'm telling the truth even though she thinks I'm lying. So I just look deeply into her eyes and wait for her to choose.

I find myself mildly distracted by her eyes. At first glance I see brown, but then they seem to change to greenish, with a brown center, and then they change again. *Hazel eyes are so cool*, I think.

She stares at me, and I think maybe she's looking at my eyes the same way I was just looking at hers. Then she's all business. "Okay, I believe you. For now. But you can bet I'll ask Samuel about this later, so you'd better cover your bases if you haven't already."

I can tell I'm smiling again. And nervous. And loving every minute of it.

"So, *Raven*"—she emphasizes my stage name—"why are you here? What do you want?"

"Well, Trudi, see, I realize that the last time we met I wasn't in the best mental state. I feel like I may have made a poor impression, especially with that whole spontaneous marriage proposal thing and all."

"Not to mention the three goons who were trying to perform plastic surgery on you. Without anesthesia."

"Right. Not to mention those guys. But that's why I'm here. I'd like to ask for a second chance to make a first impression."

"What?"

I take a deep breath and exhale quickly. I've been working hard the past few days, honest work, twelve hours a day out at both Piedmont Park and Freedom Park. Performing magic tricks, making tips, and saving every penny just to be able to do this, what I'm doing, right here, right now. I think of the thin collection of bills hidden in my wallet, and that bolsters my confidence. I may spend it all, but at least I can afford what I'm about to suggest—and for once I earned it all honestly. I inhale again, taking in the thrill of the uncertainty before me.

Mom always said I was an adrenaline junkie. I guess she was right.

"Trudi," I say, "I was wondering if you might like to have dinner with me tonight. Someplace nice?"

12

BLISS

Atlanta, GA
Little Five Points
Friday, March 24, 9:49 a.m.
21 days to Nevermore

It'd been a week since Max Roman's surprise visit, and Mama Bliss could tell that Darrent was still mad at her.

He'll get over it, she told herself. *He always does.*

Trouble was, Darrent had been more than just a worker for William. He was, in the most practical sense, a true believer in Bliss's now-deceased husband. The work they'd done had been about more than the money. Darrent had made plenty of that over the years. If he'd wanted out, he could've gotten out and lived comfortably at any time. But he stayed because William asked him to stay, because William convinced him they weren't just smuggling guns. They were changing the world, they were making the planet a better place—making Little Five Points a better place. And Darrent believed it. He'd spent most of his

110

adult life believing it, and working for it, and making it happen with his own blood, sweat, toil, and tears.

I got to do what I got to do, Darrent, in the time I got to do it, she told herself. *Mama Bliss won't last forever, you know.*

She sat on the sidewalk in front of Sister Bliss's Secret Stash and wished it would rain. The day was uncomfortably warm—not summer "Hotlanta" style, but spring-heat style. Muggy, air full of moisture but without any actual precipitation to relieve the discomfort. Bliss could see dark clouds to the north and west of her and was fairly certain they were getting rain over there, but that little storm had stalled. Maybe it would die out without ever reaching the Stash, or maybe it would suddenly shift and dump buckets of water.

"Make it rain," she whispered to the sky. There was no answer.

After a few minutes, Darrent came out to sit beside her on the sidewalk, carrying his own folding chair and setting it up next to her blank canvas. No one said anything at first, and then he peered at the chalky white and said, "Not painting today, after all?"

"Nothing asking to be painted," she said.

He nodded. "Sold your last painting today," he said. "Some tourist from New York City. Said she was going to use it as part of an exhibit at a gang rehabilitation facility in Brooklyn."

"Huh."

"It made her weep when she saw it."

Mama Bliss didn't know what to say.

"Anyway," Darrent continued, "I get it now. After seeing that woman weeping in front of your painting, I get it."

"What you talking about, Darrent?"

"I understand why you let Max Roman take those guns. I get it now. I'm sorry I didn't trust you, that's all. I thought I should say so."

"I got to do what I got to do, Darrent."

"I know."

"The time is coming, Darrent." *I won't be 'round forever.*

"I know."

"You gonna be all right after Mama's gone?"

"I'll figure out something."

"I know you will, honey." She patted his knee. "Now go inside and change the world. I'm just going to sit here and wait for rain."

"Okay, Mama." Darrent stood, collected his folding chair, and went back into the Secret Stash. Bliss nodded to no one in particular and let her mind go back over the complicated relationship that William had begun with the Romanenko family.

"Ms. Mama Bliss," Max had said last Friday night, just after Mama had agreed to let him take seventy-eight war weapons and plant them in Riverdale, only nineteen miles south of her home in Little Five Points, "would you like to see the favor I did for you today?"

She'd engaged the little motor on her wheelchair and followed him out to the alley that ran alongside the loading dock. To her left, she saw he'd brought a white box-truck to carry his guns. This one, she noticed, was painted with insignias of a large commercial carrier based in Fayetteville, North Carolina.

At least he had sense enough to disguise his truck as one that regularly brings shipments in and out of the Stash, she thought. But she'd never considered Max Roman anything less than shrewd anyway. He and his family had been around too long and been entrenched in power for too many decades to make stupid mistakes.

"So," she'd said as they turned the corner into the alley. "They tell me you're going to be the next mayor of Atlanta."

"That's the plan," Max said cheerily. "Come November 7, you may have a friend in very high places, at least as far as Atlanta is concerned."

She'd seen his car then—well, one of his cars—parked in the alley. Max kept a fleet of about half a dozen cars, trotting out his favorite one to suit whatever campaign setting he was in. For working-class neighborhoods, his driver chauffeured him around in a Ford Expedition EL. Among Atlanta's "old money" elite, he arrived in style in a Cadillac CTS-V sedan. Tonight, though, his vehicle of choice was a black Escalade ESV.

The street lamps had felt dim back there, shaded by night and concrete and the odd assortment of refuse that tended to collect in places like that. The tinted windows on the Escalade gave no hint of what might be inside.

Max had stopped a few feet from the car, and Bliss mirrored his movement. "Your William was a good man, Mama," he said, and she couldn't tell if he admired her dead husband or if he was just feeling nostalgic. "He was smart to reach out to my father back in 1995, after the ETA terror group in Spain got ahold of some of your guns. After they used your guns in that attempt to assassinate José María Aznar. That really shook things up with your CIA, didn't it?"

"We've been over this before, Max. Nothing conclusive ever connected us to those guns. And besides, that was a temporary setback. The CIA is still my biggest customer."

"Yes, yes, I know. Just remembering your husband. And just reminding you that, without me, even your CIA would have trouble laundering guns through the Secret Stash."

"Seems as though you've always benefited from the arrangement."

"I've always kept the terms of my father's deal with your husband," he said.

Until tonight, she thought, but aloud she only said, "Just as I have."

"But times, they are changing. It takes money to do what I do. And there is a long-term plan in place, which also takes money. Lots of money."

"You have lots of money."

In the darkness, Bliss thought she could hear Max smiling more than she could see it happening.

"Regardless," he'd said, "I need more. And that means buy low, sell high."

Bliss was feeling impatient. "Well, in your case, that means sending your Kipo boys to create havoc until real estate prices plummet so you can buy devalued properties, renovate entire districts with shopping malls and overpriced office buildings, and then sell at inflated prices."

"And clean up the gang problem in that area. You forgot that part."

"Right."

It was a pretty good scam, Bliss had to admit. Siphon money from your family's deep-pocketed, multifaceted real estate development company. Use it to fuel the gangs with drugs and cash and women from your shell-company strip clubs until the Kipo boys were dependent on you. Then make the gangs your weapon of choice to chase away unwanted property owners, retail establishments, business entities, and whatever else stood in the way of your lucrative development projects. And after you'd pretty much confiscated other people's homes and businesses and retail empires for pennies on the dollar, use your position on the Atlanta City Council to "crack down on crime" in your freshly acquired areas. Then "revitalize" the area like you did for the 1996 Summer Olympics in downtown Atlanta.

Of course, what that really meant was just ordering your

gangbangers to wreak havoc in a different part of the Atlanta metro area, then building new, high-visibility architecture and infrastructure. After that, watch real estate prices and asset investments soar in your formerly devalued neighborhoods. Make a killing re-selling your holdings at absurd prices and start all over again in some other corner of the ATL.

Max Roman was a millionaire dozens of times over. Still, in spite of that, no one seemed to question why a man with that much money wanted so badly to get elected to an office that paid an annual salary equal to what a competent dental hygienist might make.

Long-term plan, Bliss had thought. *Atlanta is just a stepping-stone for this muck.*

From what she could tell, Roman's ambition held few boundaries. She could see the path as easily as he could. Four years as mayor of Atlanta, followed by eight years as governor of the great state of Georgia, and from there . . . well, pretty much anything was possible from there.

"But I need you, Ms. Mama Bliss," he was saying. "You are my secret weapon, and so even when I must disappoint you, like tonight, I am always working to make you happy, as well. You believe this about me?"

"Of course, Max," she'd lied. "Our families, we go way back together."

"Good," he said. "My father promised your husband we'd keep Little Five Points clean of gangs, especially the Kipo sets. No guns, no gangs, not in William's home. That was the deal. And the Romans always keep their promises."

He'd leaned over then and opened the back door of his Escalade. The pale overhead light had startled the body nearest to her inside the car. It had taken only a second for Bliss to understand the circumstances.

The back seat of Max Roman's Cadillac was covered, top to floorboards, in a sheet of clear plastic. *Easier cleanup for the mess*, she'd thought. The boy nearest to her was shirtless, bound hand and feet, arms behind his back. There was plenty of blood.

Across from him was a dumpy Ukrainian guy, hammer in one hand and a leather-bound set of knives sitting close to his thickened thigh.

She'd recognized the Ukrainian as one of Max Roman's enforcers, a relatively recent émigré from Ukraine, family to Viktor Kostiuk, Max's right-hand man. Pavlo Kostiuk had been in the States less than a year but had already demonstrated a unique talent for clinical violence.

Under the tiny dome light, the battered teen had blinked frantically, forcing his eyes to adjust to the light, peering into the alley with the look of a cat being shoved into a canvas bag. She'd seen his face glint in recognition and knew what was coming next.

"Mama!" he'd gasped. "Mama Bliss, thank God, thank God. Help me, Mama. Please help me. They broke my arms. Both my arms. I can't feel my hands." He was sobbing now. "Please, I need a doctor. Please help me, Mama."

Pavlo had casually tapped the flat of the hammer against the teenager's temple. "You don't speak unless spoken to."

The Kipo kid closed his mouth then, and his eyes, but he kept whimpering, maybe even praying.

Max had leaned down beside her wheelchair. He was grinning. "He came up to celebrate a birthday with some little girlfriend of his, even though he knew Little Five Points was off-limits to Kipo. My man at the Planet Bombay saw his orange gang colors all the way from across the street."

Mama remembered this boy's face. He'd come into the Secret Stash with—what was her name?—well, with Sugar. *"Mama, please,*" the boy had whispered. Pavlo had looked crossly at him but didn't strike this time.

He'd known he didn't belong in her place, not at all, and he'd come sauntering in there anyway. Orange shoes blazing, an offense to her eyes.

"Kipo is what killed my grandson," Mama said to the car.

The teen in the backseat had groaned. Bliss reached out and slammed shut the door.

Max had stood and stretched lazily. "You see, Mama? I keep Little Five Points safe for you, for the Secret Stash. No Kipo is coming back here for a long time, not after they hear about this little fish. Now, what do you want? Should I have my boys drop this one at a hospital curb? Or someplace where maybe he doesn't come back ever?"

Bliss had grimaced. He knew the answer to that question already. He was just asking it to rub in the truth, make her feel somehow responsible for it.

"You let that boy see you," she said, "and fixed it so he'd see me too. You and I both know what that means."

Max Roman had signaled the driver then, and Bliss pushed her wheelchair back as the Escalade started up and rolled away. Someday, maybe in a month, maybe years from now, someone would find the bones of that Kipo boy swallowed by concrete inside a construction site or in the foundation of a high-rise building. They'd wonder what happened, why one so young had been taken that way, but no one would ever know.

No one will ever know.

Bliss had felt both sad and angry. She'd started the electric motor on her wheelchair and headed back to the loading docks. Max Roman walked silently beside her. Before they reentered the warehouse, Mama Bliss had stopped and turned her face up toward Max. He'd grinned, like he was expecting a compliment or some trite expression of gratitude. The grin froze when he saw her eyes.

"Remember, Maksym, no matter what you do for me, you need me more than I need you." The muscle in his jaw had tightened. "I can bring you down in a heartbeat. I don't even have to be alive to do it. I can take from you everything you've ever taken from anybody else, everything you worked for. It's all handwritten in a logbook, updated as needed, hidden, ready to appear any time, any place, for any reason. You understand what I'm saying, Max?"

"If you've got so much power to ruin me, Ms. Mama Bliss, why don't you use it? Are you worried that maybe I own too many dirty cops? That maybe my money spread between the cracks of our American legal system might be too much for your flimsy little logbook? That maybe I even have my hands in the pockets of influential media outlets?" She'd seen his anger rising then, but she didn't flinch. "Why don't you bring me down," he'd hissed at her, "if you really think you can do that? You wouldn't be the first to try."

It's too good for you, she'd thought. *Financial ruin, public humiliation, even a life spent in a jail cell, all that is better than you deserve.* But out loud she'd said, "Maybe I like having a friend in high places."

She'd forced herself to smile.

Max Roman had stared at her, assessing her. For the first time that night, she'd seen a flicker of worry crease his face. He knew she wasn't bluffing.

"I think we understand each other," Maksym Romanenko had exhaled at last. When he turned to enter the warehouse, he wasn't smiling anymore.

Now Mama Bliss sat on the sidewalk outside her store, remembering the events of the night before. Max Roman had his guns, and that was that. He was going to deliver them to his Kipo lieutenants down in Riverdale, only nineteen miles away, but that couldn't be helped. Maybe, in the big picture, it wouldn't matter anyway.

She reached inside her shirt pocket and pulled out the worn picture of Davis. She flipped it over and read the writing on the back. It was the same as it had been for years. She put the picture back in her pocket and instead produced a business card from one of the pouches on her wheelchair.

"Maybe," she said quietly to herself, "it's time to give Samuel Hill a call."

13

TRUDI

Atlanta, GA
West Midtown
Friday, March 24, 9:50 a.m.
21 days to Nevermore

"Trudi," The Raven said, "I was wondering if you might like to have dinner with me tonight. Someplace nice?"

She tried not to roll her eyes.

"I know a great Spanish tapas restaurant in Buckhead. They have live entertainment on Friday nights," he said. "Could be fun."

"How old are you, Raven?"

He looked a little taken aback by that. Before he could answer, Eulalie appeared in the doorway, holding a bottle of Perrier water with a napkin around the glass.

"Excuse me," she said, twisting off the cap, "I thought Mr. Deasy might like something to drink." She transferred the water to The Raven but kept the napkin and bottle cap. "Sorry to interrupt." She dimpled and left as quickly as she had appeared.

"Thank you, Eulalie," Trudi said.

Inwardly, she smiled. She knew there was a reason she kept Eulalie around the office, and it wasn't just because she needed a sparring partner at the gym.

"Thanks," The Raven called out after the assistant. He took a quick sip of the water, then set the bottle on the floor next to his chair. He turned back to Trudi. "It's just dinner," he said. "And you might like it. Eclipse di Luna was voted the Best Place to Take a Date by *Atlanta* magazine."

And you're avoiding the question, Trudi thought. She asked it again. "How old are you?"

He shifted in his seat, and she decided she liked his eyes when they weren't all bruised and blackened around the edges.

"Well, look, I can see you're worried that maybe there's an age difference between us," he said, "but why worry about that now? How about if we just put that off until you decide whether or not you like our first date enough to want a second date?"

She half-smiled in spite of herself. "I turned thirty-two this last January," she said.

"See?" he said. "We're not that far apart. I turn twenty-three next month. A few years is nothing."

"Ha," she said. "I was already married and halfway through my college degree before your voice changed."

He nodded in acknowledgment but didn't concede. "And yet, you are neither married nor in college now," he countered, "and I have since become a full-grown man." He gave a mock bow. "Come on, give me a chance. I'm more than that guy you found handcuffed to a chair last week. I'd just like a chance to show you that. To show you a little bit of who I really am. One date, that's all. If you're not crazy about me by midnight tonight, you never have to see me again."

She took a moment to think. She had no intention of "dating" this kid or anybody else, but why not have a nice meal at one of Atlanta's best restaurants? She might even pick up some valuable information. He was a street guy, after all.

The Raven reached down and took another sip of his Perrier. She noticed there was no condensation on the outside of the bottle, meaning the water had not been refrigerated. She congratulated herself again on choosing Eulalie Marie Jefferson for her assistant.

"You want some ice to go with that?" she offered.

"You're changing the subject," he said.

"Look, Raven, you seem like a nice guy. A little mixed up, but nice. You had a traumatic experience, and since I helped you get out of it, that causes you to fixate on me. My assistant is studying psychology, and she'd call what you're feeling 'affection-transference' or whatever head-shrink majors call that kind of thing."

When he didn't say anything in response, she continued. "Why don't you go out there and chat up Eulalie? She's pretty and very smart. She's earning her master's degree in night school right now. Dedicated. Plus, she's a lot of fun. And she's just about your age. Match made in heaven, if you ask me."

He stood but didn't make an exit. Instead, he let his eyes wander over the room, first taking in the bookshelves behind her, then the contents scattered around the top of her desk. He nodded, then nodded again. Trudi wasn't sure if she was supposed to stand as well or just wait it out. Finally, he smiled at her.

"Well, Trudi," he said, "you're saying a lot of things at me. But the one thing you haven't said yet is no. I think that means you're trying to talk yourself out of going on this date as much as you're trying to talk me out of it."

"Okay, then. No."

"I notice you were reading about me," he said. He gestured toward the book on her desk, *The Complete Tales and Poems of Edgar Allan Poe*, still opened to "The Raven" from when she and Samuel had been looking at it.

"Oh, that, no," she said. "I was looking something up for my ex-husband. Background for a case he's—"

"No need to explain." The Raven cut her off. "I'm flattered, but I didn't take my stage name from Poe."

"Really?" Now she was curious.

"Nope, though a lot of people think that. When I was starting out, I spent some time in Baltimore. Didn't take me long to figure out that a street magician in a football town could benefit from being associated with the sports team there, so I tried to get a job as Poe, the bird mascot for the Baltimore Ravens."

"That would've been something to see."

"Hey, I was great at it, for your information. But they already had a Poe they'd contracted for the foreseeable future. Still, the human resources lady liked me. She said that if I wanted to perform magic outside the stadium on game days, they wouldn't stop me, and maybe someday if the other mascot quit, then I'd be around when there was an opening."

"So that's when you became The Raven?"

"Well, technically, I was The Amazing Raven at first. But I shortened it to The Raven when I came to Atlanta. But that's how it started, yeah, and that's why I wear a purple cape and black eye mask. Just trying to match the colors of the home team up in Baltimore."

"So if you'd started out in Denver you'd be The Amazing Bronco?"

"Well, no, not that." He wrinkled his nose. "Guy's got to draw the line somewhere."

"Right." Trudi nodded. "So why'd you leave Baltimore?"

"My father—" He stopped himself. "You know, maybe that's a conversation to save for our second date."

"I haven't agreed to any date."

"Tell you what," he said, and he reached down to pick up *The Complete Tales and Poems of Edgar Allan Poe* off the desk. "Are you the gambling type?"

"Depends," she said.

He turned a few pages, then fanned through the rest once or twice, pausing every now and then as if he were shuffling a deck. Finally, he clapped the covers shut, leaned over the desk, and held the book out to her. After she'd taken it, he crossed his arms and grinned.

"I'm betting you want to go to dinner with me. And the reason I know that is because I can read your mind."

"What? Be serious."

"I am serious. Enough to bet on it. Are you willing to gamble that I can't read your mind?"

"What are the stakes?"

"I'll read your mind and tell you what you're thinking. If I'm right, you meet me tonight, at seven-thirty, at Eclipse di Luna for dinner, a little music, and at least one dance. My mom always told me I was a great dancer, and she never lied to me."

"And if you're wrong? If you can't read my mind?"

"Well, then my fate will be in your hands."

Trudi was starting to enjoy this guy in spite of herself.

"All right," she said. "How do you suggest we go about reading my mind?"

14

BLISS

Atlanta, GA
Little Five Points
Friday, March 24, 10:04 a.m.
21 days to Nevermore

Somewhere in this city, Bliss thought, *someone is falling in love.*

She wheeled her chair over the wood floor of the Secret Stash, past the book displays and the stacks of old hardcovers that had been die-cut into the shapes of numbers and letters in the alphabet. A recent customer had arranged a few of the die-cut tomes so that the counter now proclaimed "MN + AW" in book art.

Right now, someone is laughing and holding hands with a lover, she thought. *Someone is welcoming a child into her arms. Sharing a Coke with a teenager. Dreaming about the future.*

She nodded to Darrent as she passed the cash wrap.

And according to Samuel Hill, here in this city, in my home neighborhood of Little Five Points, someone is making plans to kill those innocent people.

She frowned, paused, and turned back to her manager. "Darrent," she said, "no interruptions this morning, okay?"

"Sure thing, Mama."

She turned and completed the little journey back to her office. She closed the door behind her but didn't bother with the lock. It was time to change the site of her insulin pump, and that was never terribly pleasant. Still, it was better than the alternative. She'd suffered some nasty bouts of diabetic shock in the past, and that was enough to make her diligent in managing her insulin levels from day to day. The pump certainly helped.

Bliss had been using a pump to regulate her blood sugar levels for years now. It was a small black box that had a narrow, flexible tube and needle attached. Bliss would use the needle to implant the flexible catheter just under her skin. Then the pump would deliver a steady drip of insulin into her bloodstream, helping to keep her blood sugar from getting too high or too low. Using the pump, she'd been able to eliminate most of the severe symptoms of hypoglycemia that were common to diabetics: dizziness, shaking, confusion, and sometimes seizures and fainting. The only problem was that the site for the insulin pump had to be changed about every three days.

It was never a thrill to wad up a roll of fat between her fingers and insert the needle under her skin to start a new three-day cycle. But she'd grown used to the ritual, and she liked being able to function almost normally when the pump was on.

Today she completed the procedure without incident, but before clipping the pager-sized box inside the waistband of her rayon pants, she paused to examine the life-giving little contraption.

Between meals and at night, the pump constantly delivered a small amount of insulin to keep her blood sugar levels in a healthy range. Before each meal, though, she had to input the number of carbohydrate grams she was about to eat into the pump display. Then it would increase the amount of insulin it delivered to her body to accommodate her food consumption.

Once, some years ago, she'd typed in the number of grams for a bowl of macaroni and cheese along with some sliced apples and a brownie—a quick lunch on a busy day. Only she'd been interrupted before she got the mac and cheese out of the microwave. Some minor emergency on the sales floor that needed her attention. Then she forgot to eat. By the time she got back to her stale lunch, the pump had already begun flooding her bloodstream with insulin. Since there was no food in her system, the result was insulin overload. Diabetic shock hit, and she'd fainted in the hallway.

Fortunately, one of the sales clerks had seen her drop. A quick trip to the hospital had fixed her right up, but Bliss had never forgotten how this little insulin pump was a two-edged sword. Handled diligently, it was a lifesaver. Handled carelessly, it could put her in a coma, or even kill her.

She attached the clip inside the waistband of her slacks and rolled her chair to the desk. It was time to call Samuel Hill, she decided. Time to fill him in a bit, as best she could at the moment.

Samuel's cell phone rang four times before she heard his voice on the other end.

"This is Samuel. Mama, is that you?"

"I'll never get used to that calling-ID thing," she grumbled. "I miss the good old days when people were polite and filled with happy surprise to find out I was calling."

"Of course I'm happy to hear from you. I'm just in the middle of a little bad news right now, so I was slow getting to my phone. But you've got my full attention, Mama. Is everything okay?"

"Yes, Samuel, thank you for asking."

"What can I do for you?"

"You told me to call you after I did some snooping about your problem."

"You have information on Nevermore? Well, that's good news. What have you got?"

"Samuel," she said, "I don't know if you'll think this is good news, or bad news, or no news at all."

"Well, tell me anyway. I'm sure it's going to be more than I've got right now."

"All right. Here's the news: There is no news."

She heard him shift the phone in his hands. "What do you mean, Mama?"

"I mean, I've put the word out, asking for anybody to tell me anything they know about something called Nevermore. Samuel, nobody knows anything. Nobody's heard anything. It's an invisible story. I mean, maybe it's not a story at all."

"You think it's a hoax?"

"You're the detective, not me. I'm just an old lady who keeps an ear to the ground in Little Five Points."

"My source says, well, my source said . . . Hmm."

"Maybe you should go back to your source and dig for more."

"Yeah, that'd be the thing to do at this point. Except my source is no longer available."

"That sounds cryptic."

"Well, this is confidential for now, but it'll be public knowledge by the end of the day, so I guess it won't hurt to tell you. My source was sitting in the pre-trial detention center at the federal penitentiary here in Atlanta. He was one of the Kipo gang members arrested in that big arms bust a few weeks ago. I just got a message from my captain about him. Apparently he still had friends on the outside."

"What do you mean?"

"Last night somebody posted bail for Andrew Carr. Just for

him, not for any of the other Kipos. He walked out the front door of the prison and disappeared. No one thought to have him followed or to keep him under surveillance. He's turned into a ghost. Might not even be in Georgia anymore."

"I see."

"That's the phone call I was dealing with when you called just now."

"Sorry to hear that, Samuel. But maybe that boy was just trying to make himself seem more valuable to you. Maybe he was angling to make a deal to lessen his sentence by trying to convince you there was some big plot going on."

"Maybe it was all a big lie, you're saying. A smokescreen sent up by a desperate kid facing jail time? Maybe it was that."

Mama Bliss felt herself relaxing a bit. If Samuel Hill could stop worrying about Nevermore, then maybe she could stop stressing about it too. Maybe they could both relax and get on with their lives.

"Or," he was saying now, "maybe that kid was telling the truth, and whoever is behind Nevermore found out about it. And maybe that was enough to find a way to silence the mouth that was talking."

Bliss suddenly felt a headache coming on. "What you want me to do, Samuel?"

"Just keep doing what you're doing, Mama. Just keep listening. Be my ears and eyes out there in Little Five Points. If you hear anything, even if it seems far-fetched or only mildly related, you let me know, okay?"

"Sure, Samuel. You know I got nothing but love for you and your little Trudi."

"Thanks, Mama. And Trudi really liked your gift, by the way. Said to tell you so."

"Good. Thank you. Got to go now, Samuel. You take care."

"You take care too, Mama."

Bliss ended the call and watched the cold telephone do nothing for a minute or two afterward.

The timing was bad for this. But she owed Samuel, as much for who he was as for the things he'd done. Often, when the CIA was involved, he didn't even know he'd been helping her. But she knew. Now she was worried that he might be getting in too deeply with this Nevermore situation. Samuel Hill was relentless, she knew. And smart. Resourceful. He'd lost one informant, but he wouldn't let that stop him. He'd keep digging until he found another, maybe several others, and that could put him in the path of danger.

Of course, Samuel thrived on danger. Leonard Truckson, his CIA handler, had introduced him to that emotional drug and kept him happy with it until Truck's untimely death about a year and a half ago. She frowned at that thought.

That man was both a blessing and a curse, she told herself.

The man they called "Truck" was a soldier, a spy, a farmer, and who-knew-what-else. William never said how he and Truck had met up, and Truck never offered it, either. Bliss could only guess until finally she gave up guessing. Truck was part of their lives, and that was that.

It had been Truck who'd helped William first set up the weapons laundering infrastructure under the cover of Sister Bliss's Secret Stash. And it was Truck who had somehow managed to make that whole covert operation a "black ops" project, meaning it had initial funding from the CIA but no direct oversight from the CIA. In fact, there were only a handful within the agency that even knew of the CIA's involvement in the Stash—Truck had seen to that. "Plausible deniability," he'd called it.

Now, decades later, the Stash was a twice- or thrice-removed pathway, an avenue the CIA used to export weapons to friendlies without having to have the United States government attached. Untraceable guns fighting in foreign wars was good business for both the Stash and the United States espionage agency, especially now that everyone was living in the age of terror.

Money from running guns had secured financial stability for Bliss and William, had paid for the broad expansions of the retail business going on at the Secret Stash, and had given them the ability to find influence in the greater community of Little Five Points. But all that money had a cost, an emotional price that sometimes felt like too much to bear.

For William, though, it had never been about the money.

It was about patriotism and, corny as it sounded, about keeping the world safe for democracy. That was what Leonard Truckson had really given her husband—purpose and meaning to his life, the idea that he was making a real difference in the world, the thought that he was doing right by helping to undermine and topple oppressive foreign governments. After Davis's death, though, Bliss hadn't been so sure.

Still, back at the beginning, it had all been a great new, patriotic adventure. They started importing guns and other small arms, cleaning serial numbers and laundering them through several ports of call until they were virtually untraceable. Then they'd export them out again, secretly supplying arms to rebels in Venezuela, Kurds in Iraq and Syria, freedom fighters in the former Soviet republics, spreading the wealth to those needing relief from oppression and a chance at self-government.

Guns go through here, William had insisted, *but no guns stay here*.

Those were his terms. His home was his home, and he didn't want to learn that even one of his guns had been responsible for harming anyone in the ATL. Of course, he couldn't have predicted the problems that would arise after Truck went off the grid and turned his dealings over to freelancers. And he certainly hadn't counted on dying at the young age of fifty, leaving Bliss and Darrent to carry on for him. *No guns stay here*, he'd said time and again. But sometimes your dead husband's good intentions just weren't good enough.

It's best you passed before Davis did, *Willy*, Bliss thought to herself. *Before you could find out that one of your guns would cost your grandson his life*.

She reached into her shirt pocket and retrieved the picture once more. Davis, arms spread wide, smiling like an angel. Keys to a new car flashing in his hand. Keys to a new life, he'd thought. The whole world ahead of him.

She turned the picture over and reread the printing on the back.

There were six names.

15

TRUDI

Atlanta, GA
West Midtown
Friday, March 24, 10:09 a.m.
21 days to Nevermore

"How do you suggest we go about reading my mind?"

Part of her thought she should just stop this little game, that she should smile, thank The Raven for his kind invitation, and then usher him out the door. That was the professional side of her. The side that was practical and hardworking and successful in her job.

Another part of her was kind of enjoying this guy. He was a two-bit crook, but a charming one. *Besides,* she told herself, *The Raven is out in the streets of Atlanta every day. Maybe he's heard something—maybe something he doesn't even know he's heard—about Nevermore. This street magician could turn into as good an informant as any other I've got.*

Out loud she said, "Do you want me to think of a number or something?"

"So it's a bet, then?" he said, sitting back in his chair. "All I have to do is read your mind and then we have a date tonight?"

Dinner at a nice restaurant. In pleasant company. She could think of worse ways to spend a Friday night. Plus, she was maddeningly curious to see if this guy could pull off a mind-reading trick. He certainly didn't lack for confidence, she'd give him that.

"Fine," Trudi said at last. She was still holding *The Complete Tales and Poems of Edgar Allan Poe*, so she set it on the desk beside her. "You read my mind, and I'll meet you at seven-thirty tonight at the restaurant of your choosing."

"Eclipse di Luna."

"Right. In Buckhead. I know the place."

"All right, then." He rubbed his hands together. "Do you want to make this easy for me, or hard?"

Trudi guffawed. "Hard, of course. I want you to work for it."

"Sure, sure. Then we'll start by getting you a random number."

He pulled out his cell phone and tapped an app. When he handed it to Trudi, she saw he'd brought up a calculator for her to use.

"Pick any three-digit number you like, we'll call that your 'triad.' Now, you can choose anything as long as it's a triad, but if you want to make it hard on me, use a number where the first and last numbers are at least two digits apart. You know, like 846, or 117, or something like that. But it's your call."

Trudi picked up his cell and tilted it so he couldn't see her typing. She chose the number 921.

"Got your triad?" he asked. She nodded. "Okay, let's mix it up. Reverse the order of your triad so the first digit is last and the last digit is first."

She cleared the display and then tapped in 129.

"All right, you remember both your triads?" She nodded again. "Now subtract the smaller triad from the larger one." She cleared the display again and subtracted 129 from 921.

792, she thought.

"Got a new number?"

"Yes. So are you going to guess it?"

He smiled. "Sure. You ready to give up that easy? Good, good. That's great. Now, Eclipse di Luna is a nice place, but dress is fairly casual. I'm going to wear jeans, but—"

"No," she said. "Let's keep going."

"Wait a minute, you said we could stop here, and I already read your mind to win the bet. What if I used up all my mind-reading energy and I can't read your mind again later? That doesn't seem fair."

"Deal with it. Keep going."

"Oh, so you really aren't going to make it easy for me, are you?"

"Nope."

He spread out his hands, palms up. "All right. Have it your way. Go ahead and take the triad you've got now and reverse the digits."

297, she thought.

"Add the last two numbers together," he said, "and we'll go from there."

792 plus 297. She did the math in her head instead of using the calculator app. *It equals 1089.*

"Okay," she said. "I've got it."

"Still a triad?" he asked.

"I'm not going to tell you," she teased. "You figure it out."

"Unless you're lying to me in your thoughts," he said. "I already know."

"Prove it," she said.

He nodded toward *The Complete Tales and Poems of Edgar Allan Poe*, sitting on the desk beside her. "All right. Make the first three digits of your number a page in that book. Turn to that page."

Trudi raised an eyebrow but did as he'd instructed, turning to page 108. She found herself in one of Poe's more obscure short stories, "The Thousand-and-Second Tale of Scheherazade."

"Now take the last digit of your number and count down that many lines on the page."

Trudi counted, *One, two, three . . . nine.*

"Read the first word on that line silently to yourself, then close the book."

She read *been.*

She closed the book.

That was a fairly innocuous word, she decided. If he could pull that one out of her head, maybe he did deserve a dinner date. She found herself thinking about what she liked best to eat at a Mexican restaurant.

He sat up in his chair and leaned forward a bit. "Now," he said, "look deeply into my eyes and, without speaking, tell me that word."

She started to comply, but then stopped. "Wait a minute," she said. She leaned over and pressed the intercom button on the telephone. "Eulalie, would you come in here just a moment?"

The Raven looked curious but said nothing.

"Right away, Ms. Coffey." A moment later her assistant joined them in the office. "What can I do for you?" she said.

Trudi stood up and walked to the side of her desk, motioning for Eulalie to come closer. "Sit in my chair, Eula," she said, "and think of this word." She held out "The Thousand-and-Second

Tale of Scheherazade" and pressed a thumb underneath the word *been*.

"Okaaay," Eulalie said, taking the seat behind the desk.

The Raven laughed. "Sneaky, but you're too late. I already read your mind. The word you're both thinking of now is *been*."

Trudi tossed the book onto the desk.

"Okay, I think I missed something," Eulalie said. "Do I care what I missed?"

The Raven stood, smiling. "Admit it. That was your word, wasn't it?"

Trudi searched his eyes. That was pretty impressive, she had to admit, and he'd made it look easy. She knew it was just a trick, something magicians do, but she had no idea how he'd done it. It was such a random word, pulled out of such a random place, in a book that she herself owned. He couldn't have doctored it before coming in here today. What was the secret?

Her eyes narrowed. "Do it again," she said.

"Oh no, this is a one-time-only mind-reading."

"He read your mind?" Eulalie said. "That's kind of cool."

"No, he didn't read my mind," Trudi said. "He did a devious little magic trick with smoke and mirrors and *The Complete Tales and Poems of Edgar Allan Poe*. And now he's going to do it again, this time for you, Eula. You'd do that, wouldn't you, Raven? Show your amazing mind-reading trick to my favorite assistant and wow her with your supernatural ability, right?"

"Ms. Eulalie," he said, bowing slightly, "you must forgive me, but I cannot perform this mind-reading exercise twice within the same hour." He feigned like he was fanning himself with a handkerchief. "It simply taxes my brain too much, and I wouldn't want my head to overheat all over the Coffey & Hill Investigations office floor."

Trudi didn't know whether to laugh or throw the stapler. "All right, then," she said, "tell me how you did it." She was like a cat readying herself to catch a mouse.

"I can't do that. A magician never reveals his secrets."

"Tell me how you did it, or you can eat by yourself tonight."

His smile grew even broader. He leaned over toward her as if to whisper something out of earshot of the assistant. "Trudi," he said loud enough for everyone to hear, "I read your mind." He gestured toward Eulalie. "And hers too. That was actually helpful, so thanks for asking her to come join us. Two minds add strength to the mental frequency."

Trudi stalked back to her desk while Eulalie jumped up and came around the other side.

"Um," Eula said, "I think I hear the phone ringing in the reception area. Maybe I should go check that out."

"Hold on," Trudi said.

Eulalie stopped before getting to the doorway. The Raven stood smirking near his chair. Trudi looked from him to her, then back again. She stood, started to say something, then decided against it and sat down. Finally, she sighed, shook her head, and allowed a small smile to sneak onto her face.

"Eulalie," she said, never taking her eyes off the magician, "please add an appointment to my schedule. Seven-thirty. To-night."

"With him? I mean, with Mr. Deasy? Seven-thirty on a Fri-day night?" Now Eulalie was trying not to grin. "Did you lose a dinner bet?"

"Stop gloating," Trudi said to The Raven. "You too, Eulalie. For all I know, you had something to do with this. Dinner at seven-thirty." She eyed both of them, then turned back to Eu-lalie. "Put it on my calendar, please."

Eulalie looked at The Raven with eyes that showed new re-spect. "Should I ask where?" she said.

"None of your business," Trudi said, but not unkindly. "Just put a seven-thirty appointment on my schedule."

"Consider it done," she said. She nodded toward the visitor on her way out. "And have a good time."

"Oh, don't worry, we will," The Raven said. "She has to watch me dance."

16

RAVEN

Atlanta, GA
Old Fourth Ward
Friday, March 24, 11:41 a.m.
21 days to Nevermore

My father used to say that joy is a gift from God, a minor proof that he not only exists, but that he also cares about his creation. I never really understood what he meant when I was younger, but right now it almost makes sense.

I have a date tonight with the woman of my dreams.

That thought fills me with a certain kind of joy I haven't felt in a long, long time. It's at once terrifying and exhilarating, like the feeling you get from walking onstage to perform in front of a thousand people, or the giddy excitement you have just after you've been strapped into the Goliath roller coaster at Six Flags Over Georgia. I just feel . . . happy. And it's nice. Makes me want to revel in a moment of gratefulness for the good things that can happen in a life.

I feel the strength of my legs pumping on the pedals of my Jamis Coda Sport bike, breathe in the air of mid-morning, and feel somehow more alive than I did two hours ago. Traffic is sweeping precariously around me, but at this moment I am nigh invulnerable.

"Yeaahh-haa!" I shout, and I don't even care that the guy in the Camry on my left had to slam on his brakes to avoid clipping my back tire before completing his right turn. Let him honk, I tell myself. He's not in love.

I do feel grateful, and somehow that makes me aware of the idea of God. *"In moments of hardship we learn to trust in God,"* my daddy used to preach, *"but it's in the moments of raw gratefulness that we finally begin to know him."*

Is that really true? I wonder. Is he present in these moments of joy? Can he be near enough to notice? Does he even care whether I'm happy or not?

This thought sobers me a little. If God is the source of all joy, as Daddy used to say, and if I'm caught up in a taste of that joy—however fleeting it might be—am I actually intuiting his presence in this moment? If I feel this otherworldly sense of gratefulness right now, doesn't it stand to reason it's because there is something, or Someone, to whom I am instinctively grateful?

My mind races like my legs on this bike, remembering my father's faith and the way he lived it out. He had plenty of hard times, more than his share of sorrows. Yet he also seemed to find some kind of joy in almost everything. His laugh is what I remember most about him. Full, open, trusting. He laughed easily and often.

Maybe the annoying old guy did understand what it meant to know God. At least just a little.

I zip through another intersection, shoulders down low, imagining my legs as pistons firing on all cylinders. The wind dries my eyes and tickles my ears. I feel like laughing too, but the sound doesn't quite come out.

"I never stopped believing in you," I shout to the sky instead. *I just stopped believing you cared.*

Even I don't want to say that last part out loud. But it's okay to think it, I decide. It's not like God would be surprised by my opinions about him. At least we're on speaking terms right now, and that's an improvement. Today maybe God is thinking of me, after all. Or maybe not. I never can tell with him. But this much I know:

Tonight I'm going to meet Trudi Coffey at Eclipse di Luna in Buckhead. And we're going to laugh and talk and maybe even dance. When it's over, Trudi Coffey just might start falling in love with me, but even if she doesn't, tonight will still be everything I've hoped for. Even if it lasts only for tonight.

"Yeaahh-haa!" I shout again, and I finally let up on the pedals of my bike. I'm breathing hard, but I'm almost home. And I can't stop grinning.

There are only a few cars lining the street when I get to my apartment. A Nissan Sentra. A beat-up Honda Civic. Some kind of Toyota hybrid. A Cadillac Escalade ESV. And even a Ford F-150 truck that seems way too big to fit on this little street.

"I should get flowers," I say to myself. But it's getting closer to lunchtime, and my empty stomach is complaining, reminding me that I skipped breakfast because I was too nervous to eat. The stomach wins. It won't take long to grab a bite anyway.

I'm tempted to leave my bike at the bottom of the steps just long enough to run up and get a sandwich. It'd save me from having to carry it back down again in fifteen minutes when I go out to get roses or something. But I've lived too long in a big city. I know it takes only sixty seconds for something you need to get stolen, and I need this bicycle to get me around Atlanta. I picked it out just for city riding, just so I could make it around to my chosen performance sites at Freedom Park, Piedmont Park, and sometimes even Centennial Olympic Park. Without my Jamis Coda, I'm unemployed. Best to bring it in.

Upstairs, I stash the bike in its normal place on the balcony and then hit the refrigerator. It's nice to have food in here again. Not much by some standards, but enough for me. I've been working hard all week, and that does have its benefits, namely a bunch of frozen dinners, lunch meat, bread, some grapes and—rare treat!—a twelve-pack of Mountain Dew.

The Dew gets my attention first. Then I find myself trying to decide between a roast beef sandwich or Stouffer's spaghetti and meatballs.

Before I can finish the first swallow of my drink, I hear a knock at the door.

"Pizza delivery!" a voice sings.

I feel my heart seize a split second before I hear the blood flooding into my eardrums.

Did I lock the front door when I came in?

I set my drink on the counter and try not to breathe. There's no rattling of the doorknob, no sound of shuffling feet in the hallway. Nothing.

Did I imagine it? Am I going crazy?

I risk tiptoeing across the apartment to peek out the balcony window. The street is empty, except for the same random cars I saw when I got home. In my head, I hear Trudi's voice from when we first met. *Those guys might come back. Are you prepared for that?*

Still no sounds. No new noises. Nothing. Every second feels like an hour passing. My hands are trembling, so I stuff them in the pockets of my jeans. I turn to face the door, but I'm not sure what to do about it.

Maybe, I think, *Trudi's warning has just got me spooked. Maybe it was nothing, or maybe it was a delivery for the lady across the hall.*

I skim over the fact that the lady across the hall is a nurse who works twelve-hour shifts on Fridays. *Maybe she skipped work today. Maybe she got sick. Even nurses get sick, right?*

Then I know it's not my imagination, because I see the knob on the door twist, just a little bit, jiggling left to right as someone tests the lock.

All right, I locked the doorknob for once. Wish I'd locked the deadbolt too.

Then another series of knocks, lazy and bored, like I'm wasting somebody's time.

One.

Two. Three.

Four.

"Might as well open up, Raven," the voice says. "I saw you go in, so I know you're there."

Now I don't hesitate. Trudi is practically screaming in my head. *If those thugs come back, remember your best exit is out that balcony door . . .*

I don't bother to collect anything. I just turn and burst through the curtains onto the balcony. The street is still empty of people. I think about tossing my bike over the railing, but even that seems too time-consuming. *It's about a ten-foot drop*, Trudi's voice reminds me, *so hang by your hands first. Don't just jump off the top.* Easy enough.

I'm over the side and measuring distances with my eyes in seconds. Kneel on the edge, grip the base of the railing, let myself down like I'm doing the back end of a clumsy little chin-up. When my head dips below the balcony floor, I realize all is lost.

"Hello, Raven."

Pavlo is underneath my balcony, on the porch of my downstairs neighbor. Standing there, he was hidden from my view above, but now I see all of him, grinning evilly, leaning with his back against the wall next to my neighbor's back door.

I'm hanging with my arms outstretched and my feet about twenty-four inches off the ground.

So close.

I'm thinking maybe I could still drop to the ground and make a run for it. *This guy obviously eats more than he exercises. I'm pretty sure I could outrun him.* But before I can make a move, Pavlo detaches from the wall and steps toward me. He doesn't bother with pleasantries this time, just plants his knuckles next to my left kidney. He hits me with a casual ferocity that makes me crumple into a heap at his feet. I'm lying there trying to breathe when he gives me a kick for good measure.

"He down there?" someone calls from the balcony above us.

I recognize the voice now. It's the football player looking down from above, the guy I nicknamed Scholarship at our last meeting. *Maybe I need to learn that guy's real name*, I think absently. Apparently Scholarship got tired of waiting for me to open the door and either broke it open or picked the lock. Now he's leaning over the edge of the railing on my balcony, and I hear him swear at the goon hovering over me.

"Pavlo, you big, dumb idiot, didn't I tell you not to break him? Didn't Viktor tell us both that?"

"He fine," Pavlo says defensively. "He was trying to run. I just stopped him running. That's all."

"Well, give him a minute to catch his breath, then get him up here," Scholarship says. And to me he adds, "You shouldn't have tried to run, kid. But my sister hits harder than Pavlo. You'll be fine."

Underneath the balcony, where Scholarship can't see it, Pavlo grimaces and makes an obscene hand gesture. When the football player disappears, the brute reaches down and hauls me to my feet. It's hard to breathe, but I'm able to rasp, "He said to give me a minute." I don't know why that really matters, but every moment counts to me right now.

"Minute over," Pavlo says. "Up."

"I can't breathe."

"How about I choke your head? You want that?"

"I'm going."

At the top of the stairs, I see that Scholarship didn't waste time with lock picks. The doorframe is busted out where the knob normally latches into the trim. My guess is that the beast just kicked the knob with one of his monster feet, and the old construction of this building didn't fight much before opening for him.

Pavlo ushers me into the kitchen, where Scholarship is busy at work. The microwave is running. *Why is this guy always eating my food?* I wonder. *Doesn't Max Roman pay him enough to buy groceries?*

There's a bag of ice on my kitchen floor and another bag being dumped into my sink.

"Stand here," Pavlo says, pushing me in front of the sink.

The timer dings on the microwave.

Pavlo shoves my hands onto the ice that's already in the sink, then he reaches down and tears open the other ice bag. Five seconds later, my hands are buried in freezing cold. The goon leans over until he's nose-to-nose with me, eyes narrowed and looking up into mine.

"Don't move, got it? You move and I hit you more. Got it?"

I nod.

Scholarship opens the microwave and pulls out a cup filled

with hot water. He reaches in a pocket and produces two gourmet tea bags.

"You like chamomile or Earl Grey?" he says to me.

"Uh . . ."

Is he inviting me to a tea party? Should I bring out my dollies or something?

"Let's go with chamomile," he says, studying me. "It's calming."

He rips open the wrapper and starts the tea steeping.

"You miss us?" Scholarship says by way of conversation.

"Not really," I say. I brace myself for a smack from Pavlo, but he's passive now.

"You know," the football player says, "we got interrupted before we could finish our discussion with you last time."

"What do you mean? I gave you everything you wanted. And you beat the living daylights out of me just for fun. Good times, right?"

Pavlo chuckles, and Scholarship just shakes his head. I realize I'm losing all feeling in my fingers, and I notice that standing with your hands stuffed into a big pile of ice cubes is kind of hard on the spine too. Something about the awkward posture, I guess.

Scholarship raises the cup to his lips and blows on the liquid a bit before removing the tea bag. He drops the wet bag onto the counter.

"That's going to leave a stain," I say. It's something my mother used to tell me, and I guess I felt it was necessary to impart that little bit of kitchen wisdom to the guy threatening to torture me again. To my surprise, he nods and picks up the tea bag, wiping the counter with his truck-sized hand to clean off the stain.

"My apologies," he says with a friendly air. He turns and drops the bag into the trash, then blows on the hot tea again, swishing the liquid in the cup to help it cool. "Still too hot.

Pav, hand me a few ice cubes. Don't want the kid to burn the roof of his mouth."

"Listen," I say. The cold of the ice is moving up my hands and making me shiver a little. "I learned my lesson already. You guys were very convincing last time. I'm on the straight and narrow now. No more stealing for me, not from Max Roman or anybody. I'm a new man. Honest."

Pavlo tilts his head and looks amused. Scholarship nods, interested but distracted by the cup of chamomile tea. He lifts it to his lips and touches the liquid to his mouth. He nods.

"I think that's about right," he says to Pavlo. The dumpy guy nods and looks bored. "Here," he continues, putting the cup up to my lips now, "drink this."

"Not thirsty."

Pavlo immediately grabs the back of my neck with his left hand and reaches toward my jaw with his right.

"No, no!" I gag. "I'll drink it! I'll drink it."

The goon looks to the other man, who nods. "Let him go, Pav. He's a new man, remember? He won't give us any trouble, right, kid?"

I nod. What else is there to do?

With Scholarship as my nurse, I swallow the first few gulps of the tea. He pulls back to let me catch my breath. "Needs sugar," I say, and he laughs out loud at that.

"I like you, kid," he says. "We're going to get along just fine."

Going to get along? I wonder. *What does that mean?*

He lifts the cup again, and before long all of the tea is gone. There's a strange aftertaste I can't place, but I'm also under a lot of pressure at the moment, so I figure I can give myself a break on that point.

"Good," Scholarship says. "How long now?"

"What?" I check the clock in the kitchen. It's high noon.

"About fifteen minutes," Pavlo says. "Maybe twenty for a boy his size."

"Wait. What? What are you talking about?"

Scholarship pats my shoulder. "You're doing great, kid. You just relax for a bit, okay?"

Suddenly I feel like crying. I didn't like it the first time these guys visited my apartment, but I was never really afraid of them then. Now I look at this football player, and then at the dumpy one, and this visit seems different. They're calm, all business. Like they've done this a hundred times. I suddenly notice that their boss, Viktor, didn't join them this time. I worry that the reason Viktor's not here is because they don't need Viktor here. Not today.

I'm not sure why, but I can't quite stop my heart from racing. I finally confess to myself what I've been trying hard not to admit. *I'm scared.*

"What do you want from me?" I say quietly. I can't keep my voice from quivering.

Scholarship turns and opens my refrigerator door. I can tell he's happy to find food in there.

"Well, you see, kid," he says, leaning down to remove my last container of strawberry yogurt, "you owe Max Roman ten thousand dollars. And we're here to collect it."

17

TRUDI

Atlanta, GA
West Midtown
Friday, March 24, 12:01 p.m.
21 days to Nevermore

"I'm going to sneak over to Taco Bell," Eulalie said to her boss. "I can't stop thinking about a Chicken Fresco Burrito Supreme and a Diet Coke."

Trudi clicked the mouse on her computer. "Mm-hmm."

"Want me to pick something up for you?"

"Mm-hmm." Click. Click.

"How about elephant tacos with shredded cardboard seasoning? That sound good?"

"Mm-hmm. That's fine."

Eulalie leaned her shoulder against the doorframe and waited. After a moment, Trudi looked up, surprised.

"Oh," she said, "sorry. What were you saying? You want to go on an elephant ride? Is there a circus in town or something?"

Eulalie moved to one of the guest seats in the office. "That Raven guy is all up in your head, huh? He is kind of cute. A little skinny for my taste, but I can see why a girl would look twice. He's funny too. I always like a guy who can make me laugh."

"No, it's not that," Trudi said. "Well, okay, yes, he is cute if you're a co-ed. But what's got me stuck is how he did that mind-reading trick. It was just so random."

Eulalie laughed. "You are always a detective," she said. "You can't live unless you know everybody's secrets. It was a magic trick. Why not just enjoy it?"

Trudi wanted to argue, but her assistant was right. Why fight it?

After The Raven had left earlier, Trudi and Eulalie had gathered in her office. Eula had brought in a resealable Ziploc bag and another napkin.

"That was good thinking," Trudi had said. Eulalie seemed to appreciate the compliment.

"Should I empty the water bottle first or just seal it with the cap again?" She leaned down and picked up the Perrier from where The Raven had left it.

"Let's empty it out, then cap it," Trudi said. "Don't want to take a chance that the cap will leak and smear the bottle."

"Got it."

"What made you think to get his fingerprints?" Trudi said as they both walked to the tiny break room in Coffey & Hill Investigations. It wasn't much but was still plenty for the two of them. There was a short table, two folding chairs, a mini-refrigerator, microwave, sink and counter, and random shelves holding office supplies and other equipment.

"He said his name was Marvel DC." Eulalie rolled her eyes. "Did he think I never read a comic book in my life?"

"Yeah, right." Trudi returned the eye roll but felt a little sheepish that it had taken her a few minutes longer than either Samuel or Eula to catch the joke in The Raven's supposed name. That was embarrassing.

"I figured, if a guy wanted to be that obvious about using a fake ID, then you'd want to dig deeper into what he was trying to hide." She held up the Perrier bottle. "So, fingerprints! I thought the glass would hold the prints better than plastic."

"Good thinking," Trudi said. "I love it when I hire smart assistants."

Eulalie hadn't said anything at that, but Trudi could tell she'd been pleased. They'd sealed the Perrier bottle and stashed it back in Trudi's office for the moment, on top of the desk.

Now Eulalie was eying her with a combination of curiosity and admiration. Her assistant nodded toward the Perrier bottle, expertly sealed and waiting. "You want me to call Mr. Hill about that?"

Samuel was always good about helping her with things like identity checks, but Trudi didn't feel ready to call him about The Raven yet.

"No. Other than my own curiosity, I can't think of a legitimate reason why I need Samuel to run those prints. Not yet at least."

"I bet if Mr. Hill knew you were meeting that guy for dinner, he'd want to run a full background check. Maybe more."

Trudi smiled inwardly, but on the outside she said, "You'd lose that bet. Samuel and I have been divorced for years now, and even when we were married he was never really the jealous type."

Eulalie shrugged.

"I think he just assumed no man could compete with him, so he didn't worry about it."

Now a laugh escaped her assistant. "That sounds about right," she said.

Trudi decided it was time to move the conversation away from her ex-husband. "Are you going out tonight?"

"Well . . ." Eulalie looked suddenly uncomfortable. "Sort of."

"It is Friday." Trudi smiled, feeling a little jealous. "Of course one of your many admirers is taking you out tonight." Trudi looked up at the clock and felt a grumble in her stomach. "How about some lunch? I'm buying. Taco Bell? I could use a Chicken Fresco Burrito Supreme. Maybe a Diet Coke too."

Something about that offer seemed funny to her assistant, but Trudi didn't know why. All Eulalie said was, "That sounds great."

They stood and headed toward the door, but before they could leave the office, Trudi stopped and came back to the desk. She picked up *The Complete Tales and Poems of Edgar Allan Poe* and waved the collectible hardcover toward Eulalie. "While we're there," she said, "we're going to figure out how to read minds."

Sitting in the corner booth at the Taco Bell across the street from Coffey & Hill Investigations, the remains of their delicious lunches littering the table, Trudi almost hated to bring out the Poe book. She'd set it on the bench seat while they ate, but now she was ready to work on the magic trick.

What if I get taco sauce or some other kind of fast-food smear on my fancy collectible book? Maybe we should just go back to the office?

Before she could make that suggestion, though, Eulalie sprang into action. "Let me clear out this mess," she said, sweeping the wrappers and napkins into a pile, "and then we can work in a clean, well-lighted place."

Trudi appreciated both the cleanliness of her assistant and the offhand reference to Ernest Hemingway. *Not bad for a psychology major*, she thought. While Eula was dumping trash into the receptacle, Trudi took another napkin and wiped down the table until she felt comfortable laying the book on it. She opened it to page 108 and looked again at line number nine.

Been.

That was infuriating. She flipped the book shut and waited for Eulalie to return. When her assistant sat down, she spoke. "All right," she said. "We know he didn't really read our minds."

"Right."

"And we know he couldn't have tampered with my book."

"Uh-huh."

"But he did pick up my book and thumb through it."

"Yeah, but could he have memorized the whole thing that fast? Maybe he has an eidetic memory or something? And how could he have known which page you'd pick for the word?"

A lightbulb flashed inside Trudi's head.

"He forced the card on me."

"What? I didn't know he used cards for this trick."

"No, it's just a saying. I mean, when a magician does a card trick, he often knows ahead of time which card the mark will choose because he forces that person to choose the card he wants. The Raven must have done something like that with my book."

"He forced you to pick *The Complete Tales and Poems of Edgar Allan Poe*?"

"No, but the book was already on my desk. Maybe he just took advantage of what was available to him at the moment?"

"Seems a stretch. How could he know which word you'd pick out of the entire book? Or where that word would be? Or even what the words would be in a book he'd never seen before he walked into your office?"

"Mm-hmm, mm-hmm," Trudi said. Her mind was clicking

now. "Let's try this. Let's try the trick again and see if I can read your mind."

"Seriously? That guy is a professional magician. You think you can do his trick after just a few hours?"

"I think I've figured it out, yes. Want to try it?"

"Let's go for it, boss."

Trudi handed Eulalie a napkin and a pen from her purse. "Okay, first you have to pick a triad—that is, a three-digit number. Write it on the napkin."

Eulalie wrote "111" on the napkin.

"Hmm," Trudi said. She ran the next steps in her head. *Reverse the digits, subtract the lower number from the larger number . . . but 111 minus 111 equals zero. That can't be right.*

"What's next?" Eulalie said.

"Something's messed up. I've missed something."

"Did I pick the wrong number?"

Yes! That's it!

"Oh, that guy was sneaky," Trudi said. "He manipulated me like nobody's business."

"What do you mean?"

"He said I could pick any three-digit number, but then he challenged me a bit." She mimicked his voice, adding an annoying nasal sound to the performance. "'If you want to make it hard on me, use a number where the first and last numbers are at least two digits apart.'"

"That was important?"

"Yep. Of course I wanted to make it hard on him. What I didn't know was that he was needling me into making it easy for him."

"Okay, so what's next?"

"Let's start over. Eula, pick a new triad, any three-digit number, but if you want to make it hard on me, use a number where the first and last numbers are at least two digits apart. Write it on the napkin."

This time Eulalie wrote "357."

"Good," said Trudi. "Now, if I'm right about this, it's all in the math. Ready?"

"Okay, I'm ready."

"First we reverse the digits of your triad, so now you've got 753. Then we subtract the smaller from the larger."

"753 minus 357," Eulalie said. "I've never been great at math. Is that 386?"

"396," Trudi said. "Good. Now we reverse those digits and add the last two triads together."

"So, 396 plus 693? What is that? A thousand something?"

Trudi did the math in her head. She felt triumphant. She reached over and took the pen from Eulalie and wrote the number on the napkin.

1089.

"That number is important?" Eulalie said.

"It's the same number I got, even though I started with a different triad."

"Ahh," Eulalie's face lit up with understanding. "So it really is all in the math. Pretty clever."

Trudi pushed the napkin away and leaned back in her seat. "So no matter what you start with, you always end up with the same number: 1089. That's the 'card' he forces on you. 1089. Then he uses that to make you choose page 108, line nine."

"So," Eula said, "when he was just"—she made air quotes in front of her—"randomly flipping through your book, he was actually checking out page 108, line nine. He knew he could make you choose the word in that spot, so he memorized that one word and waited for you to fall for the bait."

"Hook, line, and sinker." Trudi felt the corners of her lips beginning to tug upward. She liked that she'd figured out the mind-reading exercise, and she found herself liking that The Raven had been able to trick her with it.

He is pretty clever.

"Gotta like a guy who can use something as simple as math to trick two college-educated girls like us," Eulalie said.

"Yeah, I guess," Trudi said. She tried to appear casual about the whole thing.

But she couldn't stop grinning.

18

RAVEN

Atlanta, GA
Old Fourth Ward
Friday, March 24, 12:05 p.m.
21 days to Nevermore

Nobody says anything for a few minutes while Scholarship digs around the drawers of my kitchen, looking for a spoon. When he finally finds one, he dips it into the strawberry yogurt and then lets his eyes return to me.

I'm trying to swallow, but for some reason my throat is too dry. I want to say something, but it just comes out as a slight "uuuh."

Did he say I owe Max Roman ten thousand dollars? How is that possible?

Pavlo reaches into his coat pocket for something, but Scholarship stops him. "Don't be in such a hurry, Pav. Maybe this magician kid will just pay the ten thousand dollars and we can all go home happy."

"Huh," Pavlo snorts. "No matter how hard you try, the bull will never give you milk."

Scholarship tips his head to the side. "Is that some Ukrainian proverb or something? Is it supposed to be some kind of wisdom? Because it's kind of stupid. Why would you even want to milk a bull?"

"I think," my voice croaks, "it's symbolic. Like, I'm the bull, and asking me for ten thousand dollars is like asking a bull to give you milk."

"Mm. That what you meant, Pav?" The dumpy one shrugs, and Scholarship shakes his head. "Anyway, ten thousand dollars isn't that much money. Not like Max is asking for a million or something. So what do you say, kid? Do you want to give us ten thousand dollars so we can just call this thing done?"

I feel like making a wisecrack, saying something about the dismal state of education and declining math abilities in American children, but my mind is blank. All I can think to say is, "I don't have ten thousand dollars."

Pavlo turns his back and walks into the living room.

"Yeah," Scholarship says, "that's what I thought. Oh well, we tried, right, kid?"

"Look," I say, "There's $238 in my wallet, in my back pocket. Take it all." I start to pull my hands out of the ice so I can get to my wallet, but the look on Scholarship's face tells me that's a bad idea.

"Trouble is," he says, "that still leaves us $9,762 short of what you owe."

Okay, so Scholarship is pretty quick with math. Good for him.

"I don't have ten thousand dollars," I say again. I don't know what else to say. I think I must be hyperventilating because I'm starting to feel a little lightheaded.

"I see," the football player says. "Well, that's not good.

Because Mr. Roman always insists that his debts are paid in a timely way."

"How do I owe Max Roman ten thousand dollars?" I say. My voice sounds a little shrieky even to me. "I mean, I gave back the pictures."

"You cost him time, and you embarrassed his, um, personal assistants. Plus, he can't let word get around that a petty thief off the street such as yourself, no offense intended, got the better of him."

"None taken," I say automatically, though I've never really understood how saying "no offense intended" makes it okay to insult somebody to their face. But that's a philosophical problem for another day.

"I didn't get away with anything. My stupid plan to blackmail Mr. Roman backfired. All I got out of it was blood and bruises. He won. I lost. End of story, right?"

"Not as far as Max Roman is concerned."

Scholarship looks at me placidly, and I suddenly realize how much I've underestimated this guy. I let his athletic frame and jock-star demeanor trick me into thinking he's something other than what he really is. Mr. Scholarship is a businessman. Everything for him can be totted up in accounting columns, profit and loss, expenses and revenue, bottom line. The stereotypes don't apply, and I'm a little ashamed that I thought they did.

You see a large black man in Atlanta, you automatically think sports figure, I scold myself. *What if he's just a black man in Atlanta—one of many who are more than their skin color and physique can define?*

"You really did go to college on scholarship, didn't you?" I say. He grins, like he's proud to see that I'm finally starting to get it. "Yep. Full-ride, four years."

"Football?"

He snorts.

"Wrestling?"

Now he rolls his eyes. "I did play football as a walk-on in college. Tight end. But that was just for fun. I went to school on an academic scholarship. Made a 33 on the ACT. That score, plus my 4.0 in high school, was all I needed for Georgia Southern University. Earned a bachelor's degree in Economics, with emphasis in International Business. Thought I was going to get an MBA, but Mr. Roman made me an offer I couldn't refuse. Now here I am."

He spreads out his arms and smiles. I feel like he expects me to applaud or something, but I don't think my frozen hands will cooperate.

"So this is all just business to you?"

"Always has been."

"And from a business perspective, Max Roman thinks my failure to blackmail him means I owe him ten thousand dollars?"

Pavlo reenters the kitchen. "No," the Ukrainian says, walking to the counter. "He thinks you owe him twenty thousand. But this guy"—he jerks a thumb in the direction of Scholarship—"he talks Maksym into letting you off with half."

"I like you, kid." Scholarship shrugs. "I think you've got talent. I see potential."

"Thanks?" I say, but all I can think is, *How am I supposed to get ten thousand dollars?*

"Everything is ready in there," Pavlo says to his partner.

I definitely don't like the sound of that.

The Ukrainian reaches into his jacket pocket and produces a zippered leather wallet that reminds me of a shaving kit my dad used to pack when he went on trips. He sets the wallet on the counter beside me, then he looks hard at me, studying me clinically, like an optometrist during a vision exam. "Did you eat breakfast today?" he says out of nowhere.

"An empty stomach can speed things up," Scholarship says.

"No," I say. "All I've had today is Mountain Dew."

Scholarship curses under his breath. "You got to take care of your body, kid. That's a finely tuned machine you've got there. Treat it right, and it'll treat you right."

"I can't feel my arms," I say. It seems appropriate.

"What did he say?" Pavlo asks.

"Something about his arms," Scholarship answers.

My head hurts, and I'm starting to feel like my brain is churning through mud.

"Better move things along," Pavlo says.

"Look"—Scholarship nods—"you owe Mr. Roman ten thousand dollars. You say you can't pay it. So that means we have to take it in trade. Understand?"

I feel a wave of relief, almost like euphoria. "Sure," I say. "Anything you want. Take everything in the apartment if you want to. I'll even help you cart it down to your car, once I can feel my hands again."

"No, you don't understand," Scholarship says. "We're going to take it in *trade*."

He emphasizes the last word like it's something different than what I think it is. He nods to Pavlo, and the dumpy one unzips the leather wallet. Inside is a neat little row of sharp tools of varying sizes.

"Are those scalpels?" I ask, but even I hear the slurring in my speech now. It sounds kind of like, *Arethozse zcalbles?*

"You know," Scholarship says, "you look at Pavlo and it's sometimes easy to underestimate him. It's the language barrier, mostly. He's been in the States less than a year, and really he's still learning English, and it's not an easy language. Especially here in Georgia where people say southern things like they're fixin' to do something or the way we mash you all into y'all, things like that."

I'm feeling a little dizzy now, but I think it's going to be pretty important for me to hear what this guy is saying. *I hope I don't throw up all over the ice cubes.* Then again, there's nothing in my stomach, so what am I going to spew anyway?

"But back in Ukraine, Pavlo actually went to school."

"Medical school," the Ukrainian interrupts.

"Right, medical school. Pav here was going to be a doctor."

"Top five percent of my class when I left."

"Two more years and he would've finished medical school. Become a doctor. Lived happily ever after in the Ukraine with a fat wife and seven chubby kids, right, Pavlo?"

"You know it, man."

"So why did he come here?"

"Family," Pavlo says simply. "To see family, no road is too long."

"Now that's a Ukrainian proverb I can get behind," Scholarship says. "Viktor—you remember Viktor, right? Viktor calls his cousin, says he's needed here in Atlanta. And Pavlo puts family first. Leaves school, comes to America, and starts living out his own version of the American dream. Kind of sweet, actually."

"Like sugar cookies and hummingbirds," I mumble.

"Anyway, his instructors said Pavlo showed natural talent in surgical testing. Steady hands, ability to concentrate for extended periods of time. He was actually one of the better students over there, which can be surprising when you watch him work over here. But, again, the language thing is a big deal. He speaks it well enough, I guess, but he still can't read much in English. And the tools we use here are somewhat different than what they use over there." Scholarship shrugs. "Plus, he never did actually finish school."

"What are you telling me?" I say. My head feels heavy, like a thundercloud has bloomed in there, soaking my thoughts in rain. *Am I drunk from chamomile tea? How is that possible?*

"Mr. Roman wants payment. Ten thousand dollars. He said if you don't have the money, he'll take it in trade. He'll credit you one thousand dollars for a finger. At that rate, ten thousand dollars requires ten fingers, and then your debt is paid. That's what I'm telling you."

I lurch away from the kitchen sink and feel my arms flailing until Scholarship wraps his tree-trunk biceps around me in a bear hug, pinning my arms to my sides.

"No, no, no." I can't say anything else. *No, no, no.*

They're going to cut off my fingers. They're going to leave me helpless and savaged and broken. What's a deception specialist with no fingers? How will I work? How will I live?

How will I eat?

"No, please, no."

I hear myself sobbing.

"You won't remember a thing, kid," Scholarship says kindly, still holding me in his impenetrable grasp. "I put Rohypnol in your tea. That's why you feel like passing out right now. Roofies will make it easier for you. And the ice bath will help to limit the bleeding. You won't feel a thing. Pavlo is an artist, I promise."

"No, please. I'llgetthe money. I cangetthe money. WhatcanI do toget the money?"

My legs are limp beneath me. The football player is holding me up now, bearing my entire weight, making it seem like it's no big deal to carry a full-grown man in your arms. Pavlo looks up from his collection of pretty knives and makes eye contact with my captor. Slowly the Ukrainian closes the leather cover.

"Well, now," Scholarship is saying, "Mr. Roman often hires men of unique talent to assist in his business dealings. Free-lancers, mostly. As luck would have it, I heard of a freelance job opening up recently, and you are definitely a young man of unique talent. I think you could do the job. How much did they say it pays, Pav?"

"Ten thousand dollars."

"Well, that's perfect, isn't it?"

"Yes, I'll do it. Whatever it is, I'll do it."

"I see."

Scholarship carries me into the living room. My couch has been cleaned off, and a pillow from my bed is situated at the far end. The coffee table is shiny, like it's been wiped down with alcohol or some other disinfectant. All the garbage and detritus of my sloppy living style has been shoved into a corner, just to the side of the balcony door. The football player leans over the couch and lets me fall. I can't seem to move my head, let alone the rest of my body. He lifts my legs onto the couch and arranges me so I'm not hanging off the edge.

"All right, kid, the job is yours. But you've only got one week to finish it. We'll be back a week from today. Five o'clock sound okay?"

"Whastha job?" I say through a stiffening tongue.

"I'll leave details for you in the kitchen. Right now, you just get some rest. You'll feel better when you wake up."

"Okayokayokay." *Okay. Okay. Okay.* I think I might have just wet myself.

"One more thing, though. We can't leave today without a down payment on your debt. Mr. Roman would never allow that."

"Whatdoyou mean?"

"One thousand dollars for a down payment. That's all. Just ten percent to show Mr. Roman that you're serious about paying off your debt in the next seven days. You have that somewhere in the apartment?"

"No. AllIhave is $238. Inmywallet."

"Don't worry about it," he says. He pats my cheek affectionately, like we're family and he's taking care of me while I'm sick.

The room spins so suddenly I have to close my eyes. I see
blackening stars creeping in from the edges of my vision. And
then there's my dad, looking at me over the top of his reading
glasses. *Why are you so sad, Daddy?* And my mom. She won't
speak to me. She doesn't speak to me at all. She just stares past
me, looking at nothing, seeing everything.

From a faraway distance, I hear Scholarship's voice, reassuring me. Comforting me.

"You won't remember a thing."

19

TRUDI

Atlanta, GA
Buckhead Neighborhood
Friday, March 24, 7:22 p.m.
21 days to Nevermore

Eclipse di Luna was busy on this Friday night.

The sweet smell of *pollo a la plancha* and *calamares fritos* hung like perfume in the air, intoxicating people in the restaurant lobby with a strange kind of hungry desire. Trudi breathed in the aroma of freshly grilled Spanish tapas and couldn't help licking her lips.

The Raven has good taste in food. She had to give him that.

Trudi searched the little crowd packing the lobby but saw no sign of the magician. She hoped he'd had enough foresight to get a reservation for tonight. She scanned the tables in her view, but again, no Raven.

"Just one tonight, or will you be meeting someone?"

The blonde hostess was blandly sweet and welcoming. Trudi

glanced around her and saw that just about everyone else waiting here was in an even-numbered group—two college kids on a date over there, a middle-aged double date next to them, even what looked like an after-work party that divided easily into four men and four women. *So this is one of Atlanta's most popular places to take a date*, Trudi thought.

"Meeting someone," she said. "I think he might have made a reservation." She hesitated. What name would Marv use when booking a table at a restaurant? The girl looked both expectant and bored, waiting. This clearly wasn't her first night on duty at the front of Eclipse di Luna. "The Raven," Trudi said at last. "Or The Amazing Raven?"

The hostess ran a polished fingernail down a clipboard, stopped partway, looked up at Trudi, and gave a plastic smile. "Of course," she said. "Table for two. Would you like to be seated now or wait until Mr. Raven arrives?"

Trudi felt the crush of bodies tightening around her. "Now would be fine. Thank you."

It was a nice little table, situated just far enough from the performance stage to make talking manageable, but still close enough to allow lulls in conversation to be covered by "Isn't this band great?" type of comments. Trudi was also pleased to discover that the perspective from her side of the table gave a clear view of the crowded lobby entrance. When The Raven showed up, she'd see him fairly easily.

A waitress in stylish Spanish attire flitted by with a tall glass of ice water, said her name was Arianna, offered a drink menu, and then disappeared. Trudi checked her watch. It wasn't quite seven-thirty yet, but she hated being late to anything. *Always better to be an hour early than a minute late*, she said to herself for probably the ten thousandth time. But she still expected The Raven to be late anyway. He just seemed like that kind of guy, like someone who was never too worried about the rigors of punctuality.

At 7:35, the waitress returned. Would Trudi like to order a drink while she waited? A few moments later, a tall glass of cherry lemonade decorated the table. Trudi sipped and waited.

At 7:45, Trudi tried not to feel annoyed. Her personal rule was that she'd wait fifteen minutes for anyone, and sixteen minutes for no one. But she'd wait a little longer for this guy. *He rides a bicycle everywhere*, she reasoned. *So maybe tonight he had to take the bus, or maybe he missed a MARTA train.* She sipped the cherry lemonade and watched happy couples falling in love all around her. She tried not to roll her eyes.

When 7:50 came, Trudi declined Arianna's invitation to "order a little something for the wait." She checked her cell for text or voice messages, found none, and decided to pass a few minutes deleting outdated emails.

At eight o'clock, Trudi put down her phone. Why had the magician pulled a disappearing act?

She looked down at her dark denim jeans and the cream-colored, crochet, scoop-neck top with red camisole. She clicked the heels of her tan, ankle-length booties under the table and couldn't keep from muttering, "There's no place like home." She could almost feel the comfy pajamas and warm couch waiting for her.

All men are pigs, she told herself cheerfully, and even though she didn't really believe it, just thinking it made her feel a little better. She checked her watch. *8:07.* She'd waited long enough.

She reached for her purse and dropped a five-dollar bill on the table to cover the lemonade. She slid back her wooden chair, but before she could stand, a familiar face caught her eye, looking out through the entryway to the lobby.

Eulalie? Here?

Trudi ducked her head and slid back toward the table.

Eula was a popular girl, and she enjoyed a steady stream of attention from the men in her church and at her night-school classes. And from guys lucky enough to wait in line near her at Trader Joe's. And from guys who happened to be shopping at Macy's when she was out looking through the end-of-season clearance sales. And from men in general.

If I didn't like her so much, I'd hate Eulalie Jefferson, Trudi thought absently. She waited for her assistant to disappear back into the lobby, then tried to plot a clean exit.

She slid back in her wooden chair and grabbed her purse—then froze. Eulalie was in the doorway again. Standing next to her, with his hand resting lightly on her elbow, was Samuel Eric Douglas Hill.

Trudi felt color draining from her face, was vaguely aware that her mind was emptying itself of coherent thought.

Her assistant and her ex-husband were looking away from the direction where she was sitting, a small grace for which she was grateful. Then the blonde hostess stepped in front and led them away to a table on the other side of the restaurant. Nothing was ever certain in a situation like this, but Trudi felt reasonably sure they hadn't seen her. At least not yet.

Coast is clear now, she thought. *So why aren't I gone?*

Arianna breezed by without stopping. It had taken only a few recitations of "No, I'll just wait until my friend gets here" before the waitress had realized it was a waste of time to stop at Trudi's table. She parked instead at the double-date table a few feet past where Trudi sat.

The menu lay open on the table before her, and Trudi let her eyes drop to the Spanish lettering that proudly announced the delectable gastronomies of Eclipse di Luna. She suddenly realized that she was very, very hungry. She waved Arianna over.

"Ready to order?" the waitress asked.

"Yes. I'll have the cumin-crusted Ahi tuna." Arianna started to leave, but Trudi caught her. "And a cup of coffee."

"I'll get that started for you."

So, she thought to herself, *Eulalie is having dinner with Samuel. What am I supposed to do with that?*

When it came to Samuel, things were complicated. He and Trudi had been married for seven years before she'd finally pieced together the evidence of his infidelity. It was worse than she'd imagined. Not only had her husband had an affair while on assignment in the Middle East somewhere, that adultery had led to the birth of a child.

Samuel refused to tell her whether it was a boy or a girl, or even where the child lived. He would only say that, in that culture, the mother would be imprisoned, and likely executed, for her sin—unless she were married. So, even though he was already married to Trudi back home, Samuel had wed his Arabic lover, as well. He said it was just a formality, a way of protecting her from his mistake. But Trudi had never gotten over the fact that her husband had another wife, another family, somewhere in the great wide world.

"Eulalie knows this about Samuel," she muttered to herself. "So why is she out with him?"

Samuel was handsome, she knew. And charming. Why should she be surprised that her assistant would be attracted to a man like him? And of course Samuel would be drawn to Eulalie—she was just his type. Young and pretty. Trudi was surprised to feel pressure welling up behind her eyes. She clenched her fists in her lap and blinked her lashes several times.

I will not cry over you anymore, Samuel Hill. I will not. I w—

A cloth appeared in front of her. Arianna, delivering a cup of coffee and a makeshift handkerchief. She leaned over and patted Trudi on the shoulder. "He's not worth it, honey," she said kindly. "No man is."

Trudi sniffed and laughed at the same time, taking the cloth napkin and dabbing it on her face. "Yeah, I know. Thanks."

Arianna smiled. "Dinner is on the house tonight. Enjoy."

Now Trudi really felt like crying as she watched the thoughtful waitress walk away, but she also knew Arianna was right.

Okay, she told herself, *time to be a grown-up. Samuel is free to do whatever he wants in his romantic pursuits. Our divorce finalized that. And it's really none of my business who my assistant spends her time with outside the office. Probably even against some kind of human resources law for me to meddle in that part of her life. So grow up. It's their business. Deal with it.*

The little pep talk didn't really make her feel better, but at least it stopped her from feeling worse.

"This really is a nice restaurant," she said to herself softly. "I'm just going to try and enjoy it." She tilted her chair toward the stage and let the live Latin salsa band capture her attention. They were energetic and joyful and fun to watch. If Trudi hadn't been thinking about Samuel, she might have felt like dancing.

She frowned.

Something didn't fit here. The Raven had seemed so sincere this morning. Although Trudi wasn't a human lie detector, she did have a pretty good idea of when someone was being less than truthful with her. She'd watched The Raven fairly closely in her office. He'd given none of the signs of a liar when he was asking her out.

He is a performer, she thought. *Maybe that date invitation was just a performance?*

But why? What would he gain by getting her to come to Buckhead tonight? It didn't make sense.

Arianna delivered a beautifully plated Ahi steak that tasted even better than it looked. Trudi took a bite, then another, and let her mind begin to work through possibilities.

One thing was for sure, she decided, it was time to get those Perrier-bottle fingerprints run through the system. Of course, she'd have to call Samuel about that, but why not? He didn't know she'd seen him tonight, and she certainly wasn't going to tell him. She wasn't going to say anything to Eulalie, either. It would just be business-as-usual on Monday morning, and that would include asking Samuel to check the databases to see if they could find out who The Raven really was—and find out if it mattered.

Lost in thought and delicious tuna, Trudi didn't notice that a man had stopped beside her table. When he cleared his throat, she saw two hands holding two glasses of red wine. Then she saw dark hair, pale skin, and a medium build, taut and wiry. From her seated perspective, she could also make out the butt of a gun peeking out from a shoulder holster inside his suit coat.

Then she registered the face.

The Ukrainian's gray eyes were flat, but attentive. He was attempting a small smile.

"I couldn't help noticing you're eating alone tonight," he said, extending a glass as a peace offering. "Would you mind if I joined you?"

20

RAVEN

Atlanta, GA
Old Fourth Ward
Friday, March 24, 9:03 p.m.
21 days to Nevermore

I wake up thinking of Natalie.

Had I been dreaming of her? I can't remember, but I do feel the rush of air that comes from just picturing her in my mind. I don't want to open my eyes, not yet. I don't even want to breathe in, to risk losing her face because of the jostling that comes with inhaling. I just want to remember, to see her again, to experience the warmth, the safety I used to feel when she was near me.

We'd decided to meet on a Friday in October, at the Penn Square Mall food court in Oklahoma City. It was going to be just a quick lunch. She had to get to a one o'clock class on campus at Oklahoma City University, and I'd promised to take my mom to a doctor's appointment soon after.

She came up the escalator wearing a yellow sundress that showed off bronze shoulders and accented her thick, red hair that danced like fire above it all. Drove me crazy, she was so pretty, with eyes like emeralds and a smile that made men stand in line just to see it. I wanted to stop and stare every time I saw her.

"You brought your mother to our date?" she said when we met.

Mom was already seated at a table behind us, waiting for us to join her. I shrugged at Natalie and grinned.

"She wanted to meet you. Said that after six weeks, she'd had enough with cell phone pictures. Wanted to see the real thing."

Natalie nodded, frowned, then smiled, then nodded again.

She took my hand and led me over to the table to meet my mother, finally, for the first time. We had gyros for lunch, the three of us, and those two hit it off right away. Mom peppered her with questions about her voice studies at OCU and was appropriately impressed with Natalie's musical knowledge and performance accomplishments at such a young age. For her part, Natalie was the perfect daughter-in-law-in-waiting. She complimented my boyfriend skills, thanking my mother for "raising him right." She laughed at Mom's silly jokes and made her tell stories of me growing up.

It felt good. My two best girls, getting along like best friends. I think, for a few minutes, I was truly happy. And, for a few moments, I could see that kind of happy becoming a lifetime habit.

Then, too soon, it was time to go. I stood to walk Natalie back to the escalator and loved the feeling of my arm encircling her waist as we walked.

"Can I see you tomorrow?" I said. Her eyes were distant, like she was already thinking about how much homework she had to complete over the weekend.

"Yes," she said at last.

"Dinner?" I said. "I'm off tomorrow night. How about I take you to dinner and a movie? Do you have enough time, or is Dr. Van Eck demanding more ensemble practice to get ready for competition?"

"No," she said, but I wasn't sure which question she was answering. "Let's get breakfast. Meet me at Alvin's Café on campus? Seven-thirty-ish?"

"Sure, I'll be there."

She stopped before we reached the escalator and gave me a kiss, a nice kiss. Soft and deliberate. One that tasted faintly of sweet-tea lip gloss, and that lingered just a second or two longer than usual. When I opened my eyes, she was looking at me, searching my face. Then she pulled away.

"See you tomorrow," she said.

She closed the gap to the escalator, and something inside me began to crumble. I felt my heart start to pound and my breath turn choppy.

"Natalie, wait," I said. She was at the top of the escalator, ready to step on the first revolving stair.

I saw it in her eyes then and felt like a fool. Her eyes had been saying it all along, all during lunch, every time they strayed from my mother and sneaked another look at me. She'd been too kind to let her mouth say the words her eyes had formed, not in front of my mother. She was too classy for that.

"Natalie . . ."

I wanted to step to her, to wrap her in my arms, to hold her long enough to let her know all the reasons why we were together. To make her smile again, that natural, effortless smile she had when I first delivered pizza to her dorm room, the one she used to treat me to regularly when we first started hanging out after that.

She waited.

My feet were frozen, iced to the floor. A lame instrumental version of "It's Not Over" played on the mall speakers overhead. I hated that song. It was the soundtrack for my life at that moment, so I hated it even more.

"Natalie," I said slowly, "that . . . felt like goodbye."

She didn't say anything at first, just let her eyes drop to the floor. Her toes, with nails painted a cheerful sunshine color that matched her dress, were clenched inside her sandals. Then she said, "You always could read my mind." She sighed, eyes still glued to the floor. "Yes. Goodbye."

"Natalie."

"I was going to tell you at breakfast tomorrow. I'm sorry." She looked at me, searching.

There was a thick silence between us, filled only with a hateful saxophone chorus trying to imitate Chris Daughtry's rock vocals.

"Ah, don't go, Nat. Whatever it is, we can fix it. I can fix it."

"No."

That was all she said, just "no." She tried to smile, but I could see it hurt her, and she didn't let it last long. In my mind I ran through all the reasons why she might leave me, why she could leave me. In my mind, there were too many reasons. A sharp pain lanced through my head, just behind my eyes.

She turned and stepped onto the escalator. I watched her descend, hoping she might look back at me, knowing that if she did I'd go running after her. I'd beg her to stay, I'd become a better person, a better man. I'd make sure she never regretted that one last look back. But she never turned. And then she was gone.

I don't remember walking back to the food court, but I do remember my mother smiling at me and saying, "That Natalie is a delightful young woman! You hang on to her because I want to see her again, okay?"

"Come on, Mom," I said. "Let's get you to your doctor's appointment."

Lying on my couch in Little Five Points, I feel that sharp pain lancing through my head again and piercing into my beating heart. *I must have dreamed of Natalie, and of Mom,* I think. *I like to punish myself, I guess.*

I force my eyes open and stare for a moment at the dirty ceiling of my stale apartment. I know it must be late. The shadows and darkness that surround me are testament to that. I know I've lost more than just time. I was supposed to meet Trudi at seven-thirty. It was going to be the beginning of happily-ever-after, a second chance at the life I missed when I let Natalie walk away from me four and a half years ago.

I'm sorry, Trudi. In my mind, I think of all the reasons Trudi is better off without me, why it's a good thing I left her waiting alone at Eclipse di Luna restaurant.

Mom was in a good mood during the drive to her doctor's office, despite the fact that she had to ride in my beat-up 2000 Ford Mustang. Chatty. Happy. Making plans for the future.

"Why don't you come by on Sunday for lunch? I'll make beef stroganoff, just like you like it."

"Sure, Mom. Sounds good."

"If you want to come by early, you could go with me to hear your dad preach. He's on a series about Jesus's parables. Really interesting. You might like it."

I remember that the mention of my father's sermon made me feel annoyed. Hadn't I heard enough of his lectures already? Pretty much every day of my life until I graduated from high school was a sermon from my dad telling me how to do better at this, how to make up for that, how to find what he'd found in God. He wasn't happy when I told him I didn't really believe in his God anymore, at least not the way he did. He didn't get angry, though, I'll give him that much. He just seemed disappointed. And he kept preaching at me until I moved out and took a job delivering pizzas for Domino's to pay my part of the rent on a tiny apartment shared with four other guys.

"Yeah, I'll think about it," I said to my mother, figuring it'd just be easier to give her false hope than to explain I never intended to go back to my pop's old church and hear him preach another sermon at me again. I was sure I'd hear a recap of the message over beef stroganoff anyway. But it was a small price to pay for free food and Mom's cooking again, wasn't it?

"Bring Natalie!" she said suddenly. "I'll make a special dessert for her. Does she like cherry cobbler?"

"Yeah, Mom. I'm sure she'll eat whatever," I said. But inside I knew better.

Natalie was never coming back. She'd never have a nice dinner at my Mom's house, never hear my dad explain some obscure theological point, never make fun of the fact that I still kept a few hundred worthless comic books stored in my parents' basement.

We rode in silence for a minute or two, Mom chirping along to a song on the radio. When we arrived at the doctor's office, I pulled up to the door to drop her off. She looked surprised.

"You're not coming in to wait?" she said. "It's just a checkup. I'll only be thirty or forty minutes."

"No, you go ahead," I said. "I have to run a quick errand. I'll be right back."

She looked dubious. "You'll be right back?"

"Sure. Promise."

She leaned over and kissed my cheek. "Okay, baby. I'll see you in half an hour." She opened her door and started to get out.

"Oh, hey, Mom." I tried to sound casual and spontaneous. "I just remembered I have to work Sunday afternoon. Rodney asked me to work extra because they're getting a lot of football orders on Sundays and they're having trouble keeping up."

I saw disappointment fall like rain in her eyes. She pursed her lips.

"Sorry," I said. "But maybe Nat and I can come by another day."

"Okay, baby." She sighed. I could tell she didn't believe me any more than I did, but she didn't want to argue about it. She patted my hand on the gearshift. "You and your father, you'll work this out. You know that, right?"

"Sure, Mom."

"He still loves you very much. He tells you that every time he sees you."

"Sure." *He tells me that because he has to, not because he means it.* "Sure, I know. We're fine. I just have to work on Sunday. That's all."

She nodded and climbed out of my beat-up old Ford Mustang. "I'll see you in half an hour," she said before closing the door. "Please don't be late."

I nodded and waved, but in my head all I could think was *I need a drink.*

Throbbing spreads through me, pulling me away from my memories. It arcs across my chest, down through my arm, with such intensity I find it hard to breathe for a second.

My left arm.

Isn't this what a heart attack feels like? But no, my heart is pumping fine.

Still, my hand, my left hand is on fire. At least that's what it feels like. I hear a groan and know it's me. A siren drones in the distance outside, faint and faraway. My stomach clenches, reminding me of the jolting hollowness that burns inside me. And in spite of my best efforts, I remember why I'm lying here on my couch, why I don't want to wake up, even when my dreams are unpleasant.

I know what my nightmare really was.

I wasn't dreaming of Natalie, or even my mom. I was just wishing. Longing for the power to go back in time, to change one moment in my life and, in doing that, change everything.

Everything.

I should have run after you, Natalie, I tell myself. *I should never have let you walk away from me without a fight.*

A thick wad of gauze is wrapped and taped over the empty spot where my little finger used to be. It's stained a deep, dirty red. Just looking at the blood-soaked rag makes my entire arm tingle with shock.

I sit up on the couch, feel dry heaves shudder through my torso but, thankfully, nothing spews out of my mouth.

There's a note scribbled on a yellow pad, left for me on the coffee table.

> *Change the bandage and clean the wound every four hours for the first day. After that, change and clean as needed. Take Tylenol for pain. We'll be back in a week to collect your next payment.*
>
> *Sincerely,*
> *—S*

21

TRUDI

Atlanta, GA
Buckhead Neighborhood
Friday, March 24, 9:06 p.m.
21 days to Nevermore

"Would you mind if I joined you?"

Trudi didn't say anything at first, and the Ukrainian took that as an invitation. He set one glass of wine in front of her and then slid comfortably into the open seat across the table, balancing the second glass between three fingers.

"We've never been properly introduced," he continued. "I am Viktor, Viktor Kostiuk."

She pushed the wineglass away from her, sliding it across the table until it stopped in front of him. "Trudi Coffey," she said.

He eyed the rejected glass of wine, then shrugged. He set his glass next to hers and left them both untouched.

"I know who you are. Trudi Coffey, private investigator," he said. "Owner of Coffey & Hill Investigations. You're not on the internet, but your office is over in West Midtown, on Howell Mill Road. By that Arby's, right?"

Trudi heard an echo of a Ukrainian prostitute's voice in Viktor Kostiuk's words. It gave her a sour feeling in her stomach, but she tried not to let it show on her face.

"But I have to admit," he continued, "you caught me by surprise when we last met."

"Yeah, I was a little surprised to walk in on a crime scene too, so I guess we're even."

"Oh no," he said, and his left eye twitched involuntarily, "you misunderstand. We were just doing the boy a favor. No real crime going on."

Trudi snorted. "A favor? Like what, removing his spleen for half-price surgery?"

Viktor smiled, and Trudi felt like he was genuinely amused by her accusation.

"The boy, The Raven, he is a little thief. You knew this already. But he's a good boy. Talented. Much potential. We caught him in a petty theft. We thought that instead of turning him over to the police, we'd give him a little homespun lesson in ethics. Maybe we could keep him from going down a bad road, you know?"

"So the beating you gave him was just tough love, is that it?"

"See, you do understand." His smile grew wider. "A little preventative medicine. He who licks knives will soon cut his tongue, as they say."

Who says that? Trudi wondered.

"So we were just trying to help the boy see the dangers of licking knives." He shrugged. "Maybe my cousin got a little overexcited in giving the lesson, but I don't think The Raven will be pickpocketing tourists again anytime soon. It was all meant for good."

"I think we're going to have to agree to disagree on this one," she said. Then Trudi had a suspicious thought. "Where's The Raven tonight?" she asked.

Viktor shrugged again. "I haven't seen him since last week, when you and I met."

She studied him, looking for signs of falsehood, but he was relaxed and his face was open. He seemed to be telling the truth.

Arianna breezed into their orbit. "Well, hello again," she said to Viktor. "Would you like me to move your dinner to this table?"

"No," Trudi said. "He's leaving soon."

The waitress took the cue. "Of course," she said. "I'll just leave your check at your other table."

"I'll pick up this check too," Viktor said, motioning to Trudi's plate and barely looking at Arianna.

The waitress glanced at Trudi, who gave her a short nod. "Okay, then. I'll leave both at your table over there. Thank you for coming to Eclipse di Luna."

Trudi watched Arianna walk away and wondered if she should be worried about her safety with Viktor here at her table. *No*, she decided after a moment. *For starters, this place is packed with people. There's nothing he can do that won't get noticed. And second, I think I can take him. Or at least take that gun away from him, and that would be enough. For now.*

"Well, Viktor, it's been lovely meeting you, but I think I'd like to get back to my dinner. I might even order dessert now that I know it's free."

"Be my guest," he said. "There's plenty more where that came from too."

That was unexpected. "What do you mean?"

"Well, you see, Ms. Coffey, I'd like to offer you a job."

Trudi was at a loss. *The Ukrainian Mafia is hiring private detectives now?*

"I've done a little homework on you since our last meeting," he said. "You're very good at what you do. Your past clients recommend you highly. You have a good relationship with the Atlanta police department—"

"How would you know that?"

"My employer is a patron of local law enforcement. He made a few calls about you. Stellar reports all around."

"I see."

"And you have proven to me in person that you can handle yourself in stressful situations. I'm an admirer of your work. I'm hiring, and I think you'd be perfect for the job."

"Maybe you should tell me what you do and who you work for."

"I'm a political consultant. I was active in New York for a few years until I came to Georgia about five years ago. Right now, I'm in the employ of Councilman Max Roman. The future mayor of Atlanta."

Trudi took a moment to let that name sink in. She'd heard of Max Roman, of course. He was a high-profile city councilman, and he was running for mayor. Came out of a family of real estate developers, if she remembered correctly. Multimillionaire philanthropist type. But what did Max Roman's politics have to do with her?

"You realize the risk you've just taken," she said. "I know about your, um, extracurricular activities at The Raven's house last week. I witnessed them myself. And now you've just tied Max Roman to the Ukrainian Mafia in Atlanta. One phone call to the police or, better yet, to the media, and Max's mayoral campaign is torched."

Viktor reached inside his pocket and pulled out a cell phone. He placed it on the table in front of Trudi.

"Make the call," he said. "Call your ex-husband if you want, or the *Atlanta Journal-Constitution*. Or CNN. Whoever you want. We have nothing to fear."

So he knows Samuel is a police detective. And apparently they've bought influence at both the police department and the news bureaus.

"We have nothing to fear," he said again, "because we have nothing to hide. Max Roman is of Ukrainian origin, yes, but he has nothing to do with any Ukrainian Mafia. To suggest that he does smacks a bit of racism, if you don't mind my saying it. His family has been in the United States for more than a century, and his record fighting against crime in Atlanta speaks for itself."

"I think The Raven would feel differently about that."

"Max Roman had nothing to do with that little lesson I was giving to The Raven last week," he said, looking up to the ceiling in slight exasperation. "That was entirely my doing. I brought along my cousin and an old friend from college to make it seem convincing. Mr. Roman knew nothing about it—he's never even met my cousin or The Raven. And as I said, we were just trying to help the boy, to keep him off a dangerous path. He was never in any real danger at all."

She pushed the cell back to him. "Mm-hmm. Well, thanks for the offer, but I'm going to have to decline. And because I have nothing to fear either, I'll tell you why. I don't trust you, Mr. Kostiuk. I think you're a liar and a crook, and now I think Max Roman must be one too. So, no thank you and good night."

Viktor retrieved his phone but made no move to leave. "See, this is why you're perfect for the job," he said. His eyes took on a pleading look. "May I at least tell you about the job?"

Trudi hesitated, then shrugged. "It's a free country, I guess."

"Max Roman has nothing to hide, but he's a politician. It's a business of dirty tricks and smear campaigns. Right now, Mr. Roman's political opponents are scouring the earth for anything they might be able to use against him in the campaign. You know, 'Max Roman once yelled at a waitress' or 'Max Roman once got drunk at a party' or anything they can use to drum up rumors about my boss." He nodded in her direction. "Some, like you, have even tried to link him to organized crime. But as I said, he has nothing to hide."

"What's that got to do with me?"

"I'd like to hire your detective agency to investigate Mr. Roman. To do the most thorough background check possible on him."

"And why would you want me to do that? Seems counterintuitive to your goal of making Max Roman the next mayor of Atlanta."

"Right now, other private detectives and political operatives are doing the same thing. They're trying to find anything and everything that a political action committee might drum up to use against my employer. If you investigate Max, you'll be able to alert us to anything they might try. Knowing what your enemy plans is the first step to defeating him in the general election."

"Or her."

"Of course. Or her. But regardless of who ends up being his biggest challenger, we want Mr. Roman to prevail. And we believe a thorough background investigation by a Max Roman skeptic such as yourself will yield benefits both to Mr. Roman's campaign and to the people of Atlanta as a whole."

Trudi pursed her lips. The reasoning made sense when she thought about it. If you're a politician with dirty laundry, it'd probably be best to figure out what your enemy's investigators could find out about you. Then you could either work to hide the potential controversies or preemptively strike and bring them out into the open under your own terms before your enemy could do it. If you could define the public conversation about your shortcomings, you could shape the way they were viewed in the eyes of voters and make those shortcomings irrelevant.

"There are a hundred detective agencies that can do that for you. And probably a few dozen that are already in the business of digging up dirt on politicians."

"True. And I'm going to be honest, we've already hired two. But they're political insiders, and they think like political insiders. You, on the other hand, offer the perspective of an outsider. And, if I'm an accurate judge of character, you are now one who distrusts Max Roman because of his association with me. You'll work harder to find things others might overlook, just because you want me to be some kind of bad guy. You're perfect."

Trudi didn't know what to say. Viktor took that as consent to take the next step. He took a pen from his pocket and wrote a number on a napkin.

"The election is in October, but your work would only last four months, until mid-July. We'd ask to be your exclusive client until then. After that, you'll be free to return to your normal clientele. In return for your services, we'll pay you a base salary plus expenses. This is the base salary we are offering."

He passed the napkin to her, and Trudi tried not to let her eyes go wide. It was three times the annual income of her agency at present.

Mistake, she thought. *He's misjudged me. He thinks he can buy me with a big chunk of money, but he overbid.*

"That's a significant sum of money for only four months' work," she said, testing him.

"Mr. Roman values his employees," he said. "And I believe you are worth every penny."

Test failed, she thought. *He should have countered by asking what I thought the job was worth, then explaining in specifics why he came in at a higher figure. He doesn't really want my services. He wants my silence. Paying me a large chunk of money links me to Max Roman in a way that reeks of corruption. It gives him a means to discredit me as an extortionist if I were to try and go public with my knowledge of their beating of The Raven.*

"No. Thank you. Good night, Mr. Kostiuk."

A look of surprise registered briefly on Viktor's face, then his dark eyes went flat and a quick narrowing of the eyebrows betrayed a flash of anger that was almost animal in nature.

That, Trudi thought, *was a look that could kill.*

Just as quickly as it had appeared, the anger was gone from his face, smoothed over by pretense and a placid calm.

"Well, our loss, then," he said. He retrieved the napkin, crumpled it in his fist, and stuffed it in his coat pocket. He started to rise, then paused. "Max Roman is a good man, Ms. Coffey," he said quietly. "The people of Atlanta deserve to have him as their mayor. They deserve his jobs initiative, his tax reform, his education programs, and his crackdown on crime. He will make your city a better place."

"So you're a believer, then. Good for you. I'm not convinced."

"How about this?" he said. "On April 14, Mr. Roman is going to be the keynote speaker at a combination fundraiser and charity auction sponsored by the Atlanta Society for Literary Arts."

"Let me guess, Max is a patron of the arts."

"The Roman family has supported ASLA for many years, yes, and in return they sometimes assist Mr. Roman's campaign efforts. It's a one-thousand-dollar-a-plate dinner, invitation only. There'll be gourmet food, live entertainment, and a charity auction to raise money for ASLA."

"Sounds divine. So what?"

"I'd like to invite you, and a guest of course, to attend the function. Courtesy of Mr. Roman. No strings attached."

He reached inside his coat pocket and pulled out an envelope. Trudi got a clear look at the handgun holstered inside his jacket. *A reminder of the kind of man I'm dealing with*, she told herself. *Of course, I could just as easily be carrying a gun right now too.* He removed two tickets from the envelope and placed them on the table.

She read the lettering that detailed the time and place of the event. "At the Ritz-Carlton." She nodded. "Fancy."

"Come to the dinner. Listen to Mr. Roman's vision for your town," he said, and Trudi saw his left eye twitch again, almost imperceptibly, like a salesman lost in a passionate pitch. "If you still don't want to get involved in his campaign after that, then I won't bother you again. Is that fair enough?"

"Mr. Kostiuk—"

He put out his palms and stopped her from completing that thought. "At the very least, you and a friend will have a free, elegant meal and maybe walk away with some literary collectible from the auction to boot. I understand someone has donated a first-edition copy of the *New York Evening Mirror* magazine from January 1845."

Wait, why does that sound familiar?

"*New York Evening Mirror*? From 1845?" she asked.

"Ah, I thought that might tempt you." He looked pleased. "As I said before, I learned a lot about you this past week, including the fact that you hold a degree in English literature and mythology."

"And the *New York Evening Mirror*?"

"Yes, Ms. Coffey, they're auctioning off a copy of the first publication of Edgar Allan Poe's famous poem, 'The Raven.' Very rare. You might never get a chance to see this in person again."

"So," she said, her mind now spinning inside her head, "on April 14, less than a month away, at the Ritz-Carlton Atlanta hotel, the original 'Nevermore' artifact is going up for sale. At a political gathering for Max Roman's campaign. That's what you're telling me?" Alarm bells started ringing in Trudi's ears.

Viktor smiled, nodded, and stood. "Come to the dinner," he said. "Maybe Mr. Roman's speech will make you a believer in him too."

Trudi watched the Ukrainian man walk away, then looked again at the tickets he'd left for her. *Nevermore*, she thought. *Could this be it?*

"I need to talk to Samuel," she whispered to no one. "But how do I interrupt his date?"

TWO
WEEKS
AGO . . .

22

BLISS

Atlanta, GA
Little Five Points
Friday, March 31, 12:08 a.m.
14 days to Nevermore

Bliss Monroe heard a mouse scratching against the hardwood floor and cursed the fact that she was such a light sleeper.

She peeked over at the digital clock situated on the desk in her office. It was just a few minutes past midnight, which meant she'd been asleep for barely an hour before the blasted mouse had interrupted her dreamless rest. *Should just sleep at home*, she told herself, but she knew that was just empty talk. Lately, she'd been going to her house only long enough to bathe, get fresh clothes, and catch up on the mail. She'd even stopped stocking the refrigerator with anything besides just the essentials, preferring instead to keep her mini-fridge full here at the Secret Stash. At least that way the milk didn't turn into a slightly jaundiced, curdling monster in its plastic container.

Now that I'm awake, she wondered, *how long am I awake?* She was tempted to go ahead and climb out of bed, roll over to her desk, and pick up where she'd left off in her work. Her body argued against that, though—particularly her legs, which twitched in little spasms that reminded her of itches on steroids. She exhaled and listened for the mouse to make another move in the dark.

It had been a long day, especially for a Thursday. A long two weeks, really, trying to clean up the mess Max Roman had caused with his dramatic appearance the Friday before last. But things were about back to normal now, and even though her Friday was beginning at an unreasonably early time because of that blamed mouse, Bliss took a little satisfaction in that return to normalcy.

It had been around eleven o'clock when she'd finally decided to call it a night, emptying her pockets onto the top of her desk, making a last visit to the bathroom, putting on her comfy old nightgown and twisting the locks on her office door. Out of habit, she'd paused to kiss the picture of Davis before dropping it back on the desk. Then she'd lain down in her nondescript bed in the bland corner of the office and, as far as she could tell, had gone to sleep before sixty seconds had passed. She'd stayed in that darkened, blissfully black slumber until the scratching had interrupted her solace.

It's so hard to find peace nowadays, she grumbled. William used to laugh at her when she said things like that. *"Life is always hard,"* he'd say, *"but the alternative is death, so I'll keep on with this restless little inconvenience for the time being, if it's all right with you."*

She heard the *scritch scritch scritch* of tiny claws scraping on metal and felt like murdering a rodent or two. Once she heard a sound like that, she couldn't not hear it, and it tapped against her eardrums like drops of water falling on her head. She squeezed her eyes tightly shut and tried, unsuccessfully, to ignore it.

I just want a little peace, William. I can't last forever like this. It's been too long already.

Scritch, scritch.

Bliss suddenly opened her eyes.

If that mouse is skittering across my wood floor, she wondered, *then why are his claws scraping against metal?*

Now she was really paying attention. In a few seconds, she was able to locate the origin of the sound. It emanated softly from the door of her office, from the deadbolt lock she'd turned an hour ago, just before drifting off to sleep.

She heard the mechanism shift and listened to the soft tap of the deadbolt being eased into the unlocked position. Next there was temporary scratching at the lock on the door handle. Then silence.

Bliss reached under her pillow and pulled out the Beretta BU9 Nano micro-compact pistol she kept there. The clip held eight nine-millimeter bullets inside the sleek, flat form. She'd never had to use it in here, but she certainly knew how to pull a trigger if she had to. William had made sure of that. She leaned back with her head propped up on the pillow and dropped her right hand down so it rested comfortably by her hips, disguised by the sheet that covered it. She pointed the Nano so the barrel aimed at the doorway. Then she waited.

It was only a minute or two before the knob twisted and someone on the outside gave a gentle shove, causing the door to swing silently inward. Soon there was nothing but empty space between the darkened room and the dimly lit hallway. She saw a figure crouching low but couldn't make out any features other than that it appeared to be a man and he appeared to be kneeling with his head bowed, almost as if in prayer. At his feet was some kind of power tool. A drill maybe? She couldn't tell for sure. It could've been a gun for all she knew. She made sure she was ready, just in case.

For a long moment, neither one of them moved.

Bliss was a little surprised that she wasn't afraid. She wasn't even angry. She was just watching the scene unfold, feeling curious, feeling almost as if it wasn't even happening to her, but instead was happening to someone who looked like her and who felt like her.

The man raised his head but remained close to the ground. Mama Bliss decided it was time.

"What you want, boy?"

The man stood up quickly but didn't say anything. She could see that he hadn't expected to find anyone inside this room when he broke in.

"Let me rephrase the question," Bliss said. "What you want to say that's going to keep me from putting a bullet right through you?"

"Please don't."

His voice was thin, sad. Scared? She couldn't tell for sure, but she thought his hands might be trembling at his sides.

"Turn on the light," she said. He reached over slowly, feeling the wall until he found the switch. A moment later, they were staring at each other, both blinking just a little bit while their eyes adjusted to the sudden brightness.

"You going to run?" she said. If he ran, he was going to get away. Bliss was okay with that. She certainly couldn't chase him down, and if he'd already gotten past those lazy, no-good security guards in the warehouse once, he'd probably be able to do it again.

"No."

Bliss didn't know what to do with that. "Why not?"

"Nowhere to run to," he said.

She took her finger off the trigger of the Beretta. "How'd you get in here?"

She heard him exhale. "I sneaked in through the warehouse. It was empty. Found my way down the hall until I came to your door."

"Why you come in that way?"

"I've been checking out your store all week long. I saw an alarm system out front, but no electronic security in back. Not even cameras." He shrugged. "Seemed like the best option."

No, no alarm system in back, Bliss reminded herself. *That's true. Can't risk anything unexpected—like Taurus MT-9 G2 submachine guns—getting caught on security cameras back there. No permanent records but my own log, William insisted on that. And I don't want police snooping around my warehouse in answer to a false alarm back there, either. Don't want them to accidentally see a shipment of handguns or who knows what else.*

"I got three security guards at this place during the night shift," she said. "What you do with them?"

"Nothing."

She fingered the trigger again. "Tell the truth, boy. I still haven't made up my mind whether or not to shoot you dead right here."

"I didn't do anything to them. I only saw two guards. There've only been two guards all week long. At midnight, every night, one of them takes a walk around the building. A few minutes later, the other one goes outside to smoke. I waited until that last one went outside for a cigarette. He left the warehouse door open behind him."

Figures.

Had Darrent been trying to cut costs, trimming down her guard personnel without telling her? Maybe. Or maybe he was trying to invite intruders into her locked-up world? But why would he do that? *Need to keep a closer eye on Darrent*, she told herself. *At least for a bit.*

The boy exhaled again. "I don't think he's the greatest security guard I've ever seen."

Bliss almost laughed at that observation, but she didn't want to disturb the moment.

"Well, come inside, then, and shut the door behind you. And always remember that I have a gun aimed at your testicles. Understand?"

That should scare him, she thought with wicked glee. *William would've liked that.*

23

RAVEN

Atlanta, GA
Little Five Points
Friday, March 31, 12:10 a.m.
14 days to Nevermore

"Choices," my daddy used to say, *"make the man. It's the choices you make that determine how you will handle your past, and what your future will hold."*

I understand a bit better now what he was talking about. I wish I could go back and talk a little sense into my teenage self, tell me to listen to my dad every once in a while because, even though he was hard to take at times, he usually did know what he was talking about.

Right now, though, I've got more pressing matters to deal with.

"What you want to say that's going to keep me from putting a bullet right through you?" the old woman says. I'm guessing she's the one they call Mama Bliss, and she's caught me breaking into her office in the middle of the night. I think she might be the one that finally puts an end to my pathetic life.

"Please don't."

What else is there to say?

I feel my hands shaking, but not from fear. I feel like crying, which is kind of stupid. I feel angry, because I know that if I'd had my pinky on my left hand, if it hadn't been taken away from me by a psychotic Ukrainian, I would've picked those two door locks in half the time it took me. *Never knew how much I relied on a tiny little finger.*

"Turn on the light," she commands, so I comply.

Mama Bliss is old, that's obvious by her gray hair and sagging frame. And judging by the wheelchair beside her bed, she has some measure of disability. But she's certainly not helpless, even wearing that *Good Times*-style nightshirt of hers. She's thick, but not as heavy as I'd imagined she would be. Maybe one hundred eighty pounds, maybe a few less. Her face is like burned coffee grinds, dark and grainy, like an African queen from a hundred years ago, unstained by American slavery or pawing from light-skinned slave masters. Her eyes are such a dark brown that they're almost black, but the spirit in them is alive and flashing gold. I get the feeling she sees everything and misses almost nothing. I get the feeling I made a mistake breaking into this woman's property while she was resting inside.

"You going to run?" she says to me now.

It's a good question. One I've heard before.

"You going to run away and get drunk somewhere?"

The clerk behind the counter of the Liquor Mart leered at me like he wanted to be my best friend, like he was somebody special just because he'd figured out I was underage and trying to buy alcohol. My mom was safely at her doctor's appointment.

Natalie had started her new life without me. And I just wanted to sit in my car and drink a few beers to dull the pain in my head.

"Where's Sandy today?" I said, trying to change the subject.

Sandy I could deal with. Sandy was always bored, like she hated her job and would rather be anywhere else but at the store. I appreciated that in a liquor store clerk, especially when I was eighteen years old. Sandy was disinterested in my growing addiction. She never asked my age, or carded me, or even greeted me. She just rang up the six-pack, took my money, and went back to being bored by her dissatisfying life.

"Sandy a friend of yours?" the clerk said.

He knew something I didn't know, I could tell, and he intended to use it against me.

I shrugged, trying to act uninterested. He shrugged back.

"Sandy was stupid," he said, "and she got caught. She won't be working here no more."

"Got caught doing what?" I said, and immediately I knew it was a mistake. *Never give attention-starved bullies any idea you might be interested in their lives.* Too late for me, though.

"Oh, I bet you'd like to know, wouldn't you?" he crowed. "How much is it worth to you, you little pervert? What would you pay for that information?"

I could feel the clock of my life ticking minutes away while I wasted time with this moron. This day had been bad enough already, and my mouth felt unnaturally dry, like I had to have a drink soon or my throat would turn to sandpaper.

Stupid Scott Whitney, I thought.

Scott Whitney's dad had given me my first drink when I was fifteen years old. He took a few of us to a minor league baseball game in Oklahoma City and, without even thinking about it, ordered beers for us all. I think he figured we were already drinkers, so why not? Plus, he didn't really want to be bothered with a bunch of his son's teenage friends. He just wanted to watch the game and be able to say later that he'd spent time with his kid.

After that experience, four or five of us made it our goal every weekend to try and score another six-pack, or a bottle of Jack Daniels, or whatever we could finesse as underage, budding alcoholics. Three years later, I could barely go two days without some kind of alcohol in my system. I knew that probably wasn't a great thing, but I was young, and I knew how to mask the problem.

I thought I was the exception to the rule.

Of course, nobody is the exception, not really.

"I don't really care what happened to Sandy," I said. "You can keep that to yourself. I just need to pay for this six-pack."

The pasty-faced clerk wasn't happy about my response.

"Well," he said like he was doing me a favor, "she got caught stealing. Sort of stealing. She just quit taking money from the customers. The owner made her come into work last Saturday, even though it was supposed to be her day off. For two hours, she didn't do anything but read a magazine. Whenever someone came to buy something, she just said, 'On the house today,' and kept reading."

He laughed at that thought, and I could tell he admired the girl's protest. Even more, I could tell he loved telling this story, being the center of attention with this kind of gossip, even though the only person listening to him was me—and I was anxious to get out of his obnoxious presence.

"Finally, after only about two hours on shift, she stood up, raised her middle finger at the security camera, and walked out. Just walked out! Store was empty at least an hour before anybody noticed she was gone. Owner was lucky nobody stole a bunch of stuff before he could get here."

He finished his tale with gusto and a laugh. He looked to me for applause or something, but I just wanted a drink.

"How much for the six-pack?" I said, holding out a ten-dollar bill. I thought I was smoothly changing the subject. He thought I was insulting his storytelling skills. He frowned, stood behind the counter, and made like he was going to ring up my purchase.

"Just need to see your ID," he said casually. But I could see the sneer in his lips. He knew I wasn't what I was pretending to be.

"Had my license revoked," I tried to lie. "Got caught drinking and driving."

He didn't say anything, just jerked his eyes toward my car in the parking lot, then snapped them back on me. Smirking.

"Here," I said, shoving the ten-dollar bill toward him on the counter. "Just keep the change. How about that?"

Now I had insulted him.

"Get out of my store," he said, adding a colorful nickname that would've gotten my mouth washed out with soap back when I was ten. "Come back when you're twenty-one and maybe I'll let you sip the good stuff for your birthday." He shoved the beer across the counter. "And put this back where it belongs so the grown-ups can find it."

I felt my face burn red with anger and frustration. At that moment, I hated that jerk. I wanted to smash a beer bottle across his crooked nose. Instead, I took the six-pack back down the aisle and put it away. Then I saw the clerk's back was turned and recognized a shoplifting opportunity. I pocketed a pint of Everclear when he wasn't looking.

That'll get me good and drunk, I thought as I headed out the door.

"See you when your voice changes," the clerk hollered behind me. "But don't come back before then."

See you never, I thought.

I still had a little time, so I stopped at a grocery store and bought a bottle of Hawaiian Punch, mixing it with the 151-proof liquor in my car in the parking lot. I was already halfway through the Hawaiian Punch and forty minutes late when I finally remembered I was supposed to pick up my mom at the doctor's.

"You going to run?"

Now I hear the old woman's words echoing again, somewhere in my head, and they startle me enough to bring me back from memories of my awful past. Forcing me to return to my awful present. To my uncertain future.

I should run, I think. *Fly away and hide again, like the raven in Noah's ark.*

There's no way Mama Bliss could catch me. I'd be in the hallway out of her sight before she could pull the trigger on her invisible gun. But I know I'm not going to run. It takes life to run, and I don't have that kind of energy. Not anymore.

And where would I go?

No place to run. No place to land. No place to hide.

No place to go. I tell her so.

The old woman is talking to me again, and I hear my voice answering, but my mind is drifting away, reliving the choices I made just a week ago that brought me to this awful place right now.

I never called Trudi after they cut off my finger, after I missed our first and last date at Eclipse di Luna. That was a choice. I hope she at least had a nice dinner without me.

I didn't call her ex-husband either, even though I wonder if it might've been a good idea to go to the police. Another choice. But I've been a criminal for too long, and we teach ourselves never to go to the cops for anything. Not for anything.

After I got over the shock of waking up, post-surgery, in my apartment, I did what Scholarship's note recommended. My mind felt numb, but my hand demanded attention.

I went into the bathroom and tore off the bandage over the sink. I did throw up then, green, watery bile, more liquid than I thought would be possible to keep in my stomach. When I was done, I washed out the sink and tried to clean the wound on my hand as best I could. It wasn't perfect, but at least it wasn't sticky and crusted with blood anymore. I rewrapped the wound in gauze. It wasn't as tight and secure as old Pavlo had done it, but it was good enough.

I pulled four Tylenol capsules out of the bathroom cabinet and tried to swallow them without water, like they do in the movies. That was a mistake. They got stuck in my throat, and I ended up having to push my face under the faucet to gulp from the stream there until the pills finally washed down. That whole experience exhausted me. I went into my bedroom and collapsed on the unmade bed.

But I couldn't sleep. I could only feel the agony in my left hand. A few times, instinctively, I tried to flex my pinky finger. It felt like it was still there, until I looked at the bandage and felt the shock all over again.

They cut off my finger. For one thousand dollars, they cut off my finger.

The words of Scholarship's note had imprinted themselves in my mind already, and even with my eyes closed I could see that last, terrifying line:

We'll be back in a week to collect your next payment.

"A job," I said into the darkness. "They said I could do a job and that would pay off the debt. What job? They didn't say what the job was, did they?"

My brain struggled to remember everything that had happened before I passed out, before they, before they—

The kitchen.

It came back to me then. Scholarship had said he would leave instructions about the job for me in the kitchen. It was now close to two in the morning, but I had to see if that was true.

The big man had been as good as his word. Attached to the refrigerator with a magnet was a sheet of paper torn from the yellow pad in my living room. There was another note on it.

Hey Kid,

> *First, eat something. You got to take care of your body if you want it to take care of you.*

> *Next, figure out how to break into Sister Bliss's Secret Stash over in Little Five Points. Nighttime will be best. Find the big office in back of the store. Somewhere in that office there will be a safe. Take a cordless drill and drill your way into the safe. Inside should be a logbook. Bring the logbook home, and we'll pick it up from you next Friday at five o'clock. That's the job.*

> *Oh, and don't run. You're an investment to us now, which means we've got eyes on you at all times. If you try to run, you can guess what will happen when we catch you. Now, eat something!*

—S

It was after two a.m. My hand was throbbing with pain. My head felt like a college drum corps was playing inside my skull. But Scholarship said I should eat something and, for some reason, it seemed easier to obey him than not. I made a sandwich of plain bread and roast beef slices. I was surprised at how good it tasted, how that simple act of normalcy helped my nerves to return to calm. And then the Tylenol finally started to take effect, easing the throbbing in my hand to a dull ache. I wanted to cry for a bit, to shout at God for a while, but I was just too tired by then.

I went back to my room and slept until noon. When I woke up, I started to make a plan for breaking into Sister Bliss's Secret Stash.

"Well, come inside, then," the old woman is saying to me now. "And shut the door behind you. And always remember that I have a gun aimed at your testicles. Understand?"

I think I can remember that.

24

TRUDI

Atlanta, GA
Little Five Points
Friday, March 31, 12:14 a.m.
14 days to Nevermore

"This isn't stalking," Trudi said to the passenger seat. "I'm not a stalker."

Even as she said it, she tried to ignore the fact that she did occasionally have stalker tendencies, like when she'd hacked her husband's Find My iPhone app just so she could keep track of where he was. But this was different. This was a stakeout, a business situation for a private detective. The fact that her no-show from last Friday happened to show up during the stakeout was coincidence, not stalking.

"Feels a little bit like stalking," Samuel replied.

He tried to stretch his long legs in the confined space of Trudi's Ford Focus, couldn't find the room he needed, gave up, twisted sideways a bit, and finally leaned his head back against the headrest. "But wake me up when something interesting happens anyway."

"Look, do you want my help or not?"

"Yes, of course I do," Samuel said through closed eyes. "I just didn't know it would mean stalking your new boyfriend."

Trudi knew he was just needling her, knew he thought he was being funny, but it stung anyway. She didn't know which was worse, that Samuel had learned she'd (almost) gone to dinner, or that he seemed so unconcerned about it. *Sometimes I wish you were the jealous type*, she thought to herself. *More like me.*

"You're still just a middle-schooler on the inside, aren't you, Samuel?"

"Farts, wedgies, boogers." He smiled in his pseudo-sleep.

The security guard outside the back warehouse of Sister Bliss's Secret Stash took a deep drag on his second cigarette, burning an orange penlight into the night as the tobacco lit up near his cheek. He'd been out in the lot for several minutes now, apparently unconcerned about intruders, or about anything except depleting the crumpled pack of cigarettes he kept in his shirt pocket. His partner had left a few minutes before, making a night walk to check the perimeter of the building. One of them was doing his job, at least.

"How long has The Raven been in there?" she said.

Samuel peeked out of one eye and checked his watch. "Let's see," he said. "I clocked him going in at two minutes after midnight. It's about twelve-fifteen now, so thirteen minutes?"

"Hmm."

"The better question," he said, trying again to get comfortable in Trudi's cramped front seat, "is why he's in there. Any ideas?"

Trudi shook her head.

Why would The Raven break into Sister Bliss's Secret Stash

now, after being practically invisible since he'd skipped out on dinner last Friday night? She retraced the week's events in her mind.

"Come to the dinner," Viktor Kostiuk had said before leaving her at the Eclipse di Luna restaurant. "Maybe Mr. Roman's speech will make you a believer in him too."

Was it just a coincidence? A high-profile political gathering was featuring the famous Edgar Allan Poe poem, "The Raven," at the same time that underground rumblings spoke of a home-grown terrorist plot with the code name Nevermore—the key repeated phrase from the poem.

It could be nothing, she'd thought. *It probably is nothing. But . . . what if it's not?*

The idea that she might have spotted a small clue to the Nevermore plot was something she couldn't ignore. If a new terrorist attack had anything to do with the political fundraiser for Max Roman, and if it turned out she could've seen it coming but had done nothing about it, how would she ever live with herself?

"I need to talk to Samuel," she'd whispered to no one. "But how do I interrupt his date?"

In the end, she'd decided not to interrupt Samuel and Eulalie at Eclipse di Luna. She wasn't going to let on that she'd seen them there at all. She decided instead to do a little research herself before talking to her ex-husband. She wanted to come to him with more than just a "Maybe this is important?" She wanted to make sure she wasn't just insinuating a connection because it seemed convenient.

Decision made, she'd left a tip on the table and drove herself home, turning possibilities over in her mind.

A sleepless night had stretched into a windowless weekend. Trudi had avoided going to her office in West Midtown, but that didn't mean she'd avoided work. She spent most of Saturday in her attic study, combing the internet for history and records of Poe's most famous poem. She spent Sunday afternoon lost in the stacks and research materials of the Central Library in the Atlanta-Fulton County Library System.

"The Raven" had been published by several magazines in 1845, but its first appearance with the name Edgar Allan Poe attached had been in the January 29, 1845, issue of the *New York Evening Mirror*. The work itself was almost horror in style, chronicling a slow descent into madness and despair for its unnamed narrator, all of which was punctuated by an otherworldly Raven croaking again and again, "Nevermore." It had been an immediate success, prompting more magazine printings and even the publication of a book of collected Poe poems that same year.

Tracking down the collectors' history of the January 29, 1845, issue of the *New York Evening Mirror* had taken more time, a number of phone calls to finagle access to auction records, and most of the day on Monday. As far as Trudi could tell, there were still about a dozen copies of the magazine extant in the world, maybe as many as twenty. The one that had caught her eye, though, was the most recently auctioned collectible copy.

It had been sold in a private, invitation-only auction by Heritage Auctions of Dallas, Texas, on December 18, 2009. She'd been rebuffed while trying to discover the name of the buyer or even the winning bid amount, but a little snooping and disingenuous information spread out in the right places had secured for her the address to where the item had been sent for the winning bidder.

464 Moreland Ave, NE, Atlanta, GA 30307.

Trudi hadn't even needed to look it up to know what was there. That was when she'd finally called Samuel and arranged to meet. He'd come by the Coffey & Hill Investigations office about an hour later.

"First," she'd said, "I need a favor."

"Sure, Tru-Bear," Samuel had said after sitting in a metal chair in her office. "As long as it's legal. Well, as long as it's almost legal." He grinned.

She reached in her desk drawer and pulled out the plastic bag that held The Raven's empty Perrier. "I have some fingerprints on this bottle," she said. "I don't want you to ask why, but can you run these through your law enforcement database and see if there's a match?"

"You on a manhunt or something?"

"No, just looking for information. And didn't I just say I didn't want any questions?"

He reached across the desk and palmed the bottle. "I'll turn it in to the appropriate people. Could take a few days, though. I understand they're running behind, and requests like this, with no specific case attached to them, can get put off pretty easily. Do you need this back?"

"That's fine. And no, I don't need the bottle back."

"Okay. I'll let you know when I hear anything. Now, you said you had something you needed to talk about?"

Trudi filled him in on the meeting with Viktor Kostiuk—conveniently leaving out the parts about which restaurant she'd met him at or why she'd been alone at the table when Viktor came by.

"Kostiuk." He frowned. "I know that name. It's a family implicated with an offshoot of the Ukrainian Mafia up north, New York I think. Maybe Massachusetts. I'd have to check. There was a rumor not long ago that they were looking to make a move down south, but I didn't think Georgia was a target for them.

I would have guessed Florida. I can look in to it, though. And you say this Kostiuk guy is affiliated with Councilman Roman?"

"Says he's a political consultant from New York. Working to make Max Roman the next mayor of Atlanta."

"You think he's got something to do with Nevermore?"

"I'm not sure. But here's what I do know: Somehow he's gotten ahold of a rare copy of the January 29, 1845, issue of the *New York Evening Mirror.*"

Samuel looked blank. "Good for him?"

"It's the original publication of Edgar Allan Poe's poem 'The Raven.'"

It took only about a second and a half for Samuel to make the same connection Trudi had made. "And he's auctioning it off at a high-profile *political* fundraiser, right here in Atlanta? Yeah. That could be something. A terrorist attack there would certainly make headlines."

"Now," Trudi had said, "ask me where he got the magazine. Who donated it to their cause."

"Who?"

"Sister Bliss's Secret Stash."

Empty air filled the room.

"He got the magazine from Mama Bliss?" Samuel said at last. "Where did she—well, never mind. She deals in antique-everything over there. She could have easily brought it into the store, who knows when."

"December 18, 2009. She bought it then."

"What's it worth?"

"Hard to tell at this point. Mama bought it at a private auction, and I couldn't pry loose the amount she paid. But at a public auction in 2005, a first-edition copy of Poe's book *The Raven and Other Poems* sold for $54,000. In 2009, a nicer first edition of that book auctioned for a whopping $182,500, so you can see there's potential for big money in this. Mama's magazine is not a book, but it's still very rare. At auction today, I'm guessing it'd sell at somewhere between $100,000 and $150,000."

"Hmm. Pretty big investment from a retail standpoint," Samuel said. "And Mama Bliss usually turns over her store's stock reasonably fast. If it doesn't sell in the Stash, she's got a team who'll sell slow-moving items online, or sometimes she'll just send things off to an auction house herself. So why keep this really expensive, obscure magazine for so long?"

"Maybe she bought it for herself and not the store?"

"And now she's tired of it and decides to just donate a big-money item like that to a political fundraiser?"

"Well, technically, she donated it to the Atlanta Society for Literary Arts. They're the organization sponsoring the fund-raising dinner for Max Roman. They're combining the political event with a charity auction for their organization. Two birds with one stone, I guess."

"But Mama Bliss hates politics. Says it's repugnant and corrupt. She avoids it like a deadly peanut allergy. Why would she get involved with Max Roman's mayoral campaign?"

"She's fairly community-minded. Maybe she's on the board of directors for ASLA and they asked for donations?"

"All right," he said, standing. "I'll go talk to Mama. See what I can find out."

"Samuel, wait."

"What is it?"

"Think about what you're about to do. If you go gallivanting over to Mama Bliss's and accuse her of being part of some homegrown terrorist plot in Little Five Points, how do you think she's going to respond?"

"Mm. Well, I wouldn't actually be accusing her. I've known Mama for a long time. I'm pretty sure she wouldn't . . . well . . ."

"Look, Samuel, we both know that Sister Bliss's Secret Stash has more secrets than your everyday retail location. You know more about that than I do, but the point is, we're talking about Mama Bliss. She deserves our trust, not our accusations."

"Maybe Mama's not even aware that there could be a connection," he said. "Maybe she just felt like donating something special to a charity. Or maybe it's just a wild goose chase, a red herring, and talking to Mama will clear up all our concerns."

"Sure. Maybe."

"So what are you suggesting? That I ignore her connection to this magazine?"

Trudi saw the stubborn little boy creeping into Samuel's narrowing eyes. "No, of course not," she said. "Let's just take it slowly instead of running around like a couple of bulls in a china shop."

Samuel had grinned at that, and at first Trudi hadn't known why.

"What?" she'd said. "What's so funny?"

"Nothing funny. I'm just glad to hear that you're on the case with me. It'll be a little bit like old times." He sat down again.

"I never—" Trudi stopped herself and replayed her last comments in her mind. *Let's just take it slowly* . . . Let's, as in "Let us." Without really knowing it, she'd started thinking of Samuel's case as one of her own. As theirs together. Us.

Well, that's interesting.

"All right," Samuel had said. "We'll take it slow. But we should keep tabs on what goes on over at the Secret Stash for a few days. You up for a stakeout or two?"

And so, a few minutes after a humid Friday had begun in Little Five Points, Trudi had found herself parked in a car with her ex-husband, staring down the darkened street at the back warehouse entrance to Sister Bliss's Secret Stash, watching a lazy security guard get lost in his thoughts while smoking a cigarette.

It was then that the guy on the bicycle had caught Trudi's eye. He was of medium build, wiry, with short and spiky hair. It had taken a minute for her to recognize him, but once she did, she couldn't mistake him for anyone else.

"Samuel," she'd said, smacking her ex-husband's shoulder with the palm of her hand. "Check this out."

They both watched him dismount and then hide his bicycle out of view from the entrance to the warehouse. He then stepped into the shadows and crouched, watching and apparently waiting.

"Any idea who that is?" Samuel had said.

"Yeah," she'd said grimly. "That's the guy whose fingerprints I gave you to match."

"I've seen that bicycle before," Samuel said. "Twice this week while we've been on stakeouts. Once on Wednesday afternoon. And again yesterday after closing time."

"Why didn't you say anything?"

"Didn't seem important. Just some random guy riding by the Stash. I thought maybe he lived around here or something."

"You met him in my office last Friday. You didn't recognize him?"

He'd shrugged. "I meet a lot of people, Trudi. And I've been kind of busy lately, trying to stop a terrorist plot and all."

They'd spent a few silent moments watching The Raven watch the Secret Stash.

"Wait a minute," Samuel had said suddenly, and he'd sat up so fast he bumped his head on the dangling visor in Trudi's Ford Focus. "That's the guy I met at your office last Friday?"

In the darkness, he couldn't see Trudi roll her eyes. "Are you sure you're a detective, Samuel? Because sometimes you're pretty slow."

He turned to face her, and the corners of his lips twitched upward. "So that's Marv Deasy? The guy who was supposed to be your date last Friday night?" He emphasized the word *date*.

"I . . . what . . . how do you know about that?" Trudi felt heat rising into her cheeks. Had Samuel seen her at Eclipse di Luna, after all?

"I'm a detective. I know things." He relaxed back in his seat, a look of triumph on his face. "Have a good time?"

"None of your business. And how did you—oh, never mind."

"Yep. I have friends everywhere."

"Eulalie's got a big mouth."

He just grinned.

Trudi had wanted to ask him about Eulalie then, wanted to say, *So, how about you? Did you and Eula have a nice date?* But she'd stopped herself. It still felt off-limits to her, like she'd be prying in an area that was none of her business, not really. Her stomach clenched inside her anyway. She'd turned her attention back to The Raven instead.

And then one security guard had started his perimeter walk, and moments later, the other had left his post, wandered around the corner of the warehouse, and started chain-smoking his way into irrelevance.

Samuel had sat up again when The Raven made his move. The street magician had crept like a cat, silent and shadowed, and slipped into the open warehouse door with remarkable ease. The security guard didn't even know he existed, let alone that The Raven had just walked into his fortress.

"So," Samuel had said after a moment, "Marv Deasy can now be arrested and charged with breaking and entering. I think I can move your fingerprint check up on the priority list."

He'd taken out his cell and started tapping out a message. Trudi assumed he was putting a little heat into the email box of a data tech at the police station, something to greet him or her when that person arrived at work later on this Friday morning. Samuel put away his cell and leaned back in his seat, trying unsuccessfully to get more comfortable.

"Good thing we're already stalking your new boyfriend. That'll make things go faster if he is involved in Nevermore."

Trudi's eyes had narrowed at the mention of her "boyfriend." There were a lot of things she wanted to say to her ex-husband, and some things she wanted to hear from him too. But at the moment, none of them were ready to be spoken.

"This isn't stalking," Trudi had said to the passenger seat instead. "I'm not a stalker."

25

BLISS

Atlanta, GA
Little Five Points
Friday, March 31, 12:20 a.m.
14 days to Nevermore

"If you're going to attack me, now's the time."

Mama Bliss rolled on her hip and let her legs drop over the edge of the bed until her feet touched the floor. The intruder stood just inside the door, now closed, waiting for further instructions. He held his drill in one hand, dangling to the side like a useless weapon. With the light on in the room, Bliss decided she liked this boy's look. He was young and lean, but handsome in the way that today's kids were. She thought she'd see fear in his face but found only sadness there instead.

"I won't hurt you," he said.

"I'm just saying that when I switch over from this bed to my chair, there'll be a split second when my hands will be occupied. You might get to me and conk me on the head or something. I'll probably get off one shot at least, maybe two, but my aim will be bad since we'll both be moving. So if you're going to attack, better make it now. At least then I'll have a bruise to show the police when they're looking at your dead body."

Something about that struck him as funny. She watched his lips twitch and thought she saw relief in the way his eyebrows relaxed above his eyes.

"I'm a lover, not a fighter."

She heard Michael Jackson's soprano voice sing unexpectedly through his lips, then she saw his right leg twist and spin in the familiar MJ arc—just for good measure, she supposed. She snorted in spite of herself. "Well, at least you've got a sense of humor," she said. "Pretty good impersonation too. So, what? Are you Ivory and I'm Ebony?"

Now it was his turn to snicker.

Bliss paused and looked at him. There was something about this boy, this young man. But no, he clearly was not to be trusted. She hefted her weight toward the edge of the bed, preparing to make the short leap from bed to wheelchair, holding the gun precariously in her right hand.

"Would you like some help, ma'am?" he said, and doggone it if Bliss didn't believe he was sincere.

"You just go sit in one of those chairs over there," she said, directing him to the small lunch table on the other side of the office. After he took a seat and placed his drill on the table in front of him, she slid into her wheelchair and faced him again. He hadn't moved while she'd been making the transition, something that made her grateful, for his sake. If he'd come at her, she would have killed him. That smoke-blowing about how this would be the right time to attack was just a test. She wanted to see if he meant harm—and if he was stupid.

Of course she'd been ready to shoot while making the transition from bed to chair. She was no stranger to handguns. It had been thirty-seven years since William had first put a pistol in her hand and taught her to use it, and twenty-seven since they'd begun importing and exporting firearms through the Secret Stash. That meant her little Beretta was as comfortable to her as a glove on a cold day. She didn't want to kill the boy, but if it had been necessary, she certainly had enough skill, and will, to end a man quickly.

Thankfully this boy wasn't stupid enough to try an attack at this point.

Bliss rolled her chair behind the desk, feeling the comfort that came with putting furniture between herself and an adversary. Any obstacle between you and danger was a good thing, she figured. She regarded the intruder now with a different kind of interest, like a lion-tamer assessing a cub for the first time. For his part, he seemed just as comfortable sitting there as anywhere else.

"You have a name?" she said.

He hesitated. Then, "Well, I've got several. What's your preference?"

"What's your daddy call you?"

He grimaced, and Bliss recognized that look. "Fine, forget about your daddy, then," she said. "What do people 'round here call you when you're not breaking into their private work and living spaces?"

"The Raven."

She cocked her head to the side. Was he kidding? "You best explain that one to me. Mama Bliss is old, and it's late at night. She ain't ready for another mystery so soon on the heels of your arrival."

"I'm a deception specialist. A magician, I guess. I work for tips out in Freedom Park and Piedmont Park. The Raven is my performance name, and most people still call me that when I'm not performing too." He shrugged. "But you can call me anything you like."

"Magician? You any good?"

He shrugged again.

"Show me a magic trick, Mr. Raven."

"How about the one where I keep you from shooting me in the testicles?" He grinned unexpectedly at her, and she suddenly knew what it was about this young man that caught her so.

"Good trick," she said, unable to avoid returning the smile. Inside, she felt a familiar ache. She opened a drawer on the right side of her desk and set the BU9 Nano pistol inside it but didn't close the drawer. "I don't think I need this anymore, do I?"

He shook his head and looked grateful. "So," he said, "what's next?"

Bliss leaned back in her wheelchair and put her hands on the armrests. *What's next?* she wondered. *What do I do now that I've caught me a crooked bird?*

"Do you want me to leave?" he said.

Bliss found herself shaking her head. "You're free to go if you want," she said. "I won't stop you. But I am curious about you now, Raven."

"Like I said, I got no place else to go." He sighed, and she watched his face wince as if he felt pain somewhere in his body.

"No family?"

He shook his head. "Not anymore. My fault, not theirs."

"I got no family, either," Bliss said. "Everybody's fault. My husband up and died without my permission twenty-some years ago. Aneurysm. One minute he was sweeping trash off the front porch, next he was lying in the rubbish, pawing at his head, and then gone."

"I'm sorry."

Bliss looked at him and thought he actually meant it.

"Anyway, my daughter ran off into the world, and my grandson—" She stopped herself. *Old woman*, she commanded, *you best not cry in front of this two-bit thief.* "Anyway, he's gone too."

"It's hard. I know."

"You remind me of him."

"Who?"

"My grandson. Davis. Something about you is like him." *Maybe your smile. Maybe the promise that anything is possible and there's nothing to be afraid of, not really. All that hidden inside your smile.*

"So he was a good-looking dude, that's what you're saying? Big, strong, and handsome?"

Bliss laughed in spite of herself. It felt warm, comfortable—a strange feeling considering the circumstances of this midnight conversation.

"So," she said after a moment, "why you here? What's in my office that you got to have so bad you want to steal it?"

"I don't really know what it's about," he said slowly. "Just that there's a logbook in a safe somewhere in here."

Bliss felt her face harden. So that was it. "Max Roman sent you."

His eyes searched hers, trying to understand what was going on. Then he said, "Yeah, sort of. I'm supposed to steal your logbook and give it to one of his people at five o'clock today. But I didn't know you'd be in here when I came in."

"So the power drill, that's what it's for? You're this big-time magician and the best you can do for safecracking is drill through the lock?"

"Never had to break into a safe before. They told me to bring a cordless drill, so I brought a cordless drill."

Going to have to get a new safe. Bliss made a mental note. *One that's drill-proof.*

"How much they pay you for this service?" she asked.

His face dropped. "Nothing. And everything."

She let her eyes wander over the thief in her office, trying to make sense of that statement. Then she saw the small bandage on his left hand. He had a thumb, three fingers, and then that bandage in the spot where his last finger should have been.

Fresh wound. She pursed her lips. "How much you owe them?"

"Ten thousand." He looked at his left hand. "Well, nine thousand now, I suppose."

"And let me guess: They're willing to cancel that 'debt'"—she made air quotes with her fingers—"in return for my logbook. Is that the way this is going down?"

He nodded. Then he stood up so quickly that Bliss almost reached into the desk drawer to retrieve her gun. But she decided to wait him out instead and relaxed after only a few seconds. He was standing, but the boy wasn't moving anywhere beyond that.

"Well," he said, "if this is my last day, then I've got a few things to do. A few people to apologize to."

"A girl?"

"Yeah, that'd be one of them. We had a date, and I stood her up while this"—he raised his left hand—"was going on. But, you know, that could have been avoided, I guess."

"Sit down, Raven." She reached into the desk drawer and pulled out the Beretta, after all.

"I thought you'd decided not to shoot me. I really am sorry about breaking into your office."

"Just sit down. I like you, boy. Maybe I'm going to help you."

He said nothing but let himself slowly down into his seat.

Bliss set the gun on the desk. "How many come after you?"

"Two," he said. "Well, three at first. Then two."

"You can't run," she said. "Once they got you, they keep eyes on you. You know that?"

"Yeah, that's what they said."

"You try to run, it gets worse for you, for anybody you care about. That girl you talked about? You run, and they involve her in this too. You understand?"

"I'm not going to run."

"And even if you give them what they want, they'll always come back. Sooner or later, they always come back. Maybe they leave you alone for a year, maybe two. But they got you now. And when they need whatever it is you got to offer, they come back."

He didn't say anything.

"You hearing me, boy?"

"Yes, ma'am." The look on his face was that of a former drunk wishing he could find a few dollars to buy a bottle of cheap wine. Sober, and sorrowful about being sober.

Bliss pushed her chair back and ducked her head under the desk. She slid aside a false panel to reveal a small, sturdy metal safe behind it. *Thirteen, one, eleven*, she recited to herself as her fingers twirled the lock, and then the door opened. From inside the safe, she pulled two stacks of one-hundred-dollar bills and a logbook with a dull red cover.

When she came up from under the desk, she could see The Raven craning his neck, trying to see what she was doing. She slapped the money down with her left hand, and with her right hand, she put the logbook in between the cash and the gun.

"Come here, Raven," she said. He obeyed, standing in front of her desk, looking curious and confused at the same time. "You got three choices," she said.

"One: You take this gun. It's got eight bullets in it. You go home, you wait for Max Roman's people to come visit, and then you shoot them dead, dead, dead. Make sure you put at least two bullets in each man if you really want to kill him, but don't do it randomly. If they send three soldiers, you shoot each one first, disable them at least. Then go back for the dead shot after they're all wounded and trying to survive. When you can take time to compose yourself and shoot to kill. Understand?"

He nodded, but the color drained from his face.

"You'll probably go to jail," she said, "unless you run. But with those guys dead, at least you'll have a chance to run before they can regroup and start chasing you." She shrugged. "Or you can turn yourself in and see what happens, but that still means jail time, even if you cooperate with the authorities, so you'd better be ready for that."

"And the second choice?" he said. She noticed his voice sounded dry and scratchy, like sandpaper on a wood table. Bliss pointed to the logbook.

"Two: You take the logbook. This is what Max Roman asked you to get. Take this logbook, and you make yourself my enemy. You don't yet know what that means, and I don't feel inclined to tell you. Just be prepared for Mama Bliss if you take it."

"How do I know you're not giving me an empty logbook?"

"You don't, do you?" She was glad to see he wasn't dull-minded. That made the third option more appealing to her. "Maybe it's got what Max Roman wants, maybe it doesn't. You'll have to walk out of here with it and see for yourself, won't you?"

He sighed. "What's the third option?"

"Three: I'm hiring a new security guard, night shift." She gestured toward the cash on the desk. "Comes with a ten-thousand-dollar signing bonus for a minimum four-week commitment. You quit before the month is up, and you have to pay back the bonus. You stay with me for one month, and the signing bonus is yours to keep."

He licked his lips. "And?"

"You pay off your debt to Max Roman. That will at least buy you some time to figure out something."

"What about choice number four?"

Bliss looked at him hard. What was he up to now? "What's that?" she said.

"I just walk out of here, alone, with nothing. I hurt no one, take nothing from anyone, make no new enemies. I let myself be extinguished like a candle in a rainstorm."

She searched his eyes and saw he was serious. If he walked out of this office without taking anything, suicide was his next destination.

"Take the job," she said quietly, "and I'll protect you. From Max Roman. From the police. From everybody. I'll keep you safe until you're able to keep yourself out of trouble."

"Why?" It was a whisper.

Because I miss my grandson, she wanted to say. *Because I see you taking the same road he did. Because it will hurt me to see another young man disappear with nothing to show for his life but empty promises and broken dreams.*

Out loud she just said, "Why not?"

26

RAVEN

Atlanta, GA
Little Five Points
Friday, March 31, 12:33 a.m.
14 days to Nevermore

What would Jesus do?

It's after midnight. I'm staring at a desk with a gun, a logbook, and ten thousand dollars in cash on it—and that's what pops into my mind. *What would Jesus do?*

When I was just a kid, maybe five or six, that was a big fad, everybody wearing cheap cotton bracelets with the letters WWJD embroidered in them as a reminder to live life trying to figure out what Jesus would do and then doing it, I guess. My dad was all-in on that little craze. He bought a bunch of the bracelets and gave them to my mom and me to wear, then spread them out around the neighborhood and gave them to any kid who asked for one at church. I managed to "lose" mine after I got in trouble for fighting at school and my teacher said solemnly to me, "Is that really what Jesus would do?" WWJD was too much pressure for a six-year-old like me.

"You shoot each one first, disable them at least," Mama Bliss is saying. "Then go back for the dead shot after they're all wounded and trying to survive."

Is that what Jesus would do? is my first thought, followed pretty quickly by, *This old woman, she knows something about killing. That's a little scary.*

So what would Jesus do? I mean, assuming he got caught trying to blackmail a mob boss and then had his finger amputated as retaliation. And assuming he then tried to break into a big retail store and steal a mysterious logbook. What would he do?

I have no idea. I don't know him well enough for that. My dad would know.

So what would Daddy do? WWDD?

For starters, he never would have become a pickpocket and petty thief. But that's not playing by the rules of this little game I've set up in my head. What if Dad and I miraculously switched places? What if he found himself suddenly with only nine fingers, facing a brutal deadline, and staring at the items on Mama Bliss's desk right now?

What would you do, Pops? I sigh. *I know. You'd do whatever Jesus would do.*

". . . still means jail time," she says to me, "even if you cooperate with the authorities, so you'd better be ready for that." She says it like she's talking about carrying an umbrella because it might rain, or warning you not to eat the second piece of pie because it'll go straight to your hips.

"And the second choice?" I say. My voice sounds raspy, like my throat's been rubbed with sandpaper. It's distracting, and I'm kind of wishing she'd offer me a bottle of water from that mini-fridge by the wall, but I don't want to push my luck. I tune in again midway through her speech.

". . . Take this logbook and you make yourself my enemy . . ."

Okay, choice number two is out, I think.

I don't know too much about Mama Bliss, but I've seen enough to know I do not want to be her enemy. She's an old, crippled woman in a wheelchair, and yet she's got my knees knocking harder than when I first saw Scholarship and Pavlo standing in my doorway. For those guys it's all about business, all about the money. For Mama Bliss? Well, I don't think I want to find out what matters to her, especially if I'm on the wrong side of that equation.

Also, how do I know I can trust this woman? Would she really give me exactly what Max Roman sent me to steal? If I were her, I'd keep more than one logbook in that safe. A decoy. Something I could hand out in an emergency and never miss because it would be blank, or it might have sketches of fruit bowls in it, or whatever. But it definitely wouldn't have whatever it was that Max Roman wanted it to have.

What happens to me when I give Scholarship a bogus logbook?

Now she's got a third choice, and with the stack of money she's waving, it seems like this could be the one that Jesus would do. Or at least, the one I'd want Jesus to do.

"I'm hiring a new security guard, night shift . . ."

A job? She's offering me a job?

"Comes with a ten-thousand-dollar signing bonus . . ."

A low-wage job with an abnormally large signing bonus. No way this is real. What's her angle?

"You pay off your debt to Max Roman . . ."

Maybe she just feels sorry for me. Maybe she really wants to help. Or maybe she's just as bad as Max Roman and she wants to own me so that he can't. Either way, I'm still a slave.

"What about choice number four?" I hear myself saying. I know I've been thinking about it all week long, even though I keep trying to push that plan to the back of my mind. Maybe choice number four is the only one. Maybe it's the only way a slave really gets free.

"What's that?" she says.

I feel a sense of relief at finally admitting out loud what I've been thinking. And sorrow. Twenty-two-and-done seems like a disappointing life, like barely enough time to do anything at all.

What would Jesus do?

Well, not this. I know that much. *What will I do?* That's a different question. And what happens after . . . ? That question I don't even want to think about.

If you can't even think about the afterlife, I scold myself, *how can you think about ending the present life?*

Mama Bliss is looking at me like she sees inside my head. Like the way my own mother used to look at me when she knew I needed something more than kind words or a spanking.

I'm sorry, Mama. I'm sorry, both mamas.

"Take the job." She says it so quietly I almost don't make out her meaning. "And I'll protect you. From Max Roman. From the police. From everybody. I'll keep you safe until you're able to keep yourself out of trouble."

Something about her makes me believe she can keep the promise she's making. Something tells me this crusty old lady knows how to fight a war. But my war? Why fight that when I'm ready to surrender?

She's watching me closely. Inspecting me. I think she knows I'm not breathing right now.

There's a gun, a logbook, and ten thousand dollars on the desk in front of me.

"Why?" I say.

234 • THE RAVEN

I am here in this quiet moment, my life weighing in the balance. Here with Mama Bliss. Her eyes search mine. I see the pain now. I missed that before. Is that her answer? Then the curtain falls and her face becomes a mask.

"Why not?" she says.

And now it's time for me to choose.

What would Jesus do? What would Daddy do? What would Mama Bliss do?

I hear a gunshot ring through the night air, coming from the direction of the warehouse where I entered this place. Mama Bliss's head snaps to the left, following the sound. She swears under her breath and rolls her chair expertly toward the office door.

"What's an old woman got to do to get a good night's sleep around here?"

In a second, she's gone, leaving me alone, breathing stale air, still with a choice to make.

Next to the money on the desk, I see she's left a picture.

27

TRUDI

Atlanta, GA
Little Five Points
Friday, March 31, 12:28 a.m.
14 days to Nevermore

"He's been in there a long time."

"I clock him at twenty-six minutes now," Samuel said.

"Why so long, do you think?" Trudi said. "If you're there to steal something, wouldn't you get in and out faster?"

"You'd think."

Trudi shook her head. The Raven's promises had seemed so sincere a week ago. *I'm a new man*, he'd said. *Cross my heart.* Watching him sneak into Mama Bliss's warehouse, though, she wondered how much she could believe about anything he said.

About ten minutes ago, the security guard had finally satisfied his nicotine craving and gone back inside the warehouse. A few minutes later, the other guard had returned from his perimeter walk and also gone inside, leaving the warehouse door slightly ajar. Trudi wondered why there wasn't a third guard that stayed outside but decided that was irrelevant to her. What mattered was that the outside of Mama Bliss's warehouse was quiet, and she knew that an intruder was roaming around somewhere inside.

"Maybe he's just sightseeing," Samuel was saying. "Or maybe he got trapped inside when Smokey Smokerson went back inside. And honestly, he could have left a long time ago, gone out through a different exit. Maybe we're waiting for him to come out this door and he's already gone."

"Too many maybes." She paused. "You think we should call someone?"

Samuel sat up. "Like who?"

"Police?"

"I am police now, remember?"

"You're a plainclothes detective on a stakeout. You're not here to arrest someone for illegal entry. I mean maybe we should call 911 and report a break-in? Get the uniforms out here. At least then we'd find out what's going on in there."

"Trudi, it's never a good idea to call in the Blues to Mama Bliss's warehouse."

The way he said it made her understand that he knew something she didn't, and that it was all part of a bigger something she didn't want to know about. Still, it made her uncomfortable to sit there and continue to do nothing.

"Okay," she said. "What about Mama? Why don't you call her?"

Samuel chewed on the inside of his cheek. Then he said, "What do you know about your boyfriend?"

"Would you grow up and stop calling him that?" she snapped. "He's a thousand years younger than I am."

He raised his palms in surrender. "Sorry, I carried it too far. My bad. What do you know about Marv Deasy?"

"He's a street magician. Works Freedom Park and Piedmont Park. Petty criminal, pretty good as a pickpocket."

"This is the guy you told to call me? Who turned in a few stolen items over at the station?"

"Yeah."

"There were a few nice things there, but they were all minor thefts. A bracelet or an Apple Watch, those kinds of things. Nobody has even claimed them yet, and nobody reported them stolen, either."

"Yeah. He struck me as a steal-to-pay-rent kind of guy. Not so much a hardened-criminal type."

"So why break into the Secret Stash all of a sudden? Why change your mode of operation?"

Trudi let that question linger for a moment. Why would he do that? And could that be connected to the reason he'd stood her up for their date at Eclipse di Luna?

"We're going to have to talk to The Raven sooner or later," she said.

Samuel didn't reply.

There was a long moment of silence between them, then Samuel spoke softly, keeping his eyes trained on the warehouse doors and away from Trudi.

"Listen," he said, "I'm sorry about that whole boyfriend-stalking thing. It was juvenile, I know. I just, well . . ." He stopped and collected himself. "When Eulalie told me you were meeting Marv Deasy for dinner, I guess I was a little jealous, and that was my way of dealing with it. I'm sorry."

Trudi felt her heart tighten. Part of her loved that he was jealous, and part of her just still loved her ex-husband and wished that they could be together again. Wished that she could go home again. But she knew that wasn't an option. *He's got a wife and child hidden away in the Middle East*, she reminded herself.

That thought used to make her angry. Tonight it just made her feel tired.

"Samuel—" She started to speak but then was interrupted by a gunshot echoing from inside the warehouse.

Samuel sprang upright and kicked open the car door.

"Stay here," he ordered, climbing out onto the pavement. She reached for her cell phone, but before she could dial anything, his head was back inside the car. "Don't call 911. Not yet. Just trust me. Don't. If I'm not back in five minutes, then you can call the police. But give me five minutes to check things out first."

"Samuel—"

He grinned, and she could see that he loved this part of his life. The risk-taking, the danger, the chance to be a hero. That was what he lived for. *It must've been really hard when the CIA dumped you back in the States and said, "Don't call us, we'll call you,"* she thought. He saw the look on her face and maybe misinterpreted her thinking, or maybe not.

"Yeah, I love you too, Tru-Bear. But don't worry. I'll be back in five minutes."

He slammed the door and ran toward the warehouse.

Trudi tracked Samuel as he skimmed across the parking lot. She started counting. *One two three four five six*—she watched her ex-husband pause at the door to the warehouse, then slip inside—*seven eight nine ten.*

That was long enough, she decided. He must have known she wasn't going to sit in the car like a helpless little girl and wonder what was happening inside. She slid out of the driver's seat and made her way quietly across the pavement, following the same path her ex-husband had taken. Like him, she paused at the door and tried to discern what was going on inside.

She heard nothing. No sounds of a scuffle, no shouting, not anything.

I know I heard a gunshot, she said to herself. *Didn't I?*

She unholstered her Beretta Tomcat from the back waistband of her jeans, then squeezed inside the warehouse. She found it empty, lights shining brightly overhead, everything packed, palleted, and prepared for business-as-usual in the morning. Trudi was almost disappointed. After the way Samuel had warned her about calling the police, she'd expected some kind of nefarious contents hidden in here—pirate treasure or illegal ivory or something. But there were just stacks of antique furniture, cases of books and clothes, and all kinds of oddities that soon would either populate the shelves of Mama's store or be shipped to online customers longing for that one-of-a-kind gift for a loved one.

She stepped along a wall, ears straining to hear anything. A little farther in, she wondered why neither of the security guards she'd seen outside was anywhere in sight—and how Samuel could have disappeared so quickly too.

A few more steps and she thought she heard voices. She froze and listened intently, but it all sounded like mumbling and polite conversation. *Is this the scene of a crime or not?* she wondered. She crept closer to a tall row of metal shelves, still trying to make out the sounds coming from behind there.

She suddenly saw a large form stride into view, a man talking on a cell phone.

Samuel?

". . . accident with a handgun," he was saying. He stopped short when he saw Trudi, partly crouched with her Beretta Tomcat held at the ready. He rolled his eyes and motioned for her to put the gun away. "That's right. It doesn't seem serious, but I can't tell if the bullet hit bone or just passed through. Yes. Yes. Thanks. Tell the paramedics we'll wait for them in the back, by the warehouse entrance. Okay, bye."

He ended the call and gave Trudi his "disapproving parent" look.

"Shut up," she said. "I was worried about you."

His face softened, but before he could say anything else, Mama Bliss rolled around the corner, cloaked in a worn, frumpy nightgown, followed by two security guards, one of them limping and being held up by the other. The left pant leg on the limping guard was cut into strips, and she could see a length of cloth had been cut out to hold a bandage around his ankle.

"I swear, Donnell," Mama Bliss was saying, "if you hadn't just shot yourself in the foot, I'd fire you on the spot. But now I'm obligated for worker's compens—Trudi?" She stopped and looked at Samuel, then back at Trudi. "Samuel, you didn't tell me Miss Trudi was with you. And wearing such a pretty necklace too. That from my movie collection?"

"Hi, Mama," Trudi said uncomfortably, fingering the movie prop from *The Lord of the Rings* that Samuel had given her. She was suddenly glad she'd already re-holstered her pistol before Bliss had seen it. "Nice to see you again. Yes, Samuel gave it to me. I love it."

Bliss's eyes narrowed in Samuel's direction, but to Trudi she said, "Well, come give Mama a hug, honey. It's been too long."

The limping security guard groaned.

"Give it a rest, Donnell," Bliss said over Trudi's shoulder as she received the quick hug. "You shot yourself in the ankle. You deserve a little suffering." To Trudi she said, "He was trying to spin his Colt 1911 handgun like some Wild West cowboy."

"Mama," the security guard whined.

"Dropped the gun, it went off, and next thing you know the gang's all here." To Donnell she said, "When you get licensed to carry anyway? Darrent said you failed the marksman certification test and had to carry a stick for a while instead."

"Mama . . ." Her name was a moan. "I'm bleeding."

"Hush, now. Samuel wrapped you up all good and tight, and I can hear the ambulance siren already. You going to be fine."

"He passed the test last week, Mama," the second security guard volunteered. "Darrent just authorized him to carry on Tuesday."

"All right. Go get fixed up now. Leave me to talk with our guests for a minute."

The two security guards limped toward the warehouse door to meet the ambulance. After they were gone, Bliss looked at Samuel but spoke to Trudi. "Your ex-husband said he was out on a midnight drive to clear his head. As he was passing by the back entrance to my store, he heard a commotion and came a-running to make sure I was all right."

Trudi figured it was time to throw her ex-husband under the bus. "That was the best you could do, Samuel?" she said. "You used to be an honest-to-goodness spy. What happened to you? If you're going to lie, you should at least work up a good one. You know, like you did with me for so many years."

Mama Bliss snorted a short laugh while Samuel looked betrayed. But Trudi could tell it had worked. Bliss's suspicions had been alleviated, at least for the moment.

"So tell me," Bliss said to them both, "why is Coffey & Hill Investigations sitting around in my parking lot in the middle of the night?"

Trudi looked at Samuel, not sure what to say at this point.

"Just following up on a lead," he said. "Didn't mean to intrude, but we heard the gunshot and, well, coming in to check it out just seemed the right thing to do."

"You still on that Nevermore thing?" Mama said. She didn't look pleased.

"Have you heard anything new, Mama?" Samuel said.

"I told you, Samuel Hill, it's a hoax. A dead end. A nothing. Somebody talking up a ghost just to cut a better deal with the D.A."

"Mama," Trudi said, "what do you know about a street magician named The Raven?"

Bliss shrugged. "I don't get out to Freedom Park much anymore, honey."

"How about Councilman Max Roman?" Samuel said.

The old woman's eyebrows rose at that name. "He's going to be the next mayor of Atlanta," she said. "So what?"

"He's got a fundraiser coming up in a few weeks," Samuel said. "In fact, Trudi's been invited to attend his dinner as a guest. Are you a Roman supporter?"

Trudi watched storm clouds brew in Bliss's face. "You know how I feel about politics, Samuel," she said. "It's all nonsense and corruption. I don't give a mouse's behind who's mayor of Atlanta. Might as well elect Donnell out there, far as I'm concerned."

"So you're not going to the fundraiser?"

Mama sighed. "Samuel, honey, it's late, and I'm tired. Trudi, it's wonderful to see you again, but maybe it's better if we catch up another time."

Trudi could tell that her ex-husband wasn't ready to leave, that he wasn't sure what Mama Bliss was or wasn't saying, and that he didn't want to stop this mini-interrogation without getting some answers. But she could also tell that Bliss's patience was gone, that it was nearly one o'clock in the morning, and that it was best for all if they put off this conversation until sometime during the day.

"Of course, Mama," she said. "Come on, Samuel."

Her ex-husband hesitated.

"Come on, Samuel," she said again, and this time he responded to her voice. He leaned down and pecked Bliss on the cheek.

"Good night, Mama," he said. "Sorry to have barged in this way. We'll talk again soon."

"It's okay, Samuel," Bliss said. "You're just doing your job, I know. And I know you came in here for me. I'm glad I can count on you to protect me, even in the middle of the night."

Trudi shared her goodbyes, then followed Samuel out, leaving Mama Bliss sitting in her wheelchair in the middle of the warehouse. By the time they got to the door, Donnell and the ambulance had already gone, and the other security guard was standing vigil outside. He nodded when they left, then went back inside to Mama Bliss. This time he made sure the door was all the way shut and locked.

When they got in the car, Samuel was frowning.

"What?" Trudi said.

"Did you see any sign of that magician kid? The Raven."

"No. Maybe it's like you said earlier. Maybe he got scared and went out by a different exit."

"That's possible, I guess. But judging by the way Mama answered your question, I'm betting he's still in there. And she knows it."

"How do you figure?"

"When you asked if she knew him, she said she didn't make it out to Freedom Park anymore. And the only way she'd know The Raven performed at Freedom Park is if she knew The Raven."

Trudi nodded. That made sense, but why would Bliss want to keep something as innocuous as her knowledge of a street magician hidden from them?

"I've known Mama Bliss for a long time," Samuel continued. "Sometimes she has secrets to keep. That just comes with her territory."

"And?"

"Sometimes the secrets she keeps are deadly."

28

BLISS

Atlanta, GA
Little Five Points
Friday, March 31, 12:51 a.m.
14 days to Nevermore

Bliss found the thief sitting at her table, waiting. She checked the desk and saw all three items she'd left were still there, untouched.

"I thought you'd be long gone by now," she said. She rolled her chair into the office toward the desk, then stopped.

The boy was holding her picture.

"What's this?" he said. He lifted Davis's image for her to see.

Bliss instinctively patted the place where her breast pocket would be, even though her mind told her she'd emptied that pocket before going to bed.

"You're a magician," she snapped. "Read my mind and tell me."

He stood up, slowly, asking for permission to walk toward her. She nodded. He moved to the desk and laid the picture on the edge where they both could see, but he laid it facedown, with the back clearly visible.

"Six names," he said. "Four crossed off. Two left."

Mama felt her heart suddenly beating like it would break. She wanted to lie down and let it stop its racing, let it settle back within her chest into the rock it normally was.

I'm just tired, William. I want to sleep.

"You don't have to tell me anything," he said. "It's okay. I'm sorry."

He reached over and picked up the stack of cash, then turned to face her. "If you'll still have me," he said, "I'd like to accept that job offer. Is that still an option?"

She nodded, still feeling the uncertain rumble of her heart inside her chest.

"When should I start? Do you want me to come back tonight?"

She nodded again, still unable to speak. There was an awkward silence between them.

"What time should I come in?" he said.

She didn't answer.

He shifted uncomfortably on his feet, then he said, "That fifth name on your list. Can I ask you about that one?"

"Everybody dies," she said softly. "We all deserve to die."

"My daddy used to say that's why we all need Jesus."

Bliss looked up at him sharply.

"Sorry. My dad's a pastor. Back in Oklahoma. Guess he's still preaching at me even though we haven't spoken in years."

Bliss rolled her chair slowly around the desk. *Preacher's kid*, she thought. *Always the best and the worst of us, I think.* She felt a great weight pressing on her chest, wondered briefly if that was her soul, then let her mind make the decision it had wanted to make all night long.

"Sit down, Raven," she said as she moved. He obeyed, returning to his place at the table while she spun her chair into place behind the desk. She looked at him, looked at the clock, and then looked back at the picture lying facedown in front of her.

"You want to tell your story first, or you want me to tell mine?" he said. He seemed to be reading her thoughts. Maybe he was a good little magician, after all.

She sighed and closed her eyes, not wanting to see what was hidden behind them but not able to blind herself to that view either.

"His name was Davis," she said out loud. She didn't hear any response. If she hadn't known The Raven was sitting just a few feet from her, she wouldn't have guessed he was still in the room, he was that quiet. "Davis Walker Monroe, middle name taken after my maiden name. My daughter, Lenore, got pregnant her senior year in high school. They told her she could still finish school, but she dropped out anyway. She never liked school, and Davis was her excuse to quit. Few years later, she left. My husband was already gone by then, so I took Davis, and Lenore took the rest of the world."

"Where's she now?"

Bliss shrugged. "Who knows? Haven't heard from her since . . . well, since I don't know when. Maybe she's dead too. I got no way of knowing."

"So what happened to Davis?"

"My boy grew up. Grew into a man. He was going to be the first of us to go to college, going on an ROTC scholarship that would've made him an officer in the army after he got out. Summer before he was to start college, he took an internship at Roman Development Corporation."

"Max Roman's real estate company?"

"Mm-hmm. The Romanenko family business." She opened

her eyes and stared blankly across the room. "At first I thought Max was doing me a favor, keeping my grandson out of trouble until he could go off to school in the fall."

"You and Max Roman are friends?"

She frowned. "Business associates. We do business. That's it. But sometimes that business gets complicated. Sometimes he helps me in ways he wouldn't normally be inclined, and sometimes I help him, usually with some political contribution or backdoor facilitation."

"Backdoor facilitation? What's—no, never mind. So what happened when Davis went to work for the Roman Corporation?"

"How much do you really want to know, boy?"

"Whatever you want to tell me."

Mama Bliss nodded. It felt kind of good to finally get this story out of her. Almost therapeutic. She wondered how this would-be thief could have that effect on her. But what could he do, under Max Roman's thumb and obviously on the outs with the police? Besides, maybe this was her confession. She'd never had much time for religion. Maybe this was the way she atoned for her sins.

"Max introduced Davis to some of his other 'projects' in the internship program at Roman Development Corporation. He calls it the Second-Chance Program, where he hires gang members, mostly Blood Kipo boys. He gives them jobs and claims to rehabilitate them from their criminal ways by pulling them out of poverty."

"But he doesn't really do that?"

"I guess for some it works. Enough to make the program look legitimate. But Max also uses those gang kids for other things. For work outside the law. Oh, not directly, of course. No one could ever tie Max Roman to any specific crimes or gang sets.

But if he wants to buy a certain part of the city, you can bet that crime activity will spike significantly in that area for about two years before he makes an offer."

"Gangs invade, cause trouble, and bring down real estate prices, then?"

"And when values are low, he buys low. Redevelops. Orders the gangs away. Prices rebound in his new 'safe' communities, and he sells at massive profits."

"And Davis?"

"He sent Davis in to learn business with the Kipos. That was my grandson's so-called internship. He put him in a gang, and they went out to rob a jewelry store."

Mama Bliss felt lost again for a moment, reliving the memory. The Raven let silence be their guide, waiting until she was ready. Finally she spoke.

"Police put together the timeline of events afterward," she said. "Seems about right to me." She rattled off dates and times like she was reading a report. "March 10, 2009. At four o'clock a.m. my grandson and two other 'interns' stole illegal guns from an unguarded storage facility. Guns being laundered for overseas distribution." She hesitated, then worked through the choking feeling in her throat. "Next he went to the home of one of the other gang members, where they slept until noon. At one-fifteen they went to a local bar, where they drank and played video games most of the afternoon."

"Nobody asked for ID?" he interrupted.

"Not that kind of bar. Nobody asks any questions about anything over there."

"I see."

"Around six in the evening, they went out for pizza, then back to the gangbanger's apartment. At 8:45 p.m., they arrived at Perimeter Mall up in Dunwoody. At 8:58, they stormed into

Zales Jewelers, demanding jewelry and cash. What they didn't know was that they'd been spotted ten minutes earlier by a suspicious security guard when they first entered the mall. That guard saw a trio of drunk, loud gang members up to no good, and he called the police. He also followed them to the jewelry store, talking to the 911 operator the whole time, narrating where they were and what was going on.

"At three minutes after nine o'clock, the police had them trapped inside the store, with hostages. SWAT arrived shortly after that. One of those drunk gang members panicked and fired a warning shot to keep the hostages subdued. Police thought the robbers were killing hostages, returned fire, and stormed the store.

"There was only one casualty—Davis Walker Monroe, age nineteen." Bliss didn't bother holding back the tears now. It just didn't seem worth it. "My baby. My baby boy. He was supposed to change the world. He could have changed the world. And now he's nothing but dust, dust, dust."

Bliss's head hung low, dripping moisture on her comfortable old nightgown. Her shoulders trembled, and her hands lay flat in her lap. She hadn't told that story, even to herself, in a long, long time.

My baby, she kept repeating to herself. *My Davis, my big man. I'm sorry, baby, I'm so sorry.*

She didn't hear The Raven get up from his chair, nor did she notice him walk across the room and kneel down beside her. She jumped when he took her hands in his, gently at first, then with the firmness of someone who knew her pain, who remembered it almost the way she did. She looked at him and saw mourning in his eyes too, and that made her weep even harder. She clung to his hands, and he didn't let go.

There was no need for words then, just the whisper of tears

and the cleansing of sorrow. Finally she'd had enough of crying. She patted his hand, felt the blank space where his pinky finger had been, and then felt him pull away from her.

"You a strange boy," she said, laughing through sniffles. "I think I'm going to like you."

"Well, I'm still scared to death of you." He smiled and stood. "So the names on the picture?" he asked.

She nodded and reached over to pick up her list. "All the people responsible for the end of my grandson." She put a finger beside each name as she read it aloud. "Jameis Jackson. Kipo gang member. He led the little jewelry robbery at the Perimeter Mall. Walter Evans. Another Kipo boy, part of the trio at the mall. Mark Jenson, security guard who called the police. Ashland Forney, the trigger-happy cop who shot Davis in the head."

"All four of those names are lined through," The Raven said.

"Justice done," Bliss said. She squared her jaw.

"And the other names?"

"Maksym Romanenko. The greedy, power-hungry man who used my grandson as a tool and then threw him away like he was nothing."

"And that last name?" he asked.

She looked The Raven dead in the eye. "Justice for all," she said.

Bliss watched his gaze travel from her face down to the list on the back of her picture. He reread the six names there and then paused at the notation scribbled at the bottom of the list. He nodded and read that aloud.

"Nevermore."

29

RAVEN

Atlanta, GA
Old Fourth Ward
Friday, March 31, 11:45 a.m.
14 days to Nevermore

I thought I'd sleep until noon after the night I had. After the week I've had. But here I am at 11:45 in the morning, sitting in my kitchen, sipping on a Mountain Dew and hoping those tasteless frozen waffles I ate an hour ago aren't going to cause me problems later.

I can't stop thinking about Mama Bliss. About Nevermore. About how my next meeting with Max Roman's goons is going to go.

I stayed with Mama Bliss until close to two o'clock in the morning. She told me her story, I told her mine. Then we talked about my new job.

"I think," Mama Bliss said, "after your training in the warehouse, I'm going to use you as my personal security instead of as just a security guard for the store. That means you'll work wherever I am, or wherever I need you to be."

"I don't know if you noticed," I said to her, "but I'm not really built for hand-to-hand combat. And to be honest, even though I grew up in the redneck wilds of Oklahoma City, I've never even held a gun."

"I'm not looking for a bodyguard," she snapped. "Mama Bliss knows how to take care of herself. Didn't you figure that out already?" I remembered that whole *gun aimed at your testicles* speech and had to agree. "I just need you to take that title so Darrent doesn't cause me grief over adding a new salary to the payroll."

"Darrent?"

"My store manager. Right-hand man. You're going to need to get along with him. Darrent runs anything I don't want to run, which nowadays is most everything. He makes sure there's money in the bank to pay all my new-hire thieves and petty criminals."

I knew she was just teasing me then, but that time I heard her words coming from Trudi Coffey's mouth. *Criminal. Petty thief.* For the first time, I didn't like hearing those words, because I thought maybe they were true. Maybe I'd been calling myself a deception specialist just because I didn't want to think of myself as what I really am. A petty thief.

"Sometimes you'll do errands for me. Deliver important things. Take me to meetings, that kind of stuff."

"It's never too soon for a second chance," my daddy used to say. I wonder if that's really true, and if it is, how it might work. *Is Mama Bliss giving me a second chance?*

"You'll be on-call anytime, all hours of the day and night. I take it from your activities tonight that you don't mind night work?"

If I'm going to have to be a slave, I thought, *better to be one for this woman than Max Roman.* I think she must've heard my thoughts then.

"Four weeks," she said. "After four weeks, your obligation to me is paid and you can fly off to wherever you want. And Max Roman will no longer own you. I promise. But you need to trust me and do whatever I tell you to do for the next four weeks." She held out her hand.

"Okay," I said, reaching out to shake hands and finalize the deal. What else was there to do?

After that, she told me to sit quiet while she wrote a letter. She sealed it, wrote a name on the envelope, and handed it to me. "Give that to Max's people when you see them next."

"What is it?"

"If it was your business, I would've read it to you. Just consider it the first errand of your new job as my personal security. Now go home and get some rest. You'll have to go through Darrent's guard training at first, so come in at eight o'clock Monday morning to start your new job in earnest."

I must've looked shocked, because she laughed and said, "Fine. You can start at nine o'clock. Now go home and let me get some sleep before Darrent comes singing down the hall to announce the new day."

When I got home, I put the letter and the two stacks of cash on my coffee table. Just because I was curious, I tore open the binding papers and counted out every bill, laying them flat side by side on my table. When I ran out of room on the table, I moved to the floor. There were one hundred one-hundred-dollar bills. Ten thousand dollars. More money than I'd ever seen, let alone held in my own hands. I pulled them all together in a wad and wrapped a rubber band around it, then left it all next to the letter on the coffee table.

I went to bed. And couldn't sleep. Well, I started to sleep and woke up in a cold sweat, wondering what the nightmare was that made my heart pound the way it did. I spent the whole night this way, dreaming awful things, waking up, trying to go back to sleep, where I'd dream awful things once more. Finally, around eight-thirty, I gave up and went into the kitchen, but I wasn't hungry. Instead, I took half a dozen eggs out of the refrigerator, hard-boiled them, and started practicing some of my basic sleight-of-hand tricks. Eggs Up Your Sleeve. Eggs in Your Pockets. Eggscellent Disappearing Eggs. Those kinds of things.

When I finally tired of that, two hours had gone by. It had been frustrating at first, trying to adjust to having one less finger for sleight-of-hand tricks, but muscle memory helped, and by the time I was done, I felt fairly comfortable again. It felt good.

So I ate a few waffles and tried to decide what to do with the rest of my day. When it got to be almost noon, I was finally feeling tired again.

Now I yawn, take another sip of the sweet nectar of the gods, and check the clock. It's 11:46 when I decide to take a nap. *On the couch this time*, I think. *Just something to take the edge off.*

In the living room, I see Mama Bliss's letter next to the rubber-banded stack of money. It's addressed to Viktor Kostiuk, which worries me a little bit. I'm tempted to steam it open and read it, but I also have a healthy fear of both Mama Bliss and Viktor Kostiuk. In the end, I leave it alone, dropping on the couch and counting backward from one hundred until I fall asleep.

Best I can tell, I make it to eighty-nine before unicorns start dancing in my head.

In my dreams, I think I hear heavy footsteps approaching. Then I feel a jarring thud next to my head and come abruptly awake. Pavlo has kicked the arm of the couch nearest to my head, causing tremors to rumble through me. I'm totally disoriented now, trying to make sense of that world that happens when you think you're still asleep but are really awake.

Am I dreaming? How did they get in? What time is it?

The curtains are closed now and no lights are on, making my apartment a shadowy cave. Around the rim of my windows, I see light peeking through. *Still daytime outside*, I think. *I'm so confused*.

I feel lightheaded and dizzy from lack of sleep, but I sit up anyway. Pavlo is grinning at me hungrily.

"You not going to run?"

"No, I'm not going to run."

My stomach turns somersaults inside me. *Just Pavlo this time?* I wonder. *Or are there others?* As if on cue, Scholarship walks in the open door to my apartment. I'm still confused. I know I locked the new deadbolt on the front door my super repaired after their previous visit. How did they get in?

"How did you get in?" I ask. Pavlo drops a key on the coffee table, next to all the money and the letter.

"Had key made when you were passed out last time." He jerks his head toward Scholarship. "He got tired of kicking door in."

Scholarship sees me, but his attention is focused on the coffee table.

"What time is it?" I ask. "I thought you guys weren't coming until five o'clock."

"Early bird gets the worm," Scholarship says. He doesn't look happy.

I finally find the clock in my living room and see they're actually five hours early, as it's just now twelve o'clock in the afternoon. *High noon*, I think. *Am I in a western movie?*

Scholarship turns to me now, ignoring the cash on the table.

"How's your hand, kid?" he asks. "No infections? Pain managed?" He motions to Pavlo. "Look at his hand."

"It's fine," the Ukrainian says, dismissing the order. "I did good job. You saw. Very pretty."

"Look at his hand, Pav. And be gentle. Remember, I like this kid more than I like you."

Pavlo grumbles a bit, but he obeys, taking up my left hand with his meaty fingers, peeling away the bandage to inspect the scar tissue. He re-tapes the gauze and lets my hand drop.

"Fine. Looks good. No problems."

Scholarship nods, a short single head bob that stops quickly and silences his partner. Pavlo jams his hands in his pockets and steps back toward the balcony door. The football player crosses his arms over his chest, and I see him adding the money in his head.

"You hungry?" I say. I can't resist. "I boiled a couple of eggs for you. They're in the fridge."

His face relaxes at that. I'm beginning to think this big, mean monster really does like me. He turns and takes a seat in the lawn chair I've set up next to the couch. Pavlo remains standing.

"Looks like you've been busy, kid," Scholarship says, nodding toward the coffee table.

"Idle hands are the devil's workshop," I say. "That's what my daddy used to say."

"Mine too," he says. "Right before he beat the devil out of me with a belt."

I think he's making a joke, but his eyes aren't laughing, so I don't laugh either.

"We sent you to retrieve a logbook," he says. "I don't see it here. You want to explain?"

My palms feel trembly all of a sudden, and honest to goodness, I think my elbows are sweating. "I, uh, I got the money," I say.

"Here, it's all here. Ten thousand dollars." My voice cracks on the word *here*, which is embarrassing, but at least Scholarship is polite enough to ignore that. I gather up the cash and hold it out to him.

He doesn't take it. Pavlo fidgets by the balcony window.

"What about the logbook?" Scholarship says. "You were supposed to bring me a logbook."

There's a quiet fury in his manner now that I've never seen before, not even when he was hitting me during the "This Is You, Lying" game on our first night. *Is he mad about the money? I wonder. Doesn't he want ten thousand dollars?*

"I—" I'm not sure how much I should reveal about Mama Bliss's office, about the new deal I've struck with her. I shrug, and I realize I'm pleading with him now. "I got the money instead. You said Mr. Roman wanted ten thousand dollars, so I got ten thousand dollars. Did I do something wrong?"

I watch his head tilt down a notch, studying me. I try again to hand him the wad of cash, but he still doesn't take it, and I'm left hanging stupidly, arm outstretched, waiting for him to respond. He doesn't take his eyes off me, but he does speak to Pavlo.

"Count it."

The dumpy Ukrainian grabs the cash eagerly. Apparently he likes money more than his partner. I watch his lips move as he silently paws through the bills, tallying them in his head.

"Ten thousand dollars," he announces at last. At least he's happy about it.

Scholarship holds out a football-sized hand and receives the money from his partner. He quickly counts ten one-hundred-dollar bills off the top and tosses them back onto the coffee table toward me. "Credit for your deposit," he says. He folds the rest and hides them away in a coat pocket. "Now," he says, nodding toward the letter from Mama Bliss, "what's that?"

"It's for Viktor. Uh, Mr. Kostiuk."

"I can see that, kid. What is it?"

I'm suddenly glad that I didn't steam open Mama's letter. Now I can speak without trying to cover a lie. "I honestly don't know. I was just told to give it to Mr. Kostiuk."

"Here," Pavlo says, "I'll see what it—"

Scholarship's sudden movement is surprising, but the crushing fierceness of the blow to the side of his partner's head is what takes my breath away.

Pavlo was leaning down to pick up the letter, so the hammer-fist to his right ear had downward force added to the football player's strength when it connected with the Ukrainian's skull. Pavlo is not a small man, but he's rattled by the big man's punch, stumbling like a drunken prizefighter, his left cheek smacking against the coffee table as he tumbles down onto his backside. There's a little blood mark left on my table, but I can't tell exactly where it came from. Then I see that Pavlo actually bit his own lip when he got hit and that he's now licking that lip like a dog trying to stop the flow of blood.

One punch from Scholarship can take out a meaty guy like Pavlo?

I feel stunned, as well. I realize for the first time that back when we first met, when we played our sadistic punching game, Scholarship was holding back, taking it easy when he whacked me. If he'd hit me like he just hit Pavlo, I might still be in a coma.

I'm suddenly grateful for small blessings.

Breath bursts through Scholarship's nostrils like a bull snorting in a ring. "You never, *never*, take something that belongs to Viktor Kostiuk," he says.

Both Pavlo and I nod our heads in understanding. That's a lesson learned for both of us.

The Ukrainian struggles to his feet. His eyes are glassy, and

I can tell he's still a little dazed. If this were a boxing match, the referee would stop the fight.

Scholarship is towering over his partner now. "You have something to say to me?" he says.

Pavlo nods, eyes watering and avoiding direct contact. "Thank you for correcting me," he says carefully. His speech is slightly slurred, and I wonder if he might have a concussion. Scholarship nods and settles back into my lawn chair. Pavlo stumbles back to a spot by the balcony door, clearly disoriented, hand holding the right side of his face.

Scholarship turns his attention to me again. "You are just full of surprises," he says to me, and he smiles. "Like I told Max Roman myself, you're a man of unique talent."

"So," I say after a moment more under his scrutiny, "what do we do now?" I'm honestly afraid to reach down and pick up that letter, even to hand it to him. He's made no move to take it, either. I hear the Ukrainian muttering under his breath, but I can't make out what he's saying. His face has gone unpleasantly pale, and his body is swaying just a bit, like he might pass out after all. I hope he doesn't spew all over my carpet. This place is dirty enough as it is.

"Pavlo," Scholarship orders, "call Viktor. Ask him if he might be willing to join us at our deception specialist's apartment." He looks over at his partner and wrinkles his nose at the sight. "And go vomit in the bathroom already. Don't make a mess out here, or you'll be sorry."

Pavlo nods and heads down the short hallway in my apartment. A moment later, we hear his porcelain chorus.

"Shut the door!" Scholarship yells.

Pavlo interrupts his symphony long enough to obey, and finally we're alone.

The football player stands and glances around the living

room. "That was for you as much as it was for him," Scholarship says to the room.

"What?" I ask.

"I didn't like the way he knocked you around last time we were here. Seemed unnecessary. Violence should always be necessary."

"Oh."

Now he ambles toward the kitchen as though nothing has happened, like we're old roommates just spending the day hanging out, taking it easy. "You say there's hard-boiled eggs in here? What about toast? You got bread and butter too?"

"Uh, yeah. Help yourself."

30

TRUDI

Atlanta, GA
West Midtown
Friday, March 31, 12:11 p.m.
14 days to Nevermore

"Ms. Coffey," Eulalie's voice said through the intercom, "Detective Hill is here offering to buy us both lunch at CozyFloyd's BBQ in Douglasville."

"It's worth the twenty-minute drive," Samuel's voice hollered from the reception area.

Trudi pushed aside the keyboard on her computer and leaned toward the com. "Why can't we go to the one just down the street?" she said.

"Closed three months ago," Eulalie said. "Remember?"

Trudi nodded to no one. Yes, now that Eula mentioned it, she did remember them talking about it some weeks ago. But sometimes little details like that didn't stick around in her brain, and she'd forgotten it almost immediately. Before she could respond, though, Samuel was standing in the doorway to her office, holding a manila envelope in one hand.

"Come on," he said. "I'm hungry and I've got a craving for CozyFloyd's. It'll do us all good to get out of our offices on this partly-cloudy-with-forty-percent-chance-of-rain day."

He looked clean and rested, nothing like she felt after they'd both stayed up past two in the morning discussing the events at Mama Bliss's warehouse. She could almost feel the bags under her eyes etching their way into permanence, and here he stood as if he'd never age past twenty-nine.

"You go," she said. Then, just because it seemed the polite thing to say, not because she wanted to say it, she added, "Take Eulalie with you. She'll enjoy it. But leave me that envelope. Is it what I think it is?"

Samuel hesitated, tapped the manila file on his left hand, then said, "Hang on." He went back into the reception area briefly, then returned to Trudi's office. "I told her we'd do CozyFloyd's another day," he said.

I'll bet you did, she thought grimly.

"When all three of us can go together."

Oh.

Samuel spotted the *Atlanta Journal-Constitution* on the corner of Trudi's desk. "May I?" he said. She handed him the appropriate section. He flipped through the personal ads quickly, then nodded and dropped the paper back in the stack. Curiosity satisfied, he held up the manila envelope for Trudi. "I got results on those fingerprints you gave me, the ones from the street magician." Trudi held out her hand, but he didn't pass it to her. "I've looked at these," he said, "and I'm going to tell you there's nothing really unusual in here. Nothing suspicious."

"So hand it over," she said.

"I'm telling you this because there's a point at which you

taking this information could be viewed as stalking, and you've made it clear you're not a stalker."

Trudi considered her ex-husband's words. Was she stalking a kid who had a crush on her? If Samuel had dismissed him as a suspect in the Nevermore case, then did she really need to know his true identity and criminal background? Of course she did, she reasoned. She needed to know simply because she needed to know, and that was good enough for her even if it wasn't good enough for Samuel.

"I'm just double-checking leads for your case," she covered. "Two minds are better than one, all that stuff. It's not stalking."

"Except I'm telling you I'm almost certain this guy has nothing to do with Nevermore."

"Sounds more like you're trying to hide something from me." She leaned back in her chair, eyes narrowing.

"Suit yourself." He tossed the file onto her desk. "He's from Oklahoma City. His real name is Tyson Elvis Miller."

"Elvis?"

"I know. Pretty great, huh? Wish my mom had given me Elvis for a middle name. Or Danger. That would have been fun too."

"To go around saying, 'Danger is my middle name'?"

"Yeah." He looked almost dreamy. "Ooh, Ready as a middle name would be great too. Then when people asked if I was ready to go, I could say, 'I'm always Ready.'" She could almost see a lightbulb flash above his head. "You know, it's not too late. Think I should file the paperwork to add another middle name?"

Trudi resisted the urge to say something sarcastic. "You've already got two middle names. That's plenty." She reached for the envelope.

"Well, anyway," he continued, "young Mr. Miller got arrested and had his license revoked about four years ago for drunk driving, reckless endangerment, and underage alcohol possession.

Apparently there was an accident that caused injury. He skipped the trial, so there's a bench warrant in force if he ever goes back to Oklahoma. Beyond that, he's stayed fairly clean. There was one complaint about panhandling in Baltimore, but no formal charges filed. That's about it."

She opened the envelope and skimmed the contents. It was pretty much the same as Samuel's summary, except that the mug shot from the drunk driving arrest showed him with two black eyes and a bruised cheek. *Does this guy ever not get beat up?* she wondered.

"Anything else?" she said. "Did you do a full background check or just the arrest history?"

"Fingerprint identification, arrest history, and sex offender registry. No hits as a sex offender, so that's good for you. For the rest, I figured you could do a full background check from here since you know who he is now. But honestly, I can't see any compelling investigative reason for a full background. Unless you just want to vet a potential boyfriend."

"Oh, please." She held up the pages. "Thanks for this, Samuel. I'm still not convinced that Tyson Elvis Miller isn't connected to Nevermore, but at least now we know who we're dealing with."

"Okay." He stood up. "Let me know if you uncover something. I'm going to get something to eat over at Arby's. Want me to bring a sandwich back for you?"

He was asking to spend a little more time with her, she knew. Looking for an excuse to stay around. He was sweet that way. Unless he just wanted to spend time hanging around Eulalie. In that case he was still a pig.

"No," she said. "Let me work. I'll text you if something looks interesting."

He hesitated. A few years ago, this was the moment when they'd share a little goodbye kiss. She felt like he was considering it now, so she said pointedly, "Goodbye, Samuel. Enjoy your lunch."

"Okay, I'll see you," he said sheepishly, and he headed out.

After he was gone, Trudi logged into her account on the BKGUSA website. There were a number of commercial background check companies out there for licensed private investigators, but she liked BKG best because they did a bit more robust search through a number of records, combing the less-frequented databases and social networks that sometimes yielded out-of-the-ordinary results. For a modest extra fee, they also cross-referenced relevant county court records with items in the national criminal record database, and even included brief family histories from the county records too. She entered the name Tyson Elvis Miller, along with his social security number and date of birth. Then she waited.

The initial summary report appeared after about two minutes, but it didn't give much more than the information Samuel had already provided. The report she wanted was the "Detailed Digest" that would itemize by date and event. That could take up to two hours to compile, she knew.

She wandered away from her desk and out into the reception area. "Eula," she said, "have you eaten lunch yet?"

"Not yet," the receptionist said.

"Come on," Trudi said. "I'm buying today."

Eulalie dimpled and reached for her purse. "Awesome. Where are we going?"

"Well, now that Samuel's got me thinking about it, I've got a real craving for CozyFloyd's BBQ."

When they got back from lunch, Trudi found two things waiting for her.

"Looks like we had a delivery," Eulalie said. A cardboard FedEx Letter envelope was leaning against the office door. Trudi picked it up and took it inside. She was surprised to find there was no packing slip or air bill with the envelope, something she thought was required on all FedEx deliveries. *Maybe it fell out somewhere along the way,* she told herself. *Or got lost when the courier dropped it off at our door.*

Inside, on her computer, she found the completed background check for Tyson Elvis Miller waiting in her email inbox. She was definitely curious to see that. But first things first.

She tore open the FedEx envelope and found what looked like a packet from a travel agent. There was no cover letter, no explanation at all really. But the packet included two airplane tickets to Kahului Airport on the Hawaiian Island of Maui, hotel reservations for something called the "Ocean View Prime Executive Suite" at the Four Seasons Maui at Wailea Resort, and a reservation with Hertz Rent-a-Car. The names on the airplane tickets and all the reservations were the same: Trudi Coffey and Samuel Hill.

"What in the world?"

Trudi couldn't make sense of this. Was Samuel planning some kind of surprise trip for them? Was he hoping a grand romantic gesture would make amends for his past sins?

She spread the travel papers on her desk and gave them a closer look. Everything looked legitimate and had been prepaid. Just to double-check, she logged onto aa.com, the homepage for American Airlines, and entered the reservation number on her plane ticket. It popped up as an active reservation for April, waiting for her to fly from Atlanta to Los Angeles, and then from L.A. to Maui.

Maybe his travel agent accidentally sent the paperwork to me instead of to him? She scanned over everything and suddenly thought, *Hawaii sounds really good. Why have I never been to Hawaii before?* Then she frowned. Nothing was as good as it seemed, not when it came unexpectedly like this.

"Eulalie." Trudi spoke into the intercom. "Would you please get Samuel on the phone for me?"

"Right away" came the reply. A minute later, her desk phone

buzzed to tell her a call was waiting. She picked up the receiver and heard Samuel on the other end.

"Hey, Tru-Bear," he said. "You find something?"

"No," she said. "I just wanted to check with you. Are you planning a trip?"

"Not that I know of," he said, chuckling. "Unless you want to take me to Hawaii for the weekend."

She checked the dates on the plane tickets. "Well, your reservations say we're going for two weeks. Want to explain that?"

"Wait, what? What are you talking about? I was just joking."

"Seriously, Samuel, is this all a joke to you, or what? Because it's not funny."

"Okay, I'm really confused now. Are we talking about the same thing?"

"I'm talking about Hawaii."

"Why are you talking about Hawaii? Are you taking a vacation? Because if you could wait until we crack this Nevermore case before you go, that'd be really helpful for me."

"What?"

"I mean, of course you deserve a vacation, and if you want to go, then that's great. But is that why you called, to tell me you're leaving town for a while?"

"Samuel, what are you talking about? Did you do this or not?"

There was a moment of silence on the other end of the line before he finally said, "Um, Trudi. Why don't we start this conversation over? You start, and I'll just listen this time. Tell me why you called."

Trudi rubbed her temples. He actually sounded like he had no idea what was going on. She picked up the airplane tickets.

"Right now," she said slowly, "I'm holding in my hand two round-trip tickets to Maui, Hawaii. They came by FedEx this afternoon."

A stunned silence, then, "Any clues who sent the tickets?"

"No," Trudi said. She reached over to reinspect the cardboard envelope. "No air bill was included."

"It's possible FedEx had nothing to do with it, then," Samuel said. "It's pretty easy to pick up one of their envelopes from a drop box, then just deliver it yourself if you want anonymity."

"I suppose so. There are also hotel and car reservations in here, all pre-paid. The names on everything are yours and mine. Coffey and Hill. So, what I'm asking is, did you do this or not? Are you planning for us to take a trip to Hawaii?"

He didn't respond at first.

"Samuel?" she said.

"Hold on, I'm thinking," he said.

She tapped a fingernail on the desk. "Look," she said, "why don't you call me back when you figure out a good story to—"

"Hang on, Tru-Bear. No, I didn't buy that stuff. No, I'm not planning a surprise trip to Hawaii, even though that sounds like a great idea. So I'm trying to figure out who would do this. What are the dates for the trip?"

Trudi checked the plane tickets again to be sure she got them right. "Flight leaves Atlanta on Saturday, April 8, returning two weeks later on April 22."

"Hmm. Now could you check your tickets to that fundraiser dinner for Max Roman? What day is that?"

Trudi opened a desk drawer and pulled out the tickets that Viktor Kostiuk had given her. Her lips went thin when she saw the date. "April 14," she said. "Smack-dab in the middle of our free Hawaiian vacation."

"So . . ." Samuel said, and Trudi finished his thought for him.

"Somebody wants us out of the way when Max Roman holds his gala event."

31

RAVEN

Atlanta, GA
Old Fourth Ward
Friday, March 31, 1:01 p.m.
14 days to Nevermore

"What's his problem?"

Viktor Kostiuk enters my apartment like it's his own property. He doesn't knock, doesn't even expect it to be locked. Just walks in, surveys the room, and immediately takes command.

"He's got an upset stomach," Scholarship answers him.

"Yeah," Pavlo echoes from the couch next to me. "Sick."

Viktor pauses to look at the football player, who shrugs and stands up from the lawn chair in my living room.

"All right, then," Viktor says. "If you're going to throw up, get to the bathroom. No Ukrainian mamas here to clean up after you, cousin."

Pavlo almost smiles. Apparently they have some kind of shared history from the old country, something that Pavlo counts as an asset.

I feel fidgety and clumsy, but I'm not sure what I'm supposed to do right now. Scholarship is standing, but Pavlo is still planted firmly on the couch. Do I stand? Or wait to be told to stand? Do I speak, or wait to be spoken to? I decide that silence is golden and keep my mouth shut. I also try to stop my right knee from bobbing up and down nervously.

Viktor gives me an appraising glance, then turns back to the football player standing beside him. "You want to catch me up? Where's the logbook?"

"No logbook." Scholarship shakes his head. Viktor's eyes snap back to me, and I see his nostrils flare out wide. "He brought us this instead."

The big man pulls my folded cash out of his pocket but doesn't open it up for counting.

Viktor nods slowly. "How much?"

"Nine thousand."

Now the boss man rubs the bottom of his chin with manicured fingers, and I see his eyes widen slightly. "Mm," he says. He steps toward me and puts a foot up on my coffee table. "Well, that's what we asked him for, isn't it?" No one says anything, so he continues. "Good for you, boy. You're more resourceful than I thought."

Scholarship looks pleased at that. "I told you he was unique," he says.

"Yes," Viktor says, still looking at me. "You're an excellent judge of talent."

"There's more, Vicky," Pavlo pipes up. He doesn't want to be left out of Viktor's approval, I guess.

"I can see that, cousin." Viktor taps his foot on top of my coffee table, gently disturbing the envelope next to his high-gloss, imported leather shoe. "What's this, Raven?"

"A, uh, it's a letter. For you."

"Who's it from?"

I have to clear my throat, it feels so dry right now. "It's from the woman who caught me trying to steal her logbook."

Viktor smiles like a wolf and takes his foot off the table. He turns and walks to the window overlooking my balcony. "What's it say?"

"I don't know. I didn't read it." Once again I'm very happy I didn't give in to the temptation to steam open that letter. I glance over at Pavlo suffering in silence next to me. "Nobody did."

Viktor nods at the gray skies outside. I think he's trying to make it rain, just because he can. But the clouds hold back on him, at least for now. He holds out a hand, still staring at the sky. The football player leans over and scoops up the letter, depositing it into Viktor's open palm. The boss man tears off one end of the envelope and then reads the words meant for him. No one moves while he reads. After a moment, he shoves the paper toward Scholarship, who also reads it.

Pavlo stands up, eager to see what the other two have now seen, but Viktor folds the letter into thirds and taps it on his left palm, thinking.

"All right, then," he says suddenly. "Nice doing business with you, Raven."

He drops the folded letter on my coffee table and motions for everyone to leave. I can see it's killing Pavlo, not knowing what's going on, and to be honest, I'm pretty confused by it too. But I see three dangerous men leaving my life, so I've got that going for me.

"Come on, Pav," Scholarship says. "Time to go." He leads the dumpy Ukrainian toward the door. After they're gone, Viktor and I are alone for a moment in my apartment. He nods approvingly toward me, a motion that seems like grudging respect.

"See you on April 14," he says. Then, like the others, he disappears through my front door.

"April 14?" I say to the empty living room. "What's that about?"

I reach down and unfold the letter Mama Bliss sent to Viktor Kostiuk. The handwriting is deliberate, maybe a little shaky, but the words speak with authority and confidence.

Viktor,

  This magician boy is working for me now. That means he's under my protection. This is non-negotiable. If your boss has a problem with that, tell him to come talk to me about it and I will explain it to him so he understands.

  As a gesture of goodwill, though, I will make my magician available, free of charge, to perform as table entertainment at your boss's upcoming fundraising dinner and charity auction. Consider it a charitable donation from the Secret Stash.

    Bliss J. Monroe

I know what table entertainment is. It's the guy or girl—or mariachi band—at a restaurant that travels from table to table doing two-minute routines to entertain the guests having dinner. If I'm TE, I'm doing little card tricks and simple mind-reading games for customers.

"April 14?" I say again to nobody. "I guess that's when I'm performing at tables for a Max Roman fundraiser." I kind of wish Mama Bliss had mentioned that to me when we were talking in the wee hours of the morning. I wonder why she didn't.

I hear a sound, and Scholarship is suddenly standing in my doorframe again. "Forgot my drink," he says. He heads to the kitchen and comes out a second later with a can from my stash of Mountain Dew. He stops and gives what appears to be a look of paternal approval.

"That was a good play," he says to me. "Unexpected. Your best trick so far, I think."

I'm not sure what to say, but I don't have to respond because he continues as if he's talking to himself.

"Not even Viktor would have predicted that." He raises the Mountain Dew in salute. "Still, you should be aware that Mama Bliss can be a mixed blessing. She'll protect you from Max Roman, for sure. Even from Viktor and me. But if she wants to, she can make your life a living nightmare."

He heads to the exit. "See you on April 14." He closes the door behind him, and I'm alone again.

"Thank you, Jesus."

Did I really just say that out loud? And mean it? I almost grin.

Dad would be happy to know God and I are on speaking terms again, I think. Then I remember. *Of course, my daddy and I still aren't on speaking terms.*

I don't blame him, really. I wouldn't speak to me either.

I was already halfway through the Hawaiian Punch, about a third down in the pint of Everclear, and forty minutes late when I finally remembered I was supposed to pick up my mom at the doctor's.

"I'm fine," I told myself. "Maybe she won't notice. Maybe she had to wait for the doctor anyway."

Ten minutes later, I pulled into the parking lot and saw her, waiting, sitting on a metal bench situated beside the front door of the doctor's office. I think she might have been praying because her eyes were closed and she didn't notice my car at first. Either that or she was angry and trying a little meditation to calm her nerves.

I tapped lightly on the horn, and her eyes flew open. The first emotion I registered on her face was relief, followed quickly by irritation.

"Where have you been?" she said breathlessly when she got in the car. "I was worried you might have been in an accident or something."

"Nah," I exhaled. "Just lost track of time. I'm sorry."

"Lost track of—" She stopped. "Why do I smell alcohol in here?"

"Who knows? It's your nose, not mine." I thought that was pretty funny at the time. Mom didn't share my drunken sense of humor.

"Tyson."

"I'm fine, Mom," I said, straightening in my seat and cutting off my sluggish laughter. I made a left turn and headed toward the I-35 freeway. "I'm sorry. I lost track of time. I'll get you home real fast, though, so you and Dad can get on with your painless, boring lives."

"Honey, don't. Your father and I both love you. There's no need to be angry at me." There was hurt in her voice. She reached out and touched my shoulder gently. "Pull over and let me drive, baby. You can rest awhile at my house. Your dad won't be home until late tonight, and we just won't tell him about this, not this time, okay?"

"I'm fine." I didn't shout at her. I never shouted at my mom, not like I shouted at my dad at least. But now I was getting irritated. I shrugged her hand off my arm. *I'm fine*, I told myself again.

"Tyson—"

That was the last word I ever heard my mother speak. *Tyson.* My name. That was it. Up to that point, I'd always kind of believed that a person's last words would be important, that they'd mean something significant, like "Give me liberty or give me death." I never thought that they could just be an interrupted sentence. Just a lost moment trying to talk sense into your stubborn eighteen-year-old son's head.

I still don't believe there was a traffic light at the corner of Northeast 23rd Street and Martin Luther King Avenue.

And if there was a light, I can't fathom how there was no car stopped at the light in front of me or how I missed seeing that it was red.

All I remember is seeing the Ralph Ellison Library coming up on my right, hearing my mom say, "Tyson," and then feeling the impact as that lady's northbound SUV plowed into the passenger side of my rusty old Mustang.

There was shattered glass everywhere.

I must've blacked out a little, because when I blinked my eyes, my car was stopped and lights were flashing and people were yelling and there were suddenly prickly little shards scraping my neck and in my hair and covering the driver's-side airbag that was already deflating in my lap. The window beside my left ear was cracked and broken where my head, or the airbag, I wasn't sure which, had smacked into it. I felt woozy, but I couldn't tell if that was from the accident or the Everclear. And I felt exhilarated. Almost giddy. I'd just had a near-death experience and, from what I could tell, had only suffered some minor cuts and bruises.

"Whoo!" I said. "That was something, huh, Mom?"

She didn't answer.

I looked at the passenger seat, and it slowly registered with me that my mother's airbag had failed to deploy.

"Mom?"

She wouldn't speak to me. She didn't speak to me at all. She just stared past me, looking at nothing, seeing everything. There was an ugly red gash that ran across the side of her head, into her temple, and across part of her forehead. Blood spilled down the right side of her face, and I knew instantly what I'd done, what I could never change, what I could never forgive.

"Mom."

Her skin was eerily pale. Her body stayed upright, held in place by the seat belt. I smelled alcohol and copper and the awful stench of fear.

Beside me, someone finally wrenched open the driver's-side door, said something about getting me out to safety. But I heard only one word, repeated over and over in my concussed head.

Tyson.

My father and I didn't talk after the accident. We've never talked since that stupid, stubborn, awful, drunken moment that took my mother from us all.

The police arrested me for drunk driving and a few other random crimes. They threatened to charge me with involuntary manslaughter, but in the end, they went with reckless endangerment. I never knew exactly why. Either way, that night I found myself in a jail cell with the beginnings of a nasty hangover.

I heard that my father came unhinged when they told him what had happened, that he was in his office at the church when the call came, and that his secretary found him crumpled under his desk, weeping uncontrollably, lost to the world.

There was only one person to blame: me.

My dad left me rotting in jail overnight. After one of my roommates finally bailed me out the next morning, I did what came naturally. I ran, from everything and everybody. I put all my earthly possessions into one oversized backpack, got on a bus to Nashville, and never looked back. When Dad's private investigator tracked me down in Nashville, I paid off the PI to keep quiet and sneaked away to Baltimore during the night. When I ruined Baltimore, Atlanta was next.

And now what?

Maybe it's time to fly away again, I think. *That's what I do best, after all.*

Now that I'm free of Max Roman, the impulse to run is strong. I've done it before, I can do it again. Fly out of this town with not much more than the clothes on my back, land someplace new, someplace big where I can get lost. Change my name. Again. Start over.

I look at the coffee table, and there's ten one-hundred-dollar bills telling me to go. But something inside is holding me back.

You have a restless little soul, son.

My daddy used to tell me that.

But whose voice is this now, speaking silently into my being?

Like that raven in the Great Flood.

I've heard this soundless voice before, I think. *It's been a long time.*

My living room is still, the air stagnant around me, the sounds of the day outside distant and dim. I find myself sitting on my couch again, straining to listen, wishing I could hear . . . anything. In front of me is a letter from Mama Bliss and a thousand dollars in cash. I hear myself exhale.

"So what do you think, Jesus?"

It's a hoarse whisper, but I know we both hear it. I'm surprised at how easily I can fall back into praying, even after all these years.

Nobody says anything.

Not me, not him.

But I feel something I didn't think I was ready for.

Before I can stop myself, my chest shakes with choking

tremors and my stomach clenches like it's doing push-ups without my consent. I can't cut off the flow of tears. They drip down my face like little rivulets of pain, soaking my cheeks and the front of my shirt.

Why am I crying?

I tell myself I want to stop, but something inside won't let me. I realize I haven't cried since . . . since I left Oklahoma City four years ago, when I was eighteen. When I had to run.

"I'm sorry."

I mean it this time. I have no excuses, not anymore. I have no backup options, not now. No escape plan. Just me, finally facing me.

I'm sorry, Daddy.

I'm sorry, Mom. I'm so, so sorry.

And the hardest of all. *I'm sorry, Jesus. For blaming you, for hating you. For running from you.*

The world is silent, save for a stupid, stubborn street magician—deception specialist—quietly losing his all, and gaining back something he thought he'd given up long ago.

Finally the waterworks begin to dry up. My circumstance hasn't changed, not really. I'm still the drunk who caused the car crash that killed my mom, and the guilty criminal who ran away from judgment instead of facing it. I'm still the child who can't, who won't, call his own father to make amends, at least not yet. And I'm still looking at a table with a thousand dollars and a protection letter, trying to figure out if Mama Bliss is actually looking out for me or just using me as cover for something else.

But somehow, even though my broken life is the same as it was five minutes ago, everything feels different inside. Hopeful, maybe? I'm not sure, but it's definitely not the same.

"So," I wonder aloud, wiping tear-smear off my face, "now

what?" *Maybe I should call Detective Hill after all, arrange to meet him for real?* I consider the idea for a moment, but that moment passes quickly when I realize suddenly there's one more apology I need to make. *She'll probably never want to see me again*, I think, but I send the text anyway.

Three words, and that's enough.

I'm sorry, Trudi.

I wait awhile, checking my cell phone every few minutes, hoping. But, as expected, she doesn't answer.

32

BLISS

Atlanta, GA
Little Five Points
Friday, March 31, 1:49 p.m.
14 days to Nevermore

"He's here, Mama. As you requested."

Bliss rolled her wheelchair out from behind the desk in her back office. Darrent was standing in the hallway, leaning in, trying not to intrude on her private space.

"Well, bring him in, honey," she said. "Time we met, I think."

Darrent nodded and disappeared. A moment later, he reappeared with a young man in tow. The teen was handsome, in that thug-lifestyle kind of way. She could tell he'd been coached on how to dress and carry himself when meeting Mama Bliss. His neck and hands were empty of the clunky jewelry Kipo boys often adorned themselves with, though he did have a diamond stud earring in one lobe. He wore baggy jeans and a black Falcons jersey, and under the jersey she could see a gathering of tattoos that decorated his arms. His hair was braided into neat cornrows, and his face was scrubbed and clean.

She liked his eyes. They were light brown, alive. *Shame*, she told herself, *that he got himself mixed up in a Max Roman gang.*

"Have a seat," she said.

He nodded and sat in one of the chairs at the small table in her office. Darrent took the invitation too, sitting next to him. Bliss surveyed them both for a moment.

"You know why you're here, honey?" she said.

He shook his head. "He told me to come." He motioned to Darrent. "We don't like to argue with him."

Bliss nodded. "You know who I am?" she said.

"I heard of you," he said.

"What you hear?"

"You don't like Kipo in Little Five Points."

Bliss cocked her head toward Darrent, then raised her eyebrows at the teen. "You Kipo, honey?"

"No," he said, sitting up uneasily in his seat. "Not anymore."

"Redemption come for you?" she said. "You saw the error of your ways? Turned over a new leaf? Got a new job and making a contribution to society now?"

"Something like that." He looked nervously at Darrent, then back at Mama Bliss.

"Good. Now wait in the hall." She turned her back on him and rolled toward her desk.

"Go on," Darrent said. "Do as Mama says. You wait for me to come get you, got it?"

"Yes, sir," he mumbled. A moment later, Bliss and Darrent were alone.

"So," Bliss said from behind the desk, "that's little Andy Carr. Don't seem like much."

"He's been through a few ordeals lately."

"Can he be trusted?"

"Nobody can really be trusted, can they?" Darrent said, and Bliss smiled. He was parroting her late husband, and they both knew it.

"You know what I mean."

"Yes, he knows what he's supposed to do. And he's got incentive to do it."

"I should hope so," Bliss said. "His bail money alone was a nice chunk of incentive."

Darrent nodded. "True," he said, "but now he's got more riding on this than just that. He'll do what he's supposed to do."

"Where you been hiding him?"

"After his uncle got him out, we took him up to Jasper, just south of the border of Tennessee. Isolated him out on forty acres, on a farm with cows and pigs, a racist overseer, and a few angry rednecks. Let him know that some places are actually worse than prison. He was happy to come back to civilization."

Bliss paused to take a good look at her senior manager. "You are good at taming things, Darrent," she said. "I mean, look how you got me tamed."

A short laugh broke through his lips. "Mama," he said, "nobody's ever been able to tame you. Not even William, and I know he tried."

She smiled in spite of herself. "What about you?" she asked.

"I'm all set."

"Your vacation?"

"Yep. A long cruise. Leaves in a week."

Bliss nodded. "You're going to enjoy that," she said. "Time on a boat is like time without worry."

"Well, that's what William used to say."

Bliss felt warmed that he'd recognized her husband's sentiments. "What about the other reformed Kipo boys? They in place?"

"For the last three weeks," he said.

She sighed.

"You've done well, Mama," Darrent said softly. "William would be proud of you."

Couldn't have done it without you, she thought, but aloud she said, "Well, we'll see. Nothing's done till it's done."

He nodded. "Ready to make the call?" he said, returning to his seat at the table.

"Yeah," she said, but she hesitated. "I hate to see Samuel Hill mixed up in this, Darrent. I've known him for years. I owe him a little bit, owe him in ways he doesn't even know about."

"I know, Mama." To his credit, Darrent didn't try to say anything else, didn't try to convince her that his way was best. He just waited, loyal soldier to the end.

"Almost done, though, aren't we, Darrent?"

"Almost, Mama."

"You're going to enjoy that cruise," she said again. Then she tapped the speaker button on her telephone and dialed a number.

"Samuel Hill," a voice said after the second ring. "Mama Bliss, is that you?"

"I'll never get used to that calling-ID thing," Bliss said.

"Sorry, Mama," Samuel said. "How are you feeling this afternoon? Did you get any rest last night?"

"A little. Slept in. Got up in time for lunch."

"How's your security guard?"

"Still stupid, but his ankle's going to heal, if that's what you're asking. He's all wrapped up and sitting pretty at home now, eager to collect worker's compensation from me."

"Well, that's good—except for the worker's comp thing, I mean." There was a strained silence between them. Bliss let it linger just a moment longer than she normally would have. She wanted this call to go the way she'd planned it.

"All right, Samuel," she said finally, "you waiting for me to apologize? I apologize. I was cross and cranky last night, and I took it out on you and that sweet little Trudi. I'm sorry. You happy now?"

She heard him squirming. She liked that. "Aw, Mama, hey, it was a strange situation. And I'm sorry too. I never would have come storming in if I hadn't heard a gunshot."

"All is forgiven, sugar. Now, you wanted to ask me some questions last night. I'm rested and awake now. Tell me what you need to know, and I'll tell you anything I can."

She held her breath. Now would be when she'd find out whether or not he still trusted her.

"Sure, Mama. Thanks. You want me to come by and we can talk in person?"

"No, Samuel. Believe it or not, I got other work to do today than babysit you." She kept her voice light, teasing, trying to keep him off balance without antagonizing him. "What is it you want to ask?"

"All right, Mama. Now, some of these questions might seem odd, considering our friendship. But I'm just trying to follow all leads and rule out things that need to be ruled out."

"Sugar, do you think this is the first time a police detective ever questioned me about something going on in Little Five Points? Ask your questions. I'll answer with the truth." She was lying, of course, but he didn't know that.

"All right. First let's talk about that street magician."

"The Raven. What you want to know?"

"Well, I saw him last night. He broke into your warehouse, but he never came out."

She raised her eyebrows in the direction of Darrent, who shrugged in response. *The truth on this one, then*, she decided. "We caught him coming in," she said. "We talked some sense into him. He was just looking for a quick score, I guess. Said something about owing people money."

"Who does he owe?"

"Samuel, I'm not the boy's mother. How would I know who he owes? Maybe you should talk to him directly."

"All right, Mama."

"Tell you what," she said, "you can come here to talk to him if you want. He'll be working the night shift for me until Donnell gets back on his feet."

"You gave him a job?"

"He don't seem like a bad kid, Samuel. I figured he could use a second chance. And I suddenly needed a security guard."

Samuel chuckled. "Always trying to change the world, aren't you, Mama?"

"Well"—she let a smile appear in her voice—"you can't do it alone, now, can you, Samuel?"

"All right. What about Nevermore? Have you heard anything new?"

"Nothing, Samuel. I still think it's just a hoax, but you got to do what you got to do."

"Funny thing," he said. "There's a political fundraiser coming up for Max Roman. And there's a charity auction as part of the event. Mama, it looks like you donated a rare copy of an antique magazine with that Edgar Allan Poe poem 'The Raven' in it."

"What you trying to say, Samuel?"

"Well, it seems unusual that you'd be involved in politics in the first place, and that you'd be contributing the poem that made Nevermore famous to Max's campaign. And now you've hired a guy who actually goes by the name The Raven. It just feels odd."

"Samuel. You thinking Mama Bliss is your Nevermore problem?"

"No, Mama. Of course not. Like I said, I'm just trying to rule out things that need to be ruled out."

Play this right, sis, she told herself, *and maybe you can save Samuel Hill's life.* She sighed. "All right, Samuel. As for the street magician, I got no control over what he calls himself. I'm just trying to help a young man stay out of trouble and get his life right."

"I understand, Mama. What about that Nevermore antique?"

She sighed again. "Well, if I'd known it was going to be used for a political fundraiser, I never would have given up my own personal copy of the 1845 issue of the *New York Evening Mirror.* I bought it for myself and planned to keep it for myself. But you know I'm on the board of directors for the Atlanta Society for Literary Arts?"

"No, I didn't know that."

"Oh, well now you do. Anyway, Geneva Sims came 'round telling me it was my turn to head up the annual charity auction, and gosh, wouldn't it be nice if I donated something really special to this year's auction and blah blah blah. So I gave in and donated the Poe magazine. I thought it might be a treat for somebody, and I'm getting older anyway. What am I going to do with a fragile collectible when I'm dead?"

"So you're actually heading up the fundraiser?"

"No, Samuel. You're a detective. Maybe you should listen when I'm talking to you. I'm heading up the charity auction for ASLA this year. That means I coordinated the auction lots and I'm handling the entertainment, mostly. But after we got the auction scheduled and moving, Geneva had this harebrained idea that we should invite Max Roman as our keynote speaker. Well, then Max's people suggested that we combine our auction with his fundraiser, and next thing you know, I'm outvoted at the board meeting and suddenly my charity auction has become a 'combination event.' Now we have this foolish political fundraiser first, with Max Roman speaking, and then my charity auction afterward."

"That's a strange combination. How do they keep straight who gets the money?"

Bliss looked at the phone as if Samuel was speaking Chinese. "I'm no accountant, Samuel," she said with a snort. "I just donated something to the Atlanta Society for Literary Arts. They've got suits who figure out money."

"Right, sure. And the antique magazine?"

"Well, I'd already donated it before the whole political thing was added on. I couldn't exactly ask for it back, could I?"

"No, Mama, you couldn't."

"That answer your questions, Samuel?"

"Yes, Mama. Thanks. Glad to be able to rule out the Secret Stash."

Inside, she felt relieved. *Time for the misdirection*, she thought.

"Samuel, here's one little thing," she said casually. "I don't expect that it means anything, but I thought you'd want to know about it. The Edgar Awards are coming to Georgia on April 28."

"What's that?"

"Book awards named after Edgar Allan Poe. Usually in New York City, but this year they're having them in Athens. Probably nothing, but I'll send over the ad I saw so you can check it out."

Now, the final step.

"Hold on just a minute," she said, interrupting herself. She pretended to speak to the door. "What is it?" Then, "One second. Samuel, Darrent just walked into my office, and he says he's got something for you. Want me to put him on?"

"Sure, Mama. Thanks."

Darrent strode over to the desk, leaning toward the speakerphone and playing along. "He's on the phone right now?" he said as if Mama had just told him. "Hello, Detective Hill?"

"Hi, Darrent. And, as always, you can call me Samuel."

"Thanks, Detective. I think I may have good news for you."

ONE WEEK AGO . . .

33

TRUDI

Atlanta, GA
Downtown
Friday, April 7, 11:04 a.m.
7 days to Nevermore

"Not another one."

If not for the constant interruptions, Trudi Coffey would've almost liked seeing the way her ex-husband squirmed with every new "contestant" that came by. But this was supposed to be business, and they probably had better things to do than sit in the lobby of the Ritz-Carlton hotel sipping espresso and waiting for a gang member to walk by.

She barely listened while the latest crooner tried to impress her ex-husband with his shaky rendition of a Sinatra ballad and watched with disinterest as Samuel nodded politely and then sent him away. This was starting to get old.

Trudi and Samuel had arrived at the Ritz-Carlton in time for brunch. Samuel had led her directly to Jittery Joe's Coffee

Bar in the lobby, where he'd been greeted like an old friend by the perky brunette barista behind the counter. "The usual?" the brunette had said, and in response Samuel had gone ahead and ordered for Trudi, as well.

"Two today," he said, smiling.

Trudi thought the girl might have blushed a little, and Trudi grudgingly admitted it was kind of cute on her. For once, she wasn't jealous of a random beauty flirting with her ex-husband. That was progress, she decided. She smiled at the barista, as well, and was pleased to see the favor returned.

By ten-fifteen she and Samuel were seated on plush chairs atop a marble floor, sipping Jittery Joe's signature coffee drink. The White Orchid was an iced espresso made with cold half-and-half cream and a hint of vanilla syrup, shaken and then poured over ice. Trudi had to admit it was pretty good. She could get used to this kind of life.

The first contestant had shown up around a quarter to eleven, sliding in conspiratorially to greet them. She was a local girl dressed in a Jamaican style that didn't quite match her deeply southern accent. Boy, was she glad to happen across Mr. Hill today, she said. Then, without much more by way of introduction, she swept herself into a soulful rendition of a classic Beyoncé hit. Samuel took it in stride, but Trudi could tell he was obviously confused by the impromptu concert.

"Here's my name and number," the girl had said, handing over a napkin. "Now I'll let you get back to yourselves. Thanks for the opportunity!"

"Well," Trudi had said, "that's an interesting way to hit on a handsome man."

"I don't think she was hitting on me," Samuel said, turning over the slip of paper. It did indeed have the girl's name—Crystal Jones—and her phone number, as well as an email address, but it also included a little note that read, *I just love* America's Favorite Artist*!*

"What's that supposed to mean?" he'd asked.

Trudi shrugged.

Samuel had tried to talk the next two girls out of singing, but no matter what he said, they didn't believe him. "They said you'd say that." The contestants would wink conspiratorially. "And that you're just testing to see how much we really want it."

Then they'd broken into song, despite his protests. After the fifth audition—that time it was an aspiring young comedian just getting off from working the morning shift as a bellman in the lobby—Samuel had started to go with it, nodding, pretending to listen. Trudi had to stifle a laugh when she heard him tell one would-be vocalist, "That was a little pitchy but had some good moments. We'll be in touch."

Every time it seemed like it was over, someone new would come trotting up, ready to launch into an a cappella version of the latest pop hit or classic Broadway song or, occasionally, a stand-up comedy routine. Trudi had finally provided a yellow legal pad, and people started leaving their names and contact information with Samuel there, as well.

Fortunately, there were breaks in the auditions, and it was during those breaks that Trudi and Samuel had tried to get some business done.

"Tell me again why we're here," she said to Samuel.

"Because I want Andrew Carr to see me watching him. I want him to know I've got eyes on him, and if he tries to disappear again, I will find him."

"But why wait here? Why not wait back by the workers' entrance?"

"Because I like it out here." Samuel smiled and spread his

arms wide. "It's nice. Civilized. Makes me feel happy, and like there's still hope for an old, washed-up spy like me." He sipped his espresso contentedly. "So I told Mr. Carr I expected to see him walk through this lobby every day at eleven o'clock in the morning on his way to work in the catering kitchen, and if I didn't, he'd find himself on the wrong end of an APB with my signature at the bottom."

"Is that all you threatened him with?"

Samuel shrugged and gave her a look that reminded her of a teen caught stealing the keys to his dad's sports car.

"Right. So you've been here every day this week?"

"Yep."

Trudi let that ruminate. According to Samuel, Mama Bliss had been the one to find Andrew Carr for him. After Carr and a few other Kipo gang members had been arrested in a gun-smuggling raid, Carr had been the informant to first bring the Nevermore plot to light. Then someone had unexpectedly posted bail for him—but not the others. They said it was an uncle, or some other relative, who put up the money, but after Carr had left the penitentiary, he had disappeared. No one had thought to notify Samuel that his prime informant was being released, something that had infuriated her ex-husband. He'd turned to Mama Bliss for help, and she'd gotten involved, doing her old friend a favor by working her network to find the lost gang member.

A week ago, they'd found him.

Well, Mama's right-hand man, Darrent Hayes, had found him.

Apparently Carr had gone to visit an aunt somewhere in rural north Georgia while his family in Atlanta pulled some strings to try and get him a job working in the catering kitchen at the Ritz. He'd come back last week to take the new job, to turn over a new leaf, he said, and start a new life. He was done with gangs and guns and all that, he said. By all measures, he was cooperating with authorities in the gun-smuggling bust—except that he'd now changed his tune about Nevermore. That also was a frustration for Samuel, and it was a problem he was determined to solve. Samuel's voice interrupted her train of thought.

"Mr. Carr, surprisingly, has been as good as his word. In fact"—he nodded toward a handsome young man with dark skin and hair braided into stylish, neat cornrows—"there he is now."

Samuel lifted his espresso and motioned toward the young man, who nodded grimly in return. After getting Samuel's acknowledgment, Andrew Carr turned and sped through the lobby toward the catering kitchen of the hotel. Apparently he was running late today.

"So that's your informant for the Nevermore case. And he says Nevermore is just a joke he made up to get out of jail, is that right?"

"He's lying."

"How do you know?"

"Because I think he might be lying."

"Samuel, you're not a mind reader."

"No, I'm not. Apparently I'm a talent agent and TV producer, secretly hunting for contestants to appear on the next season of my hit show." He sat up straighter as a new contestant approached.

He's actually enjoying this, she thought.

This contestant was a little older than some of the others, which Trudi appreciated. She also liked that this girl was here to sing, not to flirt with Samuel in hopes of somehow improving her chances of making *AFA*.

"Somewhere over the rainbow . . ."

Nice, Trudi thought in spite of herself. *Clear, rich vocal tone. She'd do great on national TV. Too bad Samuel can't give that to her.*

"You have a lovely voice," Samuel said to the current singer.

"Thank you." The girl had a shyness about her that was appealing. Humble. Trudi liked that too.

"Leave your name and contact information here," Samuel said, pointing to the yellow legal pad. "If a spot opens up, I'll be sure to mention your name. But the competition is fierce. You understand very few people actually make the show, right?"

"Right, yes, sir," she said. "Thank you for the opportunity. Hopefully I'll hear from you next season." She smiled and shook his hand and walked away with a bounce in her step.

He shook his head. "That one deserves it," he said.

"How would you know?" Trudi laughed. "You're not really a producer for *America's Favorite Artist*. You have nothing to do with auditions for that TV show."

"I know. Of course I know that," he said. "But we've had, what, a dozen or so people come up and tell us they want to audition, right? Somebody in this hotel keeps telling them that I'm a producer, here to secretly pick new contestants for *AFA*. A practical joker is out there, I get it. Hotel staffs have warped senses of humor. Someone has probably seen me here all week and decided to have a little fun at my expense. Regardless, of all the people we've heard today, *that* girl is the best. It doesn't take a music producer to notice that."

"Point taken," Trudi said. When he was right, he was right.

"And besides, I know people. And people I know also know people. Maybe I can get"—he paused to glance at the yellow pad—"Miyasa Nichols an audition for *America's Favorite Artist*, after all. You never know, right?"

Trudi laughed in spite of herself. "Samuel Hill," she said, "if anybody can do that, you can."

He grinned and held up his empty cup. "Want another?"

"No, thanks." Trudi already felt the caffeine tickling her nervous system. "You go ahead."

"Maybe I'll wait a little bit," he said.

There was something about the lobby of the Ritz-Carlton, she decided, that did look good on him. He was relaxed, open. A lot like the guy who'd swept her off her feet back in those halcyon college days when they first started dating. She liked that guy. Loved him, really. She wondered why she could never stop loving him.

"Anyway," he was saying, "it just feels like Andrew Carr is lying to me now. My gut says he was telling the truth then and is lying now."

"Hunches can be wrong, you know."

"My hunches are never wrong. Well, almost never. Mostly never." He sighed.

Trudi didn't know how to argue that point.

"Plus," he said, "is it just a coincidence that Mr. Carr suddenly has a 'rehabilitation' job at the same location as Max Roman's upcoming fundraiser on April 14?"

"Honestly? It could be. The Ritz does run a second-chance program to help kids get out of gangs by giving them jobs."

"You just want to go on a Hawaiian vacation tomorrow," he teased.

"An island vacation does sound wonderful," she said slowly. To herself she added, *A Hawaiian getaway with you, just the two of us, actually sounds great. Like good times we should've had but didn't.* But she refused to say that out loud. Of course, the fact that they even had a Hawaiian diversion as an option lent some credence to Samuel's theory that Andrew Carr might be lying. Still . . .

"Samuel," she said, "have you considered that maybe you think Andrew Carr is lying because you *want* him to be lying? Eulalie would call that a reality distortion to fit your personal narrative."

"You and your assistant should do more detective work and less psychology homework."

Yeah, that's probably true. "Let's look at the facts, Samuel. Just the facts. What do they tell us?"

He sighed again.

"Okay, maybe you're right," he said at last. "And maybe Mama Bliss is right. At this point, all facts seem to indicate that Nevermore is just a myth. If I tried to convince my captain to station SWAT at the fundraiser based on the circumstantial evidence I've got right now, he'd probably kick me out of his office. I just can't seem to shake the feeling that I'm missing something, though."

"Well, the Hawaii trip is suspicious." *Why am I trying to encourage him?*

"Yeah. The thing is, this Hawaiian vacation could be legit too. I've made some enemies in my life, sure. But there are some folks out there who love me as much as my enemies hate me, some folks who are grateful I've got enemies. Grateful people are sometimes extravagant."

Trudi had to admit that was a possibility. She started thinking out loud. "So Mama Bliss, she's all cleared as far as you're concerned?" she said. Samuel had told Trudi of his conversation with Mama about The Raven and the antique edition of the *New York Evening Mirror*. It all made sense, but it also left them back at square one.

"Everything checks out. The ASLA board of directors did indeed assign her to handle the entertainment and auction for their charity event, and she did indeed donate the Poe collectible before the auction was changed to be a dual event. As for The Raven, he's never really been a suspect."

"And Mama did find Andrew Carr for you," Trudi said thoughtfully. "Why would she do that if she was implicated?"

Samuel nodded. He reached inside his jacket and pulled out a folded newspaper clipping. "There's also this," he said. He laid it on the table, and Trudi saw it was an advertisement for an upcoming event. "Mama found it."

"The Edgar Awards?" she said.

"Big literary festival, named after Edgar Allan Poe and sponsored by the Mystery Writers of America. Every April they have a gala banquet in New York City—"

"But this year they're partnering with the University of Georgia"—she scanned the advertisement—"to hold the ceremonies in Athens, on April 28?"

"Right," he said. "Something about encouraging young authors to achieve greatness in mystery writing. And a contract dispute with the big hotel that's their normal venue in New York."

"Wow, that'd be fun. Why didn't they ever do something like this when we were going to UGA?"

"You're missing the point, Tru-Bear."

"Right. Okay. So Mama thinks the Edgar Awards might have a connection to Nevermore?"

"No," he said. "She thinks it's just as much a dead end as the Max Roman fundraiser. But she thought I'd want to know about it anyway."

"So what do you think?"

"Well," he said, and she could see him searching out logical conclusions in his head, "maybe I'm just paranoid. Maybe these are all red herrings. There is no real evidence of a threat, none that I can find—and you know I *have* been looking. Maybe the fundraiser is just a fundraiser, and the Edgar Awards are just the Edgar Awards." He shrugged.

"Look," she said. "I'll just go to the Max Roman fundraiser and check it out, how's that?" She didn't have the heart to tell him she'd already RSVP'd for her and one guest to attend. It didn't seem like good timing to reveal that. "I'll be your inside man, your spy. I'll take Eulalie with me, teach her some imbedded surveillance techniques and enjoy a little taste of luxury for once. It actually sounds like a fun and fancy-free girls' night out. If we spot anything that seems mysterious, I'll text you and you can come save the day. Buzz Lightyear to the rescue and all that."

He laughed at the Buzz Lightyear reference, and Trudi felt the warmth of his joy. They fell silent, each losing themselves in their own thoughts.

It didn't take long before Trudi's mental synapses wandered from the possibly mythical Nevermore plot to curiosity about The Raven. Ever since he'd stood her up, he'd lived in the background. She understood he was working as a security guard for Sister Bliss's Secret Stash now, which she figured was a good step for him. And she'd eventually gotten what she thought was an apology from him, sort of. It had come in a text from an unknown number, saying just, *I'm sorry, Trudi*. She couldn't say for sure it was from him, but she assumed that was who it was. Trudi had opted not to respond.

She also had read his background file from BKGUSA. She understood some of the reasons behind his choices now. *Had to be hard killing your mother in a drunk-driving accident*, she told herself. *Had to be hard*. She also had to admit that Samuel was right. There was nothing tangible tying the street magician to Nevermore.

Samuel sat up in his seat, and Trudi had come to recognize that posture today. A new girl was approaching, a redhead this time, which was actually kind of rare in the ATL. *Out-of-towner*, Trudi thought. She spotted Samuel noticing the cocktail-waitress curves on this one and reminded herself she needed to get back to the gym today.

"Are you here to sing?" he asked when she drew near.

She smiled at him, a sultry, vampirish look that fit well with the auburn tresses surrounding her face. She glanced over at Trudi, hesitated, and then leaned down to whisper something in Samuel's ear. She pressed a folded slip of paper into his hand, then stood and walked toward a bank of elevators. Samuel unfolded the paper, and Trudi caught a glimpse of a hotel keycard inside it. He read the neat printing—a room number, she guessed— then folded it and put it all in his pocket. He looked suddenly distracted, and Trudi took the cue.

Pig, she thought. *I can't believe I wanted to go to Hawaii with you.*

"Well," she said aloud, "I'm going back to the office."

Samuel watched the redhead get on an elevator.

"I'll see you later, then?" Trudi said, standing.

Samuel stood and looked at her hard, his jaw tensing. "Okay," he said slowly. She could see the wheels spinning in his head. "I'll call you."

She started to leave, and he caught her arm. "Be careful out there, Tru-Bear."

34

RAVEN

Atlanta, GA
Downtown
Friday, April 7, 11:33 a.m.
7 days to Nevermore

Let's see, am I ready for this?

The lights are out in my hotel room, making it easy for me to blend into the darkness. I've got the washrag rolled up just right on the floor, slipped between the doorframe and the door to hold it open barely an inch or so. Just enough so I can use one eye to peek down the hallway, looking toward the elevators, without really being noticed. Also, that crack in the doorway gives me audio access to the hallway for the things I can't see. This could be helpful.

From behind my door, I can still use the little peephole to see the full view of Room 615 across the hall, so that keeps my range of vision focused when it needs to be.

I've moved my telephone to the queen bed nearest the door.

The cord doesn't reach all the way to the edge of the bed, but it's close enough. I don't want it to be right next to the door anyway. I take one last look at my preparations and finally exhale.

I think I'm ready.

I hear the elevator go *ding!* and peek through the tiny opening in the doorway. It's her. Now I feel my heart rate starting to pick up. She starts to tap lightly on my door, but I open it before her fingers can land. She greets me with a warm smile.

"Okay," she says. "I think he's coming."

Her red hair is skimming the shoulders of her dress, *business casual* I think they'd call it. Flattering, but also practical for travel.

"I feel like I'm a secret agent in a spy movie or something!" She giggles conspiratorially.

"No." I smile. "Nothing that exciting, Cherise. Just trying to get him away from the crowd for a private audition."

"I think he'll have to be crazy not to put you on the show. Your act is amazing. At least the parts of the act that you showed me."

I give a mock bow. "Well, you were a good partner."

"Ah, you're just reading my mind again."

There's an awkward moment of silence between us, and I have to fight the urge to look down the hallway. If Cherise has done her job, then Samuel Hill should be coming up that elevator any minute.

She takes a little breath and flips a strand of hair behind her left ear. "I'm glad we bumped into each other in the lobby this morning, Marv. How else would I have known to try The White Orchid espresso?" It seems like she's stalling.

"I know, right?" I say. I'm trying to be patient, but I can't help sneaking a glance down the hall now. *Time to leave, Cherise,*

I think. I'm hoping I can Vulcan-mind-meld that message into her pretty little brain.

"Well, anyway, I guess I should be going," she says at last.

It worked!

"Thanks again, Cherise," I say. I cross my fingers and hold them in the air for her to see. "Here's hoping!"

She smiles at me again, and I realize some men would be overjoyed to have this woman's attention. She's attractive, obviously successful in her work, funny, and generous. So why am I so uninterested in her?

All your fault, Trudi, I tell myself. *The heart wants what it wants, I guess, even when it can't have what it wants.*

"Anyway," she says again, "I'm flying home to Tampa today. Already got my stuff in the rental car"—she gestures to Room 615 across the hall—"so the room is all ready for your talent agent. He can just throw the keycard away after your audition. I have automatic checkout, so the card won't work after noon anyway."

She keeps saying *anyway*, which I think must be a nervous habit.

"Thanks again," I say. "Remind me to call you when I'm rich and famous."

"Well, here," she says, fishing in her purse. She pulls out a business card and looks positively shy handing it to me. "My company is sending me back to Atlanta in two weeks. Maybe you could call me and we could get together for dinner or something when I'm back in town?"

"Sure, yeah," I say, and I cringe inside because I know I'm lying. *You deserve someone a lot better than me, Cherise.* I hope our Vulcan mind-meld is broken, and that she didn't just hear that in my head. "That'd be great."

"Okay, anyway . . ." She holds out a hand, and we shake. She's professional about it, but I feel her fingers linger just a little too long. "You're definitely my favorite artist! Now I'd better get out of here before your producer shows up. I'll go out the back stairs so we don't cross paths again in the hallway."

"Thanks, Cherise. You're the best."

She heads down the hall, away from the elevators. I catch her looking back at me as she walks away. "Was great meeting you, Marv," she says. "Call me."

"Absolutely," I say, and I feel like a big jerk because I know I'm never going to call Cherise Amagan, Corporate Trainer, but I just don't know what else to say. She disappears into the stairwell, and I'm alone again.

In the darkness I can still make out the shapes of the various boxes and random artifacts that Mama Bliss has stored in this room. Apparently she didn't want to keep all the auction items for the upcoming political dinner at her store, preferring to keep everything here at the Ritz-Carlton instead. "Besides," she'd told me, "they're giving me a discounted room rate as incentive for using their facilities for the big event. Be a shame not to take advantage of that. I'll probably stay there myself the night before the ASLA charity auction."

Still, she hadn't wanted her auction valuables to go unguarded, even locked up in a Ritz-Carlton Deluxe Room. "I got me a personal security guard now," she'd said, winking in my direction. "And I don't think you'd mind it too much if you had to spend a week or so living in the lap of luxury, keeping watch over antique books and collectible paintings, now, would you?"

Well, she didn't have to ask me twice, even though a couple of her regular security guards weren't happy about "the new kid" getting such a plum assignment. Sad to say, I didn't feel sorry for any of them. After nine months in my ratty apartment in the Old Fourth Ward, I was looking forward to a downtown situation like this one.

A few of Mama's warehouse guys and I moved in a load of the auction items this morning, even before check-in time at the hotel was supposed to start. I guess Mama Bliss gets special treatment here, which works out fine for me. Then they left me on duty, with instructions to go downstairs every once in a while to get something to eat, or just to stretch my legs—but that I should never be gone more than half an hour from Room 614 until next Friday, when everything would be transported downstairs for the event.

They also left behind some of Mama's papers for the fundraiser, and I saw the RSVP list for the dinner. Trudi Coffey's name, "plus one," was on the seating chart. That got me a little concerned.

My first unpleasant thought was *I'm to be the table entertainment for Max Roman's fundraising dinner. There's going to be no way for me to avoid seeing Trudi—and whoever the muscle-bound dork is that she's bringing as her date.*

But more importantly—and I don't know exactly how to feel about this—I have a strong suspicion that Max Roman's big event is not going to be just a political fundraiser and charity auction.

For starters, there's that little list on the back of Mama Bliss's picture of her grandson. Six names on the list. Four crossed out, and the last two—both of them—will be in the same place on April 14.

At Max Roman's fundraiser.

Knowing who those two names belong to, I can't see that this is a coincidence.

Second, Mama Bliss keeps peeking at that picture when she thinks no one's watching her. It worries me, because I remember the flat tone of her voice when she hinted to me about the meaning of those last two names. "Justice for all," she'd said. I can understand that, but I also know enough of war to know that sometimes "justice" includes collateral damage.

If something bad is going down at Max Roman's fundraiser, will Trudi get caught in the crossfire?

Third, over to the side of the auction boxes, someone—I don't know who because I didn't see it happen—has placed five long, sturdy canvas bags reinforced with leather on the ends. They're locked shut with little padlocks on the zippers, but I can tell there's something heavy and metal inside each padded bag. It doesn't take a genius to know that those are rifle bags, and to guess what's probably inside them. Maybe they're selling antique guns at the charity auction? I hope that's all it is.

I was thinking about those long bags when I took a break and went down to the lobby to get coffee and a pastry. I met Cherise, and maybe I lingered a bit too long because of her, and because she was nice and friendly, and because she seemed so delighted when I started showing off with some of my close-up magic tricks. But if I hadn't stayed, I never would have spotted Trudi Coffey and Samuel Hill coming into the Ritz-Carlton.

Cherise and I slipped into a corner out of sight and watched them for a bit. She thought it was some kind of game, so when she asked who they were, I just made up the first thing that came into my head.

"Well," I said, "he's a talent scout for *America's Favorite Artist*. She must be his assistant. Or mistress maybe."

"Ooh, that's kind of exciting," she said. Then a girl sitting near us leaned in.

"Excuse me, I couldn't help overhearing." She was a brown-skinned young woman, dressed like she'd just flown in from Jamaica, but with a deep southern accent that sounded right at home here in Atlanta. "Did you say that guy over there"—she pointed toward the detective—"works for *America's Favorite Artist*?"

"Yeah?" I said.

"I love that show," she said.

"Me too," Cherise said.

Then, before I could react, the faux-Jamaican stood up, scribbled something on a napkin, and said, "Wish me luck."

Cherise and I had sneaked to another spot so we could see better what happened and, yep, the girl sang a little song for a confused-looking Detective Hill. And suddenly I thought, *Maybe I should take Trudi's advice, after all. Samuel Hill is good at helping, she said. Maybe he can help me to help Trudi stay safe.*

After that, we started quietly spreading the news about the big-time TV producer taking auditions right here in the lobby of the Ritz-Carlton Atlanta hotel. It was an easy sell, and pretty soon there was a steady stream of people interrupting Trudi and Samuel. And then Cherise said to me, "You should go audition. Why not?"

"Ah," I said, "I think they take mostly singers and comedians. And besides, there's too many people pestering him down here. My act is better without distractions."

Yeah, my evil plans work best when I make it seem like they're someone else's ideas, when I can make my words come out of their mouths. Next thing you know, Cherise—with my strategic input—came up with the whole scheme. She'd go over and get Samuel to come up to her room. *I know how to work Hollywood men like that*, she'd said. Then I'd wait for him up there and wow him with my magic.

I had a feeling Detective Hill wasn't the type to fall for a typical honey-trap, even one with Cherise's skills, so I told her to whisper something special in his ear. Then I ran upstairs to get set up for the show.

What is taking Detective Hill so long? I wonder suddenly in the darkness of Room 614. *Shouldn't he be here by now? Maybe he didn't take the bait?*

Then, as if on cue, I hear the elevator ding.

I practically hold my breath as I return the door to its prearranged position. I test it quickly to make sure I still have the right sightlines, then kneel down and fade back into the darkness, trying to see who is walking down the hall.

It's Detective Samuel Hill.

He doesn't look happy.

35

TRUDI

Atlanta, GA
West Midtown
Friday, April 7, 11:47 a.m.
7 days to Nevermore

"I've seen that guy before."

Trudi Coffey lost sight of the black Ford Ranger on Northside Drive when she got caught at a stoplight outside the Georgia Dome. But before that, she'd driven close enough to the truck to see something that had jogged her memory. The other driver was of medium build, dark skinned, maybe late twenties. He wore a plain T-shirt covered by a light gray hoodie, and sunglasses. When he saw Trudi watching him, he gunned through a yellow light and disappeared north of Joseph E. Boone Blvd.

"Where have I seen that guy?"

It was only about a fifteen-minute drive from the Ritz-Carlton to the Coffey & Hill Investigations office, but Trudi used most of that time trying to place the guy in the Ford

Ranger. It helped to take her mind off what she assumed her pig of an ex-husband was doing with that sexy little redhead back at the hotel. At a stoplight, she couldn't contain herself anymore. She slammed the meat of her palm against the steering wheel a few times. She knew she was just blowing steam off her anger toward Samuel, so she used it to focus her mental energies on the other driver.

"Arby's," she said aloud. "First it was Arby's. Across the street from the office. Just a few days ago."

She remembered now. Eulalie had noticed him after coming in from lunch on Tuesday. He was sitting at the outdoor tables with a large burrito in front of him, facing toward the front doors of Coffey & Hill.

"Trudi," Eulalie had said, "come look at this." After Trudi joined her, she pointed across the street. "That guy was there when I left for lunch an hour ago. Still there now, and it looks like he hasn't eaten any of his food. What do you make of it?"

She stared through the plate glass at the sunglasses. "Maybe he just likes to suffer through hot, muggy days outside?" Eulalie had looked at her, surprised for a second, before she realized Trudi was joking. "Or more likely, he's keeping an eye on somebody in our little strip mall and reporting back to somebody higher up."

"Us?"

"Yeah."

Trudi had gone back to her office and resumed her work. She couldn't stop anybody from watching her, and as long as he didn't do more than that, she'd leave him alone. But she did keep open the drawer in her desk that held her loaded Beretta Tomcat. Just in case.

He was gone the next day, and she hadn't seen him again until this morning.

"And he was at the Ritz," she told herself as she steered her Focus into the parking lot at Coffey & Hill Investigations. "Back by the bellhops. Maybe he was the joker sending contestants over to Samuel. But I'm not really fond of the idea that he left the same time I did."

She checked her surroundings before getting out of her car, just to be safe, but everything seemed normal. No black trucks nearby, no watchers in sunglasses stalking the area. She went toward the front door and saw a FedEx Letter envelope leaning against the glass.

"What?" she said to nobody. "The office is open, and Eulalie's inside. How lazy does a FedEx guy have to be to just toss our delivery toward the front door?" She was already in a bad mood, and this day was just getting more annoying by the minute.

When she picked up the envelope, she noticed something peculiar. There was no packing slip or air bill with the envelope. *Just like the Hawaiian vacation delivery*, she told herself grimly. *It really must be easy to steal these envelopes out of those FedEx boxes all over the city.*

"Hi Tr—" Eulalie started to say when she entered the office.

"No calls," Trudi interrupted her. "And take the rest of the day off."

"Is everything—"

Trudi didn't wait for her assistant to finish. Instead, she just went into her back office and shut the door. She tried not to slam it, but maybe it did hit the jamb a little harder than normal anyway.

"Ms. Coffey?" Eulalie's voice came softly through the intercom. "Is everything okay? Did something happen at your meeting with Mr. Hill this morning?"

Trudi sighed. Maybe she should tell Eulalie everything. After all, Samuel was stringing her along too. She ought to know about his, um, extracurricular activities, right? But in the end she just said, "Everything's fine, Eula. Just take the afternoon off and enjoy a long weekend. I've got a lot of work to do, and I need to concentrate on it. Alone."

There was a moment of silence on the other end, and then Eulalie said, "Yes, ma'am."

Trudi leaned over and looked at the video monitor feed of the reception area. She watched Eulalie quietly gather her things and then go out the front. She was grateful to see that her assistant paused to lock the door behind her. At least she wouldn't get surprised by any unexpected visitors. Not this time.

Trudi studied the FedEx envelope for a moment, then dropped it on her desk without opening it. She wanted to be a little more prepared for what might be inside. She clicked an icon on her desktop computer and in short order had called up the surveillance footage files from her outside camera. The direct-to-digital surveillance feed had been a little more expensive when they were installing the security system, but as far as Trudi was concerned, it had paid for itself a dozen times over—including this time, right now.

She started the replay at one hour ago and was pleased to see that at 11:03 a.m. the FedEx delivery had not yet been made. She fast-forwarded through the footage until, at 11:51 a.m., a black Ford Ranger pulled into view. She watched the guy in the gray hoodie jump out of the truck and then casually drop the envelope at her front door. He was gone again by 11:53, and then she saw her own car pull in the lot at 11:56. She shut off the video playback and hunched down in her chair.

She stared at the envelope, still unopened, on her desk.

An unbidden image of Samuel doing unspeakable things with a trampy redhead flashed in her mind. She stamped it out quickly, then stood up behind the desk.

"It's not fair," she said through gritted teeth. "Why do I have to be the one who forgives?"

She felt like being angry, but no fury came. *Grace doesn't have to be easy, I guess*, she told herself, *it just has to be grace*. She sat up and spotted the FedEx envelope again. *All right, then*. She reached over, tore open the top, and dumped the contents onto her desk.

She actually jumped when the phone rang.

"Coffey & Hill Investigations," she said without looking at the caller ID.

"Trudi."

Just the sound of Samuel's voice made her head ache. "What is it, Samuel. Your redhead leave already?"

He sighed. "Get your mind out of the gutter, Trudi. I'm not with any redhead, and I never was. I had to follow a lead."

For some reason, even knowing that he might be lying about it, this made her feel suddenly better. She perked up considerably and tried not to sound relieved.

"Okay," she said. "I retract my accusations and humbly offer an apology." She reached over to finally examine the FedEx contents still lounging on her desk.

"Forgiven. But listen, Trudi, about that Max Roman fundraiser next week?"

"Mm-hmm. I think Eula and I will have fun, so don't worry about—What is this now? Hold on, Samuel."

"What? What is it?"

"Hold on."

"Everything okay over there?"

"I'm fine, Samuel. Just hang on for a second."

"Okay, good. Listen, I need to run down a few things this afternoon, but about that Roman fundraiser? I want to be your 'plus one' at the party. You don't think Eulalie will mind, do you?"

"Samuel."

She found two things in the envelope this time. The first was a sheet of paper that held a printed itinerary for the supposed Hawaiian vacation she and Samuel were scheduled to take tomorrow. She had to admit it looked great. There was a couple's massage on the calendar. Surf lessons. The requisite luau and a few other touristy, romantic options.

"I can't really tell you why," he was saying, "so I'm just going to ask you to trust me this time . . ."

But she didn't spend much thought on that because the second item from the envelope demanded most of her attention.

". . . but please, I'm asking nicely, may I be your date next Friday night?"

It was a 5x7 photograph.

Samuel's voice faded into the background as she stared at the picture, slightly grainy, as if taken from a distance and enlarged.

She guessed that the boy featured in it was five years old, maybe six. His face was cherubic, with tinted skin that reminded her of a freshly baked pumpkin loaf. His eyes were a light chestnut color, with slivers of dark pigment flaked within. He had long lashes, chubby little jowls, and a delighted smile. On his head was a square head cloth, red-and-white patterned, with a double circle of black cord. She couldn't make out much of what was in the background, but the desert browns and reds told her all she needed to know.

He was looking up at someone, arms reaching out as if to receive a gift, or like he was asking to be lifted up in a mother's arms. A mother who was not Trudi Sara Coffey.

". . . Trudi? Are you still there? Tru?"

"Sorry, Samuel," she said brusquely. "I think you should probably come over here, after all. You'll want to take a look at this."

"Okay," he said. "How about if I stop by later this afternoon? First I want to—"

"No, come now," she said. She kept all emotion out of her voice. "It looks like this Hawaiian vacation isn't just an invitation for us to get out of the way."

"What do you mean?"

"Samuel, you need to see this."

36

RAVEN

Atlanta, GA
Downtown
Friday, April 7, 11:47 a.m.
7 days to Nevermore

Detective Hill stops in front of Room 615, listening. I'm grateful he doesn't give a second look to Room 614 across the hall, where I'm hiding.

At first I think he's going to just use the keycard Cherise gave him and go inside, but this guy is apparently a gentleman. He knocks, then waits for a response. Only after knocking a second time and still getting no answer does he finally swipe the keycard through the lock and open the door.

He also seems to be the cautious type. He swings the door inward but doesn't follow it right in. Instead, he studies the opening, checking the room before entering. He reaches in and turns on the light, then dips his head in before finally allowing his body to follow. When the door to Room 615 finally clicks shut, I run to the telephone on one of the two queen beds in my room and dial the phone across the hall.

I hear it ring. Once. Twice. On the third ring, he picks up.

"Hello," he says.

It suddenly hits me that I didn't think about what voice to use for this call. If I use my own voice, will he recognize me? He only met me once, and it was a brief meeting at that. But is it worth the risk?

I'm blessed with fairly decent skills at vocal impressions. My Michael Jackson imitation has gotten me more than one date. I'm not bad at Arnold Schwarzenegger, either, or another half a dozen or so people. I can even do a spot-on impression of Marge Simpson. But I don't think MJ or Arnie or Marge is a good choice right now. *What's the right voice for this call?*

I take too long to respond. Samuel Hill hangs up.

I hear Room 615 open and, before I can stop myself, I've redialed the number. The phone rings in my ear, and I also hear it through the crack in my open door.

Room 615 clicks shut. A moment later, Samuel Hill picks up the phone again.

"I'm listening," he says. "But not for long."

"Don't hang up," I say. Even I'm surprised to hear Scholarship's voice come out. But then I like it. It sounds strong, powerful. Like somebody you don't want to mess with.

"Who is this?" he says.

"That's really not any of your business, now, is it?" I say in Scholarship's voice. I feel like I'm starting to get the hang of this. Voices are about more than just inflection and pronunciation; they're about imbuing inflection and pronunciation with personality. I think, after my recent meetings with the football player, I've pretty much got his personality down pat.

"Just don't hang up," I say again.

"Give me a reason," he says, and I have to say I'm impressed. He's not imitating anybody but himself, and he still sounds just as intimidating as Scholarship.

"It's about Trudi Coffey," I say.

"That's what your redhead said when she whispered in my ear. And that's all she said. So what is 'it,' and why is it about Trudi?"

"Next Friday, Trudi Coffey is planning to attend the Max Roman fundraiser at the Ritz-Carlton hotel."

"Mm-hmm."

"I'd suggest you go with her," I say.

I think it's funny that I'm actually sweating right now, like Samuel Hill is going to come crashing into my room and bust me for making an anonymous phone call. Plus, what if I'm wrong? What if there is no secret dangerous plot that involves the fundraising dinner? Well, no harm, I guess.

But if I'm right, I may just save Trudi's life.

"Does this have something to do with Nevermore?" he says suddenly.

Okay, that's surprising.

"I, uh . . ." I don't know what to say. How did he hear about Nevermore? Is it something bigger than just a note on the back of Mama Bliss's picture? If I remember right, Trudi said he was working on a case that used "The Raven" poem as a background. Maybe it's tied to this fundraiser?

"It's . . . I mean . . ." I'm struggling now, and we both know it.

He waits. I want to ask him questions, to find out what he's talking about when he says "Nevermore," but I think it's probably time to bring the conversation to an end.

"Just go to the party with your ex-wife," I say eventually. I figure that's enough. "Consider this good advice from a friend."

I hang up fast, before I can stumble over anything else. Then I sneak over to the door and peek out through the crack. The room across the hall is silent. It's hard not to count the seconds while I'm waiting for something to happen, but I force myself to breathe and think about anything but time passing. Then two things happen simultaneously.

First, Samuel Hill strides briskly out of Room 615 and into the ornate hallway on the sixth floor of this fancy hotel. Second, the elevator goes *ding!* and I hear someone get off. Before the elevator passenger comes into view, though, I see Detective Hill stop and stare toward the new person on the floor. He has a wary look on his face, but his voice is calm and conversational.

"They let you bring a gun into the Ritz?" he says.

I wonder if I can close this door without anybody noticing, I think. The mention of guns in the hallway has me panicking just a little bit.

"That's really not any of your business, now, is it?"

No way.

I can't believe he said those exact words, though it does mean my impersonation of him was spot-on. I'm torn between congratulating myself and hoping nobody gets shot in the hall outside my door. Then another thought hits me.

What's Scholarship doing here?

Through the crack in my door, I see Samuel Hill grin. *Okay, this is a guy who thrills on confrontation*, I decide quickly. He's about as big as Scholarship, so I think he'd probably hold his own in a fight. But still, I've seen what the football player can do with his fists. I want to close my door, but now, like a guy who can't take his eyes off a car wreck, I can't look away.

"I'm just asking," Detective Hill says, "because the sign in the lobby asks for all guns to be checked at the front desk." He flips open his jacket to reveal an empty shoulder holster. "And yet here you are with a full rifle bag in plain sight. Makes me curious, you know?"

"Curiosity can be dangerous," Scholarship says, and now he's ambled into view.

"Maybe. But that's why I get paid a miniscule salary from the good people of Atlanta. To be curious, especially when it comes to unlicensed guns in public places." Detective Hill reaches into an inside pocket of his blazer and pulls out a badge.

Scholarship nods slowly.

"You don't have to worry, officer. I'm not carrying a gun. Not today. And all my guns are licensed anyway. Now if you'll excuse me—" He starts to push past, but Samuel Hill blocks his way.

"What we have here," he says, "is what's termed as suspicious circumstances with probable cause for investigation. So I'd like to look inside your bag, if you don't mind."

"And if I do mind?"

"I'd like to take a look anyway."

From my perch inside Room 614, I can see Scholarship's face over the back shoulder of Samuel Hill. Even though Detective Hill is a good-sized man, the footballer has at least an inch on him in height, and probably ten to fifteen pounds in muscle.

"No," Scholarship says. "Now get out of my way before you and your tin badge get embarrassed."

He starts to push past the detective, and then, faster than I would've thought possible, it's all over. When Scholarship lunges forward, Samuel Hill reacts with a speed and grace that's rare to see in a big man like him.

First he leans back slightly, balancing easily on his left leg while his right foot delivers a choppy, straight kick at Scholarship's left knee. The footballer drops his rifle bag and swings out wildly, his knee buckling before he can catch himself enough to straighten up to protect himself. Just as he's rising back up, Hill presses his attack and jams four stiff fingers into his throat.

Now the baller is both stumbling and struggling for breath.

The detective grabs his left arm, swings it behind, then pushes hard on the wrong side of the man's elbow. At the same time, he chops another kick to that same gimpy knee.

Scholarship goes down face-first, still gagging, with Samuel Hill on top of him.

It seems like I barely blink twice before the detective has a knee pressed into the bigger man's back and an arm-bar locked in to keep Scholarship from resisting any further.

"Hurts like anything, doesn't it?" Detective Hill says from behind the other man's head. "Spear fingers to the larynx are just no fun. If it makes you feel any better, I know this from experience. My wife taught me."

Scholarship gurgles what I think is a bad word.

"I also know how to spot an old football injury. I'm guessing you blew out that left knee in college, and it never healed up quite right. I could see you favoring it just enough to guess that it wasn't as strong as you like to pretend it is."

Scholarship's voice is coming back. This time he definitely says a bad word.

"Now," Samuel Hill says, "we have a choice. You can cooperate while I put on your bracelets, or I can break your arm and then handcuff you."

There's a tense moment, and then Scholarship swings his right arm up and behind his back. Two seconds later, both wrists are cuffed and the detective has released his captive from the floor. The football player rolls, grunts, and leans his back against the wall beside Room 615. I see his eyes flit from Samuel Hill to his rifle bag, and then they rest for a split second on the door to Room 614, where I am.

I take a step back. *Did he see me, watching through the crack in the door?* If so, he doesn't let on. He just lets out a whoosh of air and turns his attention back to his opponent.

"It's clothing," he says, and his voice sounds raspy from the spear-fingers thing. "You going to arrest me for carrying concealed laundry?"

Samuel Hill doesn't answer. Instead, he slides the bag over between them. He crouches down, unzips the canvas, and starts pawing through the contents. Even I can see it's a bunch of shirts and pants, black, like waiters' uniforms or something. He shoves everything back into the bag but doesn't stand up yet.

"Why a rifle bag?"

Scholarship grins and shrugs. "Packer's choice, I guess. You use what's nearby when you pack for a trip."

They stare at each other, and I have to give Scholarship credit. Even though he's been defeated, he's not beaten, not by a long shot.

Samuel Hill motions for him to get up, then he removes the handcuffs. "Okay," he says, "you're free to go. Next time just try a little cooperation with a police officer. Better for everyone."

Scholarship rubs his wrists absently, then picks up his bag, but he doesn't leave yet.

"Want me to walk you to your room?" the detective mocks. "I hear these halls are full of unsavory people."

The football player snorts a laugh in spite of himself. "I think I'll come back later," he says, "in case a little birdie is watching."

Is he talking about me?

He walks out of my view, heading back toward the elevators at the end of the hall. Samuel Hill doesn't follow him. He just stands in the hall outside my door, watching the other man leave. I hear the elevator ding, and then, before the doors close, I hear Scholarship again.

"Detective," he says, and his voice is calm now, though still a little hoarse from its earlier trauma. "You caught me off guard today. That won't happen again. And believe me, there will be a next time."

Trudi Coffey's ex-husband grins, and I think he means it when he says, "Looking forward to it, big fella."

After the elevator leaves, Samuel Hill pulls out his phone and walks slowly down the hall. I hear his voice, apparently speaking into his phone. "Trudi." There's a pause while the elevator doors reopen. "Get your mind out of the gutter, Trudi—" he says, and then the elevator closes.

I find myself breathing hard, like I've just run up the stairs from the lobby to the sixth floor.

"All right," I mumble to myself. "At least I gave him the warning. Trudi says he's good at helping, and I guess I can see that now. I just hope he's good at helping her."

I sit in the darkness for a minute longer, then the elevator down the hall lets out another *ding!*

I don't hesitate this time.

I pull out the washrag and shut my hotel room door.

37

BLISS

Atlanta, GA
Little Five Points
Friday, April 7, 3:31 p.m.
7 days to Nevermore

Bliss June Monroe saw the black Cadillac Escalade ESV and knew it was coming for her. She held it in her gaze when it stopped at the red light where Mansfield Avenue North crossed Moreland Avenue, but just for a moment. Just long enough to make sure.

She adjusted the brake on her wheelchair and settled in again on the sidewalk outside her store. The canvas beside her was mostly done by now, and judging by the thunder echoing lightly in the distance, she thought she should probably take it inside before the afternoon rains came, but she waited outside anyway.

She'd planned to draw a sparrow today, something light and airy, with blue sky and white clouds as background, but she'd put down only a few strokes before she knew that painting would have to wait. Today it was a different bird, a large, sooty one with a glossy sheen, thick throat feathers, and a beak like a Bowie knife.

Bliss saw the Escalade ease into the parking lot. It wasn't too crowded today, and the car parked only about thirty feet from where she sat. She saw him exit the vehicle and make his way toward her. He nodded serenely when she greeted him by the front entrance of the Secret Stash.

"Viktor Kostiuk," she said. "You'll have to go inside and get your own lawn chair if you want to sit down."

"Not necessary, Bliss," he said. "I won't be staying long."

"So," she said, "did your man make my delivery?"

He nodded. "Left it around lunchtime, in an anonymous FedEx Letter envelope."

Bliss let a little space fall between their words, listening to the sounds of rain building up in the distance.

"I wonder what your boss would say," she said, "if he knew his little spy was working for me now." Viktor shrugged, and she felt suddenly irritated. She continued, "If you'd just done your job, we wouldn't have this situation to deal with in the first place."

"I *was* doing my job," he said. "She was a threat. She still is a threat, and even after April 14 she'll be a threat. She was a witness to circumstances tying every one of us together. If she opens her mouth to her ex-husband, to anyone in law enforcement, my work gets compromised. Your work gets compromised. That's a problem, and I found a clean, permanent solution. What better way to eliminate the threat than to have her sitting in the audience at Max Roman's fundraiser next week?"

"But you forget, she's connected to me."

"Every war has collateral damage. She won't be the only person in the audience."

"Yes, but she'll be the only innocent person. The rest of

those people, they're all Max Roman sycophants. They ply him with money and favors and flattery and power. They keep him untouchable. They're complicit in his crimes. They deserve what's coming to them."

"We all do, I suppose." He shrugged again. "Anyway, I think my approach was the best way to handle your detective lady, but I'm willing to be proven wrong. Maybe she'll take the job offer. Then I can just steer her away from everything else."

"I hope so. But there is a backup plan just in case."

He gestured toward the bird on the canvas. "What about him?"

"My problem, not yours."

A light mist began to fall over the parking lot. Viktor stepped closer to Bliss's wheelchair, maneuvering to get fully under the awning of the store. She reached into her pocket and produced a small logbook with a gray cover.

"I suppose you want this?"

"It would be helpful," he said. "Max Roman is expecting me to get it somehow."

"All you had to do was ask. No need to send a thief."

"Trying to keep my cover was all. What's in this logbook?"

"Enough to make your boss think he got what he wanted, but not enough to keep him clean and safe. A week from now, though, hopefully it'll all be irrelevant." She handed over the logbook.

"Speaking of next week," he said, "what about my Kipo?"

"I got no love for any kook in puke orange." She felt like spitting, but she also knew Viktor's soldiers would serve a purpose next week. *A necessary evil*, she thought. "How many you going to have onsite?"

"Nine. Plus Andrew Carr makes ten."

"What are they expecting?"

"They think it's all about money. Smash-n-grab job to steal cash and valuables from a bunch of rich people at a high-class banquet. Except for Andrew Carr, of course."

"Then they deserve what's coming to them too."

Viktor didn't respond to that. Instead, he changed the subject. "Where's Darrent today?"

"On vacation," she said. "A cruise somewhere, I think. He'll be out of town for a few weeks."

"Week from now I might join him."

"Maybe we all will."

They watched the rain begin to pick up in the parking lot around them, staining the world with a fresh, wet wonder, making the air taste warm and sweet.

"You know, it's not too late to back out," Viktor said into the storm. "Call the whole thing off. Let Nevermore be just another almost-thing in the back of our minds."

Bliss grimaced. "I expected better from you, Viktor Kostiuk. You feeling sentimental about your family or something?"

"Pavlo is a dog of a man," he snorted. "I plucked him out of Ukraine just for this purpose. Why would I feel sentimental about that? I only wanted to give you one last opportunity to avoid an apocalypse. You're sure it's worth it?"

"How long did it take me to get you inserted into Max Roman's organization? And then to move you up, into his inner circle, without raising suspicion from anyone?"

"All together? Seven years, give or take. Including the time spent in New York building my reputation."

One year after Davis's death, she remembered. *That was the beginning.*

"So what makes you think I'm going to invest seven years and then walk away empty-handed?"

He nodded. "Sure, sure," he said.

"Besides, you and your little partner, you want to walk away from a lifetime's worth of money just because I get cold feet?"

Now he really grinned, a wolfish look that she'd grown accustomed to seeing on his face. "No, Bliss," he said. "We definitely do not want to do that."

"All right, then," she said.

"All right, then," he echoed.

The rain was steady and warm now. Bliss almost felt like rolling into the parking lot, lifting her chin, and letting the cleansing water pour down her face and into her mouth. Instead, she went over the checklist in her head for the thousandth time.

"Is the narrative set?" she asked.

"Mm-hmm," he said. He too seemed to find a little peace in their own private thunderstorm. "Computer diary dating back at least a year. A few Facebook rants. Pictures with guns and flags. Incriminating receipts. Weapons stash. Maps and photos pinned to a closet wall. Even a compromising nationalist tattoo on his shoulder. Those things will all turn up when the police investigate."

"How will it read in the papers?"

"Ukrainian terrorist recruits disaffected American gang members and stages a violent protest to raise awareness of Russian atrocities in Eastern Europe."

Bliss felt the muscles in her back relax. It was all coming together—after all these years, justice was finally going to be done—and it would be blamed on Russian politics and American fears.

"How long do you think it'll be before we'll know whether or not Darrent will be able to come back to Atlanta?"

"He wants to come back? Why? Aren't you paying him too?"

"That's none of your concern, now, is it? I'm just asking if you think he'll be able to come back."

"If Nevermore goes according to plan, he gets to come back from 'vacation,' as scheduled, express shock and dismay to the media, then get back to work for America. If there are any hiccups, well"—he shrugged—"maybe he never comes back."

"There are always hiccups."

"Your manager knew what he was getting into. I'm sure he can take care of himself."

True, true, she told herself. "Yes, Darrent can take care of himself," she said.

Now Viktor turned to meet her eyes. "Everything has been planned and schemed and practice-run down to the minor details. The only thing we don't know about is you. What happens to Bliss June Monroe when this is all over?"

She takes care of herself too, she thought. Aloud she said, "What you don't know can't hurt you."

"Right," he said. "I understand that. But you'll have to leave the country, at least for a while. There are too many of your fingerprints that'll show up in an investigation. Darrent Hayes can plead ignorance if he has to. Most likely you won't have that luxury."

"What you don't know can't hurt you," she repeated.

"Okay," he said, taking the hint at last. There was a lull in the conversation, then he said, "Well, it looks like the rain is letting up. I'd better be going."

"All right, then," she said.

He nodded toward the raven painted in blacks and grays on her canvas. "Beautiful art today," he said. "I'm going to miss seeing your paintings."

"Take this one," she said. "Remember me forever."

"Oh, I could never forget you, Bliss," he said. But he still reached up and removed the canvas from the easel.

"Careful of the paint, it's still a little damp. Turn it facedown when you walk to your car, then faceup inside the car. After the rain stops, let it set somewhere to dry for a day or so before you touch it."

"Will do. Thank you."

"I won't see you before next Friday," she said as he prepared to leave. "Make sure you get your work done. And try not to make any more problems for me between now and then."

The wolf was back on his lips. "Don't you worry, Mama Bliss," he said. "Nevermore is going to go exactly according to plan."

TODAY . . .

38

TRUDI

Atlanta, GA
West Midtown
Friday, April 14, 4:44 p.m.
Three hours and forty-three minutes to Nevermore

"You hear anything from Samuel?"

Trudi stood in the reception area of Coffey & Hill Investigations, badgering Eulalie for the fifth time today. The assistant was still patient nonetheless.

"Nope, nothing yet. But he said he'd be there, so I believe he'll be there."

"Ah, you poor, unsuspecting girl," Trudi mocked, "so unwise in the ways of men."

Eulalie dimpled and ignored the insult. "I did pick up your dress from the cleaners," she continued. "Stunning. You're going to look great tonight."

Trudi tried not to feel a flush of pride. It was a pretty dress. Samuel had bought it for her as a surprise gift when they were on the run during the early stages of the Annabel Lee case. She'd stuck it in her closet and then never had an excuse to wear it. When she'd pulled it out a few days ago, it was dusty and slightly wrinkled, but still the best thing she owned on a hanger. She kind of liked that she had something worth sending to the cleaners in preparation for the gala event. And, though she wouldn't admit it out loud, she liked that in a few hours she was going to get all prettied up and go out to a big party, even if it was just a political fundraiser and even though her ex-husband had insisted on being her date for the event.

"Maybe I should just take you instead of Samuel tonight," Trudi said.

"Ooh, don't tempt me!" Eulalie replied. "I love getting dressed up and going out. Will there be dancing?"

"Doubtful."

"Ah, forget it, then. Besides, he'll be there. He said he'd be there."

Trudi was glad that things were back on a normal setting with Eulalie, and even with Samuel, at least as normal as they could be.

He'd come when she'd asked him to last Friday around noon. She was still at her desk, staring at the picture, when he'd knocked on the outside door.

"Locked," Trudi had said to herself, stuffing the picture and the accompanying itinerary for the so-called Hawaiian vacation back into the FedEx Letter envelope. "Forgot Eula locked the door when I sent her home."

She went out front and let Samuel in. Together they'd walked back to her office.

"So what's the big threat?" he'd said, settling formally into his regular chair on the visitor side of her desk. He looked concerned. "What's going on?"

She'd handed him the FedEx envelope and waited while he inspected the contents. She wasn't surprised that he ignored the Hawaii itinerary, leaving it inside. She too had been consumed by the picture when she first saw it, just as he was now. He pulled it out and stared at it in stunned silence. She could see a thousand thoughts synapsing through his brain, and then he looked up at her. There was worry fixed in his gaze. She saw his jaw muscles tense.

"He's beautiful, Samuel. He's got your eyes and chin."

He'd nodded, speechless.

"What do you need to do?" She had swallowed her heart then. "Whatever it is, we'll do it."

He'd nodded again, more slowly this time. She thought his hand trembled where the thumb and forefinger held for dear life on to the bottom corner of the photo.

"Trudi," he'd said. Then nothing.

She'd wanted to ask the boy's name, wanted to know more about the child with her husband's smile. But she knew he'd never tell her too much. In his line of work, with the enemies he'd made, it was too dangerous to spread that kind of information around. She waited until he was ready.

"He is a beautiful boy," he'd said at last. He set the picture and the envelope on the edge of her desk. "He laughs a lot. You'd love his laughter, you really would."

"I know."

Samuel had blinked his eyes blankly, and she could see his mind processing the possibilities. Then he seemed to return to the moment and take in her presence.

"Trudi," he'd said again, "I know what you think of me. I know you thought I was with that redhead back at the Ritz. That I jumped at the chance."

"Samuel—"

"That's not me, Tru-Bear." His eyes had searched hers. "I'm not that guy. I followed her upstairs because she suggested you might be in danger. I had to see if she was right."

Trudi didn't know what to say, so she just said nothing.

"I made a mistake seven and a half years ago," he'd said, "I know it. The worst mistake I could make. I was young. I thought I was indestructible. I thought, 'everybody does it, and Trudi will never know.' But that was just stupid. Even before you found out, it tore me up. It made me wake up sick at night. I ended it, and I made a promise never to do anything that could hurt you, not ever again . . ." His voice trailed off.

"We've been through this before, Samuel."

"No, not really. Because you think I'm still the same stupid pig who had an affair just because it was convenient, just because it was easy." His voice went deathly soft. "I'm not that guy."

"Well, you still look like him." Trudi had been surprised at how quickly she could jab that knife into her ex-husband's heart. But it was the truth, and in a way, it felt good to talk about it openly with him for once.

"I know we'll never be together again," he'd said slowly, "not as husband and wife, at least. This is my punishment, and it's just. But I want you to know there's no one else for me. Never will be."

Trudi tried not to grimace. She'd felt a familiar pain welling up within her rib cage. "Samuel, you have another wife. A secret lover hidden away somewhere in the Middle East."

"No, not her either. I told you, we married just to protect her safety. We've never been together since she got pregnant. I see her when I visit my son, but there's nothing going on between us. That's the truth. We both learned from that mistake."

"It's hard to believe you, Samuel."

"You don't have to believe me," he'd said. His chin dipped,

watching his feet shuffle uncomfortably on the floor. "I'm not asking you for anything. I just wanted you to know."

She stared at his eyes and saw truth in them, but she also knew the facts. He'd made a vow on their wedding day and broken it. And what about Eulalie?

"I saw you, Samuel," she'd said. "At Eclipse di Luna. I know about you and Eulalie."

The look on his face had been one of pure confusion.

"I see the way you flirt with her around the office. And I saw you two on your date three weeks ago."

The corners of his eyes had wrinkled merrily at that, and his lips teased a brief smile. "Trudi," he said, "there's nothing going on between me and Eulalie. She's almost a decade younger than me."

Trudi had felt mildly embarrassed.

"If you saw Eulalie and me together last month," he continued, "it was homework. She was writing a paper on the Distinctive Psychosis of Law Enforcement Personalities or something like that. I had to take a written survey and then let her ask me a bunch of strange questions about my mother. I told her she had to at least buy me dinner for that."

Of course! Trudi thought all at once. *She asked me to take a survey for her too, but I passed it off. Maybe she got Samuel to take it instead?*

A sober look had reappeared on Samuel's face. "Listen, because I need to tell you this now. I love you, Trudi Sara Coffey. All of me loves all of you. I always will, whether you want me to or not."

It's crazy when a man's words both hurt and heal you, she'd told herself. She blinked, then sighed.

"So why are you telling me this now?"

"For a long time, I thought I could never love anything as

much as I love you. And then he came along." He'd picked up the picture from the desktop. "I'd do anything for you, Tru-Bear. And I'll do anything for him."

"I understand," she had said. "And I'm here to help you. What do we need to do?"

"That's the thing. You can't do anything. But I'm going to have to leave for a few days. And if I don't come back, well, I wanted you to know that I love you. Always."

She had felt an all-too-common frustration. "I can help you, Samuel. If you love me, let me help you."

"Trudi," he'd said, "this picture was taken outside my son's home in—well, in an unnamed country in the Middle East. The home is guarded day and night. I saw to that. It has electronic security as well as armed guards. But these people still got close enough to take a picture of my boy in his backyard. That means they know me, they know how to get to me, and they're dangerous. There's nothing you can do. There's nothing I'll let you do."

"So I'm just supposed to sit here and worry about you?"

"No, I want you to sit here and solve Nevermore for me while I'm gone. Figure out what's going on so we can stop it when I get back."

If *you get back*, she'd thought. Then, *Wow, I'm such an optimist.* "What are you going to do?"

He'd stood. "Thanks to my old buddies at the CIA, I'm on the international no-fly list, so it looks like my first stop will be Langley, Virginia, to get that obstacle taken care of."

A new concern had wrinkled his face then. "But I'll be back in time to be your date for Max Roman's fundraiser. Promise you'll take me."

"Samuel, don't worry about it. I'll take Eulalie with me. We'll check things out for you and let you know if we uncover anything."

"No, Trudi." His voice had been insistent. "I'll be back. Promise me you'll take me as your date."

"Fine," she'd said at last. She knew he was thinking something he wasn't saying, but she decided to let it go. "It's a date."

"Okay." He had scooped up the photo and returned it to the FedEx envelope, then tucked it all underneath his arm. He paused.

"I heard you the first time," she'd said. "Just go and save the world already."

He'd grinned, and then she'd watched him go, first through the door to her office, then on the security camera feed from the reception area, and finally on the security feed from the parking lot.

A week later, he still wasn't back in Atlanta, but she'd gotten a phone message from him saying he'd meet her at the dinner party tonight, that he'd be coming straight from the airport but would dress appropriately before boarding his flight so she wouldn't be embarrassed by his beat-up old boots.

It almost felt like a real date, a long-overdue reunion. She was actually excited.

"You're right," she said to Eulalie. "He said he'd be there, so he'll be there." She smiled at her assistant and felt the glow returned to her in Eula's face. "Come on," she said. "Want to help me pick out shoes to go with my red dress?"

39

RAVEN

Atlanta, GA
Downtown
Friday, April 14, 5:29 p.m.
Two hours and fifty-eight minutes to Nevermore

Mama Bliss is alone when I return to Room 614 of the Ritz-Carlton.

Even though I have a keycard, and even though we've spent the last two days as de facto roommates, I still stop to knock before entering.

"If I know you," she shouts, "you've got a key."

I slide the card through the lock and walk in, finding Mama organizing her diabetic instruments in a drawer of the dresser. I reach out stealthily and scoop my cell phone off the end table. One button-push shuts everything down. She glances up at me.

"Thirty minutes on the dot," she says. "I do appreciate a timely magician."

Deception specialist, I tell myself, but at this point I'm not going to correct Mama Bliss.

Mama had been as good as her word. The Monday after I broke into her office, I went to Sister Bliss's Secret Stash and found a job waiting for me. Her manager, Darrent Hayes, took me down to the warehouse and told a beefy, friendly-faced man named Sam that I was his new security guard. *Give him the one-day orientation*, he'd said. *Mama doesn't want him in the warehouse yet, just wants him to know the basics of being a security guard. She's got a special assignment for him.*

That special assignment had turned out to be the easiest job of my entire life. She set me up in Room 614 at the Ritz-Carlton hotel, started loading it with valuable antiques to be sold in her charity auction, and told me just to sit here and make sure nothing got stolen.

This is the life, I'd decided. Watching TV, playing video games on the hotel network, taking breaks from time to time to go down to the lobby to eat gourmet food, all paid for by Sister Bliss's Secret Stash. *I could live like this for a while.*

That's not to say there hadn't been any excitement. The whole Samuel Hill/Scholarship confrontation in the hallway had made me jittery and nervous for at least a day and a night. But nothing had happened after that, and I returned to my life of ease.

At one point, on Tuesday I think, Mama came by with a few guys from the warehouse to take some of the auction items somewhere else. She told me to take a break while they sorted through things, and when I came back from the lobby, one row of boxes had disappeared, along with Mama and her workers. I noticed the long, canvas bags that had occupied the far corner of the room were also gone, all five of them. For some reason, that made me feel relieved. Those bags had made me nervous.

On Wednesday afternoon, Mama had called and informed me she was moving into the hotel room with me for the next few days, to coordinate the final preparations for the Max Roman gala onsite. She didn't want to have to travel back and forth from her house to the Stash to the hotel. She just wanted to have a place close by where she could go rest if she got tired. So I had a roommate.

Sharing a room with a seventy-one-year-old woman is not without its adventures. For starters, Bliss Monroe snores like a cyclone on holiday. Even foam earplugs were no match for her, so eventually I just turned up the music on my cell phone, stuffed my earbuds in, and hoped that exhaustion would make up for lack of peace at night. Mama Bliss is also not shy about things like dressing and undressing or going to the toilet. After a few pleas, she finally conceded to closing the bathroom door when she was doing her business in there, but when it came to changing clothes, she was unfazed.

"You don't want to see," she'd said while swapping a shirt and pants for a nightgown the first night, "then don't look." So we reached a tacit agreement. When I saw she was getting ready to change clothes, I'd find a reason to spend some time in the bathroom. Then she'd holler a few minutes later, "Safe for young eyes," and I'd come out again. I think she enjoyed making me feel a little embarrassed, but otherwise we got along fine.

Mama Bliss was busy most of the day on Thursday, working downstairs getting things ready in the Grand Ballroom, but she still came back and took a nap in the afternoon. Then she went back downstairs and worked late into the night. On Friday, she slept in, almost until noon. When she woke, she still looked tired, and she asked me to go get breakfast for her even though it was basically lunchtime already. When I came back with her eggs and toast, I found a parade of about half a dozen warehouse workers taking boxes and artifacts out the door in assembly-line fashion.

"Getting close to the end of this business," Mama had said to me then. "Why don't you help the boys take these things down to the Grand Ballroom on the lower level? They need to be set up so Max Roman's guests can inspect them before the auction starts." So I did that, and by the time I was done, it was close to four o'clock and I'd missed lunch. I snacked on a candy bar and decided that was going to have to be enough.

Back at the room, Mama was going full steam again, full of energy, barking commands into the hotel room phone, laying out clothes for the evening, and generally running the world the way she wanted it.

Just before five o'clock, she started to put on her velvet pantsuit in preparation for the evening's festivities, so I went in the bathroom and tried on the rental tuxedo I'd gotten to wear for tonight. If I was to be table entertainment for the rich and famous, I wanted to look the part. Mama had been appropriately admiring when I stepped out of the bathroom.

"You clean up all right," she'd said, grinning.

I needed to add a few little surprises to my pockets, so they'd be ready to magically appear at tonight's party. I'd stashed them inside a small drawer in the end table near the hotel room door, along with my wallet, keys, and cell phone. I started lining my pockets with items from the drawer while Mama busied herself with some paperwork. Then I heard a knock at the door.

"Pizza delivery," a deep voice said.

I froze. My left hand started trembling, and I must've looked kind of doe-eyed in Mama's direction. She laughed out loud.

"Open the door," she'd said. "He's just doing that 'cause he knows you're here."

Sure enough, Scholarship was on the other side of the door,

along with Viktor Kostiuk. The football player was grinning at me like he was a stand-up comedian who'd just delivered the perfect joke. I wasn't laughing. The scarred spot on my left hand tingled like it'd been poked with needles.

What does Mama Bliss have to do with these guys? I had asked myself, and even in my head my voice was shaky. *These are Max Roman's guys.*

"Can I help you?" I said. I stood in the doorway, blocking them from coming in. I'm not any kind of bodyguard, but I knew personally what these men were capable of doing, and I wasn't about to let them work their trade on an old woman in a wheelchair. At least I wasn't going to make it easy for them. *Fingers to the throat,* I coached myself. *It worked before, right?*

Scholarship had raised his eyebrows at me. "You have a new bodyguard, Mama?" he'd called out over my shoulder. "'Cause this tuxedo kid of yours is scaring me."

"Leave him alone and come in," Mama said.

I didn't know what to make of that. *She's expecting them? This is getting strange.* I stepped aside, and they both pushed past me and exchanged greetings with Mama Bliss.

I turned back to the end table and started reorganizing my pocket contents again. I set my cell phone on the corner of the table, then noticed the Voice Memo app on the home screen. *I wonder what would happen if I recorded this conversation,* I thought.

Just then I heard Mama give me an order. "Why don't you take a break, Raven? Go downstairs and get yourself a snack."

I had looked up to see they were all settling into chairs at the little round table that Mama used as a desk, over at the foot of her bed. It looked like a business meeting was about to begin.

"Sure thing, Mama," I said, returning a few items to the drawer and replacing them with my wallet. "You want anything?"

"No, you go on. Come back in thirty minutes. We'll be done by then."

"Okay," I'd said.

"Wait," she told me. She pulled a small padded envelope off the desk and tossed it to me. "Mail this for me," she said. "Important that it goes out today, okay?"

"Sure," I'd said. The padded envelope was flat, but thick, like it held a notepad inside. *A logbook*, I thought. *The logbook?* I noticed the address on the envelope. It was being sent to the Atlanta Zone 6 police station. I turned the padded envelope over in my hands, determined not to ask questions.

They had all turned their backs on me then, ready to get down to their business. I was invisible, it seemed. I took the opportunity and tapped the app button on my cell. The Voice Memo function kicked in. I secretly hoped it'd keep recording until I got back.

"I'll see you in a half hour," I'd said. Then I went downstairs—tuxedo and all—and treated myself to a couple of chicken biscuits at the Atlanta Grill. When I came back to the room, Mama was all alone.

"Thirty minutes on the dot," she says when I come in. "I do appreciate a timely magician."

"Everything okay, Mama?" I say to her.

"'Course it is," she says. "Why wouldn't it be?"

"Well . . ." I shrug. "My experience with those guys has never been pleasant."

She gives me a look that says she hadn't thought of that. "Don't you worry, sugar," she says. "Those men won't ever bother you again. Understand?"

I nod. I think she's telling the truth, and I feel almost relieved. "Besides," she continues, "they like you. You won them over."

"Thanks?" My phantom pinky burns like a bee sting.

She's not talking anymore, but she's still looking at me. Staring. Thinking. Studying me with those all-seeing onyx eyes of hers.

"What time do you want to head down to the ballroom?" I say, trying to change the subject. "Doors open at six-thirty, so I thought maybe we should get down there around six o'clock? Be there when people start coming in?"

"Tyson," she says to me, and it's jarring to hear her speak my real name. She notices me flinch. "What, I'm not allowed to call you by name? You gave it to me when you broke into my office and told me your troubles, remember?"

"No. Sure. Yeah. You can call me by my name, Mama. It's just been a long time since anyone actually used it."

Tyson.

I hear a faded version of my mother's voice and suddenly feel tired.

"No, it's okay. I'll call you Raven. That's what you go by now anyway." She sizes me up again, and then she says, "I got four things for you, Raven. Four things I want to give you, okay?"

"Sure, Mama. But you've already given me—"

"Hush. You let Mama talk for a minute." She rolls her wheel-chair over to the dresser and opens one of the middle drawers underneath where the TV sits. "First," she says, "you're fired."

Fired? "Wait, what? Did I do something wrong, Mama? If so, I can fix it. I'll do better."

She's grinning. "No, let me say it differently. You're not fired. You're free. Your debt to me is paid. You got no more reason to stay."

"I don't understand. I've only been working for you two weeks. You said I had to stay for a full month."

"Just wanted to make sure you were who I thought you were. But two weeks is enough. You're free to go."

"What about the table entertainment at tonight's banquet? I

can finish out the night. I've got all my tricks ready. I'm happy to do it for you. You don't even have to pay me."

"No, honey. I don't want you for that anymore. You're done. You can go." She looks kind of somber now. "I need you to go. Do this for Mama Bliss, okay?"

I have no real idea what's going on, but I know what the right answer is. "Okay, Mama. If you say so."

"Second," she says quickly, and I think she's glad that part of the conversation is over. "I want you to have this."

She reaches into the drawer and pulls out a puffy manila envelope. I can see from here that it's been stuffed full of something. She tosses it to me, and I catch it in my right hand.

"There's ten thousand dollars in there," she says. "Your severance package. Use it wisely, and you'll be fine. Understand?"

"You don't have to do this," I say. *Why is this woman being so generous to me?*

"I know I don't have to do it. I'm doing it anyway. You going to argue with me about it, or are you just going to do what Mama Bliss tells you to do?"

"Yes, ma'am."

"I also want you to have this." She reaches into the drawer and pulls out an antique magazine. It's encased in a sturdy, sealed plastic case that I assume is used for both protection and display. "This is a first-edition copy of the *New York Evening Mirror* magazine from January 1845. This is the magazine that first published your namesake, 'The Raven' by Edgar Allan Poe."

"Wow. I don't know what to say."

"Just say thank you. I was going to let it be auctioned off tonight, but I changed my mind about that. I want you to have it. I want you to keep it, and sometimes when you look at it remember that old Mama Bliss Monroe wasn't all bad."

"I don't think you're bad, Mama."

"That's because you don't know me yet." She smiled, and I almost wanted to give her a hug. "Anyway, you take it and you remember me when you look at it, okay?"

"I will. And thank you. It's amazing."

"Fourth," she says, and now she's holding up a folded slip of paper torn from the pad of hotel stationery. "This last thing is for you."

"What is it?"

"It's for you."

I nod and move toward her, but she pulls the paper away before I can take it from her hand. "You may not like this," she says, "but that's not my fault."

"Okay."

She's still holding the paper out of my reach.

"After I give this to you, I'm going to leave. You can borrow my laptop here for a little while, but I need you to be out of this hotel by seven o'clock tonight. Gone-long-gone, okay? I'm coming back up here around then to take a quick rest while everybody else is eating dinner, and I don't want you hanging around here when I get back. Got it?"

"Okay, Mama. I'll be gone when you come back."

"Good." She hands me the paper, but before I can unfold it, she grasps both my hands in both of hers. "Tyson," she says softly. "He's gone now. But he left you something."

"What are you talking about?"

"Your father, sugar. He passed away seven months ago."

"What?"

The air behind my word feels frail, like it might shatter if I speak my question above a whisper. My stomach feels like I've swallowed a stone, and the earth shifts suddenly to the left and then back again. I sit on the corner of one of the queen beds in the hotel room to avoid that dizzy feeling again.

"I tried to call him for you. I wanted to talk to him, find out what he was like. The people at his church said cancer claimed his body back in September. But he left you that." She nods toward the paper in my hand.

I'm speechless. *My father, gone? But I never had a chance to . . . I never got to . . .*

"You take a little time now. You use my computer. And then you get out of this hotel, out of this town. You use that money I gave you, and you go back to Oklahoma City, just for a few days. You pay respects to your father's grave, and you settle his affairs. Then you can get on with your life, knowing at least you done what you could."

"Why are you doing this for me, Mama Bliss?"

"Because I got me a child that flew away too," she says. "And when I'm gone, I hope someone will help her come back here and pay her last respects for me."

She releases my hand and then wheels herself toward the door. She leaves without saying goodbye and, in the silence that's left behind, I feel hot tears begin to press out of my eyes. I don't bother trying to stop them.

My daddy used to say . . . I tell myself, but for the life of me I can't remember a single one of his long-winded sermons right now. I just remember his voice, and how I broke his heart over and over again. And only now that he's fully gone from me do I realize how much I needed him, how much of me is a part of him and how much of him became a part of me.

I open the slip of paper Mama Bliss gave me, and I read the careful lettering she left behind there. There's not much on it, just the URL of a website.

TysonComeHome.com

40

TRUDI

Atlanta, GA
Downtown
Friday, April 14, 6:55 p.m.
One hour and thirty-two minutes to Nevermore

Trudi found two things waiting for her when she reached the placard that announced her seat at the banquet table. One was a flute glass made of fine crystal, filled with a deep-cherry-colored wine. The other was her ex-husband, dressed in a sharp, if slightly wrinkled, charcoal-gray, four-button suit, sipping contentedly on his own glass of the same.

"You thought I wouldn't be here, I know you did," he said happily. She noticed half his glass of wine was already gone. She figured he'd be on a second glass pretty soon, as well. "Yet here I am, dressed and happy, and I beat you to the table by a good twenty minutes. Maybe half an hour."

"I got stopped by security. They were searching bags, and I had my Beretta in my purse."

He flipped open his suit coat to reveal an empty shoulder holster. "They don't like you to bring guns into the Ritz-Carlton hotel," he said, grinning, "unless you give prior notice and get authorization."

"You're a police detective. You couldn't get authorization?"

"Well"—he shrugged—"actually I did this time. But I saw Mama Bliss on the way in, and she asked me nicely if I would check my gun at the front desk. Apparently I spooked her a bit with my questions last week, so she hired extra security for this event, and she's being especially vigilant about anything and anyone who comes into the Grand Ballroom tonight."

"So you checked your Glock?"

Trudi noticed a few eyes widening on the other side of their table. There were settings for ten people at each table and, counting Samuel and her, eight had already arrived. "Don't worry," she said quickly to the stuffed shirts and expensive gowns tinkling priceless jewelry around them. "He's a cop. A detective with the Atlanta PD."

They nodded at that but weren't fully at ease until Samuel pulled his badge out of an inside coat pocket and verified it for them. Then they went back to their conversations and determinedly ignored Samuel and Trudi.

"As a favor for Mama, yes, I checked my gun." He leaned in close and winked. "One of my guns."

"Well, Mama didn't give me the option of checking my gun," she continued. "I brought my concealed-carry license with me, thought that would be enough, but apparently it wasn't. So I had to go back to my car and stash my Tomcat in there."

She started to pull out the chair to sit down, but Samuel stopped her, rising to his feet. He swiftly slid the chair out for her. "Ms. Coffey," he said formally, "it's truly a pleasure to be your date tonight."

He does like being a gentleman, she thought. *Even if it makes him a little overbearing at times.*

"Thank you, Mr. Hill." She played along. "Why did you order wine for me?"

"I didn't." He shrugged. "It was here when I sat down." He took another sip from his glass.

Trudi scanned the room and saw nothing out of the ordinary. Lots of black-clad waitstaff were bustling around the room, serving and clearing. A four-piece jazz ensemble had set up on the right side of the platform, just in front of a black curtain that decorated the edges of the stage. And hundreds of rich, sophisticated people were filling up the tables all around the room. She did a quick head count and figured there must be about 450 people attending this event. At one thousand dollars a plate, that meant Max Roman was going to gross nearly half a million dollars from this fundraiser alone.

I wonder how much money it takes to run for mayor of the ATL? she thought absently.

Still, she had to admit that her previous worries seemed out of place now that she was here at the fundraiser. *I'm the most suspicious-looking thing in this room*, she thought. *One of these things is not like the others . . . and it's me.*

"Have you noticed anything out of the ordinary?" she said.

"Nope," Samuel replied. "I took time to scout the room when I came in. Even 'accidentally' wound up in the kitchen. Nothing unusual, at least nothing I can see."

Trudi had to agree with her ex-husband. Everything seemed like just the workings of another high-society party in downtown Atlanta. She frowned. Sometimes normal just didn't feel right. This was one of those times, but she couldn't put her finger on what made her feel that way.

Samuel, on the other hand, seemed to take it all in stride.

He was starting to look downright relaxed next to her, patting his thigh in almost-rhythm to the smooth sounds coming from the jazz band.

"So what do you think?" she said. "Should we be worried?"

He looked around the room again, then came back to her, smiling. "I think Mama Bliss has things well in control. Maybe we can take tonight off for once."

She leaned in close. "What about Nevermore?"

"Look around you, Tru-Bear," he said. "Where's the threat?" He sighed. "It looks like Mama's intel was right. Maybe Nevermore is just a hoax dreamed up by Andrew Carr. I'll still keep an eye on the Edgar Awards happening in Athens a few weeks from now, but tonight's fundraiser seems safe enough. Honestly, I'm kind of relieved."

She nodded. It did look that way, but Trudi couldn't shake the feeling that not everything was as it seemed. She decided to keep her wits about her, just in case. She pushed her wineglass toward the center of the table and took a sip from her water glass instead.

"You look great, Trudi," Samuel said. He was admiring her with glittering eyes, as if she was a precious jewel. "Stunning. Most beautiful woman in the room. As usual."

He tipped his glass in her direction and took another drink. In spite of her defenses, her ex-husband's compliment made her feel good. Made her feel pretty again. She liked that.

"You're drunk," she said, laughing lightly. Then she remembered why she hadn't seen him for the past week and frowned. "How are things with, well, how was your trip?"

He nodded as he downed the last of his cabernet. "All taken care of. All fine. Well, will be fine."

What does that mean? she wanted to ask.

"Moving," he added, as if reading her mind. "We're going

into a communications blackout for six months so they can work through a set of 'disappear' stages. It takes a little time to do that kind of thing well, but I personally picked the Fader for this job. She'll do it right. Meanwhile, everyone is safe for the moment, and they'll be fully secure again soon. The Fader will contact me when everything is in place."

Trudi suddenly felt like changing the subject. "Mama Bliss looked nice tonight," she said. "Did you see her in the pre-function area just outside the ballroom?"

"Mm-hmm. Seems like she's over being mad at me, so I was glad about that. Gave me a hug and a lecture, just like normal."

"That's good. She actually seemed kind of cheerful," Trudi said. "I think she must be excited about the charity auction. There are some really cool antiques up for sale tonight."

"Maybe I'll bid on something for you. Anything special that you liked?"

"No, thank you, Samuel." She found herself actually having a nice time. She caught movement in the corner of her eye, and it made her curious. "Who are those people wandering around?"

"Table entertainment," he said. "You just missed the Trivia Guy. He gives out little prizes to anyone who knows facts about Atlanta history, or Max Roman, or classic literature. By the way, who wrote Homer's *Odyssey*?"

She rolled her eyes. "Homer."

"No, that's part of the title. Who wrote it? I thought maybe Shakespeare, but that was wrong."

"Samuel—" She started to argue with him, then gave up. "I don't know. We didn't study that in college."

He shot her a look, and she could see he knew he'd made a mistake. He returned to his introductions. "That guy on the other side, over by the back exit, he recites funny poetry. Shel Silverstein and Rudyard Kipling, that kind of stuff. Some people here like him a lot, but I thought he was too melodramatic." He pointed to a nearby table. "That woman over there, in the black dress, she's a caricaturist. Draws her pictures on cocktail napkins, which I thought was clever. I hope she comes over here because I think it'd be fun to get a picture of the two of us."

Did he just giggle?

"How much have you had to drink, Samuel?" she asked.

"One glass of wine. That's it." He snickered again. Then he slid back in his chair. "I'm really tired, though. Been up for about twenty hours straight. Guess I'm a little loopy from jet lag and lack of sleep."

He muffled a chuckle and reached for her abandoned glass. "Since you're not going to drink this . . ." he said by way of a toast, then he swallowed a third of her wine.

"Pay attention, Samuel," she hissed. "We're here for a reason."

He shook his head. "It all checks out, Tru-Bear. The place is clean. I told you I went through it all before you got here. And judging from security out front, nobody who's not a cop is getting a weapon into this room. Mama Bliss knows a thing or two about security. Maybe we should just trust her to do her job, relax, and let ourselves have a good time for once."

Trudi looked around the room again and couldn't find any reason to disagree with him.

"I feel good," he said to nobody, stretching out that last word so it sounded like *goo-ood*.

"Well, we still should be vigilant," Trudi reprimanded.

"You're right." He sat up and scanned the room. Then he definitely giggled. "Vigilant," he said. "That's a funny word. Ever notice that? Vih-juh-lent. Vigilantvigilantvigilant."

She decided to ignore that little detour. Jet lag was really a bear, she knew. "Where's Max Roman?" she asked.

"Not here yet," he said. "But look who's working tonight."

She followed his gaze and saw Andrew Carr, wearing the black shirt and pants that were the uniform of the waitstaff here at the Ritz. He was clearing a table of empty glasses while a girl followed behind him with Caesar salads for diners. She watched him take his load past an empty bussing cart near an exit and deposit it on an already-full cart farther down the wall. She wondered vaguely why he didn't just use the empty cart closest to him and then decided she didn't need to know all the details of a busboy's job. There was a reason she'd avoided restaurant work while earning her way through college.

"Watch this." Samuel nudged her. "This'll be fun."

He waited until Carr was working his way back to the next table, then made eye contact with him. When Carr looked at him, Samuel pulled his police badge from his coat pocket and waved it toward the former gang member. Then he did the two-fingered I'm-watching-you signal, motioning from his eyes to Carr's eyes for emphasis. Andrew Carr looked angry, but he just turned and strode off to the kitchen without collecting the next table's glasses.

"Samuel, stop taunting that boy," Trudi snapped. She snatched the badge from his hand and stuffed it into her purse, out of her ex-husband's reach. Samuel was snickering again, laughing at what he apparently thought was a great practical joke.

"Grow up, Samuel," she said.

"Hoo," he said suddenly. "I don't feel quite right."

"Well, stop drinking this, then." She put the wineglass out of his reach. "When was the last time you ate?"

"What time is it?" he said.

"Seven-thirty," she said after checking the clock on her cell phone.

"I had a sandwich, maybe twelve hours ago," he said.

"Alcohol on an empty stomach? Not really a good plan, you know."

"You're right," he said. "I probably should eat something."

"Well, they're serving soup and salads now. Why don't you go to the bathroom and splash some water on your face? By the time you get back, food will be here. You can start catching up to the wine."

"Good idea." He stood up, and Trudi was slightly embarrassed that he was already a little shaky on his feet. He paused to look at her again, and she saw his warm smile, the one that always made her heart flutter just a little bit. "You really are beautiful, Tru-Bear. Lovely."

Says the drunk man, she thought. But she just smiled and waved him toward the bathroom.

Max Roman and his entourage finally arrived, fashionably late, at the gala event just as Samuel left the room. She watched as Max, his stately wife, and two mildly trashy assistants half his age were ushered into seats at the table up front, next to the stage. She wondered why the councilman didn't have a body-guard with him. That seemed unusual.

She studied the layout up front. *If I were in charge of Max Roman's security tonight but didn't want to alienate potential campaign contributors, how would I handle it?*

She scanned the room again and this time let her eyes target each of the exits. *Five*, she noted to herself. *Two that go out front to the pre-function area. One on that left wall. And two exits into the service corridor back behind the stage.* She followed the visual lines from the two exits behind the stage and stopped at the black curtains, which were opened and gathered at both edges of the stage.

There, she thought. *If I'm Max Roman, I have my bodyguard slip into the room through one of those service-corridor exits and then station himself behind one of the side curtains. That way I can see him, he can see me, but no one else has to know he's here.*

She was curious now to know if she was right. She thought about waiting for Samuel to return, but then she caught one of the women across the table giving hints that she was going to be polite and start a conversation with her. *Can't have that*, she thought wickedly. *People might think I'm friendly or something.*

Before the socialite could break the ice, Trudi stood and started sauntering toward the front of the room. She walked at an angle, toward the far left corner. From there, she figured she'd be able to see behind the right curtain. On the way, she passed the exit on the left wall and nearly brushed against a grimacing busboy standing next to his cart.

"Excuse me," she said automatically. He ignored her, and she kept walking. *Rude*, she thought. But her curiosity kept her moving forward.

Before she got too far, though, she stopped in spite of herself. Like the one she'd seen Andrew Carr avoid earlier, this busboy was standing next to another completely empty bussing cart. She scanned the room again.

Five exits, she counted to herself. *Five empty bussing carts with just some lumpy tablecloths on the bottom tier. And five angry young men, one stationed beside each cart.*

She felt her heart rate pick up.

A waitress came skimming by with a tray full of roasted chicken and wild mushroom truffle risotto that smelled heavenly. *Hope that's the one I ordered*, she thought.

"Excuse me," the waitress said, smiling cheerfully as she passed by.

That's more like what you'd expect from banquet workers, she thought. *Not like . . . hmm.*

She checked her watch. It was now 7:45. Samuel had been

gone for fifteen minutes, which seemed longer than necessary for the task at hand. She thought about going out to look for him, but again her curiosity had to be satisfied first.

On the big screen behind the stage, a countdown clock was ticking for the guests, announcing there was only five minutes before the program was to begin. *Please be back in your seats by 7:50 so as not to distract from the evening's exciting festivities*, it read.

Trudi pursed her lips. Where was Samuel?

She continued walking, a little faster now, toward her destination. When she reached the left corner, she tilted her head and took a peek behind the right curtain.

Her eyes went wide.

41

RAVEN

Atlanta, GA
Downtown
Friday, April 14, 7:20 p.m.
Sixty-seven minutes to Nevermore

"I'm late."

I've been sitting here at Mama's laptop for so long that I forgot she told me to be out of here before seven o'clock, before Max Roman's fundraising dinner was underway. It's now 7:20 p.m., and I've failed to keep my final promise to my previous employer. But I couldn't help myself.

TysonComeHome.com.

It was my dad's last legacy for me. Judging from the blog entries—letters, really—he started it a few days after Mom's funeral, more than four years ago.

The homepage is mostly just a collection of pictures—beautiful pictures. My dad and me sitting on the kitchen floor, eating ice cream out of the carton. My mother and me waving to the camera while waiting in the rain for a parade. My dad and me dressed up like Mr. Incredible and Dash for a fifth-grade Halloween party. My first "real" performance as a magician, at a Sunday-night church service when I was thirteen. Dad handing me the keys to my first car. High school graduation. Random holidays and happy times. Dozens of pictures, all different sizes, spread on the browser screen like art in a personal gallery.

The only words on the homepage of the website are these: *I Love You. I'm Sorry. Tyson, Please Come Home.*

There's an email address and a place for comments, along with the phone number and address of my dad's little church in Oklahoma City.

There are also links to his blog entries. They are all, every one of them, letters to me. He wrote to me at least once a week, usually on Sunday afternoons, I gather. Sometimes he wrote me more often. Around the anniversaries of Mom's death, he wrote me three or four times in a week. The first letters are full of grief and sorrow and regret, telling me he loves me, asking me to call him, or email him, or anything, really. Then, after a few months, he started telling me about what was happening around OKC, what his new sermon series was going to be, asking me—me!—questions about God and faith and life. And he started remembering things, days when I was young. Times when he and Mom were first married, when he was in seminary and they were flat broke. And he told me stories, memories from his own childhood, about his own relationship with his father, about how and why he decided to follow God.

I know some of these stories, but not all. I have some of his memories from my childhood, but not all of them, either. And while reading his thoughts, I realize I'm only now beginning to understand that my dad wasn't just my father. He was a man who struggled with fear and faith and hope and love. He was a man who was a lot like me.

I feel unreasonably grateful to God for the gift my father left behind, even though he never knew for sure that I would find it, never knew whether or not I would want it or would even receive it. I don't deserve this gift, just like I didn't deserve the gifts Mama Bliss gave me. But, I decide, I'm not going to question any of it. I'm just going to be thankful.

There are too many letters to read in one sitting, especially now that I've missed Mama's deadline to get out of the hotel room. "We'll talk more, later, Dad," I mumble to the desk. "Right now I've got to get moving again."

That's when I see my cell phone, sitting off to the side where I left it. I forgot about that too. And about its secrets.

The phone still holds the voice memo I recorded earlier, the secrets of Mama's little tête-à-tête with Viktor and the football player. I look at my watch and feel torn. It's 7:22 already. I want to hear what went on while I was out of the room, but I also don't want Mama to catch me lingering after she told me to get gone. *I've got ten thousand reasons to get out of here before she gets back.* In the end, I opt for the best of both worlds.

First I start the playback on the voice memo and turn the volume almost all the way up, then I set the cell on the desk to let it play. Next I pull out my duffel bag and start stuffing my clothes and extras into it, packing up while I listen to their meeting. Of course, the first thing I pack is the envelope with ten thousand dollars in it. I wait to add in the antique magazine because I want to cushion it a bit with my clothing.

From the cell phone speaker, I hear myself say, "I'll see you in half an hour," and then the hotel room door opens and shuts with a solid *click.* It's just the three of them in the room then, and I'm hoping they spoke loudly enough for me to hear what they said.

"I like that kid," Scholarship says with a chuckle. "He's special. Got big things ahead of him."

"Mm-hmm," Mama says. "Good kid. Deserves a chance to do better. Maybe he'll get it."

"I think we have other things to discuss right now," Viktor says.

I'm pleased to discover that the microphone on my cell has surprisingly good range, picking up all three voices without too much in the way of ambient noise or intermittent audio breakup. It helps that the hotel room is quiet, no air-conditioning running in the background or people banging around on the furniture, and that Mama Bliss runs this little conversation like a business meeting.

"Tell me about the wine," she says, which I think is an odd question. But then again, I wasn't there and I don't know the context.

"It'll be at the table, waiting. I'll deliver it myself right before the doors open." It's Scholarship speaking. His voice is strongest on the playback, so I'm guessing that he was either standing or sitting near the end table by the hotel room door.

"Are your people in place?"

"Carr met them at the service elevator on the lower level half an hour ago." That's Viktor speaking, but I don't know what he's talking about when he says *Car*.

"Uniforms?"

"Yes, he had all the black waitstaff uniforms with him. By now, the Kipo are all dressed to blend in, but they won't be roaming the halls. They'll stay mostly out of sight until after the dinner is under way."

"Where?"

"We've got a back room off the service corridor," Scholarship says. "They'll sit tight there until the time is right."

"Busboy carts?" Mama Bliss seems like she's going down a checklist.

"Carr has them in place in the room," Viktor says. "The Taurus MT-9s are hidden under tablecloths stored on the bottom of each cart. Five total, one near each exit. I checked them personally ten minutes ago."

"I thought we were using AK-47s," Scholarship offers.

Okay, this sounds bad. At the mention of AK-47s, I stop shoving dirty jeans into my bag. *This sounds really bad.*

"We changed it after Max stole from my shipment a few weeks ago," Mama says. "Poetic justice, I suppose. Plus, these are the same guns being used to wage war in the Ukraine right now. We want the police to make that connection, with a little help from us. You set up the email chain, Viktor?"

"Yep," Viktor says. "Police will discover private correspondence that shows Pavlo arranging to have the guns smuggled into Atlanta three months ago."

"How did you backdate the emails?"

"Maybe I learned a few things from your street magician," he says.

Hey, I think, *that's not fair. I don't know how to backdate emails, and even if I did, I never showed Viktor anything like that.* Of course, then I realize it doesn't really matter whether or not I showed him. He apparently knows how to do that kind of thing and just doesn't feel it necessary to explain to Mama how he learned to do it.

"Where is Pavlo right now?" Mama Bliss says.

"He's assigned to be Max Roman's bodyguard today," Scholarship says. "He was pretty excited about it."

"He has instructions to stay out of sight, but within twenty feet of Max Roman at all times," Viktor says. "We showed him where to enter through the service hallway and where he can stay behind the black curtain at the right side of the stage. He'll be able to see Max from there, and Max will be able to see him, but he should be out of view from most everyone else in the ballroom."

"And the briefcase?" Mama Bliss says.

"Handcuffed to Pavlo's left wrist," Viktor says. "He thinks it holds some really valuable artifact that Max is going to donate to the charity auction as a surprise. A last-minute addition to wow the constituency. He says he'll guard it with his life."

Mama Bliss snorts in derision, then says, "Show me the remote." There's a shuffle in the room and then, "Why is it red? Isn't the light supposed to be green?"

"That just means Pavlo's not in the building yet," Viktor says. "The remote detonator—"

Detonator? What? Now I'm sitting on the bed, all thoughts of packing driven from my mind.

"—has a range of two hundred feet in all directions. About twenty floors. We're on the sixth floor here, so plenty close enough for the radio frequency to connect to the Grand Ballroom on the lower level. But Pavlo has to bring the briefcase into the Ritz before the remote can register the connection. You'll see it turn green when Max and Pavlo arrive around seven o'clock, at the start of the fundraiser. It'll be in range then."

I check my watch. It's 7:31, which means the detonator must be flashing green right now. *Not good.* I start throwing things in my bag again, faster this time. I think now might be a good time to hurry.

"It's tamper-proof?" Mama Bliss is saying.

"Right. No buttons or controls on the remote. Display info only. The computer chip inside can't be reprogrammed unless it's inserted into the base unit. A sensor inside also monitors the integrity of the remote. If it detects a crack in the casing, or an attempt to break it open, it automatically resets the timer to zero to complete the countdown."

"So if I accidentally run over the remote with my wheelchair?"

"Then you'd better hope you're far away from Pavlo's briefcase."

"All right," Mama says. "Run me through the rest of the timeline one last time."

Viktor takes the lead on this, and he lays it out like he's reading bullet points.

- 6:30: Doors open at the Grand Ballroom.
- 7:00: Dinner is served to all the guests.
- Sometime between 7:00 and 7:15: Councilman Roman and his entourage arrive. Pavlo will arrive with them and take his place behind the black curtain.
- 7:40: The video screens show a countdown clock and announce ten minutes before the program begins. People are encouraged to "be back in your seats by 7:50 so as not to distract from the evening's exciting program."
- 7:50: Geneva Sims does her pre-auction presentation as president of ASLA, welcoming guests, explaining the mission of ASLA, showering praise on Max Roman for his support of the arts, and spotlighting a few of the upcoming auction lots.
- 8:00: Geneva Sims gives a flowery introduction of keynote speaker, Max Roman. Max begins his speech. At the same time, my partner here makes an anonymous phone call to the front desk, saying there's a bomb in the Grand Ballroom.

- 8:01: Police are called. The Ritz-Carlton goes on lockdown protocol. They'll begin preparing for police to seal the area around the Grand Ballroom. Next will be an orderly evacuation. They'll shut down all the elevators, and security personnel will rush to station people at every floor's stairwell. Once security is in position, the switchboard will start rolling robocalls to every room in the Ritz, announcing the lockdown and telling all guests to stay in their rooms until security arrives to usher them safely out.

- 8:05: Kipo take over the Grand Ballroom, conveniently shouting slogans like "Free Ukraine! Death to Russia!" and that kind of thing. Five gang members use the MT-9s to block the exits and scare the people in the room into submission. Four others use their Glocks as enforcers and start shaking down the guests for money and valuables. They have no idea there's a briefcase full of C4 explosive in the room. They think they're just on a high-class smash-and-grab job, and they've practiced it dozens of times in our simulations over the past month. They think they'll be able to sweep the room and get out in under seventeen minutes. They're kind of proud of that.

- 8:15 to 8:20: By now the first responders should arrive. They'll work to fully secure the perimeter and assess the situation. Then they'll wait for whichever SWAT team is on call to assemble and make it to the hotel.

- 8:20 to 8:25 or so: While everyone is distracted by the marauding Kipo, Andrew Carr unexpectedly breaks away and shouts "Long Live Ukraine!" He pulls his own Glock and assassinates Max Roman. If Pavlo tries to stop him, he kills my cousin too. We promised Carr a load of money, safety out of state, and even his favorite call girl from

Roman's strip club, but he doesn't know we were lying. And he doesn't know about the bomb either. He thinks he'll be able to murder Max Roman and still get out with the rest of the Kipo when they break for the door. He doesn't know he signed his death warrant when he told the police about Nevermore, when he was stupid enough to try and cut a deal after his arrest. Of course, he might not have survived the raid anyway, so either way, it was probably over for him.

- 8:27: The timer goes off on the remote detonator. The C4 in Pavlo's briefcase explodes, making sure Max Roman is dead. This'll probably kill Andrew Carr and about half the guests in the room. Kipo too. Maybe a few people unlucky enough to be on the floor above the Grand Ballroom. But the explosion should be localized to the nearest two salons of the banquet room, if that matters.

- 8:29: We all disappear, never to be seen or heard from again.

- 8:30 to 8:40 or so: SWAT finally arrives, just in time to start picking up the pieces. But we're all gone, and Nevermore is finally complete.

There's a moment of silence when Viktor is done speaking. No one says anything, and it's so quiet I think maybe my recording has cut off, but then Mama Bliss picks up again.

"Justice for all," she says.

"And hopefully," Scholarship finally chimes in, "the police blame Ukrainian terrorist Pavlo Kostiuk. Just another extremist waging an insane war to make a statement about Russian aggression in his homeland."

"That's what we hope," Viktor says. "But even if they don't stay with that theory, by the time they connect the rest of the dots, we'll all be long gone."

And Mama has a backup plan. A logbook that I mailed today that'll arrive at the Zone 6 police station tomorrow. I don't know for sure, but I'm guessing that logbook will have all kinds of documentation of Max Roman's organized crime activities and his lewd network of enterprises. *For Mama Bliss, it's not enough just to kill her enemy—twice. She intends to murder his reputation too.*

"All right, then," Mama is saying on the recording. "I believe I owe you gentlemen some money."

I hear fingers tapping on a laptop keyboard. It must have been the same laptop she loaned me, the one I've just been using to read my dad's letters. *How can this woman be so kind and generous toward me yet so cold and cruel toward everyone sitting in the Grand Ballroom downstairs right now?*

"It's done," she says. "The money is split between your accounts in Switzerland, Luxembourg, Lichtenstein, and the Isle of Man. May you enjoy the lap of luxury in ways that I never could."

There is shuffling of feet and mumbled thanks and congratulations, and then Viktor says, "Well, I've got to be going. I've got a few planes to catch." He then apparently speaks to Scholarship. "You know what to do?"

"Of course," Scholarship says. "By this point, I could do it in my sleep."

"I don't like that he has to stay behind," Viktor says.

"Then you never should have taken certain matters into your own hands," Mama says evenly. "You know that."

"I'll be fine, Viktor," Scholarship says. "First I help Mama with her little errand. Then I drive north for a bit, pull over and make a panicky phone call, and then I ride off into the sunset."

"Be sure to dump the phone after the call."

"I got this, Viktor. You go disappear. I'll be gone right after you."

There's a brief moment of silence, and then Viktor's voice says, "Pleasure doing business with you, Bliss."

"Mm-hmm," she says. I hear the sound of shoes on carpet, then the door to Room 614 opens and shuts with a heavy metal *click*. After Viktor's gone, Scholarship speaks.

"You need anything before I go downstairs?"

"No, you go on. I'll meet you down there later."

"Okay," he says. "I'm going to go pick out a nice bottle of red wine."

"Mm-hmm," she says.

Again the door opens and shuts, and I hear Mama shuffling around lazily in the hotel room. Maybe she's reading, or judging from the clicks and sighs, maybe she's inserting a new insulin pump, I can't tell for sure. But I know the conversation time is over. I check the recording, and even though there's about twelve minutes left, I figure it's safe to turn it off. I tap the pause button, then turn to make a final sweep of the room.

Got all my clothes, I think. *Don't need to get my bathroom stuff, I can buy a new toothbrush anywhere. Got my money. Don't need anything else, really. Just have to fly away again, like the Raven of Noah's ark.*

Now I lay the Poe collectible magazine gently into the duffel, and a thought I had earlier returns like a hammer to my head.

How can Mama Bliss be so kind and generous toward me yet so cold and cruel toward everyone sitting in the Grand Ballroom downstairs right now?

It didn't register with me before, but it does now.

Trudi Coffey is downstairs, sitting in the Grand Ballroom. Right now.

At 8:27, a bomb will explode in there, killing at least half the people in that room. Maybe killing Trudi.

I'm standing with one hand on my duffel bag and another

pressed against the headache that's suddenly creasing through my temples. It's 7:45 now. Only forty-two minutes until Nevermore.

I have to save Trudi, I think. *But how?*

As if in response to my unspoken question, a keycard slides into the lock on my hotel room door.

42

BLISS

Atlanta, GA
Downtown
Friday, April 14, 7:33 p.m.
Fifty-four minutes to Nevermore

Bliss saw Samuel Hill exit the ballroom and head toward the bathroom. She sighed and tapped the football player's arm, but he'd already seen it too.

"Finally," he said. "I was getting a little worried."

"What took him so long?" Bliss said.

"Apparently he's got a higher tolerance for Rohypnol than I expected. His mass is good-sized, but I didn't want to overdose him, so I only put one pill in his wine."

"So where's the girl?" Bliss snapped. "She's half his weight. Did you overdose her?"

He stepped to the door and peeked inside the ballroom. "She's not in her chair. Maybe she left already and we missed it?"

Bliss felt tension spreading through her shoulders. Where was Trudi Coffey? Was Viktor Kostiuk going to get his way, after all? Was Trudi going to get caught—and killed—in Nevermore tonight?

Nothing to be done for it now, she thought grimly. *Collateral damage, like Viktor said. Going to have to take what I can get.* She sighed. *At least I can still save Samuel Hill.*

"Get in position," she ordered, "and be careful."

The football player obeyed, standing just outside the door of the men's room. It was only a moment or two before Samuel left the restroom and walked right into her muscle.

"Nice to see you again, detective," he said as he wrapped a chokehold around Samuel's neck.

Stupid, Mama Bliss thought. *He obviously doesn't know who he's dealing with.*

Even impaired by alcohol and roofies, Samuel Hill knew how to protect himself.

In a flash of speed and strength, Samuel dipped his head to the right and down, instinctively taking the other man's left-handed grip into account. He pulled them both into a crouch. Then he stepped sideways to the left and skipped his right leg behind the other man's left knee. Samuel twisted his head inside, then slid it deftly out of the chokehold while simultaneously twisting the footballer's left wrist painfully behind his back. Then Samuel kicked the back of his attacker's left knee. When the football player dropped to the ground, Samuel leveled a punch across his cheekbone that sent him sprawling.

"Samuel!" Mama Bliss shouted. He turned glazed eyes toward her. She stood up and started walking toward him. "Samuel, what do you think you're doing?"

"Mama?" The detective was stunned by the sight of Bliss. "I've never, not ever, seen you out of your wheelchair."

"This chair of mine is a convenience, not a habit," she said tersely. "I told you that before, didn't I?"

"I guess so, Mama. If you say so." He shook his head. "What's going on here?"

"Stop fighting," she ordered, and Samuel let go of the other man's arm. "Somebody dosed you with Rohypnol. You need to lie down."

"Are you . . . Am I . . . Am I hallucinating?"

"Yes, Samuel. You're hallucinating. Now just—"

At that point, her football player had recovered enough to retaliate. He delivered a crushing fist to the side of Samuel's head. The detective stumbled but didn't go down. Before a second blow could land, though, Mama gave an order.

"Stop," she said. "Give him a minute."

Samuel Hill tried to say something, but the drug was now taking full hold on him. "I don't feel right, Mama Bliss," he mumbled. He sank down to one knee.

"Pick him up and put him in my chair," she said, "or, big as he is, we'll never get him upstairs in time."

The football player spit blood out of his split lips. "I say we leave him down here, let him take his chances."

"He beat you fair and square. Now let it go and do your job. You're enormously rich, and he's just a workaday cop, remember?"

The linebacker was still breathing hard, but he nodded. He wrapped his arms around Samuel's torso, and this time the policeman didn't resist. A moment later, Detective Hill was slumped in the chair, slowly passing out and mumbling something about Mama Bliss and wheelchairs.

"Use your belt to strap him in," Bliss said. "And let's get him upstairs before we run out of time."

It was 7:44 by the time they got up to the sixth floor. Samuel Hill was out cold before the elevator ride was over. She could tell that her companion was itching to leave, but she admired his unwillingness to say anything about it to her.

"Help me get him into the room," she said when the elevator stopped, "and then you bug out. You need to get off the premises before you make that call."

He nodded and led her to Room 614, pushing the wheelchair ahead of him. She slid the keycard through the lock, then stepped back for him to deposit Samuel in the room.

"You want me to put him on a bed or something?" he said.

"No," she said. "Just go."

The football player nodded. He didn't bother to say goodbye.

After the hotel room door shut, Bliss let a deep exhale slide through her lips. She was already feeling the effects of the insulin, and she instinctively longed for the comfort of her wheelchair. But there was no way she was going to be able to move that mountain of a man now sleeping in her chair. She left him by the half-shut bathroom door where the football player had deposited him.

The room was quiet.

She looked at her watch, saw her hands shaking instead. She checked the alarm clock on the nightstand by the bed. *Seven-fifty*, she thought. *Time for Geneva Sims to begin blowing hot air about Maksym Romanenko.*

She sat on the edge of one of the queen beds in the room and closed her eyes to let a dizzy spell pass. She felt dampness on her forehead and under her arms. Her stomach complained for food, but she ignored it.

When she could, she walked over to where Samuel sat. She leaned down and pecked his cheek fondly.

"You were a good man," she whispered. "I'm sorry."

She reached into a pocket on the wheelchair and fumbled for the remote detonator she'd hidden in there. The status light on the rectangular little box burned a steady green, as it had for almost half an hour now. She turned away from Samuel and momentarily forgot what she intended to do next. Then her stomach leapt inside her, and she remembered.

She stumbled over to her bed, irritated at herself for timing this so close. She lay herself down and set the remote beside her right hip. She heard someone breathing hard, a labored gasping like she remembered from when she was a girl, gone swimming, who'd stayed underwater too long before coming back to the surface.

She repositioned herself on the bed, pulling her head up higher on the pillow, feeling the familiar lump of the Beretta BU9 Nano pistol she always kept there. She willed her breathing to slow down to almost normal. Her mind wandered.

It had been relatively simple, really. Just before five-thirty, after her last meeting with Viktor but before The Raven had come back to the room, she'd inserted a new catheter into a spot by her hip and attached a fresh insulin pump, one full and ready for three full days of use. Then, about half an hour later, she'd begun slightly increasing the insulin drip on her pump, inputting data that told it she was about to eat a new snack but then forgoing the snack. Around seven-thirty she told the pump it was time for dinner. Now she could feel the effects of the insulin overdose flooding her system, clogging her mind, taking away her consciousness. At her age and in her health, she wouldn't last much longer. Diabetic shock would first send her into a coma and then—well, then the end would come.

If I've figured this right, she thought dizzily, *I'll be gone before Max Roman is. I won't even hear the blast.*

That thought gave her a little comfort, but also, for the first time, she felt a little fear.

She reached into her shirt pocket and pulled out the picture of her grandson one last time. *So handsome*, she thought. She placed four fingers on the front of the image and felt the tears drip from her eyes. She turned it over and, through bleary eyes, read the list on the back.

There were six names, all lined through.

~~Jameis Jackson.~~

~~Walter Evans.~~

~~Mark Jenson.~~

~~Ashland Forney.~~

~~Maksym Romanenko.~~

~~Bliss June Monroe.~~

"Everyone responsible for Davis's death," she mumbled to herself. "Justice done. Justice for all. Including me."

She pressed the picture against her breast, closed her eyes, and invited the darkness to come. "I'm sorry, Davis," she whispered. "I should've protected you better. Should've watched over you better. I just should've been better."

Behind her eyes, Bliss saw a light flicker and dim.

What have I done? she said to herself suddenly.

That was her last thought.

43

TRUDI

Atlanta, GA
Downtown
Friday, April 14, 7:51 p.m.
Thirty-six minutes to Nevermore

Trudi felt her eyes widen and her heart race.

I know that guy, she told herself. *I almost had to jab him in the throat with spear fingers about a month ago.*

There was no mistaking it. Sitting placidly behind the black curtain, maybe ten or fifteen feet away from Max Roman himself, was a heavyset Ukrainian. He was someone she knew personally to be a mafia enforcer employed by Viktor Kostiuk. A cousin or something, if she remembered it right. He was also someone who supposedly had zero connection to Max Roman, yet here he was comfortably ensconced in the councilman's inner circle, playing what appeared to be the trusted bodyguard role tonight. Max's guard was dressed in an uncomfortable gray suit, eyes blank and bored, holding an expensive, hard-shell briefcase.

Trudi tried not to stare, and simultaneously tried to fade into the background. She didn't want to be noticed by this guy. Not now, not ever.

She stepped away, out of sight of the man behind the curtain, then halted herself. *Is he holding that briefcase? Or is it tied to him?*

She risked getting close enough for another look. Sure enough, the briefcase was attached to his wrist by virtue of heavy silver handcuffs. Despite what her ex-husband had said earlier, she knew this was suspicious.

A mafia enforcer handcuffed to a mysterious briefcase? Samuel should have trusted his instincts. This could be Nevermore, after all.

A prissy old woman, powdered with garish makeup and a plastic smile, was onstage now. She was thanking everyone for coming, droning on with praise for Councilman Max Roman and his support of the arts. Trudi slid away from the front of the ballroom and began working her way unobtrusively back toward her seat. Almost everyone else had settled in at their tables, ready to give rapt attention to the show happening up front. Trudi felt a little conspicuous. She tried to shadow a nearby waitress, hoping that might mask her rude walking tour through the ballroom while Old Priss was speaking.

She slid into her seat, welcomed by the disapproving frowns of her high-society tablemates, and she noticed immediately that Samuel still hadn't returned. Alarm bells went off in her head. Then she realized something equally important.

Viktor Kostiuk is not in this room.

She forced herself to breathe slowly, calmly, through her nose even while her lips pursed with worry.

Kostiuk had called himself a true believer, had personally invited her to come to this political fundraiser out of his passion for Candidate Roman. Said he wanted to recruit her for the Roman campaign and yet, now that the moment was here, he was not.

Instead, Viktor's cousin, the mobster, was here. Alone. With a briefcase.

Perhaps Viktor Kostiuk had skipped this party because he knew something bad was going to happen, and he didn't want to be there when it all went down?

Trudi couldn't wait any longer, couldn't take any more chances.

I need to call the police, she thought. *I need to find Samuel. And I need my gun.*

She scanned the exits and saw the same five busboys standing next to the same empty bussing carts. There were no more waiters or waitresses in the room, though. Just the busboys at the exits, and a few more busboys standing back near the entrance to the kitchen. She noticed Andrew Carr standing among that crowd.

None of the busboys looked happy.

Now Old Priss was spotlighting some of the items to be auctioned off later, but Trudi ignored her completely. She snatched her purse off the floor and headed for one of the exits leading out to the pre-function area, where the bathrooms were located. This time she didn't care if people thought her rude. It was time for action, not good manners.

She hurried to the door, but before she could get out, an angry busboy stepped in her way.

"You need to go back to your seat," he said gruffly.

Thoughts flashed like lightning through Trudi's brain. She could disable this cocky young kid with a well-placed kick followed by an expertly applied elbow . . . but that would bring too much attention to her. And it might warn the mob enforcer behind the curtain that someone was on to him. That could set off events before she had an opportunity to get help.

She took a chance on her acting ability instead. "I know, I know, Councilman Roman is about to speak," she said lazily. She made herself wobble a bit in her boots, and she bent forward, draping an arm across the angry boy's shoulder, letting wet lips smear on his cheek. She stage-whispered in his ear, "But I've been drinking wine since four o'clock, Mr. Waiter Man in your fancy black pants and matching shirt. So either you let me go to the bathroom right now, or in about two seconds I'm going to throw up all over your neck." She added a little gulp and hiccup for effect.

The busboy looked disgusted. He shoved her aside and stepped out of her way. She pushed through the door and ran out toward the lobby. *Where are you, Samuel? And why are you never around when I really want you?*

She skidded to a stop at the front desk but couldn't get the white-faced clerk to put down the telephone long enough to listen to her. She quickly understood why. Even from where she was, she could make out the sounds of a panicky man on the other end of the line, and she heard the word *bomb* at least once among the garbled prose. The desk clerk ignored her completely and waved toward a co-worker. "Call the police," he rasped as he covered the receiver with his hand. "Tell them we need a SWAT team. And a bomb squad. Call them now!"

That was good enough for Trudi. She sped from the lobby and out to her car.

Inside, behind the steering wheel, she worked through the situation. There was a bomb in the Grand Ballroom, and she had a pretty good idea of who was holding it. She reached under her seat and retrieved her Beretta Tomcat. She'd never had to actually use this particular gun in a real-world situation, but just feeling its familiar contours helped settle her nerves.

Okay, she thought. *Nevermore is about to happen, after all. Police have been notified. Do I go in and try to take out the bomber? Do I wait for the police?*

She stuffed the handgun into her purse, saw Samuel's badge

that she'd stuck in there earlier, and remembered the thing that really worried her.

Where is Samuel?

She let her face fall into her hands, forced herself to take deep, cleansing breaths. *Think, think, Trudi!* she commanded herself. And she heard herself cry out silently to God. She wasn't even sure what she was praying, it was pure emotion and a plea for help. She opened her eyes and saw her purse again. She suddenly knew what to do.

Trudi grabbed her cell phone out of the purse and tapped on the Find My iPhone app button. She logged in as her husband and activated the Urban Enhancement—Atlanta Edition extension that overlaid city blueprints on the map on her screen.

Where is he, where is he? she fretted, looking for the icon that would tell her where his cell phone was located at this moment. She really hoped he was with his cell.

"There," she said out loud when the icon finally appeared. She zoomed in for a closer look. "Still in the Ritz-Carlton. Sixth floor. Room 614."

She was out of her Ford Focus and running toward the hotel entrance so fast that she couldn't even remember if she'd closed her car door. It didn't matter, not now. The clock on her cell phone told her it was 8:03 p.m.

At the front door of the Ritz, she ran into problems. Hotel security had already taken up stations at the entrance, and they were turning away anyone who tried to enter. Trudi didn't waste time. She reached in her purse and plucked out Samuel's detective badge.

"Atlanta police," she barked at the security guard. "Out of my way. I've got to get to the sixth floor."

"Wow, you guys got here fast," the guard said. He seemed relieved to see her.

"I was, uh, already in the neighborhood. More are coming. But I've got to get to the sixth floor right now."

"That way," the guard said, pointing. "You'll have to take the stairs. They've already shut down all the elevators. They'll start evacuating as soon as all of our security team is in place."

"Evacuating?"

"Yeah. They'll start at the lower floors and work their way up to the twenty-fourth floor."

"Good," she said. "Good plan."

"When will SWAT get here?" the guard asked. "We've got a few guys watching the Grand Ballroom, but they can't really do anything without SWAT."

"Any minute now," Trudi said. She could see he wanted to ask her more questions, but she didn't want to waste any more time. "Keep up the good work," she shouted as she ran away.

She hit the stairwell jogging and didn't stop. *Just another workout on the Stairmaster*, she told herself. The physical exercise actually felt good, relaxing, though running uphill in her fashion boots took a little getting used to. Her fancy red dress was surprisingly responsive, despite the way it clung to her like a glove.

She checked her phone. It was now 8:09, and Samuel had left Room 614, though he was still on the sixth floor. *Hallway*, she told herself. *Hurry, Tru-Bear!* She passed the sign for the fourth floor, then the fifth, and the icon for Samuel's phone was still motionless, right above her on the next floor up.

She reached the door to the sixth-floor hallway and paused to collect herself and prepare for what she might find on the other side. Out of habit, she smoothed the sides of her dress and wiped the dampness off her face. She was absentmindedly glad she'd worn perfume.

Is he alone? she thought. *Not likely. But this isn't a time for caution.*

The clock on her cell phone now read 8:11 p.m. In the distance she thought she heard muffled sirens, but she couldn't be sure that wasn't just wishful thinking. She dropped her phone into her purse but left the clasp undone, just in case she needed to get to her gun in a hurry.

A deep breath.

A quick prayer.

And she opened the door.

44

RAVEN

Atlanta, GA
Downtown
Friday, April 14, 8:01 p.m.
Twenty-six minutes to Nevermore

From my hiding place inside the bathroom, I have a clear view of Mama Bliss lying on the hotel room bed. It seems like she isn't moving. The clock on the nightstand tells me she's been here for seventeen minutes, but it feels like longer than that.

When Mama Bliss and Scholarship had come barging through the hotel room door, all I could think to do was hide. I snatched my duffel bag and dove into the bathroom, lights out, door partly open so I could keep an eye and ear on what was happening outside. It was a mild shock to see Mama walking across the room as if she did it every day, as if she never really needed that wheelchair. Her sheer commitment to the ruse, for years and years if I understood it correctly, was impressive. Many magicians use similar ploys, appearing to be weak in certain ways in order to deflect attention from what they are really doing, from what are really their strengths.

You'd have been a good deception specialist, Mama Bliss, I thought to myself. Then I realized that's exactly what she was, an expert deception specialist, playing for much bigger stakes than I ever dreamed.

Those revelations were crowded out of my mind when I saw Scholarship push Trudi's ex-husband into the room in Mama's wheelchair. Detective Hill was unconscious, which couldn't be a good thing. Scholarship had a thick bruise starting to swell on his cheekbone. I could only guess how that had happened.

"You want me to put him on a bed or something?" Scholarship had said.

"No," Mama Bliss said. "Just go."

He was gone before I could blink. And suddenly it was just me, Mama, and the sleeping Samuel Hill in Room 614 of the Ritz-Carlton hotel.

The room was quiet.

From my vantage point inside the bathroom, I had a clear view of the alarm clock on the nightstand. I watched the illuminated little green numbers change from 7:46 to 7:47. *I have to get out of here*, I thought. *I have to save Trudi.* But something about Mama's presence made me wait. I knew she kept a gun under her pillow. If I tried to confront her now, would she use it on me? Could I get out before she could shoot me?

She leaned over and whispered something to Samuel Hill, then pulled something out of a pocket in the wheelchair.

A small plastic box, about the size of a deck of cards. A bright green light burned at one end.

Remote detonator, I thought. And then I knew what I had to do. Somehow I had to get that detonator from Mama Bliss. I had to get it more than two hundred feet away from here. *If the detonator is out of range*, I told myself, *it can't make the bomb explode. If I do that, I save Trudi—and everyone in the Grand Ballroom downstairs.*

I knew that meant saving Max Roman and Pavlo Kostiuk too, but I didn't care. Collateral criminal rescue was worth the cost of saving Trudi Coffey.

I peek out of the bathroom again, and now I'm certain she's not moving anymore. I can't even tell if she's breathing at this point. About ten minutes ago, she laid herself down on the bed, putting the remote detonator right next to her. Then she'd folded her hands across her chest and gone to sleep.

She'd said she wanted to come up and rest during the banquet. Maybe she really is doing that now. Maybe.

The alarm clock rearranges its numbers until it reads 8:03. I decide to risk being seen.

I reach out and pull on the bathroom door, opening it wide. Mama doesn't notice. I step softly into the opening between the bathroom and the rest of the hotel room, but again, she's unmoving.

"Mama Bliss?" I say quietly. She doesn't respond.

I leave my duffel in the bathroom and walk into the main hotel room. Samuel Hill is groaning faintly, and I see him twitch in the chair like he's fighting something in his dreams. I step around him, and still Mama doesn't move. In a moment, I'm standing beside her, looking down on her still form. Her face looks pained, but her body is at rest. Suddenly she takes in a deep breath and exhales.

I freeze. *Does she know I'm here?*

Her breathing returns to a shallow, almost insignificant thing. *You don't look well, Mama.*

My plan isn't fully formed yet. I know I'm going to steal

Mama's remote and get it out of here. But go where? If I head downstairs, I'm actually going toward the bomb. By this time, Scholarship has made his panicky call to the police, and any minute now, the Kipo are going to storm through the ballroom.

If the hotel is on lockdown, will I be able to get out of the lobby in time?

The room phone rings, startling me so much I nearly wet myself. Mama Bliss doesn't react to the piercing sound jangling next to her head. The phone rings four times, then goes silent.

I notice that I'm breathing through my mouth, and that my mouth feels much too dry. The phone suddenly rings again, and this time I pick it up.

"Hello?"

"This is a hotel emergency call," a recorded voice tells me. "Please stay calm. A—" I hang up.

The lockdown has begun, I think. *That means they're going to start evacuating the hotel, flooding the lobby with people. But the upper floors will be quiet while guests wait to be evacuated by security.*

The plan finally completes itself in my head.

Up, I think. *Viktor said the remote had a range that went up about twenty floors from the Grand Ballroom, so I should go up higher than that. To the roof. On the roof it'll be out of range, and nobody dies.*

I reach across Mama Bliss and palm the remote detonator in my left hand, feeling the coldness of the plastic on the empty spot where my pinky finger used to be. My wrist brushes against Mama's arm when I pull away, and I feel a sudden clamminess inside me.

That didn't seem right.

I touch her hand.

Mama Bliss is unexpectedly cold.

I wrap my fingers around her wrist, and I can't find a pulse. She's still breathing though, and now I'm torn. This isn't sleep, after all. She's dropped into a coma, maybe some kind of diabetic shock. If I leave her here, Mama Bliss will surely not survive for long.

She's been nothing but kind to me. Can I leave her to die here, alone?

But if I don't leave . . .

Samuel Hill groans, louder this time. The alarm clock skips to the next number.

A picture falls from Mama's hand.

Davis Monroe.

I don't have to pick it up and turn it over to know that. I recognize it by what's written on the back of the photograph. And I see the lines drawn through all six names.

The burning green light on the remote catches my attention, and I see there's a timer display on here, as well. According to this, the bomb downstairs will explode at 8:27 p.m.

Exactly twenty-one minutes from now.

"I'm sorry, Mama," I say.

I know I've got to go, but first I take out my cell phone and synchronize my timer app with the clock on the remote detonator. I set it to beep every minute between now and then, so I can keep track of the time without having to look at it. I store the cell in the inside pocket of my tuxedo jacket while I get everything ready to go.

Too soon the timer next to my heart beeps.

Twenty minutes.

I stuff the remote detonator in the left coat pocket of my tuxedo and, before I can talk myself out of it, I reach under Mama Bliss's pillow and recover her Beretta pistol. That goes in my right coat pocket.

"Now, what to do with you?" I say to Samuel Hill. The timer on my cell phone beeps again, agitating me because time is slipping by faster than it feels like it should be, too fast for me to keep up with it.

Nineteen minutes.

"Come on," I say, turning the wheelchair toward the door. "It's time for you and me to take a ride."

45

TRUDI

Atlanta, GA
Downtown
Friday, April 14, 8:11 p.m.
Sixteen minutes to Nevermore

The first thing Trudi Coffey saw when she entered the sixth-floor hallway was her ex-husband, drooling and unconscious, slumped in Mama Bliss's wheelchair. The second thing she saw was The Raven, dressed in a tuxedo, standing beside her husband, pushing the call button for the stalled elevator.

He stared at her with genuine surprise, then his face reshaped to express what appeared to be relief. She scanned the hallway, found it empty, and turned back to the street magician.

"So, Raven," she said, "this is interesting."

"Don't call me that, Trudi," he said. "I mean, you don't have to call me that. You can call me—"

"Raven," she interrupted. She wasn't about to get friendly with this guy, not now. All she cared about was getting Samuel, then getting as far away from this hotel as she could, as fast as she could. "I can't help noticing you've got my ex-husband, unconscious for some reason, strapped into Mama's wheelchair."

"You look great, Trudi," he said. She felt like smacking him, but she restrained herself. She needed a minute to assess what was going on. "I mean, wow, Trudi," he was saying. "Spectacular. You should dress like this all the time. Are those Vince Camuto boots? Very nice."

"We're talking fashion now? That's the best you can do?"

"I'm just saying, you're dressed nice today. It's a compliment."

Just then Samuel twitched and groaned in the wheelchair. She frowned. *What is his game?* she thought. Aloud she said, "This doesn't look good, Raven."

Something in the hallway beeped, a high-pitched sound like a smoke alarm running low on battery. *Did that come from his pocket?* she wondered.

"What's that?" she said to him, though it was more of a command than a question.

In response, he reached nervously for the elevator button and pressed it impatiently three or four times.

"Raven," she said. She took a step closer, positioning herself close enough to disable him if it came to that. "They already shut down the lifts in the whole hotel. SWAT's going to be here any minute. So . . . you want to explain what's going on, or do I step out of the way and let them take you down? I'm giving you a chance here. Maybe you should take it."

He didn't answer. A deep exhale split his lips, and he closed his eyes.

Trudi heard another smoke-alarm beep come from his vest pocket. *Timer?* she thought. *Those beeps come about a minute apart.*

He opened his eyes and smiled at her. "Trudi," he said, "I hope you'll forgive me for what I'm about to do."

She started to react, but he pushed the wheelchair toward her, putting Samuel's body between them. She hesitated to catch the chair, and in that moment, he pulled a gun from a pocket in his tuxedo. He held it unsteadily aimed at her, both hands wrapped around the grip.

"You've got to let me go," he said. "You don't understand, and I don't have time to explain. But I've got to get up to the roof. So, you know, back off or I'll shoot."

Trudi almost laughed. She stepped around the wheelchair until there was only empty space between her and The Raven. She took another step, closing the distance between them.

"Give me the gun," she said, holding out a hand. "You don't know how to use it anyway. And that way I don't have to break your fing—" She stopped.

He tried to cover it, but she'd already seen the gap on his left hand.

No pinky, she thought. *Mob justice. Oh, Raven. Why didn't you listen to me?*

"Trudi, please," he said. "Just let me go. Please."

She sighed. She nodded and let her head drop, keeping her eyes focused on the gun pointed at her chest. She saw his grip relax and his arms slacken just a bit.

That's my cue, she thought.

She dropped to a three-point stance and swept her left leg toward him, fast. She heard the sickening *crack* from where her chunky heel hit his left ankle but kept her leg moving for solid follow-through. He toppled over instantly, totally caught off guard by the leg sweep. The gun fell from his hands, and she'd recovered it before he could reach down to grab his ankle in pain.

She put a boot under his chin, pressing just enough to threaten his breathing without actually suffocating him.

"Seriously?" she said. "Pulling a gun on me? Is that your way of apologizing for standing me up? Because if it is, it leaves a lot to be desired."

He choked a laugh, in spite of himself. He raised his hands above his head and waited. She stared into his eyes, and something in them made her relent. She stepped back. He sat up on the ground, rubbing his ankle with one hand and holding his neck with another.

A beep sounded from inside his coat.

"Trudi"—his voice was pained—"you've got to let me go. You've got to, or hundreds of people are going to die."

Trudi didn't say anything, but her brain was working in overdrive. She finally put it together.

"When this is over," she said, pointing at the amputation on his left hand, "I want to know what happened there. But right now just tell me how much time is left."

He sighed and reached into his left pocket. Trudi saw the little lights on the plastic box, saw the timer display counting down, and recognized it as a remote detonator. She assumed it was for the bomb downstairs.

"Thirteen minutes," he said.

"Then?"

"Boom."

Samuel jerked in his chair. *Some kind of bad dream*, she thought. *Or maybe he's hang-gliding in his sleep. Hard to tell with an adrenaline junkie like him.*

"Are you involved?" she said quickly.

He shook his head. "Trying to stop it. Trudi, they're going to kill hundreds of people."

"Who? No, never mind. That's a question for later."

"You've got to let me go." He held out the remote so she could see the timer ticking down. Too soon it hit twelve minutes, and she heard another smoke-alarm beep come out of The Raven's tuxedo.

"What's your plan?" she said.

He struggled to his feet. She could tell by the way he favored his left leg that she'd given him a good bruise on that ankle. He'd have trouble walking until the swelling went down.

"It has a two-hundred-foot range. About twenty floors. I'm going to take it to the roof, get it out of range until the police can defuse the bomb."

"Give it to me," Trudi said.

"No," he said.

"Give it to me before I kick your teeth in."

"Trudi—"

"Look," she said. "I don't know if you're involved with this or not. I hope you're not. But either way, you can't keep the remote detonator. If you are involved and I let you go, then you'll just blow up the ballroom as soon as you get away from me."

Beep.

Eleven minutes. Why is time slipping by so fast?

"If you're not involved," she continued, "then you still have to give it to me. I might have broken your ankle just now. You'll never make it up eighteen flights of stairs and onto the roof before time runs out. So, Tyson, give me the remote."

He started to say something, closed his mouth, then shook his head in admiration. "We would have been great together, you know," he said. He held out the remote. "Our kids would have been beautiful and smart."

Trudi tried not to smile, but she was unsuccessful. "Now, take my ex-husband and get out of here. Security should be in the stairwells by now, so ask them for help. Go."

He started hobbling down the hall. She passed him and hit

the stairwell running. She was on the seventh floor already when she heard his voice shouting up to her.

"When this is over, are you free for lunch sometime?"

Trudi didn't see security until the eighth floor. The woman tried to stop her, but Trudi just flashed Samuel's badge and kept running. She did the same thing on the ninth and tenth floors, and on the eleventh floor she caught the last part of a walkie-talkie broadcast announcing her coming to the guards on the floors above. After that they all just stepped aside and watched her run past.

Even with her athletic conditioning, running up eighteen flights of stairs in a dinner dress and chunky-heeled boots took something of a toll. At the sixteenth floor, she finally stopped long enough to dump her shoes. *Sorry Vince*, she said as she dropped the boots on the stairs, *but I can go faster barefoot.* She kept running.

At the twentieth floor, she allowed herself to stop and catch her breath. She looked at the remote detonator.

Seven minutes left, she thought. *Made it with time to spare.* She felt mildly euphoric.

Then she noticed that the light at the end of the plastic box was still green.

Okay, she thought. *I'll keep going.*

She stopped again at the twenty-second floor. The light still burned green.

"Stupid manufacturer," she muttered breathlessly. "You and your 'under-promise and over-deliver' marketing strategy. You promised a two-hundred-foot range but delivered more just on principle. Whatever happened to shoddy American workmanship?"

She kept running.

By the time Trudi had reached the twenty-fourth floor, the timer read four minutes—and the light was still green, though now it flickered a bit from time to time.

She found no security guard on this floor and silently told herself not to panic. She dashed through the doorway into the hall and started hunting for roof access. At one point, a guest heard her and timidly opened the door of his room.

"Are you here to evacuate us?" he said.

"Stay in your room!" she commanded. He started to say something, then saw the countdown clock ticking on the remote in her hand. He slammed the door shut.

She raced to the end of the hall, searching. "Thank you, Jesus," she exhaled. Her lungs were burning now, and she could feel heat in her thighs and calves, but she'd found it. She'd found the door to the roof.

It was locked.

The timer in her hands clicked to two minutes.

She stepped back and kicked at the heavy metal door with her bare heel. It didn't budge. She took a running jump at the door, launching both bare feet into a spot just to the left of the handle. The door rattled in its hinges as she fell to the ground, but she still wasn't strong enough to dislodge it.

Now what, God? she silently shouted to the heavens, feeling new bruises forming on her heels. *Is this how it ends? Almost, but not enough?*

"Here!" She heard a voice calling out behind her. "Come over here!"

She turned and saw the hotel guest who had asked to be evacuated. She was speechless.

"Hurry," he said, "over here!"

He was standing in front of an alcove where the icemaker and a few soft drink vending machines were located. She stared at him.

"This is a dead spot on the floor," he said. "No cell service in here. Maybe no radio frequency can get through here either? Maybe that's what you need?"

She looked at the remote detonator and saw the light flicker back and forth, briefly, between green and red.

She got up and ran toward him.

"Go back to your room," she commanded breathlessly.

He turned and rushed to his room, pausing to look back at her before he closed the door. *Room 2421*, she thought. *If this works, I'll have to remember to thank the guy in 2421.*

She stepped into the alcove and saw the light flicker to red. She sighed, still breathing hard. Then it flickered back to green.

One minute left.

She started searching the room for just the right spot, holding the remote high first, then low, then next to the ice machine, then by the door. She finally found the spot she needed, wedged between the icemaker and one of the drink machines. If she crouched down on her haunches, with her back to the wall, the light turned red and stayed red. She held her position.

The timer hit twenty seconds. Then fifteen. At ten seconds she closed her eyes. If this didn't work, she didn't want to be the one who counted down to death. She waited what seemed like an eternity, and felt her heart leap. *Surely that was long enough*, she thought. *Surely that was ten seconds.* She opened her eyes and saw her heart had rushed the count. There were three seconds left.

Two seconds.

She couldn't look away.

One second.

The space between one second and zero on the timer seemed simultaneously to last forever and to take no time at all. She held her breath.

She strained her ears.

She heard nothing.

She felt nothing.

The remote stayed red. The timer had stopped. And there was no explosion.

She let her head drop and decided it was okay that she was crying all over her fancy red dress. Her fingers trembled, and her legs felt like they were cramping up, but she didn't move. She stared at the little red light, and only one thought filled her mind.

Thank you, Jesus.

She kept saying it over and over. She couldn't stop herself.

Thank you, Jesus.

TWO
WEEKS
LATER . . .

46

TRUDI

Trudi sat at her desk in the Coffey & Hill Investigations office and checked the personal ads in the *Atlanta Journal-Constitution*. She smiled. Then she flipped the paper over to the front page and read the headline again.

Mayoral Candidate to Face Grand Jury

According to The Raven, Max Roman was lucky to be alive right now, but the way his past few weeks had gone, she was willing to bet he didn't feel so lucky.

Mama Bliss had planned three assassinations of her enemy. She was the thorough type.

First, Andrew Carr was supposed to fire a bullet into Max's skull. Pavlo Kostiuk had thwarted that attempt. During the chaos of the Kipo takeover of the Grand Ballroom, he'd come out from behind the black curtain and tried to get Max out through one of the back exits into the service corridor. Problem was, there was a Kipo guarding that door with a Taurus MT-9 G2 submachine gun. Apparently Kipo working undercover on the catering crew had secretly planted five of these submachine guns in the ballroom, one at every exit, hidden under tablecloths on bussing carts stationed by each door.

Trudi had to give the Ukrainian credit. He'd charged the Kipo at the back door, actually was able to take the Taurus gun from him. His mistake was that he'd stopped to use the gun, killing the Kipo he'd defeated. That was when Andrew Carr changed his target and shot Pavlo Kostiuk in the back of the neck instead of shooting Max Roman first. Pavlo went down firing, taking out Andrew Carr before he died.

When the shooting started, Max had run back into the ballroom, where he hid under a table until it was all over. It was cowardly, yes, but it also saved his life. If he'd made a break for the door, there was a second Kipo with a Taurus MT-9 aimed and ready to shoot. He would have been killed in a hail of automatic gunfire.

Max's second assassination was supposed to be the bomb in Pavlo's briefcase. That was Mama Bliss's primary backup plan, just in case something happened to prevent Andrew Carr's success. If not for The Raven stealing the remote detonator from her hotel room, that murder attempt would have worked. Trudi had had to stay crouched next to that ice machine on the twenty-fourth floor of the Ritz-Carlton for almost an hour before the police found her, and then it was another half hour until a bomb squad officer had relieved her of the remote. It had taken almost four hours—well past midnight—for SWAT to regain control of the ballroom from the Kipo. Then it had been two more hours after that for the bomb squad to defuse the C4-filled briefcase. But it had been worth it. By the time Saturday morning arrived in force, the C4 hadn't gone off, the Grand Ballroom of the Ritz was still intact, and the only casualties in the Kipo takeover had been one Kipo guard, Pavlo Kostiuk, and Andrew Carr.

The one thing she hadn't been able to explain was the mystery man in Room 2421 of the hotel. As far as she was concerned, he was a hero. If he hadn't helped her at the critical moment, Mama's bomb would have gone off, killing hundreds of innocent people along with Max Roman. Trudi figured that man deserved some kind of recognition from the city, or at least a letter of commendation and thanks from the Ritz-Carlton.

She'd looked for him afterward, to thank him properly for his help, but he was nowhere to be seen. She'd made her obligatory report to the authorities, making mention of him specifically because she wanted his heroism documented in their investigation. Then, on the Monday after Nevermore, she'd checked with the hotel management to find out who he was.

"Which room, Ms. Coffey?" the manager on the telephone had said.

"Room 2421," she'd said. "On the top floor."

There had been a pause and the sounds of fingers tapping on a computer keyboard. "Last Friday night, you say? April 14?"

"Yes, of course."

"I'm sorry, Ms. Coffey, but there was no one staying in room 2421 on Friday, April 14. In fact, the entire twenty-fourth floor was empty on that day."

"But I saw him. He was . . ." She'd stopped herself. She couldn't remember what the man looked like, couldn't even remember the color of his skin or the style of his hair. *Too much drama going on for me to pay attention to details like that*, she guessed. *Or maybe I wasn't supposed to remember what he looked like?*

"Is there anything else I can help you with?" the manager had said.

"No, thank you." She'd hung up and spent the rest of the day puzzling over the mystery, never reaching a satisfying conclusion. In the end, she decided just to be grateful, even if she didn't understand it all.

The third assassination of Max Roman was of his reputation, and in this attempt Mama Bliss succeeded. Sometime on Friday afternoon she'd mailed an envelope to the chief of police at the Zone 6 police station in Atlanta. The envelope contained only a logbook, but that was enough. There were hundreds of entries in the book—meticulously kept records, names, even photographs, and notes about where to find hidden audio recordings, video, and more. Every new thing seemed to be more incriminating than the last. Taken together, they painted a detailed picture of a vast organized-crime operation with Maksym Romanenko at the head. There was evidence of gun smuggling, racketeering, sex trafficking, street gang terrorism, and much, much more—all of it with Max Roman's fingerprints attached.

The police had taken Councilman Roman into custody within a week. He'd posted bail and then been stupid enough to try and flee the country. Samuel Hill had caught him on the tarmac of Dekalb-Peachtree Airport, trying to board a chartered flight to Germany. Now Max was where he belonged: in the United States Penitentiary, Atlanta, surrounded by unsympathetic guards and angry incarcerated Kipo gang members.

Trudi Coffey put away the *Atlanta Journal-Constitution* and tried to get to work. She had three cases that needed her attention today, though none of them were pressing. In the first folder on her desk, one of her regular customers, a woman in Chamblee, wanted a background check on a potential domestic employee, a maid or a cook or something. That wouldn't take long. The second folder was a businessman at CNN who wanted a consultation on human resources law, which was boring but which also paid well. Corporate consultations were almost always good business for Coffey & Hill Investigations.

The third folder was most interesting. It contained a letter from a movie producer at 3Arts Entertainment in Los Angeles. They were in preproduction on a new gangster film about Irish mafia types, the letter said. They'd heard about Trudi's involvement in taking down Max Roman's Ukrainian gangsters and wondered if she might be interested in being one of the advisors for their movie. They were asking for three days of her time, somewhere near the beginning of production in October or November. They promised a reasonable fee, all expenses, and an "assistant producer" credit if she came to Boston, where they planned to film on location. She was curious about that possibility but wanted to do more background research on 3Arts Entertainment before making a commitment.

She was tempted to start on that third folder but opted to take them in order of Coffey & Hill priority instead. She fired up her web browser and started digging into the latest on human resources law and litigation. Still, her mind wandered.

Samuel had recovered reasonably well from his drug-induced experience at the fundraiser.

Well, his body had recovered, but his ego was still bruised by the fact that he'd been so easily knocked out of commission. It didn't help his self-esteem that Trudi had avoided a similar fate because she didn't drink that glass of wine. She'd been sure to needle him about that. Not a lot of needling, just enough so that he remembered he'd been bested by a woman, by his ex-wife.

They'd caught Stephen Gartrell in South Carolina. He was

that football player she'd seen at The Raven's apartment the first time she'd met the street magician.

Gartrell had slipped out of the state of Georgia without incident and probably would have made it all the way to Canada if he'd been more patient. Apparently he had something of a lead foot when driving, and he'd been clocked going eighty-five miles per hour in a sixty-miles-per-hour construction zone. When the highway patrol tried to pull him over, he'd panicked and tried to race away. The high-speed chase was over when the police punctured his tires with nails spread across Interstate 20, just west of Florence, South Carolina. He was now awaiting transfer back to Georgia to face trial as a Nevermore co-conspirator. Word from Samuel was that Gartrell had made a "business decision" and was cooperating with authorities in anticipation of a plea-bargain agreement.

Viktor Kostiuk, on the other hand, had vanished. Like a ghost, he'd evaporated into thin air.

On April 14, an airline passenger with the name "V. Kostiuk" had booked seven different international flights, at seven different times, going to places as distant as Beijing, China, or Kiev in the Ukraine, and as near as Havana, Cuba.

Someone had boarded each flight and filled each V. Kostiuk seat, but airport surveillance never showed a clear image of any of those people, nor could they prove that any of the seven was the real Viktor. Theories abounded, but Trudi's best guess was that all seven were decoys meant to distract the authorities while the crafty Mr. Kostiuk slipped away by other means. At this point, the chances of ever finding him were slim to none.

Darrent Hayes, Mama Bliss's number-one manager at the Secret Stash, had likewise disappeared.

According to Samuel, he'd taken a vacation cruise to the Bahamas one week before the Nevermore date. He'd emptied his cabin at the Nassau port on April 13, told the captain he'd decided to stay for a while, and slipped away before anyone suspected him of anything. The Bahamian government was cooperating with American authorities in trying to track him down, but again, Trudi suspected he was long gone, probably off to South America or some subtropical climate. She'd been allowed to see his pre-planned itinerary and recognized several similarities with the one she and Samuel had been given for their Hawaiian vacation temptation.

After talking it over, she and her ex-husband had reached the conclusion that Darrent was probably the one who'd FedExed the Hawaii vacation tickets to Coffey & Hill Investigations. "I think maybe Mama Bliss was trying to protect you," Samuel had said, "and me too. I think she wanted to get us out of harm's way." It made sense, even if the evidence was circumstantial.

Mama Bliss, ah, poor Mama Bliss.

According to The Raven, Mama was driven by guilt over the untimely passing of her grandson. She'd made a list of six people that she felt were responsible for his death during a robbery gone wrong—and had included herself on that list.

Four of the people on Mama's list had already died under suspicious circumstances. One, a gang member, was killed in a drive-by shooting on his way to meet his parole officer. Another Kipo was killed in a prison fight. The police officer who had shot Davis Monroe during the robbery had died in a freak fishing accident less than a year after he'd retired from the force. In an ironic twist, the mall security guard who'd called 911 during Davis's robbery was killed in an armed robbery at a McDonald's in the Old Fourth Ward. He had just been made part-owner in the franchise restaurant and was starting a new life outside the security industry.

Other than Mama Bliss, Max Roman was the last person alive

on her list, and apparently the one she held as most responsible for her grandson's death. After seeing glimpses of Roman's alleged involvement in the Kipo gang structure, Trudi could see why Mama felt that way.

Paramedics had said Bliss Monroe was already dead when they arrived on scene, victim of fatal diabetic shock. Her insulin pump had either malfunctioned or, as The Raven claimed, been mis-set to deliver an overdose of insulin into her already fragile system. She couldn't have lasted long. Trudi hoped that she'd been able to find peace at the end but had to live with the fact that she'd never know for sure.

The Raven, Tyson Elvis Miller, was in a bit of hot water in the immediate aftermath of Nevermore. Police held him as a "person of interest" for a while and considered pressing charges against him as a co-conspirator in the terrorist plot. He did, after all, have connections to Max Roman and to all three of the other Nevermore conspirators. Finally, though—and largely because of Samuel Hill's persistence—his status was changed to "material witness" and he was allowed to go free. It also helped that he turned over an audio recording of the other conspirators going through the planned timeline of events during the early evening of April 14. He wasn't allowed to keep the first-edition copy of the *New York Evening Mirror* magazine from January 1845, even though he protested loudly that Mama Bliss had "given" it to him as a present. It was now safely stored back at the Secret Stash while he made a legal claim to it as his property.

After he'd been released from custody, The Raven and Trudi had finally had a chance to talk. She learned what happened with his pinky finger, and he began to understand her relationship with her ex-husband. They kind of hit it off. Not romantically— Trudi made that very clear, much to his disappointment. But he got over it, and they discovered they shared many of the same interests. After that they started hanging out as friends in almost a big sister/little brother kind of way. Trudi liked that. It felt good.

The Raven had to get permission from the Atlanta PD before being allowed to travel back to Oklahoma, and in the end they'd opted to send a plainclothes detective and a junior lawyer from the district attorney's office to accompany him anyway. With all the new revelations spilling out every day about Max Roman, they wanted him to be both safe and available. Plus, there was a bench warrant waiting for Tyson Miller in Oklahoma, and they needed to get a plea deal worked out in order to keep him available for Georgia-based court proceedings.

Trudi understood why he'd gone back to Oklahoma City, why he even wanted to go back, and she was glad for him, in spite of the reason for his return. It would be a time of healing, a little reconciliation mixed with redemption and closure. She expected this trip might actually help to finalize the change in direction his life was taking.

She hoped so.

"Ms. Coffey," Eulalie's voice sang through the intercom and interrupted her train of thought. "Mr. Hill is here. He wants to know if you're available."

"Sure," Trudi responded. She checked the clock and was surprised to see she'd been working for more than two hours and that it was already 11:45. *Where does the time go when you get in a zone?* she thought. She said, "Send him back."

Samuel looks good, she admitted to herself when he came, grinning, into her office. *Why does he always have to look good?*

"Hey, Tru-Bear," he said, flopping comfortably into one of the guest seats in her office. "Hot out there. Glad you've got air-conditioning."

"Nice to see you too," she said, returning his grin. "What's that?"

He tossed a greeting card on the table. "Today's my Uncle Rexy's birthday. Thought you'd want to sign the card before I give it to him."

"Of course. Thanks." She scribbled an endearing *Calvin & Hobbes* quote inside and added her name at the bottom before handing the card back. "How goes the investigation?"

"Things are falling into place," he said. "The case against that football player is airtight, thanks in no small part to The Raven's testimony. Still, Gartrell's intimate knowledge of Max Roman's entire operation, and of the whole Nevermore circumstances, means he's got plenty of leverage with the district attorney. And he knows it. Got a good mind for negotiations, that guy. When all is said and done, my guess is he ends up spending less than four years behind bars. We'll have to wait and see, though."

"And Max Roman? The paper says he's going to go away for life."

"Depends on if he's tied to any specific killings, and who in the Justice Department is on his payroll. He's still a man with money and influence, so that mitigates his circumstances somewhat. But given the trove of evidence Mama Bliss turned over, the cards are not stacked in his favor."

She nodded. They'd done their job, she reasoned. Now it was time to let the legal system do its job. She had other things to worry about . . . like maybe a budding career as a film advisor. Heck, she might even try to write a screenplay someday. She tried not to think about that, though. First she had to do a background check on a maid in Chamblee.

"The Raven is back in town," Samuel said. "He got back yesterday afternoon."

"I know."

"He—" Samuel stopped himself. "You knew that already? How?"

"I'm a detective, Samuel," she teased. "I know things."

"I— " Again he was temporarily speechless.

"Have you heard from—" She paused, then decided it was no longer a secret and that she should just ask what she wanted to know. "Heard anything new from your, uh, family?"

The earlier joviality of his entrance faded a bit, but he still tried to smile. "They're in a—well, let's call it a lengthy transition period. No communication during the transition, which can take anywhere from six to twelve months. But I expect to hear some news before the end of the year. I'm sure all is fine. I made all the necessary arrangements last time I saw them." He let silence fill the air for a moment, then said, "Thanks for asking. Thanks for caring."

She nodded and looked at her hands. She'd been surprised to discover that she did care. She'd spent so many days hating Samuel's son just because she was not his mother. But after seeing his face, after looking at his cherubic cheeks and his smiling eyes, she knew she was done hating. *Bitterness is a root that only poisons me*, she thought. She felt like that new attitude was growth, both emotionally and spiritually.

Now Samuel was standing. "Hungry?" he said. "How about if I take you to lunch today?"

His eyes sparkled, and she remembered again why and how she'd fallen in love with him in the first place. But today was not the day she was going to fall down that drain again.

"Thanks," she said warmly, "but I've already got plans."

"Plans?" His eyebrows inched upward. "A date?"

"None of your business, Samuel." She laughed. Just then Eulalie's voice broke in on the intercom.

"Ms. Coffey, your twelve o'clock is here."

Samuel turned and looked curiously down the hall.

"Come on," she said. "You can walk me out."

The Raven was waiting in the reception area, right in the middle of a card trick for Eulalie. "I'll finish this later," he said, turning to Trudi and Samuel. "Detective." He nodded in greeting at Trudi's ex-husband.

"Raven," Samuel said. Trudi could tell he was trying not to let his mouth gape.

"You ready?" The Raven said to Trudi.

"Yep. Where are we going?"

"If you don't mind driving," he said, "I've really been craving CozyFloyd's BBQ lately."

47

DARRENT

Atlanta, GA
West Midtown
Friday, April 28, 12:22 p.m.
Fourteen days after Nevermore

Darrent Eugene Hayes sat in the driver's seat of his wine-colored rental car, a Toyota Corolla from Hertz this time. From his vantage point in the corner of the Bank of America parking lot at 1775 Howell Mill Road, he had a clean view to the front door of Coffey & Hill Investigations across the street.

Darrent had been tempted to skip over to Taco Bell next door while he was waiting, to grab a burrito for his growling stomach, but he resisted the urge. He didn't want to unnecessarily risk being seen—and identified—by some random video camera in the area. Maybe the bank's ATM camera or security video inside the Taco Bell. When he eventually did get out of the car, he'd do his deed quickly, hiding his face under a hoodie as best he could, but even that would be dangerous, and he knew it. A chicken burrito simply wasn't worth the added risk. He stayed where he was and let his stomach rumble.

The unsealed FedEx Letter envelope sat on the passenger seat next to him. He'd intended to wait until the office across the street emptied for lunch and then deliver it, but now he hesitated. He'd seen both Samuel Hill and The Raven go inside. A few minutes later, he'd seen Trudi Coffey and The Raven leave together. Then Samuel Hill drove away in a different direction. The receptionist had come out around twelve-fifteen, locked the office door, and walked across the street to the Kroger shopping center. From what he could tell, she'd decided to lunch at Piccadilly cafeteria today.

If he was going to do it, now was the time. He just wasn't sure anymore that he was going to do it.

"Mama Bliss said she owes you, Samuel Hill," he said to the empty car.

He let his mind work in silence for a few moments, then he picked up the FedEx envelope and removed two 5x7 photos from inside it.

He looked at the first photo and grimaced. It was a residential compound, just hours after a suicide bombing and military raid had taken place there. The charred shell of the Toyota truck used in the attack carried a now-tattered black flag. Daesh had claimed the attack was retaliation for crimes against Islam committed by the "apostate" Saudi government. Nine bodies littered the ground, seven men and two women. Three of the bodies belonged to Daesh, five had been residents of the compound, and one was a CIA Fader in the wrong place at the wrong time.

Darrent couldn't recognize the remains of the victims, but he knew one of the women had been young, no more than twenty-nine or thirty years old. She'd been an Arabian beauty too, with skin the color of fresh apple butter, deep brown eyes, and a fiery, happy spirit. He'd only met her once, but he'd liked her instantly. He had a feeling every man felt that way when meeting her.

If the attack had come only one day later, even twelve hours later, she would've been gone. They all would have been gone, moved to a new safe house, hidden in a new country, on the second leg of a well-planned Fade into obscurity. But life doesn't always go according to CIA plans.

He slid the first photo behind the second and now saw a sad little boy, about six years old. His eyes were a light chestnut color, surrounded by long lashes and the chubby cheeks of childhood. He had been crying, Darrent knew, because Darrent had taken this second picture himself.

The boy was slumped in a window seat on a private airplane, winging his way away from his home, from everything he knew. Headed to an unknown world where all would change for him, where he'd never again feel his mother's arms wrapped around him, holding him tight, protecting him from suicide bombers and bloodthirsty soldiers bent on sending everyone to hell.

But maybe his father's arms, Darrent told himself. *Someday. Maybe.*

He returned both images to the FedEx envelope and stared for a few minutes at the empty offices of Coffey & Hill Investigations.

"Mama Bliss said she owes you, Samuel Hill," he said again. "And I owe Mama Bliss. That means her debts are now mine."

That includes this boy, he thought. *And Trudi Coffey.*

He started the engine of his rental car. Maybe someday he'd deliver the pictures to Samuel Hill, he didn't know. He just knew that right now, today, was not the time for that. He would wait. He'd put off paying his debts a while longer.

It's what Bliss would've wanted, he decided. *And besides, being a secret guardian of Samuel Hill's only son might come in handy someday. Maybe someday soon.*

Darrent Hayes eased his Corolla out of its parking space at the Bank of America building, then slowly pulled into the lunchtime traffic that crowded Howell Mill Road.

EXCLUSIVE

PEEK

at Book #3 in the

COFFEY & HILL
Series!

1

DREAM

"Get. *Down*."

He's driving too fast, looking too often at his rearview mirror. The world outside us is a strange, pale kind of twilight. There's no sun in the sky that I can see, yet there's still some kind of half-light, as if day is resisting night, refusing to go to bed like an ill-tempered child.

The gun resting on the console between us is still warm.

I could take it, I think. *I could grab that pistol while he's distracted.* But the steel in his voice makes me think twice. He did just kill a man, after all. I can still smell the wet, hot, copper spray that blew from the dead man's body when the bullets hit.

The driver glances at me now, scowling.

It's a tight fit, even for someone my size, but I slide off the passenger seat anyway and try to squeeze into the leg space below. Apparently I'm not good at this.

"Farther," he snaps. "All the way down. So no one can see you, even if we stop at a red light."

If we stop at a red light?

The sedan lurches left, hard, but the tires don't squeal. He guns the engine and, briefly, I feel dizzy, like I might have a concussion, like I might throw up if I'm given half a chance. Instead, I press myself deeper into the floorboards until he glances at me and nods. Then he does a double-take.

"Don't you spew in my car. You understand?"

I nod and close my eyes. Seems a lot to ask of me at this point, not to throw up. But I really don't want to argue right now.

"You spew, and I'll put you in the trunk with everything else."

His accent is strong, harsh, and hard to follow. I'm not from New England originally. Didn't grow up here, and never quite mastered the nuances of that brash northeastern accent. For instance, to me that last threat sounded like, "Yah s'puh an ahl pudya in tha trunk wid everthin else."

It takes me a second to process what he's saying, and that seems to make him angry. He taps the brakes and leans down toward me while making another left turn. "Yah unnerstan?"

I nod again. *I understand.* There's nothing to do about it now except pay attention and make sure my mind translates his words—fast.

But there's nothing to do about that now except pay attention and make sure my mind translates his words—fast.

"Wwhat do you want with me?" I ask. My voice sounds thin, like the pale light fading around us. I try to concentrate so I can translate his accent in my mind.

"You was in the wrong place at the right time," he says. With my eyes closed, I can almost hear a grin in his voice. I have no idea what he's talking about. I'm afraid to ask.

Afraid.

The car screeches to a sudden halt, and the back of my head smacks lightly on the glove box behind me. I risk opening my eyes, and I see him tapping the steering wheel impatiently. I can't see the traffic, but I assume there's a car stopped in front of us, maybe at a red light.

Now's my chance, I think. *Shove open the door and roll out into the street while the car is idling.*

My legs feel deadened from this cramped space, but that doesn't matter. I'll just fall out of the car and crawl away on my hands and knees. Hopefully somebody out there will see me, someone will wonder what's going on, and that'll be enough for him just to let me go.

"What is that? Is that blood?"

His eyes flick in my direction, and I feel my chest tighten like thickening cement. Callused fingers flash toward me and grip my wrist. He yanks at my arm, and I suffer the needling pain of opportunity pulling away. "Di'ya geh bluhd in mah cah?" *Did you get blood in my car?*

"No, no!" I say. "It's cadmium red. Oil-based. It's what I was using when you, when you . . ."

He throws my hand back at me and hits the gas again, swerving to pass something in the street. I reflexively try to wipe at the drying paint on my fingers and tell myself again and again, *Don't throw up, Javie, don't throw up.*

The man barely looks at me, intent on speeding through the twilight streets of what I'm guessing is East Middlebury or Ripton by now. He's found a deserted route and is all business. I think we're heading out to the forestlands because I can see tall sugar maple and beech trees shadowing the sky above us.

I sneak a look in his direction while he's occupied with the road. His cheeks are Pilgrim-pale, flecked with pockmarks that suggest he had a problem with teenage acne. His nose looks like a partially inflated balloon, bulbous and angry. He's got thinning brown hair, a chin shaved clean, and clear blue eyes that seem out of place in that face. He's wearing dark brown pants, a white button-up shirt, but no tie. And now his right hand is resting on that silver gun still stuck to the console between us.

"That's how you do it where I come from," he's muttering to nobody. "That's how we do it Southie style. Whitey B., you see that? Yeah, you saw that, wherever you are."

"You're from Boston?" I say, and even I'm surprised to hear my voice ask the obvious question.

His face relaxes into a proud grin. "Born and raised," he says. Then he glances over at me and frowns. "Now stay down and shut up while I try and figure out these crazy-stupid roads out here in this crazy-stupid place."

I nod. Outside, night has finally pushed aside the last complaints of daytime and taken its rightful place. The Southie flicks on the car's headlights, but the vehicle doesn't slow.

"Head down," he barks at me. "I got no time to deal with a skiddah like you right now."

Skiddah? Oh, Skidder. Boston slang for a worthless bum. Is that what I am now? I fold my arms onto the seat and bury my face into them.

I'm going to die.

There's silence as we continue into what I can only assume is more countryside.

But if he wanted to kill me, why didn't he do it back at the workshop? Why come in with guns blazing at Henri and then stop when he sees me?

In my mind's eye I see a slow-motion explosion of bullets and flesh, a gruesome reminder of my recent past and the vivid memory-making mechanism that works in my brain. I force Henri away from my thoughts, training myself to forget, at least for the moment. I can't relive that awful killing, not yet. Another day, another time, I'll say my respects, bid poor Henri a thoughtful goodbye. Right now I have to think of other things or maybe I'll go insane.

Don't throw up, Javie. Don't throw up.

It feels like at least an hour, maybe more, until he finally sighs and tells me I can raise my head.

"Almost there, skiddah," he says. "You still beatin' in that heart of yours?"

I nod, and then realize he's looking at the road and not at me. "Yes," I say. "Where are you taking me?"

"Taking you home, skiddah. Taking you to your new home."

I want to ask what he means about a "new home," if he'll ever let me go. But all I can do is grieve. *I had a chance*, I think. *Back there, when he stopped at the red light or whatever that was. I missed it. Lord, help my poor soul!*

It seems fitting to me, at this moment, that I'm praying the last words of Edgar Allan Poe. *Lord, help my poor soul.* I've wondered often if God answered that poet's prayer, or if it was just a cry into emptiness by a man lost in the blinding night.

"We're here."

It takes a few moments to make my legs work again, to un-cramp and enliven them with blood flowing once more. It's dark, and we've parked at the end of a dirt road, surrounded by cover of many trees. To our left is a small cottage—a literal "little house in the woods." Under different circumstances, I'd probably like it, windows warm with yellow light, the scent of smoke puffing through a fireplace chimney. But right now it's only a prison scene to me.

Southie stops unpacking the trunk long enough to look at

me, hard. "Don't do it," he says, like he's reading my mind. He waves his hand, and I see he's got the gun in it. "I don't feel like killing another bazo tonight."

My legs couldn't run right now anyway, I think. *But maybe tomorrow. Or the next day. He can't watch me forever, can he?*

My captor loads me with a long leather tube and a small wooden crate, then turns me toward the door. He's got two similar tubes, and I see he's carrying my pages too, still wrapped up in my portfolio case, almost ready to send. *So close*, I tell myself. *So close to being done. Should've finished that Poe project before I took the new job, before I got mixed up in . . . this.*

A broad man with a sour expression opens the door to the cottage.

"What took you so long?" he growls, and I hear an Irish brogue that's almost musical in its sound.

"Skiddah here needed a little hand-holding." My Southie grins back. "But we got it all, no problem."

"Who's he?"

"Your new assistant."

The burly Irishman glowers at me in the dim light on the porch. "Can he draw?" he says.

"He's a forger," Southie says. "Caught him making a wicked-good copy of this one." He raises a leather tube with a rolled-up oil painting inside and waves it toward the Irishman.

"Don't need a painter," the Irishman snaps. "Not yet at least, not for a few more weeks. Maybe even a month. Need a penciler right now. A sketch artist."

"I can draw," I say suddenly. *Maybe if I make myself useful*, I think, *they'll keep me alive long enough for me to find a way to escape.*

"See for yourself." Southie shoves my portfolio into the Irishman's hands, then pushes past him to enter the cottage.

The stocky man looks hard at me for another moment, then

unzips my work. He flips through a few comic book pages, nodding once or twice, making unintelligible grunts at the images he sees. Then he slaps the case shut again. He wraps his arms in front of him, pressing my artwork to his chest almost like he's giving it a hug.

His stare is hard to hold, but I try not to wilt under his gaze. He's looking at me as though he's trying to gauge whether it's easier to kill and bury me here in the woods or to invite me inside for dinner. Finally he nods, decision made.

"Clocks," he says to me brusquely. "I need lots of clocks."

Mike Nappa is an entertainment journalist at FamilyFans.com, as well as a bestselling and award-winning author with more than one million books sold worldwide. When he was a kid, the stories of Edgar Allan Poe scared him silly. Today he owns everything Poe ever wrote. A former fiction acquisitions editor, Mike earned his MA in English literature and now writes full-time.